RUBY BUTTERFLY

SEDUCING DAVID

BOOK Eight

of the

SECRET BUTTERFLY SERIES™

A NOVEL BY

Rosemary Lightfoot Ness-Bitner

A CAUTION TO THE READER:

Sociopathy is in the process of yielding to David's journey into psychopathic madness. Chapter seven of book eight (RUBY BUTTERFLY©) contains gruesome, heinous passages. Undoubtedly, it is among the most troublesome passages in literature ever written. It is likely to trigger an emotional reaction from many readers and listeners. As the author explains: There was no other way to convey the depths of depravity and malicious, vicious evil which had taken possession of David's soul; nor how else to illustrate David's possessive hold over Marty.

Here, he leads her into his bottomless abyss of sinister wickedness. And she, ever eager to gain his approval, casts aside all remaining vestiges of her morality.

And Marty, before these passages, arguably possessed a salvageable soul. In her protesting questionings she offers a glimpse of the sort of person she wishes she could have been; but David quashes her hesitation and spurs her onward. He steals her most valuable personal property-her moral conscience; her sense of right and wrong. He purposely severs Marty's few remaining strands of humanity as he unleashes his masterful ability to manipulate her into doing the most unthinkable betrayals. He convinces her to relish and savor her horrific deeds; and to embrace and cherish her blood lust and eternal damnation.

Chapter seven of book eight is not for those who are faint of heart. If you can steel yourself to read its wretched, horribly descriptive passages; then, by all means, read them.

ROSEMARY

This book is dedicated to lovers and their dreams.

The eBook and print version layouts of RUBY BUTTERFLY© were done by Andrea Reider of Reider Books. The cover design was created by Carrie of Cheeky Covers; and I am Minna Morinette, your audio book narrator.

Rosemary Ness Bitner's Secret Butterfly Series books are available wherever books are sold.

To order RUBY BUTTERFLY©:
For print paperback: 978-1-961850-17-0
For eBook: 978-1-961850-18-7

A BRIEF PREFACE TO THE SECRET BUTTERFLY SERIES™

Why, a reader might ask, would any sane author write a preface to a Series of her books at the outset of her eighth Series book instead of at the first; or at the beginning of her introductory bookend book, ALPHA (THE BEGINNING) ©, in this case? The answer, dear readers, is that everything prior to RUBY BUTTERFLY©, BUTTERFLY MORALS ©, TROPHY BUTTERFLY©, LOVE AND LOVERS©, and the three book INSANITY VOLUME, four book REINCARNATION VOLUME, and OMEGA (THE END) ©, which follow these final four works of the PASSION VOLUME, was necessary background for the meat of our saga. Now that you know something about our main characters Marvin, Susan, Marty, David, Barbara, and Bob, and their psychic make-up, you are entitled to understand how their personal dynamics entwine, clash, and reconcile, or not, their relationships.

I cannot explain why I wrote the SERIES, other than to say I felt compelled to do so. It seemed, at many times, that my pen was guided by hands that were not my own; but compelled to put upon paper visions that I had while dreaming or near awakening. A television show that discussed extraterrestrial intelligence postulated that there is a telepathic mechanism that some humans experience. I do not know whether that was what possessed my pen, or what produced round circle marks upon my arms during my dream nights. But I have asked myself: Was I chosen by some intelligence to write these things? Were the visions I saw in my dreams and twilights of awakening real visions of actual happenings from the past; and precursors of things to come? I do not know. But I tell you this, in all truth: The dreams all seemed to be real happenings. I saw them in vivid detail, as if I was there, observing the happenings. There must be something to it. I cannot simply sit down to write because it is the appointed hour to write. Some authors can do that two hour a day routine. But I can't. Maybe I could, but I don't. I only write when I feel this content *'thing'* presenting itself from within me, which I then feel duty bound to commit to paper. That's when I write.

Mother, or perhaps her spirit soul, may have had some part in this. When I was a child, she often asked me questions which I could not answer. But her questions haunted me and came back to me many thousands of times throughout my life. Her questions sent me on mental journeys of exploration. Now, many years after Mother's death, I still go on the journeys her questions launched. After I entered womanhood and dated some, Mother asked me, point blank: *'Do you think men enjoy sex as much as women do? I mean, do you think they feel the same ways about it? Or, do you think women like it more?'* I have since listened very carefully to what many men and women said about sex. And I think the answer depends upon the person and the relationships they have. I try to answer Mother's question in my books. I am still searching for answers.

Another question Mother asked was one that has taken my life on many twists and turns. She asked: *'Why do you think Hitler hated Jews?'* That question took me aback. I never thought to ask it. I had always assumed that Hitler was an evil madman. Why would Hitler, or anyone, for that matter, hate us? I wrestle with that question, even today, many years after Mother died. It sometimes chases my mind around in my dreams. What gave rise to

Hitler's hatred? Mother's question seemed to presuppose that it was our own fault that Hitler hated us.

But how could that be? Could it be that, because of our belief in God, and our Torah stating that we are chosen by God to be an example for the rest of humanity, that we developed a superiority complex; that this complex led us to exclude others; that those others became jealous of this complex and our successes? And along comes this impish Hitler fellow who says: *'Oh yeah! I'll show you Jews who is superior!'* And he then riles up the German people into insane national hysterical group think, that phenomena Nietzsche warned about? I think so. Mother's question still confuses me. It's impossible to answer why we are as we are.

And are we Jews any less culpable of thinking in such a horrible group think way? When I see a Palestinian child, I ask myself: Is that child any less a child of God than I am? No, of course not. She is also a child of God. And can that child help thinking about Jews in any way other than how she is taught by her parents and community to think about Jews; and can I help thinking about Palestinians any differently than my community taught me to think about them?

Obviously, it is extremely difficult to change the way we think about each other. But this much I believe is certain: Each human life is a universe of hope and possibilities unto itself. It is a horrific wrong to murder that life, even if it is being used as a human shield. It is just horribly wrong for we humans to think of each other as *'them'* or *'they.'* We are not objects. We are humans, creatures of God, every one of us.

And we are all capable of thought. We all want to love and be loved. We must use our minds to change how we think about others. We simply must. We must not be killing each other. That is so wrong; such a waste of talent and hope. We must cherish all life. It is so precious. We must do better; much, much, better. I try to address this issue in my books. Perhaps some of the behaviors of my characters will repulse you. That's good. It's a start. And, hopefully, you will ask: *'Are real people actually capable of behaving this way?'* I assure you; they are. My characters are composites of traits I have seen in real people. When you identify those traits in a real person, don't walk. Run for the nearest exit! Get away! Save yourself!

I equivocated about what to title SERIES books eight and nine. I thought titles like: KING DAVID'S MURDERS; and THE SEDUCTION OF MOSES AND CHARLES might elicit more reader interest; but that would depart from the SERIES theme of recurring souls, which I have strived to maintain. So, I stayed with the book titles of RUBY BUTTERFLY© and BUTTERFLY MOR-ALS©; and used subtitles: SEDUCING DAVID and SEDUCING MOSES AND CHARLES. That's somewhat consistent and it relates to a woman's feelings. And what a range of feelings we have!

My vision dream of David and Marty murdering George and Bertie in RUBY BUTTERFLY©; had me waking up wondering whether the David of my dreams is the reincarnation of biblical King David and whether what he and Marty did in their murder scene was in some way similar to what David and Bathsheba did to those unfortunates who got in the way of their passions?

David's character is easily misunderstood. Be careful as you learn about him. You may think you've got his character pegged. But I promise you, you don't. He is a classic narcissist. And, like many narcissists, he has an overwhelming need to be in control. Many, like Marty, who enter the orbit of such a personality as David's, assume that his behavior is ego driven. That's the mask David wears. But his personality is not at all ego driven. It is fear driven. That's key to understanding David. And it must be under-stood. David is incredibly emotionally weak and needy. His life is a horribly empty void, even a deeper void than Marty's void. He is terrified of Adonai, the Hebrew God; or, Don, as David refers to him. David seeks mental comfort in his murders and his confidences with Dolly, his black sheep, and secret lover. You'll see David's mask removed and his weaknesses devolve into depravity, carelessness, and self-destruction in the second SERIES volume: INSANITY. I hope you'll enjoy that volume. I tried to write it from the perspective of someone who is going insane. While you read it, try to remember it's strictly fiction.

I cannot help but wonder, in my vivid dream about Baalezebelle's (Belle's) seduction of Moses, the murders of his wife, Zephorah, and two children, Gershom and Eliezer; Belle's copulation with the Apis Fertility Bulls; the fortnight of Belle's pornographic orgies and the gorging fests of the Nile crocodiles, was I possibly foreseeing the genocide of today's displaced Palestinians? And how casually the world seems to accept their demise, as if it's just part of the human experience? Were Belle's fornications on the tribal altar the reason why Moses needed to murder half the Hebrew Tribe and ascend Mount Sinai that second time? Were the two commandments he added to his second set of tablets his attempt to forever yoke women to marital slavery? That seems likely, since the tradition of slavery, learned in Egypt, was deeply engrained in the Hebrew psyche. Was Moses sex-obsessed? I think he was. We cannot know; but my dream had a terrifying *Out With The Old And In With The New* sort of theme. If my fictional Sinai happenings upset you, I apologize. Please remember, it's fiction.

Moses. What a guy! What sort of man was he, really? Many male Jews will tell you that Moses is *my man.* But what does that mean? I think those who would idolize Moses do so for their perception of his leadership skills. After all, he led the Hebrews out of Egypt. He defied Pharoah. He, with God's help, brought on the plagues. Really? He turned a stick into a snake and a snake back into a stick. Really? He touched a stick to a rock and the rock flowed water. Really? He parted the sea. Really? I mean: Wow! What a guy!

But somehow, in my mind, the Torah homily doesn't quite fit things together logically. I've read the Torah story many times. And the more I read it and think about it, it feels, to me, like someone is trying to force a square peg into a round hole. It seems to me that Moses really did exist. I believe he was a real person. Apparently, he also craved power. Ah, power! That's the ultimate aphrodisiac for many men, especially those with sociopathic tendencies. So, what kind of man ditches his wife and kids and just walks away from them? That's the Torah version. And what sort of man commits murder? The Torah version has Moses killing an Egyptian overseer of slaves and slaughtering the non-believers at Mount Sinai's Golden Calf scene: Remember? Those are actions of a man who seeks power. And Moses, clearly, craved his power. If you crossed Moses, he killed you.

So, while fictional, my version has some consistencies with the facts and struggles of that historic time; those crucible days when humanity struggled with the choice of worshipping many gods or one god. Akhenaten was a *One God Fits All* guy. I think he gave Moses the concept of one god. In my fictional version, Moses had a thing for Baaleezebelle. She was his favorite harem whore. He watched her, fascinated and obsessed, while she did the Apis bulls and performed her breathtaking pornography. His lusts were so strong that he had Zeporah, his wife, and his sons murdered to smooth the way for his marriage to Baaleezebelle. I also hypothesize that Akhenaten's sister and wife, Nefertiti, was totally into incest; and, as likely, Moses was their first borne son.

Nefertiti loved her power and perks. She regarded Akhenaten with increasing concern. He was showing signs of dementia; not caring about matters of state or governance; given to star gazing and babbling about there being only one god. She saw increasing risks to her power. She didn't care how many gods the people worshipped. Maybe she felt offended by Akhenaten's insistence on there only being one god, named Aten? Maybe she felt marginalized when Akhenaten impregnated her oldest daughter and had his sixth daughter with her?

Later, in another dream, I believe I saw the world through the eyes of Nefretiti. She was terrified of the plague and death. She was obsessed with keeping fleas and lice away from the palace. She had everyone shave their heads, bathe, and dust bathe to rid their bodies of lice nibs. When she discovered lice in her palace grainery, she went berserk; ordered all palace grains destroyed; all diseased animals destroyed. But what to eat? She turned first to the child of her oldest daughter; ordered her slaughtered and her flesh and entrails eaten. Then, she ordered her own fifth and fourth daughters slaughtered and eaten. She intended to survive and hold onto power, come what may.

Maybe the events of my second dream never happened? Maybe Egypt's horrible plague conditions took the lives of those three young princesses; and caused Nefretiti her mental anguish? Maybe the Egyptians practiced cannibalism of their slaves during food emergencies and the princesses died from eating diseased, bacteria infested flesh?

Maybe Nefretiti blamed Akhenaten for letting the plague get out of hand? Maybe she, like the priests, lost confidence in his leadership? Maybe she was disgusted by his weakness for Baaleezebelle and how he had offered her own son and favorite lover, Moses, to the whore? Maybe her newest son, Tutankhamun, gave Nefertiti sufficient incestuous pleasures that she no longer felt the need to keep Moses or Akhenaten around? But didn't she need to be rid of both men to keep her power? Surely, she didn't want her cushy lifestyle upset by having a priests' rebellion on her hands. Who would want that? Maybe her solution for all her problems was for her to make a deal with her son, Moses; to have him kill her husband, Akhenaten? And, maybe, for the sake of peace, she sent Moses away with half the wealth of Egypt; taking his *one god*' idea, his Hebrew friends, and his greatest love, Belle, with him? Nefertiti loved her pleasures. And her youngest son, Tutankhamen, had become her favorite consort from the time he was eight years old.

The SEDUCTION OF MOSES story in BUTTERFLY MORALS© is my own fictional version of his romantic life. It's not the sanitized version of Moses, the man who becomes celibate after ditching his wife and sons; not the version of the man presented in the Torah. That man is not my Moses. My Moses character had real needs, including the love of a woman. And his need for her was profoundly great. He murdered for her.

My dreams were vivid; so much so that I was left wondering whether I once lived a prior incarnation of myself? I heard the roaring shouts of crowd approval over Baalezebelle's servicing of the bulls and her spectacular pornography. I heard the crocodile's jaw shatter and crunch down on Zeporah's skull. It was uncanny; frightening; realistic and surreal!

My dreams had no place for Aaron, Torah's brother of Moses. Yet, Moses surely had a closeness with Aaron. Perhaps Aaron was a close friend and early convert to the *'One God Fits All'* idea? Perhaps he was like an adjutant record keeper, scribe; being articulate of voice, a cantor, a composer of hymns and praises; and much like a brother to Moses? As a true follower, Aaron would not leave Moses or their *'One God'* cause, despite knowing that Moses murdered his sons. Aaron's loyalty was thus tested and found strong, far stronger than Simon Peter's weak-kneed loyalty to his Christ, over a millennium later. I think Aaron's unwavering loyalty attests to the strength of leadership and the psychological control which Moses exerted over his followers. It's a rare, genius, leadership ability that can make a crowd go insane. Hitler possessed that same leadership ability. He also made people believe in him; and thus, exerted psychological control over them.

My fictional version of Moses is very different from the sanitized version presented in the Torah. Both versions have the commonalities of the plague; of Moses parting ways with his wife and sons; of Moses murdering; and of the *One God Fits All* concept. I wonder whether the Torah version is accurate? Might a Yiddish saying: *'If you wrap a little truth around a lie, that gives it legs and helps it walk a far way'* be what we've been told?

My fictional dream Moses is the leading male character in history's most consequential love story. Smitten and obsessed with desire for Baaleezebelle, Moses consigns his wife and sons to dismemberment and devouring by crocodiles; thus, proving his unwavering devotion to Egypt's most notorious, deliciously salacious whore. But my Moses doesn't stop there. It's not enough for him to consort with Baalezebelle. He makes her his wife!

And he determines that no other man shall have her. My Moses is about control and possession. He is so intent upon making Baaleezebelle his exclusive love slave that he changes the course of history. He reorders humanity's religious practices to ensure that Belle remains his exclusive property. Historic love and passion lusts will do that. Women can thank my Moses for ordering wives to live as slaves to their husbands.

On his second descent from Mount Sinai, my Moses presented the Hebrews with two additional commandments. He added the seventh: *'Thou Shalt Not Commit Adultery'* and the tenth: *'Thou Shalt Not Covet Thy Neighbor's Wife...'* commandments to specifically prevent other tribesmen from consorting with Baaleezebelle. This was a radical departure from the Tribe's accepted norms.

Going back to the time of Abram and Sara, I think Sara put it around for her father, Terah; and for the Pharoah and his sons;

and, she shamelessly performed orgies for visiting traveler trios to Abram's tents; getting pregnant, finally! During that time, apparently it was accepted and condoned for married women to enjoy limitless sexual freedom. Abram never complained. He was a perfectly compliant husband who benefited greatly from Sara's natural promiscuity. He even pimped her to Pharoah!

My fictional Moses issued new laws which changed tribal policy. And he murdered Arron's sons, Nadev and Avihu to enforce his new laws. The SEDUCTION OF MOSES in BUTTERFLY MORALS©, book nine of the SECRET BUTTERFLY SERIES™ is the previously untold love story that has codified marital relationships between men and women ever since. In the story, I reveal Moses as hypocrite.

He does not stone Baaleezebelle for her natural proclivity; rather, he makes excuses for her; and with his new, innovative pleasuring device he enhances their sexual bond and takes their love to a new, higher, more understanding level. He declares that only male adultery law violators are punishable. But females, opines Moses, are more like flowers, (or perhaps more like butterflies). They must have their natural freedoms! Their promiscuity is perfectly understandable, you see. He opines that men must accept a woman's natural trait. Clever Moses gets the power he demands over his fellow tribesmen and the intimacy he sorely needs from Baalezebelle. The story reveals Moses as a man whose deepest needs can only be met by Baalezebelle.

Bathsheba, Salome, Cleopatra, Isabella, and many other famous women have used their sex appeal to great advantage. And, despite their immoralities, these promiscuous women all found their true loves. We do not hold their natural desires against them; nor did the people of their times. *Au counterair!* These women were heralded and celebrated! And they held life or death power over others. Is my fictional Moses character just a lust obsessed madman? No, he isn't. I do not portray him as mad. Obsessed for power and control? Yes, certainly. In this way he is similar to leaders of the other nation states of his time; and similar to our own leaders in our own time.

As I developed my Moses character, I believe I found my answer to Mother's question: *'Why did Hitler hate Jews?'* Nietzsche's axiom that, as individuals, people may be sane; but in a crowd, they are susceptible to madness, applies to Mother's question. I believe Moses kept the Tribe in the desert wilderness for some forty years to naturally cleanse away the old religious practices of worshipping multiple gods. Through attrition by death and through years of indoctrination, Moses created Judaism, the worship of one god. He instilled in Jews the belief that we are, indeed, chosen people. My theory is that Moses instilled within Jews the notion of superiority. And this was a precursor to similar notions that gave rise to Christianity and Islam.

But Hitler could not tolerate any Jewish attitude of superiority in the new Third Reich he was creating. Hitler believed he had to have a united people, all of a single mindset that they were superior to all other peoples; and that his unified Germanic tribe was destined to rule the world. Hitler saw Jews as a people with an attitude problem. They stood in the way of his vision of world domination. They had to be first marginalized; then vilified; then destroyed by genocide. Incompatible attitudes clashed. The result was the Shoah.

But my Moses was by no means a madman. He was no Hitler. He was clever, far seeing, and calculating. And he was very unlike Hitler in that he was willing to compromise. After all, he knew of Baalezebelle's wantonness. He adored her for it and he accepted it as her condition for their lives together. Why? Because he had to! She gave him no choice. She was honest about her nympho tendency. She never tried to change her ways to his; and she made it clear to him that she had no such intentions. He knew it's nearly impossible to change the basic inherent nature of a person.

So, Moses partnered up with Baalezebelle on her terms. Love, that human dominating limbic thing, caused their partnership to happen. Moses loved her. And Moses found his true god in that love. He allowed his wife and sons to be murdered so he could make her his bride. Possessive as he was, he murdered half the Tribe of Israel to keep other men from having her. And he murdered his own brother Aaron's sons to make it abundantly clear to others in the Tribe that he would have sole possession of her favors. And he saddled humanity with his adultery commandments to keep her off limits to others.

Love held Moses in its grip from the moment he first met Baalezebelle. And, despite Baalezebelle's absence of morals, or rather because of her complete absence of morals, Moses loved her! Was he drawn to her because of her character flaw? I think he was. Some men are naturally attracted to fallen women. Some men adore that trait in a woman. I think some men seek it out because they believe they can save her by reforming her and marrying her. Other seek out that trait because they psychologically need to feel dominated by their woman's promiscuity; become beholden to it, perhaps? I don't know. But it is a powerful force that can hold a man in its grip.

My Moses didn't *just* love Baalezebelle. He was smitten by her and he obligated his life to her love. He loved her resolutely, without reservation; never equivocating; and with unbridled passion! Loving her was his life's priority.

The power element that threaded through my dreams left me wondering: Why do people, as Nietzsche tells us, suspend disbelief, and go mad when they are in crowds? And what do sociopathic leaders understand about taking power over a crowd that enables them to gain it? Is it this simple: That if you can divide a population into dogs and underdogs; and if you champion the underdogs, you can use them, and the useful idiots who go along with their spew, to overthrow the dogs? And thus, you can make yourself the ruler of the underdogs, who have become the new dogs? And, if this is true, then it matters not whether you divide people by religious beliefs; by political beliefs; or by gender beliefs. All that matters is that you divide them!

After all, we will, all of us, always have some difference with others which can be exploited, no matter how nonsensical the difference, won't we? Sure, we will. Even between the sexes! How else can one explain the pink pussy cat vagina hats that female protesters find so fashionable?

So, then it is not too farfetched, as I wrote in LOVE AND LOVERS©, book eleven of THE SECRET BUTTERFLY SERIES™. that we could be entering a period where humanity divides between those who believe in religion, any religion, and those who do not believe in any religion at all; but rather believe in nihilism. And we could then revert to our natural, pre religious worship practices, could we not? Sure, we could! And we, or many of us, could revert to some modern-day form of ancient Ashera, female vagina, worship, couldn't we? Sure, we could! I believe that's exactly what modern day pornography is telling us. In other words, our time is a great time to be a whore. It's a great time to be Marty!

Are we seeking to return to our natural worship tendency, our limbic urge? Are we yearning to unleash our deep limbic desire to once again worship the female vagina? I think we are! It is, after all, the source of our creation. We worshipped it before men devised religions that told us we needed to worship their versions of God. We did what seemed natural then; and we are doing what seems natural now.

And who is to say, in opposition, that God created the universe; rather than to accept that the universe just is and always has been and always will be; and it is unknowable for us mere humans to know how it came to be or how life relates to everything that is, dark matter or seen matter? And may we not then, soon, see the day when a sensational, beguiling and becoming, comely porn star becomes our most revered leader? Crazy? Perhaps? But why not? At least, could we finally believe in someone who has achieved Godly status by natural adoration; and not by climbing the ranks of a religious regime that made its bones by murdering others?

Well, maybe not! My bad girl characters: Marty, Attorney Marcy Adams from ALPHA, THE BEGINNING© AND OMEGA, THE END© stories, and Jen, from LOVE AND LOVERS© all murdered often. And all of these salaciously immoral vixens profited handsomely from their murders. They are all very salacious Bad Girls, indeed! My questions only elicit more questions.

But let's leave our ruminations about ancient Egyptian worship practices and the age of accepted slavery. Slavery still exists, by the way. It just assumes new forms. I'm not talking about child trafficking and prostitution; but an example which is insidious and less understood. Let's now enter a world where slavery takes the form of mind control.

Marty's tedious seduction of psychologically damaged, neurotic Charles, in BUTTERFLY MORALS©, explores a different, more subtle method of little understood human slavery; but just as dehumanizing. A selfish mother manipulates a boy's natural Oedipus Complex to control his life far into adulthood. Perhaps Nefertiti first put her moves on Moses; and later, Tutankhamen? I wonder: Is slavery a natural human trait? Must each of us be either master or slave? When we consider the way David manipulated Marty and his other employees, one cannot help but wonder: Just how pervasive is the slavery trait? Does it manifest in the very nature of corporations, generally? The trait seems, to me, to be too consistent to be unnatural.

I discovered another natural trait while writing RUBY BUT-TERFLY© and BUTTERFLY MORALS©, a behavior I hadn't considered when I began the SERIES. But I soon realized that Marty's most predicable behavior had to have originated from a natural desire to seduce. It is simply that heroine Marty studied her male quarry and schemed ways to seduce them. And Marty refined that natural trait; took it to a whole new, higher level; and made a sport of it. Hence, we label her *'Bad Girl,' 'Vamp,' 'Dominatrix,'* and *'Homewrecker.'*

Consider her seduction methods of Carl's wife, from A WOMAN'S VOICES©; Fred, and Big Ed, from PROMISCUOUS DREAMS©; and Dominick, from BUTTERFLY MORALS©. Each seduction required careful study of her mark and refinement of her tactics. Her genius emotive mind was able to perform its assessment quickly; *'On The Fly,'* so to speak, in the case of Carl's wife. I think readers will agree: That was one clever murder! But Marty was much more methodical and meticulous in her seductions of Fred, Big Ed, and Dominick. Her cunning character trait reappears in incestuous murderess Jen, the genius femme fatale heroine of TROPHY BUTTERFLY©.

Bertie and George are horribly tragic, pitiful characters who actually sought out Marty to be the instrument of their own destruction. We first meet them in PROMISCUOUS DREAMS©, and travel along in their pathetic, damaged lives as they search for meaning. In Marty they believe they have found their true purpose for living; but these two are impossibly naïve. Like flies ensnared in a spider's web, they become Marty's helpless prey.

She takes full advantage of their generosity. They teach her how to hone her acting skills to create the world's most salacious pornography. They open their hearts, their fabulous wealth, and their friends to her. She awes them by explaining her innermost feelings while she was seducing Marshawn, Josh, and her other porn partners. She shares her most evil, innermost thoughts with them. She even shares with them her joyous feelings while she's destroying Aaliyah's marriage. This naïve couple even empathize with Marty's compulsive need to destroy the other woman.

But they are so blinded by their need to love Marty and their desire to please her and dote upon her that they become blind to their own fate. Ultimately, in RUBY BUTTERFLY©, Marty betrays them. She mocks them; revealing to them that she only saw them as her victims. They nevertheless love her while she proves herself to David, during her grandest murder finale, ever. But does she succeed? Does she capture David? Have her murders really excited him? Does she finally seduce her ultimate quarry?

The SECRET BUTTERFLY SERIES is, through and through, a love story. Not just any, run of the mill, love story. This is a love story saga of a reincarnating murderess, wrapped within her ribald loves and her murders, lived by a time traveling female serial killer; and a temptress so beguiling with needs so compelling, that many readers will empathize with her. They will understand her needs and sympathize with her. And those who understand her will embrace her character and love her!

True love binds Bob to Marty and Marty to Bob. Their relationship is based upon honest romantic love. But their love is not without complications. Indian Princess Barbara and Bob were romantically involved long before David ordered Marty to seduce Bob. That seduction plot sets off a remarkable chain of events which ultimately lead back to David and reveal his evil. Barbara, with the help of Big Chief, her father, deduce that David is the ultimate Bad Boy, and that there is a nefarious corporate plan afoot. Then, with the help of Jimmy, *'The Blade,'* Checini, Barbara discovers David's world of insanity and morbid fetishes in the book, MURDER PROPERLY DONE©, which begins the INSANITY VOLUME of THE SECRET BUTTERFLY SERIES™. I wrote a separate preface to that volume in MURDER PROPERLY DONE©. It guides you through the bizarro, insane rabbit hole world that is David's mind.

Jen, Bifster, and Thor are the three main characters introduced in TROPHY BUTTERFLY©. Bifster is Jen's cat. Thor is Jen's lover. Thor acquiesces to Jen's incestuous compulsions and her calculating murder of Dominick, her father; and to LBJ's (Lolita Bunny Joyful) seductively destructive 'Bat' tactics. As male stud Thor plunges headlong into Jen and LBJ's worlds of sin and debauchery, where those two Bad Girl Vamps pillage wealth from their willing victims, I found myself wondering: Was I foreseeing a world where religion will be displaced? Has humanity begun a future where Popes, Cardinals, Archbishops, Bishops, Priests; Imams and Rabbis are seen as mere sock puppet automatons, relegated to a dying religious world order?

Will our religious worship places be repurposed, as Marty recasts them in the SERIES' fictions, for real; and become temples for the Modern Morality Standard's Pagan religious services; and for live pornographic performances? Will pornographic worship practices achieve tax exempt status? Will the hedonists among us achieve enough political power to overthrow the political order we have evolved since colonial times to make immorality our new reality?

After hearing Marty's morality philosophy and her forecast for humanity, one cannot help but wonder? Promiscuity, whoring, and pornography seem to be the growing trend. *'The trend is your friend,'* they say. So, why will it not gain political dominance? Why will debauchery not achieve preeminence? Why will the religions not be discarded? Why will we not descend into nihilism? Or, should I rather ask, ascend to it? It depends upon one's perspective, doesn't it?

Perhaps? Time will tell. It's always difficult to foresee what lies ahead, especially when you're contemplating the future. But the present trend away from religion and towards greater immorality seems, to me, very real. The Make America Great Again movement may endure. It may even reverse the immorality trend. But I doubt it. I think it likely will be seen, historically, as a mere bump in the road; on a road that is turning our history around one hundred eighty degrees; taking humanity all the way back to our ancient, Pagan morality roots, from which we all arose.

In all truth, even though few will openly admit it, many of us truly do secretly love and adore our porn stars. Even though we are conditioned and commanded to see them as hopelessly lost immoral souls; fallen women and profligate, casual, unrepentant sinners, we secretly, earnestly wish them continued success with their ribald careers. And we eagerly await their latest, most titillating, salacious film, and photo offerings.

But we should keep our minds open to the possibilities that, as our porn stars have changed many of us; they, too, can change. In LOVE AND LOVERS©, incorrigible apostate Marty, after seducing her phantom enigmas in one final, fantastical lust fest; and in the waning moments of her sordid, immoral life, desperately turns to God. Yes, she does! She becomes a true believer! She earnestly repents and begs God's forgiveness for all her sins in all her past lives.

Uncertain and confused, David listens as Marty's corporal life expires. She bids farewell to her profligate, immoral soul, flinging it into the welcoming arms of ever-forgiving; ever-accepting, ever-lasting God. And a butterfly flutters away!

For the sake of readers' sanity and my own, the preface to the INSANITY VOLUME'S three books: MURDER PROPERLY DONE©, LOVE AND MADNESS©, and BUTTERFLY LOVE© are prefaced in MURDER PROPERLY DONE©. The REINCARNATION VOLUME'S four books: CRIMSON MARIPOSA©, CRIMSON AND PINK©, LUST WHEELS©, AND

YES FOR LOVE© are prefaced at the beginning of CRIMSON MARIPOSA©.

The SECRET BUTTERFLY SERIES™ is bookended by ALPHA (THE BEGINNING) © and OMEGA (THE END) ©. Those two bookends books are a completely contained miniseries in themselves. The story concerns a profligate porn star, a heinous crime of passion murder, and a willful, highly unethical, but brilliant female attorney. Please enjoy them.

And for your ultimate enjoyment pleasure experience, I seriously recommend that readers also procure audible copies of all SERIES books, and follow along with your readings the outstanding narrations of the books. The expressiveness of voice artist Minna Morinette will, I promise you, captivate your attentions and awaken your passions.

I addressed profound questions in the SECRET BUTTERFLY SERIES™ fictional books: 'What constitutes religion for favorable tax treatment status?' 'Will pornography become humanity's newest religion?' 'Will our profoundly deep, carnal yearnings gain tax exempt status as legitimate worship choices?' 'And if not, why not?' 'Is our religious freedom to worship an abstract God any more a legitimate worship practice than the ancients' worship of fertility goddess Ashera and the female vagina?' 'Are limbic desires legally forbidden in modern worship practices; and if so, why?' 'Why couldn't ancient religious practices, long since forcibly eradicated by the religionists, be resurrected, and revived?' 'What is the true source of our creation, anyway?' 'Why isn't it the cervical opening, that mysterious passageway into the mysterious female womb?'

The truth is: We don't know. Nobody knows. The religionists insist that they do know and that you must believe them. They will tell you it is God; but in all truth, they don't know what cause creation. I think it must be what we choose to believe; not what we are compelled to believe through our forced childhood indoctrinations. So, when you hear a religionist vilify a porn star, consider motive. And ask yourself: Who has rights to the moral high ground?

I wonder: Did Abraham, Moses, Jesus. Mohammed, and Budda set humanity on the right paths? Are those paths our best paths? And where are those paths taking us? To genocides of the Americas' native Indians; genocides of Uyghurs, Tibetans, Palestinians, Armenians, Tutsi's, Cambodians, Jews? Nuclear annihilation, perhaps? Why? For what reason? Is it all just a power trip for some with a sociopathic need to be top dog? What's the point of dividing populations and fighting those who are of different minds or persuasions? What does it mean for you, if you are not one of the 'Chosen,' or not one of those 'Blessed To Be Called To The Supper Of The Lamb?'

Does it mean God has signed off on you? Does it mean God has red tagged you? Perhaps marked you down as unsuitable; to be disposed of? Does it mean you deserve getting bombed, shot, killed or maimed; or having your children taken from you? And what if you are not a Muslim? What if the Muslim's call to prayer means nothing to you? Does that mean you are an infidel? Does it mean you deserve to be raped, pillaged, and murdered? Good grief! By what logic? Oh, that's right. Religions are not logic based. They are faith based. But how can faith based be differentiated from insane based? Oh, you might say: 'We don't do that bad stuff anymore.' But we do!

Is there no way to end humanity's collective madness? I wish I knew. I imagine many millions of us wish we knew. But I know I do not know. I doubt that trusting power to nihilists or porn stars is the answer any more than entrusting power to religionists or communists is the answer. Perhaps the U S Constitution is the best answer? At least it seeks to prevent power from vesting permanently in one place or one hand for very long. Maybe shaking things up is the only antidote to power's aphrodisiac alure. I fear we will perish as a species unless we can figure out how to control the human impulse to hold power and exert it over others. There must be a way to come to grips with it. Perhaps comedy is our solution? Yes! That's it! We should laugh at ourselves. When in a crowd, we can become dangerous. We can become mad!

I wonder: What was humanity like before religions' first leaders defined right and wrong for us? What do we know about early humans' belief practices? Did they worship anything or anyone? And if they did, what, and how, did our pre-civilization ancestors worship? Does anyone really know; or are we all just imagining and guessing? How did the Torah's homilies first come into being? Does anyone know? Where is the proof? In truth, we don't know. Likely, we will never know.

How can anyone look upon pre-religions' carved images of Ashera's vagina statues and not believe that the female vagina was the object of early Pagans' adoration worship? Were the bards who created our religions being truthful; or were they spinning tales around their campfires so they could seize control of the Ashera worshippers? Did they intend to control our freedoms and our lives?

Have our homily-based religious beliefs served human progress well? Did our early faiths rely upon persuasion, or upon force? Clearly, Moses applied force. Murder is force. Was he simply acting out human tradition? Has humanity always relied upon force?

I wonder: Did the tribe from Baalbek slaughter the tribe from Gobekli Tepe? I think something epical like that must have happened. How else can those two religious sites be explained? If only ancient stones could talk! Were there early tribal clashes for the glory and favors of a female's vagina? Homer's Iliad tells us that males' vagina control motive caused the infamous Trojan War. Did entire nation states come to war over one woman's vagina?

Homer would have us believe it. So, we should ask ourselves: Are we naturally hard wired to kill each other over females' favors? Good grief!

Were our earliest clashes tribal extinction events? Was sex the reward that females offered the victors of those clashes? Perhaps the Lakota Tribes with their ancient Pole Dance rituals can teach us something? Victorious Lakota warriors were demonstrably rewarded with copious sex as bounty payments for their Pawnee scalps. Was their tradition just a nomadic Plains Indian tribe's cultural anomaly; or was it a remnant holdover from humanity's universal ancient practice?

Did men then, and do men now, murder other men for the pleasures of a female's vagina? The criminal record is filled with lust and sex as motives for murder. I think, consciously or subconsciously, we do commit murder for sex. The ALPHA© and OMEGA© bookend books tell of just such a case. Attorney Marcy Adams personifies the predatory female who cleverly uses sex for murder and profit. Do we women encourage our males to commit homicides? Do we even understand how profoundly powerful our offerings of sex motivates our males? I think the answers must be: 'Yes!' Deep down, we do know.

I believe Cain murdered Able for a woman's favors; and I believe women's favors have been the key, bedrock motivation for killings and wars ever since. Our *Survival Of The Fittest* driver is, after food and perhaps shelter, most assuredly, sex. In this vital aspect of human life, we are only different from the other animals in this respect: Most species' male animals, contesting for breeding rights, usually stop short of killing their rivals. But human males do not stop. Humans want their enemies dead. Humans kill.

Truth is elusive. But it remains standing after all lies are peeled away. The SERIES books are pure fiction. Please do not take them as factual. They may affect the way you think about some things;

but they will not enlighten you with certain answers. They are not a religious text. They are not gospel truths. Unlike archeology and anthropology, they will not unmask long-hidden truths. But hopefully, they may cause you to wonder about what really happened in times past. And they may cause you to reflect about happenings in our present-day world. After reading the SERIES books, truths about beliefs may seem tantalizingly close to being revealed; yet, still vexingly elusive.

This preface would be incomplete without mentioning Bifster. I found him sleeping in my rocking chair on my front porch one clammy, cold February morning. When I said: *'Hello, Mr. Cat,'* I startled him. He leaped to his feet, hissed at me, and bristled his fur. His tail looked like an exaggerated bottle brush. He extended his razor-sharp claws and showed his teeth. Clearly, he was ready to fight me.

I noticed that he had a wheeze in his breathing and only one eye, which was rheumy. He'd recently been in a fight. One of his ears was badly torn and some of his fur had been ripped away from his right front leg. The leg had dried blood on it. I felt simultaneous fear and pity. This boy was obviously feral wild, full of fight, and fearless. I could not imagine the hellish life he led.

I spoke softly to him, assuring him that I meant no harm. I told him he could stay as long as he liked. My calm demeanor and soothing voice seemed to settle him. I assured him that he was my welcome guest. And I promised to feed him if he decided to stay with me. Thus began our routine. Bifster guarded my abode. And I fed him. His presence on my porch reminded me that every life is precious. And no matter what struggles or challenges life throws at us, life is, nevertheless, a special, wonderful experience; and well worth living.

Bifster Cat was unlike other cats. He was far bigger; possibly part Bobcat. And he had a serious psychological issue with dogs.

Bifster seemed to think that dogs did not belong in this world. Unlike most cats who cowered and hid from dogs, Bifster hated dogs so much that he attacked them, abandoning all sense of self preservation. Seeing a dog of any size, the bigger the better; it didn't matter. Bifster leaped into action. He became suddenly fearless and obsessed. The dirt road in front of my cabin became Bifster's turf. And dogs were not allowed trespass. He shot off my porch like a lightning bolt and ran down every hapless dog. Ignoring all risks to himself, he leaped onto the dog's muzzle, and began shredding its face.

Howling, yelping, screaming; hissing and cat wailings signaled that Bifster was attacking some poor, unfortunate dog. There was no reasoning with Bifster and no stopping him. He simply had to act upon his obsessive hatred of dogs. I never had any clue as to how his canine hatred originated; but it was ever present. Dogs and their owners soon avoided my cabin. They detoured around behind it on a path through the woods.

After about three months of our acquaintance, Bifster allowed me to lightly touch his head while he ate. He even purred softly! The lost fur on his front leg grew back. I began hoping that his feral soul was ready to be tamed. I imagined he would let his guard down while I threw a blanket over him and took him to a Vet for shots and neutering. I envisioned Bifster becoming my house cat and lap companion.

But my hopes were not to be realized. As suddenly as Bifster came into my life, one morning he was gone. He left no clue as to where he was going. He simply left! I often wonder whether a coyote got him; or a cougar, or a dog that refused to put up with his antics? Perhaps an interesting lady cat came along and enticed him away? I can never know. Some creatures are just wild things. And, being wild things, getting tamed terrifies them. They refuse to trade their wildness for comfort. Bifster was one of those. He has gone away, somewhere. Now that he's gone, I think I finally understand him. I was a fool to imagine I could tame him. I accepted him. I'm certain he knew that. And I believe he accepted me. We respected our differences. I still think about him. I loved him. And I badly miss him.

Rosemary

Hello, I'm Minna Morinette, your narrator. Have you ever wondered if a nymphomaniac has honest feelings about love? Does she need to be loved in the same way other women need love? Or, is life only about sex for her? Was Marty born with her addictive condition? Was she sent to us by the Spirits to enlighten us about our own sexuality? Or, is Marty an unfortunate child who turned to promiscuity to escape her fear of never being loved? Does she actually love her many lovers, or is she seeking love with one special person? Has her soul changed, now that she's found ways to make money from her addiction; or is she still the same lonely, abandoned little girl? She strives to please David, but how wise is that?

Who is David, anyway, and why does Marty feel her deep attraction to him? What makes her want to please David; and if she doesn't, then what? Let's capture her thoughts and understand the clever ways Marty advanced her career in prostitution to become the world's most famous porn star. We'll learn how Marty uses her intimate secrets to turn a man's mind inside out. What makes a man fall in love with her? What makes him forsake all others for her? Marty's seduction skills reveal her soul's inner workings; her sweet, compelling, honest innocence; and her magnetic lovability. When will David reveal why he desperately needs Marty to return to him?

In RUBY BUTTERFLY©, our eighth novel in THE SECRET BUT-TERFLY™ SERIES, Marty has arrived. She'll reveal why she's now ranked at the world's number one star of intimate film artistry, and why her film sales exceed the sales of the next twenty porn stars, combined. She'll seduce a reclusive prince and capture the heart of a billionaire movie mogul. She'll answer many questions from her admiring fan base in a revealing tell-all interview with Consuelo

Lovely of Intimacy Artistry Magazine. It seems nothing could ever go wrong with Marty's glamorous life. But why then, does an apparition appear to Bob with its foreboding message?

What sparks Barbara's change of heart towards Marty; and what causes Barbara's sudden, intense interest in Marty's career? Why is Barbara suddenly alarmed over David's treatment of certain expense records? What does her discovery reveal about Bob, and the Firm's secret murders? In her desperate race against time, Barbara turns to an unexpected source for help. Will they solve the puzzle soon enough, or will the villain escape with his crimes unsolved?

Let's find some answers to our questions. Come flutter with me as I narrate RUBY BUTTERFLY, the eighth book of the SECRET BUTTERFLY ™ SERIES. We'll begin by listening to Marty as she reveals her grand Las Vegas adventure to Consuelo.

**SECRET BUTTERFLY SERIES ™ CHARACTERS
INTRODUCED IN "RUBY BUTTERFLY"
(MAJOR CHARACTERS ARE BOLDFACED)**
Readers reference guide to where a character is introduced.

(CHARACTER, DESCRIPTION OF CHARACTER, AND
CHAPTER WHERE CHARACTER IS MENTIONED)

**CONSUELO LOVELY, REPORTER, INTERVIEWER FROM
THE WONDERFUL WORLD OF PORN MAGAZINE
AND ITS AFFILIATE TV CHANNEL, PORN BEAT, RUBY
BUTTERFLY(RB), CH1**

**DOMINICK, OR DOM, LOVER, PROMOTER OF MARTY'S
PORN CAREER, (RB), CH3**

MARY MAGDALENE, WIFE OF JESUS CHRIST, (RB), CH3

**MISS LUST, MARTY'S VOICE THAT URGES HER TO
COMMIT MURDERS, (RB), CH6**

**ATHENA AND HERA, HANDMAIDENS TO MARY'S
CONCEPTION MIRACLE, (RB), CH6**

CHAPTER ONE

There are two kinds of whores. I don't mean young or old, thin, or full; or anything like that. I mean about how they relate to the men who love them. There are sensational, glorious, carefree whores. And there are also whores who conceal some very deep secrets. (Rosemary Ness-Bitner, author)

TRIUMPH

While seated upon the haybales at David's, Marty's thoughts traveled back to her interview with Consuelo Lovely of 'The Wonderful World of Porn' magazine and star reporter from 'Porn Beat', the magazine's television affiliate. She was explaining her newest business venture with multi-billionaire, Dominick:

"Our clothing line and film making decisions prompted Dom to take me to Las Vegas the following week. That's where Dom made his bold announcement that rocked the sex industry world. And he did it in style. He rented the entire casino and invited two thousand media people into the casino's largest ballroom. He stood on the stage as if he was a bride groom waiting, looking for me, his immoral, promiscuous bride, in anxious anticipation. He wore his beautifully jeweled blue tuxedo. He lifted his head up, searching the sky.

"That was my cue to float down from the ceiling. I wore huge Monarch Butterfly wings attached to my transparent harness.

My arms and legs were held by silk cords. I appeared to flutter in mid-air, as I came down to Dom from the sky. I wore a bikini from our new Erotica Premium clothing line. It was very tight fitting. It accented my fuck crazed tush perfectly, like I was eager to break out of it because I was so primed and anxious to make love. My top was a transparent silk string with huge diamonds positioned directly over my nipples. Dom's genius idea had an insert sleeve sewn into the V of my bottom piece. He designed it to hold a protruding fifty caret ruby.

"When I fluttered down from the sky into Dom's arms, he held me above his head. I enshrouded his uplifted face with my bosom as my wings fluttered and I flexed my ass tightly, in my MLB pose----"

"Wait," interrupted Consuelo, "what do you mean by MLB pose, Major League Baseball?"

"No, silly, MLB pose is my Magnificent Love Bunny pose. It's the strong and tight way my ass looks from behind when I flex hard with a cock captured tightly inside my VAGINA. It's my high and tight, deliciously ravishing love making fucking machine look. It's highly suggestive; like it's saying that I love being a fuck bunny. I often preview my porn films by first showing my MLB pose. I flex my tush and bend over so my fans can see my vagina. Sometimes I look through my legs and smile with my head upside down while I open my vagina with my fingers. Then I stand upright and twerk a little. That gives my fans the illusion that I'm anxious to begin fucking and Kegel squeezing every last drop of cum out of my partner's cock. It's a routine that heats up my fans' appetite for the whole film. From the very beginning of the first scene, they can hardly wait for me to start having sex."

"I see, well, do you have other shorthand terms for your poses?"

"Oh, sure, there's my IP pose."

"That doesn't mean Internet Protocol, does it?"

"No silly, it stands for Insatiable Pussy. It's the movement I make when I'm on my back with my hips up thrust and I'm bump twerking upwards, lifting my vagina high toward the sky. Sometimes I use my hands to hold myself open and rub myself seductively while I do that. The effect shocks my viewers. It's highly erotic; communicates my explicit yearning to fuck. It's explosive as dynamite. It helps fans imagine that they are about to penetrate me; like they are kneeling between my butterfly wings, bringing their cocks to me; about to feel the slippery hot inside of me; willing to abandon their moral souls in my love and immorality; make love with me; lick me; lose their minds in my vagina."

"I see-- any others?"

"Yes. There's my PB pose. That means Pussy Behind. Producers have me present my vagina from behind while I look around and smile sexily at the camera. I often hold myself open while I pose that way. I also use my eyes and my 'Come Play with Me' smile to invite my partner to enjoy the ultimate love making experience. By entering from behind me, his cock gets way deep inside me. His cock feels my incredible tight vagina sensations. He discovers he's in erotica's ultimate heaven."

"I see. Let me ask you, do you prefer having sex when the males mount you from behind?"

"Oh, yes, yes, and OH MY GOD, ABSOLUTELY YES! Yes, very, very much! I very much prefer making love that way. I absolutely love it when the penis is way up inside me, touching my cervix while that cock is all bone hard stiff and swollen up. I love going crazy twerking my ass when I have a cock all the way deep inside my vagina like that. I can get the whole feel of the entire fully erect cock throughout the entire insides of my vagina. I feel like I have millions of tiny sensitive hot lips kissing that huge swollen cock. I can fee those kisses throughout my entire body, from my vagina right to

my brain, then to this trembling in my spine. The pressure of a hard cock setting off my thousands of clitoral nerve endings, is beyond sensational. It causes me to lose my mind; I want to keep fucking forever. It's that wonderful.

"It's simply the most sensual way to fuck, Consuelo. My vagina gets all wet and juicy and swollen when I make love like that. I reach my hand down below my belly and use my fingers to push against my clit and stimulate myself while the cock is thrusting. It brings on passion sensations that always result in spectacular orgasms. I feel this ecstatic delirium. My lust cravings send me out of my mind.

"I love making love that way so much that I encourage my film producers to include scenes where I can have three or four part-ners primed to mount me in succession from behind. When several partners are doing me that way, you'll notice my facial expressions become out of this world glorious. I radiate from the splendor I feel. My face takes on this stunned, far away look because my feelings become other worldly. I orgasm to the universe while I make love that way.

"While I'm PB mounted like that I orgasm almost instanta-neously and continuously. My libido stays at its maximum high for an hour or more, easily; especially when my partners hold my hips and pull my ass tightly against them. That helps me feel their bone hard cock's way up inside me. My mind flies away to heaven when partner after partner does me that way. I desperately want to keep going, even after I collapse from exhaustion. I love it that much.

"That's why, after my last cock withdraws, you see me continue twerking. My vagina still pulsates and quivers while cum continues flowing out of me. I love the PB position so much. It's wonderful! You are seeing my vagina's reflexive involuntary action. It's natu-ral; same as my heart beating or my breathing. Copulation is my natural condition. I'm that much of an insatiable nympho! And the PB position especially satisfies me because the beauty of intimacy is

so highly intensified. It's impossible to control my urge to continue making love when I'm being done PB. My natural reflexes never want the feeling to end!"

"Thank you for those valuable insights, Marty. Where were we?"

"We were right where I had my legs wrapped around Dom's neck and I was doing my MLB pose. My ass was magnificent. You can see in some of the photos how beautiful and tight it was; and how it bulged out of my bikini bottom, like I was just begging to make love. After that, I slowly up righted myself and stood before Dom. My bikini bottom was a skimpy, transparent triangle that barely covered my vagina. It had less than one sixteenth of an inch of material extending on either side of my vagina. Dom's marketing idea is to use my vagina as our product and to showcase it at every opportunity. He designed the triangle napkin portion of my bikini to cause viewers eyes to rivet to my vagina. It's an ingenious design. Dom calls it positioning the product to best advantage. He designed a tiny slot of bikini material in the lower front of the triangle napkin. He mounted a huge fifty caret flawless red ruby on a thin piece of plastic. Then he inserted the plastic with the ruby attached into the front of my tiny napkin. He had a seamstress measure the ruby and the cloth, and sew a perfect circle in my skimpy triangle which allowed my ruby to protrude from my vagina in a very prominent way. When you see me in that bikini bottom, your eyes are instantly drawn to my vagina.

"Dom's theory of branding is to make my vagina synonymous with a priceless ruby in the minds of my viewing fans. He believes, and I totally agree with his thinking, that the more explicit scenes I create; the more scenes my fans see of me making love with cock after cock; the more cream pies (that's the scene that captures the white semen flowing out of my vagina after a cock has ejaculated inside me) that appear in my films, the more recognizable and famous I and my vagina will become. Dom wants my future films

to focus less on the actual strokes of the cocks and my vagina while I am fucking. Oh, he wants some of that for effect; but he wants my future films to emphasize the actual ejaculations and the flows of the cream pies from my vagina, after my partners come inside me. He calls that promoting our product. He wants me to create, literally, over three hundred more scenes where my vagina is featured coaxing an ejaculation from my partners. To do this, we'll use assistants who will basically prep my cocks for me. Those women will give the cocks blow jobs and have them all stimulated; so that, once those cocks are inside my vagina, they will already be very sensitized and primed to ejaculate. That way, I won't feel tedium from too many strokes before my cocks shoot off their semen inside me. Dom wants to portray me as the most debauched, immoral woman the world has ever known. As part of his project, I'm going to have ten orgies with six men ejaculating into me during each orgy. Then, Dom is going to create a compilation of my immoral depravity and set it to a romantic musical score. He's going to title the film 'RUBY BUTTER-FLY' He's convinced that males the world over will salivate over me and my vagina will become unforgettable in millions of minds. It's a very creative idea. I'm so happy to have Dom promoting my image."

"Marty, how will this film compilation differ from all other porn compilations that are already out there?"

"Consuelo, according to Dom, there are billions of fans who watch porn. But within this vast audience there is a particular sub-set of fans that Dom calls the afficionados. These are viewers who can discern the most minute differences in porn films. Just as no two women, not even identical twins, have exactly identical faces, Dom asserts that no two women have perfectly identical vaginas. He wants to market to that discerning group of aficionados. Dom said that, although I am a fully developed woman, my vagina retains the qualities of a teen aged girl's smaller and more perky vagina. He studied close up porn film scenes of hundreds of pussies while

they were fucking their partners. His conclusion is that my vagina is uniquely beautiful. It's adorable, memorable, and easily differentiated from all others."

"Really? How so?"

"According to Dom, I have perfect roundness, symmetry, and a blushing, pinkish coloration in my outer lips. My inner lips are perfectly symmetrical as well, with no sign of prolapsing or variation between the lips while I am fornicating with a cock. I fuck in perfect symmetry, according to Dom. I take in my erotic pleasure sensations evenly, through my entire vagina. My crown hood is also a distinct and pronounced feature. It's very ambitious during sex. It uniquely harmonizes and complements the rhythms of my partners' cock strokes. Dom swears no other vagina performs quite as smoothly, rhythmically, and salaciously deliciously enjoyably naughtily, as mine. Dom absolutely adores my cunt. He says he can see, in the slow-motion close-up sequences, that my vagina loves the sliding sensations that the cocks give to my hood, while sliding inward and outward. He says he can uniquely visualize the glistening inner sensation, that joyous warmth that I can feel in my hood while I'm fucking; while he's watching my vagina fornicating.

"Dom believes the aficionados can also visualize that same differential that my fornications communicate through my films. He believes these aficionados have discovered a unique rabbit hole that's a rarity in porn films. He thinks they love my films because they allow the viewer to visualize my sex addiction. They are able to empathize with my nymphomania. They sympathize with my need for sex and they adore me for it. And, here's the kicker, Consuelo. Because they empathize and sympathize with my need, they become as addicted to watching me as I am addicted to fornicating. My addiction induces the porn addiction of others!"

"Dom sees this addiction phenomena as his way to create a wider segment wedge into the overall porn market. He intensively studies

market data. He noticed that online porn watchers tended to view my explicit fornication segments repeatedly; some viewers will see them, literally, hundreds of times. Other porn stars were not getting anywhere near that number of eyeball hits on their explicit fornication scenes. Dom has concluded that these aficionados narrow their searches to find and zero in on my vagina. He's done surveys of porn watchers. And he's discovered that the men who are addicted tend to idolize a particular porn star. They memorize her most erotic scenes. They fall asleep dreaming that they are in those scenes, performing them with her. They love her. They insist on viewing only her films.

"Now, just beside my vagina, about a half inch away from my right-side outer lip, I have a tiny, almost indiscernible brown freckle. No other vagina has an identifier exactly like mine. Dom said his audience data tells him that the most discerning porn fans search out my little freckle. They identify with it like it's a seal of approval. Seeing it in my explicit close ups assures them that they are receiving exclusive, premium pornography; the very best; the most relatable and most stimulating. They are confident that they are watching the world's most amoral, incorrigible, lovable whore in the world. That's my brand image; my product positioning. They demand it because they love me. They will not accept a substitute. They have that brand loyalty. They seek me out from all the other porn stars. They adore me. Dom thinks he's hit the nail on the head."

"Why does he think this compilation idea is key to bolstering your brand identity?"

"His in-depth research. He says there are two whys. By that he means there are two reasons why that aficionado group obsesses over my porn films. The first why is because they know I'm completely immoral. They know, from my films, that I've dipped fifty wedding rings through my cum pool, meaning that I've heartlessly ruined at least fifty marriages. They know I'm completely devoid of empathy for the women whose lives I've upended. I'm without conscience; and

they love that about me. Psychologically, they wish that the cock that they see fucking me was their cock; and that, somehow, they would discover a loving relationship with me and that I would also help them upend their own existing relationships that have the trapped."

"Okay. What's the second why?"

"It's based upon questionnaires Dom sent out to my Premium Members and their feedback comments. Dom studied and interpreted their answers. He says the second why is that I have become a religion for the aficionados. It gets into the psychological reasons why people go to church, or mass. They want to believe that the service enables them to be psychologically closer to, with, and one with God and the Christ. They identify their psychological belief processing with the cross, the priests in their magnificent robes, the readings from the scriptures, the sermons, the communal eating of their wafer as the transformed body of the Christ, the icons and statues and paintings of the various religious saints, and the music. By going to services regularly, these devout people get what they believe is much needed reinforcement and assurance that the mystery of faith, which they believe in, is a valid belief. It reassures them that their belief is valid and that their religion is the right thing to believe; that they will have life after death; that they will come face to face with God and the Christ in their heavenly afterlife."

"I'm not sure I see how your porn compilation is similar, Marty?"

"According to Dom's research, my compilation will have a very similar effect for the aficionados. They need to believe that my immorality is sacred; that it is inviolate and everlasting; uncompromising. They need to believe that they can always trust in me to be conscience free and forever committed to my freedom loving, sinful ways. Watching cock after cock fornicating with me will give them the reassurance that my message is constant and never varying. They need to feel that I believe in what I am doing by my whoring, just like the religious faithful need to believe that the priests believe

in the message that they are selling. My freckle is psychologically similar to the physical setting of the church for the believers, with its statures and crosses. Dom says my freckle serves the same purpose. It assures my believers that they have come to the right place to have their beliefs reinforced. By watching my compilation frequently, like once a day or weekly, my followers will get the same belief reinforcement that the churchgoers receive. He is reassured that I am there for him; that he can count on entering the same psychological realm that my mind is in; that realm of eternal, promiscuous freedom, and endless sinfulness.

"It's my followers' psychological equivalent to a churchgoer's psychological attainment of oneness with God and the Christ. Like services assist the churchgoer in his attempts to perfect himself and act more like God and the Christ in his dealings and way of life; so, too, will regular, frequent viewings of my porn compilation and my other films assist my followers to accept and adopt my immoral ways in their own daily lives. Reinforcement of my consistent message, that my immoral ways are the right and true ways, will help them become more like me and to seek out others who also desire to be more like me."

"Okay, but why a two-hour compilation?"

"Dom's studies show that reinforcement of a message is key to behavioral changes. That's why the Church encourages people to attend services regularly. The message must be repeated, like a continuous liturgical loop, played over and over. Well, pornography is similar. Dom reasons that, by creating this two-hour compilation extravaganza of me continuously fucking sixty or so different cocks in ten unique orgy sessions, we will cause many viewers to become psychologically addicted to the message, that immoral behavior is liberating and beautiful. They will become faithfully committed to loving my pornography and regularly watching my films, just like religious churchgoers. Dom believes we will convert a huge additional

percentage of casual porn watchers into die hard aficionados; all of them becoming life-time addicted to watching me fornicate. Dom always thinks big. He sees blockbuster potential in this RUBY BUT-TERFLY compilation concept; millions more new fans, all addicted to watching me fuck."

"Won't this exhaust you, Marty?"

"Oh, no," Marty giggled, "not at all. I'll enjoy all of it. I'm fascinated by the project concept of it. I'm going to love doing it. I'll love getting my hair coiffed in all the different styles; the different make up schemes; the different erotic scenes and mood music; the fun of meeting my handsome new partners; feeling their lips as they each kiss the ruby on my bikini, accenting the theme of my cream pie compilation; then the thrills of feeling each of them removing my bikini triangle and kissing my vagina to excite me; then me kissing each of their mouths and their cocks for those first times, establishing my romantic attachment to them; and then, skipping a lot of the customary, long tedium of screenplay, and moving right into fornication, with fantastic exceptional cocks, one after the other, that are already prepped and rock hard, anxious to fuck me; and then, experiencing their hot, wonderful cum shots over my clitoris; that intimate sensation of passion and love; and then those gradual outflows of all that wonderful warm semen! It's always a thrill for me to meet and seduce new partners, Consuelo; and to achieve intimacy with them. It's my own internal blessing, for me. And I'll be thrilled knowing that each segment, each explicit ejaculation sequence, will reinforce my fans' belief that I am the immoral and eternal unholy truth that they seek and need. And, they will love me for enabling them to believe in me."

"What does Dom think about the market for this?"

"Oh, Consuelo, that's big. Dom thinks religion is a huge market. Look at how well the Pope does. Gold, art, power; the top people in a religious market segment do fantastic! Well, Dom thinks there's a

huge segment of religion that are non-believers and skeptics. That's the niche he's going to target. He's working on a strategy to create New Morality Temples where the liturgy will be Pagan worship. Instead of pitching a message that we're an exclusive group, like the religions do, we'll be non-exclusive. Instead of commandments and mitzvahs about what is forbidden, we'll have a doctrine that says 'anything goes.'

"We want our members to worship beautiful, immoral freedom; especially sexual freedom. We will insist that our members obey all secular laws; but consensual relations among adult members will be the foundation of our New Morality faith. Dom thinks we'll gain a lot of market share in the religious market. He intends to leverage our memberships into political power as well. We'll endorse candidates for office who favor legislation that gives the New Morality Standard political control over what is taught in schools and what sorts of judges we have. Basically, Dom wants to create a society that has no morality."

"And, your role in this?"

"My films will be shown at the temple meetings; kind of analogous to the scripture readings that they do in churches. We'll be using quite a few of my new orgy sequence films. Dom will have composers creating musical scores for those films to give our congregations the ethereal mood they need to participate in the services. This is why I must perform at my very best while I create these orgy films. I'm already getting psyched up for doing them.

"While I'm creating these explicit performance orgy films, I already know how I'll feel. I'll feel like I'm a little girl again, smiling for the cameras. Then, I'll soon be riding one huge, marvelous, imaginary stallion horse after the other. My mind will go into this dreamy la-la land, where I imagine I'm flying along on a cloud; twirling free and uninhibited in the air, without a care in the world. All I'll need to do is remind myself to say what I'm feeling;

to tell my horse that I love how wonderful his big beautiful cock feels while it's thrusting inside me; that I really, really want him to shoot his cum inside me; that I can't wait to taste his cock again, after he finishes. And then, when my champion comes. I'll feel his hot rush. I'll tremble, along with him, as my stallion surrenders all his masculine strength into me. I'll hug him; kiss him. I'll tell him he was wonderful.

"And then, just like that, another cock will appear. It will touch my vaginal lips and tell me it's ready. It wants me. It wants me to ride it next. It wants to be inside me. Then I'll know I'm going to go riding on another huge wonderful stallion. I'll lift my pelvis to receive him. Then I'll start to feel his strength and the rush of the wind. I'll soon be flying through the clouds again on my new imaginary stallion; riding him hard while he grasps my ass and squeezes it and fucks me so beautifully. It will be wonderful, Consuelo. It will be all so very heavenly and wonderful. Wow, I can't wait to do this gig. It will be a wonderful fun-filled blast. I'll just need to be sure I stay lubed and oiled, so my vagina reinforces its image as the ultimate fucking machine. Ha!

"Dom's theory is that the more cocks I fuck and the more cream pies I create, the more my fans will solidify their opinions that I am the most incorrigible, promiscuous, immoral, unrepentant whore; the most craven, debauched porn star in the entire world. That identity, Dom firmly believes, will make my fans love me even more than they do now. He believes they will cross over the psychological barrier from acceptance and desire, into obsession. He firmly believes that the more profligate and immoral I am; the more my fans will adore me and my vagina; and the more they will desire to date me and become my Premium Members; and, naturally, the more of my films and product line merchandise they will want to buy. Dom assures me that, through his branding, my vagina will be on the minds of millions and millions of men, the world over.

"Every man adores a woman who is an unashamed, total whore. Every red-blooded man craves the experience of putting his face into a profligate porn star's whoring vagina and giving her, her best orgasm ever with his tongue. Every man wants to hold her ass and kiss her mouth while he fucks her and surrenders all his manliness to her. It's all because, in every man's heart of hearts, deep down where he won't admit it, he loves a whore; totally swoons over her; loves her and her immoral behaviors enough to die for her. Anyway, that's what Dom says.

"And, because my vagina will frequently be shown in my skimpy, ruby jeweled bikini, those men will identify my vagina as the singularly most desired, most expensive, most promiscuous, most uninhibited, completely fuck crazed, whoring vagina in the entire world. Premium marketing is what Dom calls it.

"Well, anyway, Consuelo, there we were, on stage before two thousand buyers and influencers in Las Vegas, just beginning to promote my Premium line. My near naked body in my see-through bikini and my breasts and vagina were pressed tightly against Dom. I had my arms wrapped around his neck. I had him enveloped in my lusty presence. Obviously, I was being the unashamed total whore; giving eye candy to the audience. I stimulated Dom by massaging the back of his neck and his head while I kissed him with a soul kiss.

"I was then lifted up by my invisible ropes. I gave out a laugh and a giggle, like I was surprised to suddenly be in midair. Then, I fluttered before Dom until my jeweled vagina was suspended, tantalizingly, like a scrumptious, delicious treat, before his face. The spotlights highlighted my vagina, effectively shading away everything else on the stage. I spread out my legs and canted my pelvis, pushing my vagina invitingly close to Dom's lips; inviting him to kiss me there. The cameras began flashing like crazy when Dom clasped his hands to the small of my back and brought my ruby jewel right up against his lips. His lips engulfed the ruby. I could feel his lips hot

against my vagina. I began burning hot inside. I wanted his tongue inside me; his cock; everything. It was so erotic! I was getting wet just contemplating having oral sex with Dom, right there on stage. I then wrapped my legs around his neck a second time and supported him while he bent backwards until my ruby adorned vagina was positioned directly over his head.

"There we were. I was the butterfly with my vagina's ruby mouth and proboscis directly over Dom's lips. An overhead spotlight focused its beam on my ruby. As my body movements turned the ruby in the light beam, its facets directed flashing rays of enticing incarnadine colored light over my abdomen and legs. My legs became magical enchantresses, lavished in the reddish pink colorations. They communicated the fire I felt pulsing through my clitoral tentacles. Audience members' imaginations seized upon my message. Our viewers responded with claps and whistles.

"My ruby was visually radiating the lust I was feeling, communicating my intense cravings for sex. I twerked my hips and bumped my vagina invitingly against Dom's lips, twerking it slightly, clearly indicting that I was going out of my mind, eager to have sex. My entire body felt the electricity of the audience. My sex was literally throbbing with hot desires for a cock. The colored light rays flashed and danced over my legs. The rays were perfectly broadcasting my surreal, overwhelming urge to do it. I wasn't even a human woman anymore. I was this wild, passionate animal, absolutely needing and craving to make love. Blood rushed into my skin. I was like a human octopus, expressing my flaming desires through my skin; silently screaming to the world that I simply had to have sex. The audience became spellbound. They held their collective breath, waiting to see what I'd do next.

"Dom's mouth played its role as my succulent flower, the object of my ruby proboscis. While I fluttered my wings, Dom three times extended his tongue and caressed my ruby. With his help and loving

tongue, we created the perfect optical illusion. His tongue appeared to reach from my vagina into his mouth, like a true proboscis extending outward from a butterfly. After his tongue touches, I settled my vagina's ruby upon his lips; and lovingly bumped my vagina against them. My vagina became a butterfly, drinking its nectar.

"The audience clapped and whistled. They shouted roars to Dom to remove my bikini bottom and have oral sex with me. Photographers' cameras flashed like crazy. It was a wildly successful promotion. People howled and screamed themselves hoarse; stomped their feet; yelled hysterical commands for Dom to eat my vagina and fuck me, right there on stage. I twerked softly, seductively. pushing my vagina firmly, but gently, against Dom's lips. I couldn't help myself. I absolutely had to do it. I was so in the moment. I wanted him. I can't control my spontaneous immoral impulses. When I feel them, I just have to let go!

"That ruby, and that transparent, skimpy patch of cloth, barely covering my vagina and holding it in place, was all that separated Dom's eager lips from my vagina. Dom loves having oral sex with me. It took superhuman willpower for both of us to stay on script and not enjoy cunnilingus, right there on that stage. The photos of Dom's tongue and his lips licking and kissing my huge ruby appeared on several magazine covers. The messaging we were promoting was that a woman's vagina is far more valuable than a priceless ruby. And it is! It's the source of life! Dom told the audience we were naming my premium erotica bikinis, my 'PRICELESS' line. We had a very successful launch of my new Premium bikini line. Dom got pre orders of over two million dollars of my new see-through bikinis!

"Looking back on that day, I realize it was my erotica career's defining moment. We successfully branded my 'PRICELESS' bikini line; and millions of men now consider me to be the ultimate adult film star. Yet, despite my fame, I get wistful about that day. I think

we let those people down. They expected to see me have oral sex and get laid on that stage. And I really wanted to do it, Consuelo. I can't put into words how much I wanted to perform sex before all those adoring fans. It was one of those spontaneous moments, when I felt this limbic wave sweep over me.

"I desperately needed to fuck. I knew if Dom had put his tongue inside me, I would have had an orgasm almost instantly. I was so primed; so anxious. I wanted Dom's tongue and his cock; wanted to do it so bad. I was aching to have Dom do oral sex and make love, right there in front of two thousand people. I didn't care at all about all the hundreds of cocks I had sucked and fucked before. I get like that, Consuelo. Nothing else matters to me, other than sucking and fucking the cock I'm with when I have that limbic rush. But Dom's idea was to whet peoples' appetites for my full-length films; and drive those frenzied fans to buy advanced bundled ticket packages to my movies.

"That's where Dom showed his promotional genius. He started a slide show for those two thousand men. Each slide showed me properly dressed in a period outfit going back to the fifteen hundreds, followed by another slide of me in a courtesan's salon. I'm shown in various stages of undress, like I perform for my porn picture shoots, until I finally have my partner's cock just about to penetrate my vagina or almost in my mouth. After three of these sequences, Dom slipped in a slide where I'm completely naked. I have one partner's cock in my vagina; I'm in a compromising position with a nice background and I have my hands on another partner's testicles and on another partner's cock that's touching my lips, or taking in semen from his cock into my mouth.

"Well, Consuelo, Dom had ten slide sequences like that. First, he showed me in my porn picture poses, then he slipped in the slide where I was doing a threesome or a foursome. The men in the

audience went wild. Dom had tables around the room where the men in the audience could purchase advanced tickets to my upcoming ten feature length films. What a night! Dom is a genius! Dom sold two hundred thousand advanced tickets for my full-length films at a discount price of fifteen dollars each. We took in over three million dollars in one hour. Can you believe that?"

"Of course, I can, Marty. None of this surprises me. You are living proof of what I've always said at PORN BEAT."

"What's that, Consuelo?"

"That men can never get enough porn! Tee hee."

"Oh yes. You are so right about that. I often remember how enthused people become while watching me have live sex. Some sit through two or three shows and come back night after night. I guess the female vagina is highly addictive. It's good to have one! Ha, ha! Dom is working on having me perform live in some major venues. He's planning some outdoor concert events and possibly something like the halftime shows for football games and Super bowls where I can perform my live scenes before a stadium filled live audience. I'd like to go all the way, having cunnilingus and sex; hopefully orgy sex, on a huge outdoor stage in a large venue. I'd absolutely love promoting immorality by doing live orgy performances like that. If I could give the world an orgy performance during something like the Super Bowl, I know I could send those TV ratings through the roof! I'll keep you posted on Dom's progress with that idea.

"Dom's mission is to change the world's perceptions about prostitution and intimate film art. He feels hurt when derogatory articles call me "Cum Dumpster, Cum Guzzler, Cock Queen, Queen of Debauchery, Queen of Sin, Queen of Sluts, and other nasty names. He believes my films are beautiful, intimate artistry. Watching my vagina delightfully coax semen from cock after cock sends Dom into this state of sublime euphoria. He tells me my performances are divinely inspired artistry.

"He tells me no other feeling compares with the overwhelming rush of desires he experiences, every time he watches my films. Each time he views a film he tells me it makes him adore me more than he did before. He says my work is vital to human progress, because it appeals to the human need for freedom. There's a special place in the human brain where endorphins are boarded, like horses being kept in a barn. When they are set free, they ease tensions and promote love and harmony. Dom says I set those endorphins free.

CHAPTER TWO

Never apologize for who or what you are; and never let someone else define you. That is like inviting a hippopotamus to have dinner with you. It leaves nothing for you. (Rosemary Ness-Bitner, author)

MARTY ANTICHRIST

"Marty," asked Consuelo, "Dom's wife said he was a religious family man before he met you. She claims that you've not only pulled him away from his family, but also from God. She says you are so profligately immoral that you should be banned from polite society. Everyone knows they were a prominent social family. They did a lot of charitable giving through their foundations. The tabloids say your affair with Dom is the biggest scandal in years. Their pending divorce, I'm sure you know, is in the public eye.

"She's even been on national talk shows blaming you for her shattered marriage. On one show recently she broke down crying, hysterically. She claimed you are the Antichrist. She claimed you sleep with snakes, like Medusa. She says you are possessed; in effect she has called you the Devil. She was so upset she fainted, and they needed to carry her off the stage. Do you care to comment about that?"

"Oh, she called me that?" Marty gave a puzzled smile. "Well, that's so sad. I think religion is great. It's a real plus for people who need to believe in something good. It uplifts them. Why, I even did a recent film honoring the conception by the Virgin Mary. Of course,

I put my own interpretation into that film. A lot of scripture is open to interpretation, you know. I think God is a loving God and God would be pleased that I made that film. I think the film encourages people to study their gospels; and to think seriously about what a wonderful experience the immaculate conception must have actually been, for Mary.

"I'm NOT the Antichrist. That's silly. And, I'm not the Devil. If I were the Devil, I'd be an evil person; and I'm NOT an evil person. I definitely enjoy being a naughty girl, sometimes; that's all. I believe every woman needs to let her naughty side express itself sometimes. And when that limbic wave sweeps a woman and lights her torch, who can blame her for being naughty? It's natural. And it's fun and glorious and beautiful to be naughty. Why, I even go to church myself sometimes, so I'm sort of religious; and a lot of my partners are very religious. But, none of us are evil. None of us are the Devil. We just love making love.

"But I actually have met the Devil in person, and many of his Troglodyte friends. Yes, Consuelo, sometimes I sneak away to the underworld to party with them. They are all about twelve feet tall. And they have hairy, masculine bodies. They're much stronger than ordinary men; and they all have gorgeous penises that are three feet long; extra wide; and, they can keep their cocks hard all night long! They are fantastic sex partners. If Dom's wife would like to join me for some real fun, tell her to please call me. I'll take her with me the next time I go to play with the Devil. The two of us can go to hell together!'

"Tee Hee, oh, Marty, you can be too funny sometimes. What do you think is her real problem?"

"Stress, I think she's stressed coming to grips with her new reality. She's learning the world belongs to those who take what they want. It does not belong to the meek, the timid, the apologetic or the fearful. She calls me wicked. Okay, I get that; but I'm not wicked, I'm only human. She's unrealistic, and name calling is her childish way

of coping. That's all this is about. She's simply stressed. Possibly her meds are off? Maybe she needs a new shrink? Trust me, Consuelo, her upsets were waiting to happen before Dom met me.

"Have you taken a good look at her? She has way too many bad hair days. Have you seen the way her hair is falling out? She looks like a mange victim. Have you had a close look at her face? Her mascara is always running from all her crying. It makes her look like a sad circus clown with those black streaks down her cheeks. And, her face droops around her jowls. You can't help but notice that. And her body! Oh, yuck! Double yuck and barf-o! She has an obvious weight issue. Wearing a designer pattern tent and pretending it's a dress will not trick Dom into going back to her. She's delusional. Dom is with me now; not her. Someone needs to tell her that. Her reality is she's old. It's no big deal. It happens to every woman. She needs to move on, that's all. It's time for her to visit fat farms and go on cruises. I'll send her some brochures. That might help her think positive again.

"I realize she's twenty years older than me; but honestly, a woman should know when she needs repair work. Her lard ass and belly tire are just plain ugly; and those crow's feet around her eyes scare the crap out of a man before he even has a chance to think about sex. They're like red warning flags. They signal a man that she needs lubrication jelly, because she can't get herself wet anymore. I won't begin to criticize how badly her breasts sag. After all, she's had kids. But she should definitely get some boob work done. Some simple steps would go a long way to improve her attitude. It's too bad she didn't think of these things before Dom decided to divorce her. But it's never too late to try looking like a woman again. You know what I mean?"

"Yes, Marty. I've seen pictures of her. No wonder Dom ditched her and went with you. Your breasts and ass are spectacular! Every man would make that trade! You must be making him feel like a new man!"

"I would think so! I can feel his enthusiasm for me by the ways he squeezes me. He loves putting his hands all over me. It is amazing that Dom put up with her as long as he did. I mean, when a woman lets her body go and starts looking like a baggy old cow; and when she can't keep her husband warm at night, what did she think was going to happen? She let her marriage depend upon whatever blew into their lives on the four winds. She was not at all proactive. How stupid could she be? Well, guess what? I blew into Dom's life on a hot wind. And I happened to land on her marriage. Too bad!"

"Marty, she claims you sleep with snakes. Is there any truth in that?"

"Snakes! Get serious, Consuelo, please. I have nothing to do with them; but I am fascinated knowing that male rattlesnakes have two penises. Why aren't human men equipped like that? When one penis gets tired, the other penis could take over! It's a fantastic concept! I'll bet female rattlesnakes are well satisfied ladies!

"Look, Consuelo, that woman is bat shit crazy. She's gone total woo-woo. I think she needs to stop obsessing about whether or not I'm the devil or the Antichrist and all that mental claptrap. She has so many of her own issues. By the way, I actually think religion is wonderful! That's where I get my best film ideas. You must see my latest release. It's about the Immaculate Conception. I interpreted it differently than the scriptures, as you might imagine. My film downloads are way, way up. They're setting records and shooting my sales off the charts!"

"Do you believe your work has any redeeming social value, Marty; or do you see yourself as just a provocateur that teases men out of their money? I mean, do you honestly believe that anything good comes out of the work you do?" Consuelo probed deeper into Marty's opinion of herself.

CHAPTER THREE

Some men need instructions how to give a woman great sex. Don't make this complicated. Relate to your man like you're telling him how to drive. Tell him to go slower, or faster, or more to the right or the left. And when the mood suits you, tell him you want to be backed up and be driven in reverse. (Rosemary Ness-Bitner, author)

SOCIAL VALUES AND CROWD MADNESS

"Oh, I'm definitely helping humanity with my work," affirmed Marty. "I'm straightening out all the mix-ups that the male patriarchal world has forced upon society from the time when the Adam and Eve story laid a guilt trip on women, all the way until the present day. Dom gets it. He gets it mentally as well as physically.

"Dom says people need to see my films as elegant pathways into the most loving recesses of their minds. He believes millions will appreciate how I communicate my dedication to love. He's right, you know. My work is therapeutic for many people. And buying my films is more cost effective than working with a shrink. My work sweeps away the real evils of fear, ignorance, superstition, and hatred. Dom says the difference is that my work opens people to honest uninhibited intimacy. Very few shrinks will do that. My films give them courage, confidence and competence in their love making. I help people believe in themselves and help them become brave enough to

express their feelings of honest sexual love. Dom loves my work. He has become my biggest fan.

"I felt like I connected to humanity that day in Vegas. That was the magical day when I understood my work reaches something that people keep deep inside themselves. It happened when Dom kissed my ruby studded bikini bottom. It was an electrifying moment. I knew we were igniting fireworks in that room. After the audience applause finally died down, he made that stunning announcement. He announced he had acquired a chain of two thousand big screen movie theaters, all across the world; and he was starting a private production company to provide film content. He told all those reporters he would produce no less that ten full-length feature films, starring me. And, he will distribute them throughout the entire world. He told the crowd he'd fallen in love with 'this woman,' whom he had discovered. And, he declared that I was the only true love of his life, ever! Then he declared he would move heaven and earth to promote me and ensure my film career success."

"Wow, you are sooo lucky!"

"Yeah, Consuelo, you could have knocked me over with a feather. Dom raised a glass and toasted me as the most beautiful, most sensational Sex Goddess, ever. The loudspeakers started playing 'Twist and Shout,' that song from the Beatles. All I did was blow a kiss to the audience and then turn myself around and around while twisting my body and shaking my boobs; and twerking my tushie while putting my hand down my bikini bottom and pulling it away slightly to reveal my vagina. After all, everyone knew my vagina was the star of the show. I held myself open and smiled while I twisted and twerked, as if I was being filmed on set. I just love the bounce beat in that song. I could have danced for hours. I dance pranced, toe stepping, using steps I learned watching a Native Indian dance instructor on TV. I was pretending I was a tasty, living bon-bon treat; bouncing, twisting, twerking, shaking my boobs and my bootie. I imagined I

was a fishing lure, making all those seductive gyrations; waiting for a big bass to come and swallow me whole."

"That took some guts, girl."

"Yeah, but I was in the moment and letting myself go with the music; and I was loving it. Whenever I vagina-peek revealed and teased like I was begging for a cock to enter me the way I did, the crowd went absolutely wild all over again. They screamed their approval. They couldn't contain themselves when they heard Dom's sex goddess announcement and saw me start twerking. They were ecstatic after hearing I'd be performing full feature length explicit porn films for the big screen. Some men screamed out, begging me to marry them. It was surreal."

"I wish I'd have been there. All those sex crazed men!"

"You would have loved it, Consuelo. At least two thousand sex crazed males. They absolutely went nuts. They were screaming, stomping their feet, clapping their hands, and whistling. I felt the entire room shake. I resonated in tune with the crowd lust. I couldn't help what I did next. I had this primordial craving. It swept over me and carried my body away from my senses.

"I became like a fuck-crazed pagan whore. I wanted to give the crowd everything their most sex crazed desires demanded of me; and more. I continued holding my ruby bikini bottom away from my vagina with my hand behind it, pushing it outward to accent the ruby. Then, I did this spontaneous, unplanned naughty sexual thing. I couldn't even believe I was doing what I was doing; except, I really wanted to do this and create a lasting impression on those men.

"I fisted my hand that pushed against the bikini bottom and made it pulse; bumping my fist outward, then pulling it back; out and in, out and in, like my vagina was throbbing; yearning for those men in the audience; inviting them to come forward and push their cocks inside me, while I blew kisses to them with my other hand. Some men gasped. They were smitten by my uninhibited promiscuity."

"You got down and slutty, didn't you?"

"Oh yeah, I did! Really slutty! I felt their hearts pounding and leaping into their throats. Those men wanted me so badly. It was the most erotic, suggestive cock teasing thing I've ever done. The lust in that ballroom reached a frenzy rage. As I looked at the men's faces in the front rows, I saw many were salivating. I could read their minds. They wanted to throw off their clothes; jump up on the stage with me; lick my vagina and screw my brains out. That just happens with me when I perform. I only think of the cocks in the audience and never the men that are attached to them. When I think like that, I can tease cocks and the men attached to the cocks into a frenzy. It's all in a girl's mind set, you know.

"Anyway, my pagan lust surge grew and grew. It coursed through my body. It was self-reinforcing. I was responding to the audience by telling myself that I wanted them to become even more excited. This sensation kept sweeping through my body. It was my immoral pagan lust force. I don't know what else to call it; but it kept telling me that all these men loved me. It told me they were bonding to me, adoring me; and they all wanted to fuck me. Something just screamed from inside me that I needed to give them what they were craving. I wanted to let myself go dangerously crazy, like a bitch dog in heat. I wanted to fuck every man in that ballroom. I imagined I was doing that. Actually, I even contemplated trying to do that.

"You couldn't have. Would you have tried it?"

"I'm not sure, Consuelo, I was out of my mind. I get a little crazy and oversexed sometimes. I was in some kind of insane limbic mental state and about to try it. Honestly. I knew those men could feel how I felt. My mind entered this lovely place where it often goes while I'm fucking man after man during one of my orgies. It just kind of drifts away to these magical places. Sometimes I imagine I'm lying beside a lovely pool in a garden. There are Koi fish in the pool and they are all up close to the surface watching me making love. And I can feel

what the fish are thinking while they watch me. They are thinking I'm lovely and my love making is very special and beautiful.

"Then, these butterflies come and flutter over me, like they approve of my love making, too. And then these feelings happen. I feel these tiny fingers of the spirits caressing my skin, all over my body. And then these spirits whisper to me. They tell me that they love and fully endorse what I'm doing. They say it's necessary that I create porn and do my orgies because they set so many peoples' spirits free. They kiss my body everywhere with their spirit lips and tell me I should not concern myself with all the marriages I wreck and all the relationships I upset because the most important thing is that I spread my message of freedom and uninhibited love. And, they fully endorse my immoral behaviors. They say I am doing the divine work of the spirits; and that I need to do more of it; and they love me for being the promiscuous whore that I am.

"That's where my mind was when I realized that there was this communal recognition of my mood taking place among the men. That's when I decided to let my inner slut go. I arched my back and bent myself over backwards, letting my head almost touch the floor. I spread my legs wide enough so that my vagina with her butterfly wings was completely revealed. Then I did it. I bump thrusted my vagina outward and back; out and back, repeatedly, like I had a cock inside me, to the music beat of 'TWIST AND SHOUT.' The shameless, insatiable whore effect that I created electrified those men. They all imagined their cocks were inside me; fucking me; holding me close by pulling my vagina against them, holding their hands on my ass, pulling me tightly into them while I twerked in my contorted position. They became as fuck-crazed as I was. Their feelings contagiously affected mine; and my feelings contagiously affected theirs."

"Marty, you went way into high-risk behavior."

"I know, Consuelo. I was completely out of control, just reacting to my lust urges. I swung my head around in a circle to make my

hair fly everywhere, like I had become demonic and crazed to fuck. Then the crowd got totally out of control. Some men responded spontaneously to what I was doing. Their natural urges took control of them. They jumped out of their seats and rushed the stage. They had become so lust crazed they lost their minds. They pushed against the police line. They were salivating and screaming FUCK, FUCK, FUCK. Everyone, including me, was insane with passion lust."

"Weren't you scared?"

"Almost, but not just yet. Then, one man kneeled down next to my face and exposed himself to me. He had a huge, fat cock with a monster hard on. The men in the audience all started screaming to me: YES! FUCK HIM! FUCK HIM! Their screams became a deafening chant. They got louder and louder and more and more insistent. They wouldn't stop yelling. Their shouts of FUCK HIM resonated through my mind."

"Did you?" Consuelo was breathless. Her eyes were wide open.

"No, but something happened. It was as if time stood still. There was something about that cock. I had this feeling. I felt as if that cock was trying to talk with me. I believed that, somehow it knew me; and it had some deeply meaningful connection to me. I thought it was telling me that it wanted it to diddle me."

"Diddle? Marty, what are you talking about? This is getting very strange."

"Yeah, diddle. That's when a man loves you and he uses his cock to please you, make you feel good and happy all over. It's when he's making love with you for your pleasures, not his; and he's intent about giving you a really wonderful time. He's honoring a special friendship he has with you. It's a deeply empathetic friendship type of closeness fuck, which is a level of intimacy that's way above ordinary fucking. It's true, honest, friendship fucking; kind of like when young boys say 'Scout's Honor,' if you know what I mean."

"Oh, okay, then what?"

"Well, my diddle thought went away. I imagined I became a Congo Line's final destination. Men swayed back and forth, steadily moving forward toward me. When the head man in the line reached me, he inserted his penis inside me. I wriggled my hips while he came; then he pulled out and the next man up entered me. I shook my head, back and forth, savoring my imaginary lust fest. All the while I continued twerking and twirling my head.

"I realized I had lost control of the men's behavior. They became possessed by a mob's mind set. All of them were gripped by uncontrollable lust rage. They yelled out to me to remove my see-through bikini bottom, lie down on the stage, and fuck that man. They were ordering me to fuck him, right there on stage. They were crazy; demanding that I fuck this man. Their frenzied excitement and the sight of his spectacular cock caused my nymphomania to flare. I felt like a blow torch was shooting hot flames through my blood. His huge cock was so beautiful, and so deliciously tempting, that I imagined feeling how wonderful it would feel thrusting inside me. I tried telling myself that I was a human; not a wild bitch dog in heat. I felt desperation urges to fuck that man; let him diddle me; let myself discover love with him; but privacy is needed to diddle. A girl shouldn't let herself be diddled on stage; plus, I was fearful if I dared to do it, a hundred male hounds would rush the stage and attack me like I was a piece of raw meat. They'd all want to fuck me at once. I sensed my lusts would unleash the whirlwind of uncontrollable male passions. The situation was so out of control I feared I might get fucked to death and torn apart."

"Jesus, Marty."

"My body screamed at me, urging me to come to my senses. I was about to be gang raped by a dozen or more sex-crazed men. I needed to suppress my lust and pay attention to my fears. I trembled with fright. But I didn't know what to do. I shook visibly, fearful that those sex-crazed men would breach the security line, rush the stage

and tear the flesh from my bones. They were wild eyed; out of their minds, like crazed dogs. I had never seen anything like it.

"They worked themselves into a manic frenzy. I knew I had caused it, but everything had flown out of control; and, I didn't know how to stop it. Imagine me being afraid of having sex, Consuelo! But I was! I was terrified! I now know how a woman feels when she's about to be raped."

"Oh my God!" Consuelo feared for Marty's safety. She clasped her hand over her mouth.

"Dom realized that those men might mob the stage. Thank goodness Dom is a take charge kind of man. He whisked me up into his arms and carried me off the stage. He held me close to him until we escaped through a back door. He lifted me into his limo, then slid in beside me and kissed me. I'll always remember that kiss. It was my rescue kiss. It was special. It told me that Dom was pleased because we successfully pulled off our promotion. It also told me that he loved me and he would protect me. It told me so much, Consuelo. Without saying a word, his kiss told me that Dom understood I was a completely unrepentant, immoral whore; and he loved and accepted me for being exactly who I am. It was one of the most emotional moments of my life."

"Wow." Consuelo hugged Marty. *"I'm so happy for you. That was so touching and special!"*

"Yes, it was. We left in the nick of time, with those men howling after us. I was lucky to get out of there alive. Dom saved me. I trembled in his arms in the back seat of his limo. He held me close to him all the way to his ranch. For the first time in my life since I was a little girl, I felt safe and warm, like I was secure in my daddy's arms again."

"Thank God you weren't hurt." Consuelo's eyes teared with joy.

"Yes," Marty's eyes found sympathy in Consuelo's eyes. The two women held hands as Marty continued.

"After Dom tucked me into bed, while I drifted off to sleep, I wondered about that man with the huge penis who had rushed the stage. I tried to figure out why I had those special feelings about his magnificent, huge cock. I dreamed I had made long sweet love with that man and his fabulous cock, right there on stage, before thousands of applauding fans. The next morning, at breakfast, I couldn't get him or his cock out of my mind. That's my nymphomania effect, Consuelo. Sometimes when I get to thinking about having sex with someone, I simply can't let it go. I fixate on it until I've finally come together with that man and his cock. It's just how I'm internally wired. I can't help it."

"Did you find him?"

"Oh, yes. I decided to go back to the hotel while Dom was off doing business somewhere. I got with the hotel security people and persuaded them to search their cameras and identify him. Deep inside myself I knew there was some kind of fate or karma happening. I knew I absolutely had to find that man. I knew it was important to make love with him, like he was the last man on earth. I was out of my mind crazy; fearful I would never find him. When the security guards finally identified him, was I ever surprised! His name was Slim. He was from Montana and his wife's name was Maria!'

"Maria, from your school years? That Maria?" Consuelo's jaw gaped open. She jumped up and down for joy. *"Oh, Marty, I am so happy for you!"*

"Yes, she was my best friend from when I was in WEX School for Girls. Slim was still in the hotel, so I called him. We met for coffee. Well, it didn't take long before I was in their hotel room. Maria was surprised and overjoyed to see me, Consuelo. We screamed for joy and hugged each other for what seemed like forever.

"The three of us talked and talked, and then we kissed and hugged and made love. We made wild passionate love like the end

of the world was coming. It was beyond wonderful, doing that threesome with Maria and Slim; and especially having oral sex with Maria again. Everything Maria wrote me about Slim was true, too. He is a fantastic lover. And his darling cock was everything I imagined it would be, and more! We all agreed that we'd never be able to get enough of each other; so now we get together every month or so for a day or a weekend of fun. They are ski bunnies; so, I often meet them in Vail or Aspen. And, I also go to their ranch in Montana. It's amazing how life can come full circle when you least expect it, Consuelo. I guess that's called destiny. Yes, it is destiny. I'm a total believer in destiny now.

"That evening, after Maria, Slim and I shared our love, I went back to Dom's ranch. I was sitting there in a huge leather sofa before the massive stone fireplace sipping a coffee, feeling totally satisfied. I had my beautiful friendship with Maria again. I was feeling all warm and glowing inside. I totally love Maria. That doesn't even begin to describe how I feel about her, Consuelo. I adore her. It's like we're the same person and we know each other's feelings. It's a beautiful form of love. That's when this sudden rush of happiness swept over me. It was surreal. I had my closest friends again; my lovers; and my fame.

"It dawned on me how famous I'd become, thanks to Dom, my beautiful wonderful Dom. I was firmly established as the world's number one adult film star. I had a unique position in the entertainment world. It was like winning the Oscar for best actress; only better, because so many people would become my fans and purchase my entire film library.

"It's wonderful to be on top. All sorts of offers have come to me from everywhere. They keep pouring in. Dom's brilliant at brand identity marketing. Billions of people will see me making love outdoors in all our national parks in one of Dom's new movies; in another I'll make love in different indoor settings; in another I'll

have several orgy party scenes. There will be an orgy food scene in another; and on and on, so that whenever someone goes to a national park; or an indoor office building; or a restaurant, Dom's branding effort will associate my love making with those places. I'm getting the opportunity to make thirty to fifty realistic love scenes, with exceptionally handsome partners in those movies.

"And the music scores for the films and the musicals will be beyond fantastic! I've heard parts of what the musicians and song-writers are working on. They've created this one song called 'HER BLACK LACE PANTIES.' It's sung by this woman while I'm fucking her boyfriend. She's in a mental institution, remembering how she lost him to my whoring and my black lace panties. You'll love the song and the scene she remembers me doing with her boyfriend. I promise! It's my favorite gig in the entire movie. The musicians' lyrics and music beats are so fantastic. I know I'll love making love to all their songs. Now, when Dom tells me he loves being on top, I tell him we are BOTH on top! Dom has handed me the opportunity of a lifetime! Only love can inspire a man to do that for his woman."

"Marty, do you have any comments about how Dom's wife is taking his love affair with you? She's been saying some mean things about you in the press. I'm sure you're aware of this," Consuelo was fishing for Marty's reaction.

• • •

"At this point in the interview, Marty voices faint scorn for her victims' misfortunes." Barbara happens to be reading the transcript of *Marty's Consuelo interview to Bob. She expresses her thoughts about Marty and what Consuelo's interview reveals about her archrival, Marty, to Bob. Barbara cannot conceal her disdain for Marty:*

"She pleaded sweet innocence to the media, knowing full well her voracious vagina devoured Dominick's marriage. I'm certain

when Dominick's wife saw those photos of the two of them cavorting at Cannes, and when she saw Dominick kissing Marty's bikini ruby jeweled vagina, the poor woman became shocked and horrified. Marty lured that man to glorify her whoring vagina before the entire world! I'm certain that Marty knew the Paparazzi were following the two of them with their cameras. She had to know a photo of one of the world's wealthiest men holding her above his head and kissing her vagina like that would make a front-page splash on all the tabloids. Marty is such a vixen vamp; a totally self-promoting heartless sex obsessed nympho. She had to know she would cause Dom's wife to flee her marriage after she saw that photo. No self-respecting woman could hold her head high after that devastating psychological onslaught. She must have felt crushed and destroyed.

"I feel terribly, knowing that the woman I work with at our Firm could be such a cruel sociopath. And David completely approves of Marty's behaviors. He encourages her and rewards her for her whoring. He lets her make her porn films while giving her cover as if she is a legitimate corporate officer at a prestigious investment firm. So, to keep my own job, I must stand helplessly by; keep my mouth shut and watch while Marty inflicts her mental torture on hapless women like Dom's wife. That makes me feel ashamed of myself and complicit in Marty's sordid affairs. But I am not complicit. I'm just helpless to stop her, that's all. That's how David has the Firm set up. We must all kowtow to Marty and her whoring and her whims. And, this ruby vagina kiss display was not her first time to wreck another woman's marriage, Bob. I'm sure you know Carl, one of the top local salesmen. Marty has him pushing the Firm's product sales. His wife's car went off Mountaintop Road. She died, Bob. I'm sure that Marty was having an affair with Carl. And I think that Marty had something to do with the woman's death. She wanted Carl's wife out of the way. And she got what she wanted.

"I'm sure Dom's wife is crazed. She must feel like a runaway train smashed into her marriage and obliterated it. But Marty doesn't care one wit about her. She has no conscience or morals. She's a twisted sociopath, Bob; a total narcissist. She thinks she makes herself more desirable to her porn fans by destroying another human being. I could just visualize Marty's face during that entire interview before Consuelo Lovely's Porn Beat audience. I'm sure Marty's porn fans lapped up every word she spoke. I'm positive Marty wore her sweet, innocent school-child smile while she mocked the distress of Dom's wife to Consuelo. She's very good at playing the innocent one in the chaos she causes others. She's a very sick woman, Bob."

CHAPTER FOUR

Morality is like a tightly wound spring. Many moral women unwind those springs by blaming their upsets on whores. That doesn't work. And that's why ice cream and blintzes were invented. (Rosemary Ness-Bitner, author)

MORALITY

"I can't imagine why Dom's wife tells people I'm immoral, can you, Consuelo?" Marty pouted, turned her head, and smiled her most coquettish smile and shrugged her shoulders. She was the picture poster girl of innocence, caught up in the headlined marriage maelstrom that had nothing to do with her involvement with the other woman's husband. *"It's very hurtful to know some other woman has labeled your honest heartfelt love immoral. There's nothing immoral about two people falling in love, is there? I can't imagine how there could be, can you? I mean, love is love, isn't it? I can't understand why she has such a hard time accepting that, can you? I believe morality is a state of mind; you know. It's how people feel about what they are doing. There a huge difference between making films that champion immorality and being a woman in love who happens to also be an adult film star. Everything Dom and I do is loving and beautiful. We honestly express our deepest urges and feelings. I don't know anyone who thinks honesty is immoral, do you?"*

"No, I don't. I can't imagine it, Marty. I'm sorry that this is so hurtful for you." Consuelo agreed, giving Marty her full sympathy;

implying that Marty's honesty about her affair with Dom made their love affair perfectly moral and acceptable in polite society.

"I know my spirits instruct me to be merciful because without mercy one can not be truly creative. So, when I break a few eggs to make an omelet I try to feel sorry towards the broken egg shells. Well, a lot of people that get in the way of my film creativity are like broken egg shells, Consuelo.

"I know some people cling to their religion and their backward ideas about not accepting human progress. They get stubborn. That's easier for them, mentally, than thinking correctly as mature adults. I try hard to forgive narrow-minded people who try to block my creativity. But at the same time, it's hard to be merciful towards someone who constantly runs to the media and calls me nasty names like whore, slut and home wrecker. There's something wrong with a woman who carries on like that. I mean, honestly, all I did was fall in love with her husband.

"I've stopped being merciful to Dom's wife. I once hoped she'd welcome me into their family, after I seduced Dom; as a healthy supplement to their marriage, kind of like a badly needed vitamin. But she refused to see the beauty of that perfectly workable arrangement. So, now I view my vagina as a tent of mercy and a refuge place for poor, persecuted Dom. When his wife berates him for loving me, I'm always there for him.

"I wish she and I could be good close friends, but she doesn't want to be mature about this; and there's nothing I can do about it. I've never trash-talked about her. I've never said she was a bad wife or a bad mother. She's been a good wife to Dom and a good mother to his children. That's why I feel so badly for her.

"Dom cut off her fifty-million-dollar credit line and gave it to me. But I had nothing to do with that. It's just something Dom decided to do to make me happier. I have no idea why she started having these sudden marital problems. Her difficulties had nothing to do with

me. I can't believe she thinks I'm the cause of their separation. I've just been there for Dom. I'm not causing marital problems. Really, Consuelo, what was I supposed to do when Dom told me that he wanted me?"

"I don't think there was anything you could do. When a man falls in love with a woman, she really has no choice in the matter. She simply must go with her feelings. You did the right thing, Marty. You stayed true to your feelings." Consuelo held Marty's hand sympathetically.

"Would you say no to a handsome wealthy man like Dom?"

"No, Marty, you poor thing, of course you couldn't say no. If I had been in your position, I would have spread my legs for him, just like you did. What else is a poor vulnerable, impressionable woman expected to do? My goodness, his wife can surely understand how he swept you off your feet! She should be completely sympathetic to the terrible pressures you were under. How, on earth, could she expect you to say no to him?"

"Yes, Consuelo, like you, I thought she would also have feelings for me; but she didn't. The woman has no empathy for anyone but herself. Then, when I discovered how wonderful Dom was with cunnilingus; and how much stamina he has when we make love, I couldn't imagine ever saying no to him. After all, good lovers are hard to find. Tee Hee. What woman in her right mind would say no to a man like that?"

"No woman would say no, Marty. You did the only right and sensible thing you could do. You didn't say 'no.' You said 'yes.' You didn't try to control him by telling him to get divorced first. You didn't let ridiculous formalities interfere with your feelings of love." Consuelo voiced her full support to Marty's position.

"She must have been unable to keep him happy," Marty shook her head. *"That's what I think. A woman must be a good lover for her man. I don't know why she can't understand that, can you?"*

"Goodness, no, every woman should know that," Consuelo nodded.

"I've given this quite a bit of thought, Consuelo. I've tried to place myself in Dom's position. His wife's body is chunky heavy, with lots of baby fat. I can't imagine her twerking her hips over Dom's cock or performing erotic gyrations with it, like I do. I am still almost as thin as I was when I was a teenager; and I'm just as slippery and hot inside; so, I can perform sexually with the same eroticism I have always had. Her problem is she can't keep Dom happy; but I can. I know I can. Dom never has difficulty releasing inside me. Happiness, companionship, and a joyful experience for his cock is all Dom has ever asked of me. He's not demanding at all. And I'm always willing to give him what he wants. That's how a woman should see something like this, don't you think, Consuelo?"

"Yes, Marty. A thousand times yes. Of course, I do," Consuelo embraced her favorite porn star with an understanding hug.

"And, Dom's NEVER been thoughtless or selfish with ME. He's sweet and loving, like a man who loves a woman should be. I can't imagine what she's talking about when she says I have poor morals when all I want to do is make love with Dom. Of course, I want to make love with him. That's how love naturally expresses itself. He's done so much for my career, and I'm so grateful. So, I naturally want to make love with him every time I see him. She doesn't understand me; that's all. It's her terrible close-minded attitude. Maybe Dom discovered he's happier being with me and happy to be away from her."

"Bob, Marty artfully, by innuendo, flaunts her victims' agony in her interviews while keenly professing she had nothing to do with their turmoil," continued Barbara. *"Subtle promotion of her web site is always closely woven seamlessly into her interviews. Just listen."*

"I'm sure as Dom's kids become more accustomed to seeing him with me, they'll know I'm a sweet loving woman. All that negative stuff his wife says about my "icuminmarty.com" web site isn't the real me at all. She doesn't have to make a big deal over it. Naturally, as a porn star, it has thousands of porn pictures of me doing all sorts of reveals and sex poses. And, of course, it has a complete catalogue of my films for my fans to purchase. What would anyone expect me to have on there? She's overreacting to everything. My films are only my temporary way of making a living until I figure my life out. I'm just like everyone else, honest. I'm not one bit different. I'll admit I am somewhat promiscuous, but I can't help myself when I fall in love with a man. I just want to make love with him in every way imaginable; and I don't care if the whole world sees me with him or that their imaginations run wild about all the different ways that we have sex. I definitely love sex. I freely admit that. But sex is so much more than a business for me. It's my whole life. Some even say I have nympho tendencies. I suppose I do. I freely admit that, too. I don't make pretenses that I don't have nympho tendencies; and I love making love with my man in every way imaginable. That's just who I am. I'm no different than any other innocent girl who's figuring out her life."

"Marty," Consuelo interrupted Marty's self-promotion. "Dom's wife is saying that you're in the planning stages of starting up some sort of cult to practice Pagan worship. She's telling people that you are the Devil's favorite whore. Any truth to her claims, or are they just more of her vicious comments?"

CHAPTER FIVE

Every time someone tells me to go to hell, I go there, as ordered. It's a fascinating place. (Rosemary Ness-Bitner, author)

DEVIL'S WHORE

"Oh, my, my, she has quite the gossip mouth, doesn't she? I'm not even going to lend any dignity to her demented mind. I can't imagine why she'd say something like that. But I'll tell you what. If I ever do start up a Pagan denominational cult, I'll certainly invite her to our services. I'll reserve a front row seat for her so she'll be able to watch me and Dom making love on the Pagan altar. You can tell her that.

"Also, please tell her that the Devil and I have a terrific relationship. I'd feel terribly hurt if I learned the Devil loves any woman more than me. He loves me so much that he carries me down into hell with him, every night. It's warm and toasty comfy down there. He has fantastic digs for making love; lots of blindfolds, whips, ticklers, cuffs, straps, floggers, dildos, vibrators, ropes, lubes, collars, gags, racks, nipple clamps and leg spreaders. I adore my dear, misunderstood friend, the Devil. We make sensational love together. He has every sex toy imaginable and he uses ALL of them with ME! He's even given me private coaching sessions to make me an expert at BDSM!"

"Really, Marty, you perform bondage and sadistic-masochism?"

"Oh yes! Of course, I do, Consuelo. I am a free spirited, well-rounded, completely uninhibited whore. I thought you already knew that about me. I also teach everything I know to Dom, so he knows how to please me, whatever mood I'm in. Please tell his wife that. And, tell her that, when I spread my legs for the Devil's cock, I can feel my insides turning end-over-end with hot desire. And I feel that same excitement when I spread my legs for Dom. Tonight the Devil is taking the two of us to his orgy banquet, as his special guests. Dom and the Devil will both be flowing their hot cum into me, at the same time! I can't wait. I know I'm going to love it. The three of us, happily frolicking in hell, doing threesomes and orgies, will make me feel sinfully wonderful. Please tell her I'll be thinking of her while I'm being a very bad girl."

"Okay, I will," chuckled Consuelo. *"I'm glad you brought up the subject of BDSM, Marty. It's all the rage now. So many people are getting into it. Do you prefer BDSM or straight sex? Which is more fun for you?"* Consuelo asked. She couldn't resist following up Marty's last response.

"That question makes me think. I do love BDSM. I absolutely love being pinched and whipped and dominated and blindfolded and frightened in all sorts of ways. I love those adrenalin rushes very much, I certainly do. Dom plans to have some BDSM scenes in my upcoming full-length movies. He knows it's quite the rage; and he appreciates that I love it so much. BDSM brings out in me this special level of intimacy that's born of fear and rescue. Straight sex can't quite reach that feeling; except, sometimes with a lover who loves creating a control experience by giving exceptional cunnilingus, of course. That also can produce the adrenalin rush; but I reach that intimacy condition in a more heavenly, spiritual way with oral sex than I do with BDSM. It's a way of sharing intimate love that BDSM can't reach. Great oral sex with a dedicated partner is impossible to top.

"The type of sex I prefer depends upon my mood. Some days I crave BDSM. I just must have it. And I love having my nipples clamped while a vibrator plays with the hood of my vagina, and while I'm getting slapped or whipped. During those times I WANT to feel dominated and I MUST feel controlled. Chill run up and down my spine. And the only way I can get control of myself when that happens is by making love. It's wonderful to feel that way. I just love it when my partner does that. I release in such glorious orgasms then. It's like I'm a total woman.

'Other times I just want to cuddle and love and love and love, kind of surrender myself to love, with lots of sweet, loving, romantic straight sex, you know? I guess that's why we have so many different positions and so many different sex toys and all the BDSM accessories available to us. It's about making sure that, we, as women, can enjoy our complete range of sexual experiences.

"We women need to have available all those many different ways to express our sensuality and cravings for making love. I often think that Eve found exciting ways to pleasure herself with that serpent. She must have been a fascinating, mysteriously sexy woman; and I suspect she knew how to play her cards very well in a man's world. Rumor in the spirit world has it that God first tried to pair Adam with a woman named Lilith before God paired Adam with Eve; but Lilith was too sassy, too frisky, and an impossible woman for Adam to dominate.

"Lilith refused to cook, make homemade pasta or Adam's favorite dish: linguini with clam sauce. She insisted on dining out in five-star restaurants every night and only having sex with Adam once a week. She told God she wanted to use Adam as her Cuck and insisted that God provide her with a handsome gardener who could satisfy her sexually. God declined Lilith's demands. God realized that his matchmaking attempt failed terribly. God decided that Lilith had to go; declared her defective and issued her recall notice. She was sent *to another, more suitable, planet where bitchy women rule men with whips.*

"Thankfully, Eve proved to be more amenable to a male ordered world. But she also wanted to push boundaries and experiment. She listened to her good friend, Snake. At Snake's encouragement Eve took a bite from the knowledge apple. Speaking woman to woman, Consuelo, I think Eve secretly used Snake as history's first vibrator. When Eve saw the ways Snake tasted the air with his tongue flicks, I'm certain she invited him to perform cunnilingus with her. I know that I would have, if I was Eve. I mean, think of it! A tongue like that going wild inside your vagina! Wow!

"After all, we women are, by nature, loving, emotive, plea-sure-enjoying creatures. We also, always, try to make the world a better place for ourselves. Poor Eve, only Adam was available. She never even enjoyed a threesome or an orgy! I believe, given Eve's difficult circumstances, she needed her privacy times for Snake and her masturbations. Who can blame her for trying to make the best of such an isolated homebound situation? We women are entitled, in this man's world, to experience all the ways of love and pleasure, you know. Many of us need more than one man to make us happy. That should not surprise any men in your audience. How else are we sup-posed to feel complete satisfaction? Men should expect no less of us."

"And your Dominic understands this? I mean, does he believe you are entitled to complete satisfaction at all times, even if it's with someone else and not him?"

"Yes, definitely. We arrived at an understanding about that. He's totally supportive."

"Can you elaborate?"

"Sure. I asked him what he liked most about me."

"He responded, without hesitation: 'Your pussy.'"

"Not my personality? My character?"

"Those, too."

"But you said: 'Your pussy.' You blurted that right out. You must have meant it."

"I did. It's true."

"But every woman has a pussy. Why did you say that?"

"Because I've watched your films. I see how it thrusts up to greet the fingers that ply you, stimulating you. I see how hungry it is to fuck; how much it craves being fucked. And I see how hungry it is for the cock when you take a partner's cock in your hands and rub it against your vagina's outer lips. I see those scenes and I imagine how hungry for the cock it is; and that's so beautiful. To me, that's breathtakingly beautiful. And I love you for that craving to fuck which burns hot inside you. Do you always have that craving?"

"Yes, I think so. It's my nymphomania."

"Have you always, had it?"

"I think so; ever since I rode with a boy named Donny. We were in his convertible. I had my legs spread open; one leg propped on the door. He placed his hand on her, my Gloria, I call her. He started massaging her. I felt these urges them; like I wanted him to continue doing that; and fingering inside me; and fucking me. Those urges have never stopped since then. They've only gotten stronger with time. You said the close-up segments of my pussy in my porn scenes are breathtakingly beautiful. Tell me, Dom, how do they affect you?" Marty cooed. More than fishing for a compliment, she was eager to hear how she might improve her tradecraft.

"It's a phenomenon that sweeps through my blood. It's a spiral that takes me into this immersion of lust cravings. My heart starts pounding. My mouth salivates. Blood rushes into my penis. I get very hard. My temples start throbbing. I'm sure that's blood pressure. And then I feel this pounding in my chest. It's like I'm getting punched by this invisible fist. And my mind blocks out everything else. I feel I must take you into my arms and kiss you while I finger you. And I want to peel down your panties and take them off. And

I want to spread your legs. I feel driven to place my mouth to your vagina then; and I must kiss it; like I must worship it, because it is a holy thing; a giver of life. Even though what you are doing with those men's cocks is completely immoral, I feel I must discard all those taboos and kiss your vagina and love it, because it is part of you; you glorious, immoral you. And I must love it with my whole heart and soul because it is part of you. I feel smitten; overcome; mesmerized; unworthy to live unless I'm totally committed to your vagina and all that it does; all its glorious copulations; all its sensational erotic foreplay. I feel like I must die to please you, if that, somehow might please you more in some way. I don't know how better to describe the sensation, Marty.

"When I see your outer lips glistening with moisture; so anxious to feel the head of your partner's penis rubbing against them; seeking entry; and then seeing the head of the penis passing your lips and entering you; beginning its penetration; and then I see your face. Oh, Marty, your face is so sweetly innocent and heavenly in that moment. You have this divine continence. It sweeps over your face. Your very soul leaps from your eyes. It's glorious. It's all so glorious. And I am so happy for you; so, deeply in love with you. I want to know you are feeling pleasure. I want to feel sure that you are partaking from the biblical Tree of Knowledge; and knowing that it is your right, as a woman, to feel pleasure and not conceive. I want you to enjoy that right to the fullest. And I want to cherish you for all my days. I feel like I'm in the presence of God, or in the presence of something even more holy than God could ever be. I'm smitten, spellbound. I'm overwhelmed by these feelings of adoration for your vagina and for you. I'm like a hopeless puppy dog; a puddle of something waiting to be taken by you; shaped by you into something, I don't know what."

"And then those scenes where you lie with your head over the side of the bed; and you stroke the penises of your porn partners while you lick their testicles. You know what I'm talking about?"

"Sure. I love doing those scenes."

"Yes. And when your partner places his hand on your vagina in such a reverential way and then he ejaculates into your mouth. And then you lick his penis. Remember?"

"Yes, of course."

"Well, when I watch those scenes, I think I'm seeing the most splendid erotica ever performed. And I sort of shudder inside from my awe of you; from my realization that you can never be tamed or controlled; that you are absolutely free of inhibition or any sort of guilt feelings about your lifestyle. And I adore you for that. What's going through your mind while you're performing those scenes?"

"Oh, it's complicated, Dom. It's my way of rejecting those church teachings my grandmother forced on me. I just stopped believing that stuff. I was recalling some biblical passage about how sinful it is to spill your seed. I thought about that. I decided it was just another one of the religious misogynist's tricky ways to corral people into thinking they should only have sex to procreate; and that, of course, meant whenever people got the urge, they would procreate more children. More children, of course, means more future customers for the church. And the poor kid doesn't know any better. A child can't think for itself. So, by my way of thinking, that whole spill the seed stick is kind of cruel. It's a way of creating slaves to the church."

"And when you were doing those scenes, how were you opposing that?"

"By showing people that sex for pleasure's sake, without having children as a result of having sex, can be and is glorious and beautiful. It's very humanistic. Very loving. Very mush connecting two human souls in mutual love and pleasure. It's beautiful. Don't you think those scenes are beautiful?"

"Yes. Definitely. And you don't feel there's anything evil about what you're doing?"

"No. Absolutely not. I think it's beautiful and loving and glorious. It's my way of celebrating the majesty of the male penis. It's my own version of holiness."

Dominick kissed her mouth while his fingers began stimulating her vagina. *"Marty, you are the antichrist. I think I'm starting to understand you. And I love you. I'm falling more and more in love with you."*

"Because of how my mind works; or because you love fucking me?"

"Oh, both. Definitely both. I'd like to ask a favor."

"What?"

"My daughter, Jennifer. Jen has been so closely tied to her mother's ways of thinking. Her mother dominates the poor girl; suffocates her thinking. She's constantly forcing religion down the poor girl's throat. It's painful to watch. Jen doesn't know anything about boys or dating. She's in her mother's prison; always tightly controlled. I can feel Jen's frustration. Her eyes look at me, crying out for freedom. She desperately wants to break free of her mother's ways. I want to help her, but I don't know how."

"So, when you have your times with Jen, you want me to join the two of you? Is that it? You want Jen to become familiar with me and learn from me that there's a whole different way of seeing the world?"

"Yes, Marty. That would mean so much to me; and to Jen. Would you join us for our weekends together?"

"Yes, on the condition that I will always be my honest self. I won't be her mommy substitute; at least not in the ways she relates to her mother."

"More like a big sister, then?"

"Yes; but a big sister who performs pornography and has no shame or misgivings about her lifestyle. Think you and she can handle that?"

"I think so. I think I owe it to Jen to expose her to another way of seeing the world; another perspective."

"Okay, I'll help Jen become a mature adult. But realize, she may decide to become a porn star."

"That would be her informed choice."

"So, you'll trust her with me?"

"More than I would with any priest."

"When she discovers her sexuality, she may realize that she loves having multiple partners, orgies, experiments with different positions, lesbian sex; all of it."

"Her life. Those would be Jen's choices; not her mother's choices."

"Okay, Dom. I'm all in. I'll open Jen's eyes. I'll cut her mommy's apron strings and set her free. I'll become her truest and best friend. And I will love her as you love her."

"Thanks, Marty. You're a true friend."

"Yes, I am. And as 'my' friend, there's something you should know about me. Can I confide in you?" Marty smiled as she kissed him on his mouth.

"Sure, Babe." Dominick nodded. He loved it when Marty confided in him.

She held his penis in both her hands and whispered in her most confidential tone: *"I get these flashbacks sometimes. They frighten me. I can see myself in this previous life. I was a temple goddess and I performed fornication rituals. I had this lover who adored me. He told me how he felt while he watched me perform my fornications. When you explain your feelings and open your heart to me, like you just did, you remind me of that man in my dreams. He worshipped my vagina. The entire tribe worshipped my vagina."*

"Like a cult worship thing?"

"Yes. I was their tribal goddess. We were Pagans. Everyone worshipped me. They became animated and joyful while I performed ritual sex with the tribal members. I was on this dais platform with

my legs spread. There were drumbeats and chanting. Everyone on the tribe came to me and kissed my vagina. They paid homage that way. Then, the men brought me gifts of jewels and furs as tribute; and they all fornicated with me. Also, many women came forward and kissed my vagina. They were such loving, sincere kisses. Their kisses sanctified my fornications. Dozens of men came to me, knelt before me, and kissed my vagina; then they penetrated me with their penises."

"Did they hurt you?"

"No. I had servant girls. They put lubricants on the penises. They rubbed my shoulders while I fornicated. I loved it. I felt the sensations of each penis entering me and thrusting inside me. It was breathtaking; exciting; wildly erotic. I loved every penetration. I loved the whole ritual. My vagina had this power over everyone in the tribe. Everyone adored me."

"So, why does this dream frighten you?"

"Because one woman was against me. She's always in my dream. I have this vague recollection. She angered me. She told people I was not their God. She conspired to take people to another tribe that believed some imaginary man was God. She had a husband. She tried to stop him from giving me jewels and furs. I found out that she was trying to take him away from our tribe. I became furious with her."

Marty wrapped her arms around Dominick and kissed him. *"I need you to hold me close while I tell you this. I need you to understand my feelings."*

"As a Pagan goddess?"

"Yes, Dom. I need you to understand me and love me for what I did to that woman back then. I was so horrible and wicked. But I had to do what I did. I needed to keep my tribe together."

Dominick held Marty in his arms. He kissed her mouth with love and passion. *"It's okay, Marty. Whatever you did, it's okay. Your*

Pagan goddess isn't really you. Only you are you. You are here with me, now. Tell Dom what your Pagan goddess did to that woman. I'll understand."

"Are you sure?"

"Yes, Babe." Dominick rubbed his hand over Marty's vagina. His other arm squeezed her body close to his. *"I'm sure. Tell me."*

"Okay. Well, I was very cruel to her. I ordered the men to bring her before me. I then ordered them to eviscerate her and render her flesh from her body while she was still alive. They used obsidian blades. Like razors, they sliced into her abdomen. It seemed so effortless. She was shocked and horrified. I felt badly for her; but I knew what had to be done; and I couldn't stop her death sacrifice."

"To you? Right? She was being sacrificed to you?"

"Yes. And all the while she was being disemboweled and rendered with those sharp blades, slicing her flesh from her, I had one of the men hold her head. He made her face me. He forced her to watch me fornicating with her husband while she was being murdered in this very painful way. That was part of her punishment; that lasting impression on her mind as she was dying; knowing I was taking her husband from her. I wanted the tribal members to see I could be an angry goddess. She cried and wailed and screamed. Then, I felt this sensation. I loved knowing how much pain she was feeling. I felt this inner joy. I was destroying her world by fucking her husband and putting an end to her very life at the same time. I discovered rapture. And I loved that feeling. That's what I want you to know about me. I was destroying another woman in every way imaginable; and I loved what I was doing."

Dominick kissed her again. He looked into her eyes, as if seeing her true soul for the first time, and accepting it and all the wicked things it did. *"Oh, Babe, I love you. I deeply love you. It's all right. I accept whatever you did in your past lives. I love you. You did nothing wrong. That's how things were back then. You did what needed to be done. There was nothing wrong or immoral about what you did."*

"I find myself thinking what I did was beautiful; and those thoughts make me wet inside. They make me feel like making love. Do you think what I did to her was beautiful?"

"Yes; she deserved what you did to her; for those times, what you did was beautiful."

"So, because her murder pleased me; thrilled me and made me wet and anxious to fuck with more enthusiasm, the murder was justified? It was a beautiful thing?"

"Yes, my love. If it pleased you; if it stimulated you; it was beautiful. You are beautiful. What you did to her was beautiful."

"But I often think that the same soul of that Pagan goddess also lives inside me; that I am she; that I continue doing the same things she did." Marty nibbled Dom's lips. Her hand rubbed his penis while she sniffled: *"Would you still think I am beautiful? Would you continue loving me if it's true?"*

"If what's true?"

"If I have the soul of a really a very bad woman; a woman who was once a murderess; a woman who now enjoys destroying other women's lives? I'm just begging you to understand the real me. I love hurting other women; taking their men from them. It's just who I am." Marty pined and whimpered.

"But you don't murder people, do you?"

Marty exhaled a soft laugh: *"No, darling. Of course not."* Marty relied on her tradecraft. Never troubled by a conscience, she lied effortlessly.

"Then what are you talking about?" Dominick looked into her eyes, perplexed.

"Their marriages. I love destroying their marriages. It's all there, in my films. The proof of who I am; how wicked I am, is there, on that neckless I wear; that one with the wedding rings on it."

"I don't understand."

Marty pulled Dom's pants down and took his penis in her hands. She rubbed its head against her outer lips. She cooed while she kissed him. *"Do you remember, in some of my films, how, after I've fucked my partners; how, after my vagina has become filled to overflowing with semen; how I remove my neckless and dip those wedding rings into all that semen; like I'm drowning those marriages in my vagina's fornications? And then, do you remember how I lick the semen off those wedding rings?"*

"Yes. I noticed those scenes. I thought you had some sort of strange fetish. Tell me. What goes on in your mind while you do that?"

"It's me, declaring to the whole world that I'm a free soul. I'm telling the world that my soul is the same soul as the eternal soul of that Pagan goddess who murdered that woman who opposed her. I'm letting my viewer fans know that I'm perfectly okay with destroying marriages; that I'm absolutely willing to help free them from their unbearably tightly constraining cocoons of marriage, if they'll come to me, join my Premium Service, and surrender their frustrated, imprisoned souls to my iniquitous, joyfully immoral, guilt free soul. I'm letting them know that my wanton, fuck crazed cunt wants to set them free. Nothing gives me greater pleasure than freeing a man from his marriage yoke. I'm signaling men that I'll be delighted to fuck them until I drive their wives to split from the marriage. And I'm signaling to the males; letting the males know that they'll have me when they leave their wives; that they won't be alone during their journey to freedom. I'll be there. I'll be supportive and loving. And whenever they feel lonely, I'll be available for intimate sex with them."

"Like you've been for me, right?"

Marty guided Dom's penis past her outer vaginal lips. *"Yes, my love, like I'm here for you, now. Ohhh, how I love when you first penetrate me. Ohhhh, Dom, you're so wonderful to me. I love fucking you. Ohhhh, that's it! I love your cock. I want to feel it inside me; all of it. So strong. So manly. So beautiful! Oh, yes, Dom. That's it. Yes! That's it. Ohhhh, fuck me. Yessss. Fuck me. I love it so much when you are fucking me."*

"Oh Babe, I don't pretend to understand everything. I can only tell you how you make me feel. Your vagina has this hold on me. I'm just drawn to it. I love fucking you. I feel you are called by the universe to copulate; that your fornications, your promiscuity, your carnal lusts are sanctified; that there are forces greater than any other I have ever known. They are compelling me to adore you and everything you and your wonderous vagina are doing. I believe you are sent to us by the spirits to fuck; and that you should fuck at every opportunity. I sometimes imagine the only time you aren't fucking is when you're trapped into a situation where it would be inappropriate, like on an airplane."

"Oh no, darling," Marty held his head in her hands. She cooed while she looked into his eyes. She often did that when she was about to reveal something. *"I never feel it's inappropriate to fuck on airplanes. I often fuck on airplanes. I love fucking on airplanes."*

"In the lavatory?"

"No, Dom, my darling; never there. I always fuck in the cockpit!"

"What? That's not safe. How do you manage that?"

"It's perfectly safe, Dom. I have a pilot friend, Travis. He and Larry or Jeff, his usual co-pilots fly transatlantic. When I'm going to Europe, I match my schedules with theirs. They give me their buddy passes. I fly for free. I get invited into the cockpit and I fuck those pilots all the way all across the Atlantic from New York to Paris and back to New York."

"But that's dangerous. You're putting all those people at risk!"

"No, Dom. It's not dangerous. The two pilots share me. Only one is needed to fly the plane while the other pilot fucks me. Besides,

we're mostly on autopilot."

"I don't want you doing that."

"Dom, you know you don't own me. You know how much I love to fuck. You know about my nymphomania. You know I can't help myself. You know when there's a situation when I can be a naughty girl, I'm going to be a naughty girl. You have no idea what a thrill I feel while I straddle Travis's cock, facing outward staring into the sky; chasing the sunrises on the way back to New York."

"Sunrises? Plural?"

"Yes. We fuck until I orgasm. Then, Travis takes the plane a few thousand feet higher. The sun pops back up above the horizon. Then, we fuck some more, until I orgasm again while the sun is setting again. Then, we go up a little higher. I see the sun setting again. I feel I need to fuck again. I often have four or five orgasms that way. It's a wonderful experience; soooo exciting and beautiful!"

"I don't want you doing that anymore."

"I don't want to stop, Dom. I won't stop."

"How about if I got you your own private jet and paid your pilot and flight costs. Would you stop then?"

"Would I stop fucking Travis and Larry and Jeff?"

"Yes."

"Well, maybe I could stop," Marty purred, *"if I had my own big jet with a queen-sized bed. And if you would pay for my favorite porn partners to fly with me. I'd want Josh and Marshawn to fly with me. You know how much I love fucking them. I'd love to discover how my pussy feels while I'm fucking them high above the ocean. Would you be willing to do that for me?"* Marty purred while she kissed Dom and fondled his testicles.

"Yes, of course, you gorgeous whore. Anything to keep you and your ravenous pussy safe and happy."

"You are a love; my best love, ever." Marty lifted her vagina off Dom's penis and began performing fellatio.

As she began her sensuous licking, Dom moaned: *"You are undoubtedly the world's most incorrigible, immoral whore. You know that, don't you?"*

"Yes, I know that, darling. I love being a whore. There, I've said it. And that's what you love about me, isn't it? And you love the ways I suck your cock, don't you? Mmmmm, mmmmm; tell me that's what you love about me. Tell me you love all the ways I make you come. Tell me you love the whore that I am. Tell me that you're glad you left your wife for me. Tell me that you want me to help you raise your daughter. Tell me that you want her to be just like me."

"Yes, oh baby, that feels so good. Yesssss, yessss, a thousand times yes. I'm glad I left her. I love you. Oh, babe; I totally love you. Ohhhh. I'm coming! Yes, I want Jen to know you; to love you; to become a woman who thinks like you."

"You'll approve if I help her smash her moral compass? She may even decide there's no sin in incest. We could do threesomes. She's lovely. I'd love to be intimate with her. Will you be okay with that?"

"Oh Marty, I'm starting to come. Yes, darling. I love you. You know how much I love you. Of course, I'll be okay with that. Smash her compass. Teach her your ways; our ways. Anything you want, Marty. Ohhhh! I'm coming. I love you so much! I adore you. I'm so in love with you. Ohhhh, yessss, Ummm. You're so wonderful! My glorious, beautiful, totally immoral whore. I need you. Oh, Babe, I know I need you."

"Yes, Dom. Yessss, that's it! Come into my mouth Oh, my sweet love. You taste soooo good. I love how I feel while you fuck my mouth this way. Tell me, I need to know. I need to know your mind. What's going through your mind while you're coming in my mouth? What do you see? Please, tell me."

"I'm seeing you in one of your films; the one where two men are seated on a sofa and you approach them. You are wearing a lacey

bra and napkin panties. You kneel on the sofa. You begin kissing one of the men. You present your breast to him. He pulls your bra away and begins sucking your nipple. The second man holds you by your waist and begins kissing your back while he peels down your panties. Your hand finds the penis of the first man. You bring it to your mouth and start sucking it. The second man presents his penis to you. Each of your hands holds a penis and you begin sucking them. I know you will soon begin fucking both men; and I adore your insatiable appetite for sex. I feel this adoration for your instinctive need to fuck both men. I love you more than I have ever loved anyone. And I feel like coming forever into your mouth. I know you are the very personification of immoral sin and godlessness; and I love you all the more for who you are. My spurts into your mouth are my surrender to you and your wanton immorality; and I want to be part of that until the day I die. I know I can't live without you. I know you own my soul. I know you are everything I need; what I want for my life."

"Oh Dom, that's so beautiful. You're helping me understand your mind. You're helping me make better porn. You're bringing out sensations in me that I love feeling. I'll hold those feelings in my heart while I'm performing porn on set. I know I'll be more emotive than ever. You want me to perform the most gorgeous, glorious porn I can possibly create, don't you?"

"Yes, Marty. Of course, I want you to be the best porn star you can possibly be."

"And you want me to be known as the most notorious whore in the entire world, don't you? I'm the sin loving woman you want to be with, aren't I?"

"Yes, Marty. Of course you are. I want the world to know about you. You are the only woman I want to be with."

"Mmmmm. I think we'll go far together. Let me suck you while I stroke you. My mouth loves playing with your cock. I could mouth

your balls and suck you all day. I want all of you. Yessss, I must have all of you. Mmmmm, mmmmm. That's it. Every drop. Mmmmm, mmmmm. I adore your wonderful cock. I totally love your cock. Yummmm. You're soooo wonderful!"

Marty returned the conversation to Consuelo: *"There, Consuelo, don't you agree that a woman's pussy should always get first class treatment; should always feel appreciated and satisfied; that there's never anything that's too much or too expensive for an incorrigible, fuck loving pussy to have?"*

"Yes, I completely agree with you, Marty, as do our faithful readers." Ever supportive Consuelo segue weighed into Marty's latest film promotion: *"Your latest film, THE CONCEPTION STORY, is a sensation across the country. It's running now and available for downloads. Can you give us any insights about how you became inspired to make that film; and how satisfied you felt while making it? And will you tell us what you plan to do next?"*

"Sure, gladly, Consuelo, I got the idea for the film one day while I sat in church with my grandmother. I was in our family pew trying not to fall asleep during service when a piece of plaster fell from the church ceiling and landed next to me. I was a young girl then, but since then the thought crossed my mind that the entire church and its messaging about sin and salvation seemed kind of decrepit and old. After I became a mature woman, I decided the message needed upgrading to one with more credibility and more in line with the scientific method of logical reasoning. That got me thinking and creating. Now that film is a smash hit, not just in adult film genres, but a smash hit in box offices and movie downloads, worldwide."

"What was your mind-set while you created it, Marty?" Consuelo was intrigued with the creative processes of the film. Her interviews were read by over a million fans for the insights she revealed.

"While I made the film, I imagined entering the worlds of long ago and living in those moments. I acted out my honest feelings. I felt like I became Mary, the divine mother, making love for a special reason. I wanted to unchain mankind's thinking from something that never made sense to me. That feeling I had, that I could release freedom and truth from its chains, is what sent the film to the top of the charts. I just let myself go.

"Everyone knows the true source of eternal life is the egg seeds which a woman carries in her womb, right? Well, I then reasoned that those male constructed religions are just ways for men's' little boy minds to deny reality's truths. So, I just released my thoughts while we filmed. I let my feelings and my thoughts immerse me in the wonderful joy of love making. I made love with every one of my film partners with passions that were heavenly and filled with purpose. Every ejaculation of my partners and every one of my orgasms gave me an immense feeling of pride in my accomplishment, and immense satisfaction. That's the best way to describe my feelings during that film shoot.

"As far as what I'm planning next, I can only tell you this much. A man and woman keep running into each other at a bookstore. He asks her to have a coffee with him to discuss a book. They eventually discover they are both interested in all sorts of kinky sex; BDSM, multiple partners, those sorts of things. As the plot moves along the woman, that's me, has a secret way of going down into the underworld and meeting the Devil and all his friends; and all the evil people who've ever lived throughout history. She takes her new boyfriend with her and they explore all sorts of erotica in the underworld. Then they make a shocking discovery about the Devil. They learn something that no one throughout history has ever figured out before; and that's where it all gets very interesting. That film will be filled with breathtaking, unforgettable BDSM scenes. That's all I can tell you without giving away the plot, okay?"

"Come on Marty; don't leave us hanging like that. Can't we have a little hint about the shocking discovery?"

"Well, okay, just this little bit," Marty paused while stroking her chin and looking up in thought. *"There is a place that is much naughtier than hell. It's where hell dwellers go for vacation; but you need to become friends with the Devil to know how to get there. If I tell you more than that my producers will shoot me!"*

"Marty, my dear friend, this sounds so exciting. I feel myself getting moist again. I get like that whenever I'm around you. I wish I could be involved, somehow, in your upcoming film about the underworld. It sounds marvelous!"

"You're serious, aren't you, Consuelo?" Would you like to join me on the sets? Do you think you'd like to have a role in the film, perhaps join me in one of the orgy scenes?"*

"Yes, Marty, a thousand times yes. Oh my god! I would love it! I'd like nothing better. It would be like my fondest dream come true to perform in an intimate adult film with you. I want to do that so much!"

"Okay, Consuelo, we'll do it! I'll be sure the producer includes you. In fact, there are three different scenes that will be perfect for you. You'll do a seduction scene of a handsome male partner, a threesome with me and a male partner, and an orgy with me and seven male partners. I'm excited to perform with you also. I'm anxious to discover your delicious taste. I'm salivating at the thought of you! You're going to love doing orgies with me. They are the pinnacle of whoredom's pleasures. They are totally self-gratifying; tons of cocks all just craving to enter you; non-stop fucking you everywhere; non stop kissing you and your vagina, giving you endless pleasures.

"You'll love it. You'll feel like a giggly happy little birthday girl swimming in more ice cream and chocolate cake than you can possibly eat. You'll have so much pleasure you'll scream and beg for more. You won't want it to ever stop. You'll totally love it. You'll want to

keep fucking forever and you'll want to do more and more orgies, again and again. I promise.

"Since you asked, Consuelo, I'll let you in on another secret. Dom and I are working to produce the most sensational intimate film extravaganza ever made. The plot thread will be that Mary Magdalene, the female companion to the Christ, was his mistress; and her vagina was the actual Holy Grail! Well, after the Romans take him away, she runs off with two of the disciples, played by Marshawn and Josh, two of my favorite performers. We escape the Romans. Marshawn and Josh pimp me, Mary, as their whore and we fuck our way westward to a new land and a beautiful harbor which we call "The Port of the Grail." It's now modern-day Lisbon in the nation of Portugal. There, I open a salon called 'Heaven's Place.' We even have a song that goes with our plot line. Its lyrics say 'Bring your face to heaven's place. Bring your face to my place.' Heaven's Place is, of course, my bordello; and my place refers to my vagina.

"Dom's plot features Heaven's Place as a notoriously immoral whore house and its whores are all immortal goddesses. It's the most popular stop for wayfaring merchants and seamen who transport wines from Porto in the north, and the Azores to the south, to the European continent. Most of our orgies will take place at Heaven's Place, but we'll also stage some of them in the spectacular castles in the mountain town of Sintra. That's where the Portuguese royals went to escape the summer heat.

"You'll love the castles, Consuelo. They are enormous! Huge kitchens that can roast ten animals at a time! And the beds! They are high up off the floor. They are perfect for orgies. You can position your vagina at the edge of the bed and a man can easily enter you while he's standing. You can lay your head over the side of one corner of the bed and lay your vagina over the corner's other side in a way that enables you to suck and fuck two men while they are standing

beside you, touching you. Those beds are perfect props for incredibly erotic sex. Those kings and queens loved having their fun!

"You'll make love next to casks filled with gold and silver, Consuelo; and, here's the best part: Dom will pay us in real gold and silver coins, not paper money. Dom believes the world's only honest profession deserves to be paid in the world's only honest money.

"The movies will be a quadruple feature series, starring me in twenty orgy scenes taking place a hundred years apart; or one orgy scene every hundred years. We will make historical reenactments of orgy scenes from the time of Christ until the present day. We'll be creating twenty to fifty hours of orgy filming with a hundred different partners, all carefully chosen for penis size, handsome looks, and physical stamina. Each scene will pair me with five to ten lovers in erotic costumes of that historical period. The men will undress me, kiss, and fondle me; and then I will perform with them in splendid, colorful magnificent orgies. The productions will have outstanding lighting effects with different color shadings highlighting my vagina. We'll use some innovative slow-motion framing and close ups to capture the explicit erotic effects in many of the scenes. One hundred different male partners! Just imagine, Consuelo! Over a hundred different fantastic wonderful sex-crazed cocks for us to suck and fuck! The production process will take months! How fun!"

"Marty, will these movies have individual themes? Can you give us some hints about the things you and Dom are working on?"

"Oh, sure, glad to Consuelo. Understand that this is still in the formative stages. We've only had initial discussions with directors and screenwriters. There's just so much. I can give you some hints about the films that are furthest along, okay?"

"Yes, please. I know my fans are dying to hear what you are up to."

"Okay. Well, all twelve films will have musical scores and two or three of them are also designed to be performed as live musicals as well. I'll give you some parts of a few of them, okay?"

"Okay. Shoot."

"Well one will have this part about me playing this little cater-pillar spirit. It gets thrown out of its mother butterfly's house because Mother wants to dance with a handsome male butterfly. So, the lit-tle caterpillar crawls away feeling hurt and lonely. Other caterpillars don't want to play with it. They make fun of it and laugh at it. But then these two boy caterpillars notice it and come up to it and kiss it. Well, the little girl caterpillar stands up and takes off her caterpillar suit and shows the boys she has wings. The boy caterpillars take off their suits and they have wings, too. Then I make love with the two boy butterflies. Then all the boy caterpillars that previously laughed at me come running from the corner where they were standing with their girl caterpillar friends. They run to me! They suddenly want me! They take off their caterpillar suits and show me that they also have wings; and they all want to make love with me. So, to this really cool music, I dance this ballet dance with each one of the butterflies. The boys all kiss me and squeeze my tush and then I make love with every one of them. And I become known as the most beautiful, most desired butterfly in the entire world.

"Another film will have a scene with me fluttering with other butterflies over a desert and then an ocean. There will be sounds of howling winds and thunder and lightning. The cameras will show an angry ocean below us. We cry and become frightened, but we must keep fluttering onward, even though it hurts our muscles to continue. We finally reach this lovely jungle beneath us and we come together with these male butterflies above the jungle canopy where we kiss them and make love with them.

"Another film portrays me as this huge African butterfly. I have huge purple wings. I flutter over migrating animals. Below me are Wildebeests, Antelope, Giraffes, Zebras, Lions, Cheetahs, Leopards, and Hyenas. I flutter into a huge tent where a man and woman are making love. And I transform myself. I become the woman. You can

see me making love while I'm in this open-air safari tent and all these gorgeous wild animals are running past us.

"Another film has my butterfly spirit becoming confused about what I want out of life. My spirit guardian carries me far away to this magical land. Everything is perfect and lovely. My spirit stands me before a gigantic lust wheel. It's like a huge Ferris wheel, only it has handsome male butterfly spirits on it instead of carriages that hold people. Each male butterfly spirit is an exceptionally handsome man with a very huge, very hard and fabulously splendid cock. The men rotate before me on this wheel. Then each man stops in front of me while I perform fellatio. The wheel keeps turning to the next spirit male where I perform on him. And on and on. Meanwhile all this wonderful music is playing. It gets me in the mood to go crazy. After I suck all the male spirits, they get off the wheel and surround me. We all dance together. I love dancing. My titties are bouncing; there's lots of touching and kissing and disco lights are flashing over-head. I get hoisted into midair. My legs are spread wide, revealing my beautiful, freshly waxed, creamed, and lubed vagina. My partners kiss my vagina and touch me everywhere. It's very erotic; extremely Pagan-like. Just walking through the scene took my breath away.

"Another movie we'll do will be salaciously sacrilegious. Dom is casting me as the Whore of Babylon. I'm on this throne. I'm the love object for this fornication ritual where my tribal leaders all make love with me. Then these battle trumpets sound and I order my warriors to conquer the Hebrews because they will not worship me. So, there's this huge battle scene where my warriors storm the Hebrew temple of Jerusalem and slay lots of Hebrews; and my warriors take the Arc of the Covenant from the Hebrew temple and bring it to me as trophy tribute from their conquest. I open the Arc and take out the stone tablets with the Ten Commandments on them. Now, Consuelo, I can not tell you what I do with the Ten Commandments after I have pos-session of them. I represent everything evil in this movie and I am

antithetical to the teachings of the Ten Commandments. I am a totally naughty girl in this movie. So, I'll have to leave what I do next up to your imagination."

"Marty, you are so totally bad. You're going to make me go see that movie, aren't you?"

"Yes, of course. You won't be disappointed. I think I perform explicit sex at my very best in that movie because it has that titillating aspect of evil in it. I promise you, Consuelo. You'll love it. You won't stop talking about it. I thank Dom for all of the film ideas and the musicals. I'll be performing live sex with the musical's cast for at least a year on Broadway and on tour. Dom is such a brilliant promoter. I'll tell you another secret. He's going to insert single frame shots into every film. They will fly past so quickly that the audience will only receive subconscious impressions. Those will include still images of a giant penis erupting with cum into my vagina; images of penises erupting into my mouth; threesomes showing me with a cock in my mouth as well as one entering my vagina. Dom will also have explicit erotic images where I'm seductively kissing my partners in scenes from the other movies in the series. He thinks those will entice viewers to see all four of my orgy series movies.

"Dom is convinced there is nothing more erotic than a seductive kiss. He thinks a sensuous kiss causes the limbic zone to flare hottest, more than any other romantic act. The flash frame inserts will include the phone number for my private member service; Dom believes that will plant the subliminal urge for viewers to call my service. He predicts calls to my private member service will skyrocket."

"Marty, I can tell that you're excited by watching the way you're running your fingers through your hair. I can only imagine how thrilled you will be, enjoying a hundred different cocks. Cocks in your hands and mouth, stroking inside you, all those different positions; all that cum shooting into you. It sounds so yummy! Please promise me you'll let me share, Marty."

"Oh, I will, Consuelo. We'll both have so many cocks to fuck and suck we'll go out of our minds. It's going to take us a whole year to create all those scenes and fuck all those cocks; but it will be worth it! Here's the sweetener, Consuelo. After every orgy scene, the Great Spirit will appear to me in the persona of Marshawn or Josh. Dom then has me making love with their Spirit's souls and their Spirit's souls entering my soul and our souls becoming one soul. After each orgy the Spirits tell me that they are immensely proud of me. They confide to me that, after every one of my orgies, they love me more than ever; and that they adore my whoring ways.

"The Spirits constantly reassure me I am doing the right thing, leading humanity forward, through the centuries, with my immoral whoring. They profess that my whoring is inspiring and beautiful and they desire to see my unapologetic immorality living into the future, forever. They tell me that by making love with me their spirits and my spirit become one; and that their voices and minds become my voice and my mind; and that my immoral ways have now become the future path for our entire immoral world. They tell me that the passions I arouse in men are good for the world. They say it's good to make love and they want humanity to enjoy more of it.

"Then, the Great Spirit appears. He decides to make me immortal, to reincarnate me over and over, forever; like one of his timeless butterflies, until the end of time. Then, after every orgy, I become this renewed eternal goddess. I become an even more beautiful and more sensuous erotic whore than I was before. I spend all of eternity fucking and sucking and making passionate love. In the films, my spirit never dies. I am completely at peace with myself and my shameless whoring persona because I know the Great Spirit adores my immorality and wants more of that in the world. I feel blessed to be immersed in a sea of adoring cocks and having my soul totally immersed in whoredom."

"You'll really include me in your orgy scenes? You'll help me become an intimacy film star? You'll let me kiss your vagina? You'd let me do that with you? Please, Marty, it will be my dreams come true." Consuelo's eyes brimmed with hope and desire.

"Yes, Consuelo, of course I will. We'll have a ball! I'm thrilled that you've asked to join me. You know you're gorgeous and very sexy. You'll be perfect! With you beside me, the immorality theme of the "Heaven's Place Whore House will be totally believable and spicy delicious. Absolutely I'll partner with you. You're hired!' Each movie of the quadruple feature series will have five different orgy scenes in it. They will portray the morality and the erotic dress costumes for each of the twenty past centuries. We'll wear twenty different promiscuous time period seduction outfits.

"You'll love being undressed and stepping out from the many different styles of stockings and panties. So erotic! So sexy! What fun! I know we'll love feeling and stimulating the men's cocks through their dress garb, kissing while they fondle us; then unbuttoning their pants and taking their aroused cocks into our mouths. It will be wildly erotic and deliciously imaginative; and incredibly mouth wateringly sexy. We'll love having delicious sex with all those men in so many different positions and exotic settings. We'll constantly be making love with and sucking the most splendid, sex loving cocks of the world's handsomest men for week after week after week while we're making those films.

"Trust me, Consuelo; our performing partners make the art of love making a fantastic erotic experience. You'll love them. You'll want to make love forever! We'll have so much fun! So many orgasms! I can't wait to begin filming. We're going to love making these movies."

CHAPTER SIX

Achieving the status of sex goddess is like being the only girl on your block with a bicycle. You're accepted. You can hang around with the boys and do the same things they do. And when you take your panties down, suddenly you are extra special. (Rosemary Ness-Bitner, author)

INTIMACY'S QUEEN

"Okay, Marty. Thank you ever so much! I'm thrilled out of my mind to join you. I'm also very anxious to taste you. You'll never regret allowing me to work with you, I promise. We'll be beautiful together. I'm sure all your future films will be smashing successes.

"Before we reveal our annual survey results and present our annual awards, I want to show our viewers our current issue's photo feature layout. Our editors selected six delicious photos of my guest Marty, to grace the photo layout section. You will all want your very own personal copy of these never-before-seen pictures of Marty posing at her evocative explicit, erotic best. Marty, please discuss this first photo for us. Your partner is positioned beneath you. You are kneeling over his face. You have this most heavenly erotic expression. Can you tell us what is going on here?"

"Sure, Consuelo, I'm facing the camera during cunnilingus with Marshawn. He's one of my most favorite lovers, ever. The camera captured the moments while his tongue was massaging my clitoris. I had just popped my first orgasm. My face is registering my

innermost feeling. I call it 'My Divine Explosion.' That expression captures my understanding that my soul and Marshawn's soul have become inseparably married. It's even deeper than that. It's my realization that my clitoris and Marshawn's tongue became one; yes, one united, rhythmic organism where my flows syncopate responsive reflexes to his tongue's coaxing. He touches. He strokes. And I respond. My delayed reflexive pulse bursts uncontrollably. I pop. It's like when a balloon goes bang, but without the loud noise. There's only the changed state of me. It's my vagina, from holding all my love and feelings inside me; suddenly erupting with its love; releasing it into Marshawn's mouth, and gushing all over his face. Maybe there should be a name for that photo? Maybe call it the Pop or the Big Bang, or the Wow? All of those would express it, I don't know words capture my feelings best. The two of us are suddenly enjoying that magical harmony together. Yeah; maybe the photo should be called Harmony? Marshawn and I cherish that instantaneous moment. It's incredibly rare and Ohhh, it's soooo beautiful. I love having oral sex with Marshawn. I positively love it.

"At that moment I knew everything in my world was wonderful. My vagina was joined with Marshawn's loving mouth. His tongue was stroking my clitoris. His tongue is studded with black pearls on both the top and the bottom. That way, when his tongue strokes my clitoris, I experience this extra intensely erotic sensation. It's divine. And when he strokes me with the underside of his tongue, I positively go out of my mind from the sensations. When Marshawn and I feel intense love for each other, like that; neither of us wants to ever stop. He's often told me that he wants to lick my vagina forever. He adores my vagina; totally loves it. What a wonderful man! I'm overcome with appreciation. That photo captured that euphoric moment and the divine feeling I was having when my orgasm first exploded.

"In that instant, I realized that I'm a hopelessly fallen woman. I was accepting and embracing that realization. I had no shame about

it. I knew I had completely given myself over to sin; letting the whole world know that I am an ungodly sinner; hopelessly, incorrigibly immoral; and that I'm in love with who I am: whore; connoisseur of penises; glutton for sex and semen. I also felt immensely grateful. I had this wonderful good fortune. I was making love with this wonderful man with his wonderful mouth and his fabulous cock. I know that I'm being paid extremely well to do what I love doing most. My mind is thinking I'm living in this wonderful dream. I'll pinch myself and wake up. It's all too wonderful to be real. I'm thinking that I could do this forever! I know I'm irretrievably immersed and consumed by my euphoria. I'm loving my erotic immorality. I'm loving that I'm falling away from everything moral. I'm loving my rapture feeling. That orgasm and the loving man who made it happen were so beautiful."

"Wow, Marty, that's powerful. Now in this next photo you are sitting on the edge of the bed. Marshawn is standing before you, and the two of you are holding each other tenderly and kissing passionately. Your hand is down inside Marshawn's pants. Obviously, you are stroking him. What's happening here?"

"That's me and Marshawn just being happy together knowing we are about to make love. We have this thing for each other. It's hard to explain it, but Marshawn sends fire through my entire body when we kiss. I can not contain my excitement or my passion. He has just rubbed my body with oils and I'm highly aroused. I can't wait to remove his pants and suck his beautiful cock. I'm just crazy anxious knowing we'll soon make love. I'm imagining my body touching against his, everywhere. I adore his body and his wonderful cock. It's a photo that captures me feeling awe. I'm in the presence of a divinity. I'm brimming with anticipation of our love making. I totally love this man and I love making love with him."

"Wow, again, Marty! Now this last photo seems especially provocative and intriguing. Obviously, Marshawn has released

inside you. There's tell tale white cream seeping from you; and yet, you continue to passionately kiss him. The two of you are lying there together in a sensual embrace and you are deeply into soul kissing after sex. What was going through your mind?"

"Here, I'm simply enamored with Marshawn and what the two of us have done. We made beautiful romantic erotica. We felt each other's souls while we performed; but there's more to this photo than that. My kisses are communicating that I know he understands how he's able to hold my soul in his soul while my mind totally surrenders itself to my soul's immorality. My kiss tells him I know he respects my naughty nature and loves me for it. I know he will never belittle me or think less of me as a woman.

"My kisses tell him that I appreciate his profound understanding of who I am. He knows how much I love being a completely unrepentant immoral whore; and I adore Marshawn for his unquestioning understanding of my needs. It's me silently telling him that I love his cock so much that I could spend an entire day sucking it. It's me telling him I love it when he comes inside me four or five times in one afternoon. It's me letting him know that even though I spend almost every waking hour of my life making love with different film partners and premium members I also have a special need to be loved. I love knowing that my man loves me. My kiss tells Marshawn that I appreciate the accepting, unquestioning love he gives me.'

"But you have a steady boyfriend, too, don't you Marty? Do you love him like you love Marshawn?"

"Oh, gee, Consuelo, this is a little hard to explain. Yes, I do have a steady boyfriend. I go home to him at nights when I'm not away somewhere. I need his love more than anything. He is my anchor to the woman I am inside myself. He loves me, for me; to be with me, no matter what. We have this very deep commitment to our love. There's a sweetness feeling about our intimacy that I only know with

him. We have a special understanding with each other. We both lost our fathers at an early age. That connects us somehow.

"But with Marshawn and a few others, I can experience a different kind of love. It's erotic and passionate. It unleashes this expressive wildness within me. It overflows with physicality and passion. It satisfies my intense craving for unbridled erotic romantic intimacy. I think I'm like a lot of women, Consuelo. We are women who need both kinds of love. We can't completely compartmentalize our love, or exclude one kind of love to favor the other. We need freedom to embrace love in all its forms.

"What makes that photo sort of jump out is that it was completely unscripted. It's me in all my wholesome uninhibited, shameless immodesty. It's me being me, feeling my erotic love, unleashing it from all boundaries. It's me in my unapologetic iniquity for seducing Marshawn; taking him away from his wife. I did that, Consuelo. I'll tell you more about that some day, but not now. Let's just say my kissing Marshawn in that photo is our acknowledgement that we have an inside baseball secret between us; and I want to leave it at that. That photo captures true intimate love between a man and a woman. It's showing that love must come first in life and intimate love is far more important than everything else."

"Oh Marty, that's so beautiful, so inspiring, and so true. I now understand why you have such a huge following. Thank you for those comments. And now, I'm sure this is the moment you've all been waiting for. I have results of THE WONDERFUL WORLD OF PORN MAGAZINE'S annual survey.

"Our readership was asked to rank their favorite film stars in five categories. First, the star that creates the greatest feelings of romantic love in her work; second, the star who creates the most desire and passion with her work; third, the star who creates the most innovative expressions of intimacy; fourth, the star they'd most like to take

on a date; and fifth, the one star they would like to introduce to their family and declare her to be the woman they've chosen to marry.

"Fifteen thousand five hundred sixty-five of our subscribers responded to our survey, Marty. And here are their results: In category one, you ranked at the top of our survey. You were number one with ninety three percent of respondents. In category two, you were on top again with ninety five percent of respondents voting for you. In category three you ran away from the field, Marty. Fully ninety nine percent of respondents voted you number one innovator. Congratulations! Well done! And, in our final two categories, again you were on top with ninety six percent of respondents saying you were the star they'd most want to take on a date and ninety five percent of respondents voting you the one star they'd most want to introduce to their families as the woman they've decided to marry. Congratulations again, Marty! We have never seen such blow out results in any previous annual WONDERFUL WORLD OF PORN MAGAZINE survey.

"Now for the result of our dating drawing: Six thousand forty-three subscribers bought a one-hundred-dollar raffle ticket for the chance to be that lucky man who takes you on a dinner date to the restaurant of your choice and experiences romance with you afterwards. Here is the name and phone number of our winner, Marty. He already knows he's won. Our staff has interviewed him. He passed his blood tests with flying colors. He is very handsome, as in tall, dark, and handsome. He's in his mid thirties, divorced, not in any serious relationship, and he's anxious to meet you. He's waiting for your call. What do you say, Marty?"

"I'm flattered, Consuelo. My thanks go out to all your wonderful subscribers who voted for me. I promise everyone I will continue to do my very best, whatever it takes, to make the most appreciated intimate artistry films in the world. I'm anxious to meet this year's contest winner. I think I'm falling in love already! Thank

you, Consuelo, and thanks to your entire magazine on behalf of all sex workers world wide, for promoting the fabulous dynamic world-changing intimate artistry industry."

"And, thank you, Marty for the spectacular artistry you create, and for this insightful interview; and thank you very much from our editors and staff for being so gracious with your time and your openness about your thoughts and feelings.

"Now I'd like to present you with this check for three hundred two thousand one hundred fifty dollars, which is your half of our blind date drawing entry fees, as agreed to in our promotional contest."

"Thank you, Consuelo!"

"And now, on behalf of our magazine, the world's number one intimate artistry focused magazine in circulation, readership, advertisers, and content articles, and on behalf of our editorial board and our entire staff we want to present you with our first annual GOLDEN GALAXY AWARD. This solid fourteen inch high, eighteen caret gold engraved grail, or cup, sits atop a golden globe of the world. It recognizes you as the world's best film actress in the dynamic world of intimate erotic artistry. With this award we are also making two important corporate announcements. I am chang-ing the name of my column to WORLD INTIMACY BEAT and our magazine's name is changing to INTIMATE ARTISTRY PERFOR-MANCE APPRECIATION MAGAZINE.

"Our first annual GOLDEN GALAXY AWARD from INTI-MATE ARTISRY recognizes you, Marty, as the worlds' number one intimacy performance artist, selected by our devoted readers' poll. See, inscribed there below your name: VOTED WORLD'S NUMBER ONE INTIMACY APPRECIATION ART'S TOP PER-FORMANCE ARTIST. Congratulations for your beautiful intimacy art film achievements, Marty and for your phenomenal success at promoting the exciting, new intimate film art genre and the Modern Morality Standard."

"Oh, my goodness, Consuelo, this award trophy is three feet tall!"

"Yes, Marty, it's three times taller than an Oscar. It signifies that intimate film artistry is a three times more important medium for bringing love to the world. You'll notice the Galaxy has a wide circular base, studded with diamonds representing our galaxy and its billons of stars; and out of the base rises a golden globe of the Earth, our planet where you perfected your artistry, Marty; and then, standing atop the planet is a woman cast from solid eighteen caret gold. She's wearing a jade bikini bottom studded with rubies and diamonds and a diamond studded bikini top.

"The rubies represent the source of eternal life and the diamonds represent her sparkling sex appeal. She's holding high above her head a grail. The Galaxy Grail represents the divine nature of feminine anatomy and its power to reincarnate life through birth. You'll notice, on top of the Galaxy Grail rests a Monarch Butterfly with its wings widespread.

"The butterfly has ruby and diamond jewels studded into its wingtips; and along its back there are two ridges studded with rubies, representing a woman's vagina prepared to experience love and create life. If you'll look closely, Marty, your Galaxy butterfly is detachable. It can be worn as a broach or as a pendant on your eighteen-caret gold neckless. There's a hinge in the back that swings open revealing a clasp pin if you wish to wear it as a broach; and it also has a slot that enables you to mount it on your neckless.

"Inside your Galaxy Grail is your gold neckless chain with a mounting bar that's fitted to the mounting slot of your jeweled butterfly!

"I will now place upon your head a golden crown with seven rays of gold. Your crown symbolizes the bright light of freedom that your majestic immorality brings to the world. Its origin is pre-biblical. It was the crown worn by Ishtar, the highly revered whore of pagan Babylon. Wear it with pride, Marty. Wear it for all freedom

loving peoples everywhere. Let it inspire all who want freedom. Let it symbolize your radiant loving spirit and let it shine hope into the hearts of dispirited millions!"

"*This is so amazing, Consuelo, I don't know what to say. I'm profoundly honored to wear the crown. And this Galaxy trophy leaves me breathless. It makes an Oscar look so puny and insignificant by comparison. My goodness, it must have ten times more diamonds than a Super Bowl ring! It's stunning; absolutely, stunning!"*

Marty was overcome with joy. Tears ran down her cheeks.

"*Marty, the solid eighteen carets Galaxy Award was created by Gwendolyn's, the fine arts appreciation jewelers and donated to the Galaxy Awards by your dear friend Gwen."*

"*Thank you, Consuelo. Thank you, Gwen, my dearest, sweetest friend. I'm proud and grateful for this trophy and your recognition. And thank you to the wonderful staff at INTIMATE ARTISTRY PERFORMANCE APPRECIATION MAGAZINE, and a special thanks to WORLD INTIMACY BEAT, for this opportunity to catch up with all your intimacy art fans world wide, Consuelo. And thank you to every one of my millions of fans world-wide who download my films.*

"*I am so profoundly grateful that you voted me number one of all intimate artists. I am truly honored. I'd like to give a special thank you to......................'*

Miss Iniquity screamed into Marty's ear:

'*You were about to say it, weren't you? You were going to thank George and Bertie for their endless patience and their efforts coaching you for endless days and hours to help you become your most expressive best. You were going to say you were sorry they couldn't be here to enjoy this moment with you, weren't you?*

'*How stupid can you be? You murdered them, remember? The last thing you want is to draw attention to the fact that you worked closely with them. If that slips out, David will be furious! Get a grip!'*

Miss Lust screamed next:

'What is wrong with you? This isn't some game. This is murder and the cover up. The police have already asked you if you'd seen them and you said no, not for a long time. Are you subconsciously trying to get caught? Recover! Get a grip right now, IMMEDIATELY!'

Marty nodded her head and silently whispered her apologies to Miss Iniquity and Miss Lust. *'I'm sorry. I was so caught up in the awards and the honors I forgot I murdered them.'*

Consuelo noticed the unscripted pause in Marty's acceptance speech. Ever the gracious host, she offered aid to her friend:

"Are you okay, Marty? May I get you a glass of water?"

Marty sat briefly. After taking a few sips of water she raised her hand and shook her head, indicating that she did not need any help. She resumed her acceptance speech.

"And, I'd like to give another special thank you to my fabulous performing partners who worked so lovingly and intimately in all the films we created over this past year. Working with you was a sensational erotic and love filled experience. I thoroughly loved the intimate love making experiences I had with every one of you. There was not a single moment in all our film making when I felt anything but joy and my thrills of making love with you. And, another special thank you to my make up and wardrobe assistants who helped me look my best in every scene of every film. You were always there for me when I needed a quick change in appearance or dress, or, tee-hee, undress. And, here's another very special thank you:

"Thank you to every one of my fifty-three advertisers and sponsors for giving me the opportunity to offer my face, body, and enthusiastic vagina to represent your products and services. I am profoundly grateful to work with all you wonderful people. I'm deeply honored knowing that, because of my films, advertisers and sex workers gained satisfied customers for chat, dating, and personalized intimate experience services. I am also honored knowing that

photos of my face, body and widely recognized butterfly vagina are successfully promoting products and services from big game hunts to automobile and yacht sales to adult community home sales and exclusive club memberships.

"I promise all of you that my work in the coming year will exceed everything I've done previously. I and my film partners will shatter all barriers to shameless immorality and provide you with fresh, licentious, riveting, and naughtiest ever, must-have materials for your viewing pleasures and your advertising programs. I assure you I am fully committed to honoring this prestigious award that you have given me. I am highly honored. Through my educational offerings and new creative film ideas I intend to promote widespread acceptance of the new Modern Morality Standard and make your sponsorship investments in my work produce even greater results for you. I fully appreciate what many of you have already told me: 'SEX SELLS!'

ABOUT CHAPTER SEVEN:

A RENEWED CAUTION TO THE READER:

Chapter seven of book eight (RUBY BUTTERFLY©) contains extremely gruesome, heinous passages. Undoubtedly, it is among the most troublesome passages in literature ever written. It is likely to trigger an emotional reaction from many readers and listeners. As the author explains: There was no other way to convey the depths of depravity and malicious, vicious evil which had taken possession of David's soul; nor how else to illustrate David's possessive hold over Marty.

Here, he leads her into his bottomless abyss of sinister wickedness. And she, ever eager to gain his approval, casts aside all remaining vestiges of her morality. David's sociopathy is in the process of yielding to his journey into psychopathic madness.

And Marty, before these passages, arguably possessed a salvageable soul. In her protesting questionings she offers a glimpse of the sort of person she wishes she could have been; but David quashes her hesitation and spurs her onward. He steals her most valuable personal property-her moral conscience; her sense of right and wrong. He purposely severs Marty's few remaining strands of humanity as he unleashes his masterful ability to manipulate her into doing the most unthinkable betrayals. He convinces her to relish and savor her horrific deeds; and to embrace and cherish her blood lust and eternal damnation.

Chapter seven of book eight (RUBY BUTTERFLY©) is not for those who are faint of heart. If you can steel yourself to read its wretched, horribly descriptive passages; then, by all means, read them.

CHAPTER SEVEN

*Will all great Neptune's Ocean wash this blood from my hand?
(Shakespeare, Macbeth)*

*Though your sins be as scarlet, they shall be as white as snow.
(Isaiah i:18)*

TRADECRAFT

*"Marty," Consuelo continued her interview, "could you please take
one more minute and tell us how you achieved those perfect emotional expressions that many say are the most riveting aspects of
your erotic work?"*

*Miss Iniquity sensed the danger in the question and spoke
quickly to prevent a mishap.*

*'No mention of the hours Bertie made you practice to perfect
every movement. Throw Consuelo a cream puff. Get away from this
line of questioning. Get away fast!'*

Marty's mind raced. She vividly remembered the recent murders.
She was naked in the murder room with David. He wore his wet
work garb for these affairs, a simple pair of cut off blood splattered jeans, an old blood splattered white shirt and tennis shoes;
stored, concealed from public view in the huge cavernous killing
room. Marty's assistants had stripped the clothes from Bertie and
George and bound their arms and legs with Manila hemp rope.

Her best friends and intimacy coaches were naked now, tied from behind to upright posts near the murder table. Horrified looks streamed from their eyes. Their muffled cries and grunts strained from their throats and their taped shut mouths. One assistant had already removed their discarded clothes to the barnyard hill where the goats congregated. The goats would be hungry. David hadn't fed them yesterday or today. They would eat the evidence clothes. If Bertie and George saw goats eating their clothes, they would know what was happening to them was irreversible; but they didn't know that; not just yet. They held out hope that this crazy madness would stop; that everything that had happened to them thus far was all just a macabre joke.

David cuddled Marty from behind, pressing his body against hers. He knew what brought her body to its heightened awareness state. He did those things now. He kissed the back of her neck and ears. He knew she loved that. It stimulated her and unleashed her limbic passions. From behind her, he cradled his body against hers; wrapping his arms snugly around her waist. The two of them began swaying slowly, lovingly, back, and forth before Bertie while smiling to her.

It was suddenly obvious to Bertie that the two of them needed to do whatever they were doing or about to do; that their need was expressed in this bizarre togetherness that they were experiencing, for some unspoken and unknowable reason. Maybe they needed a kind of love that came from some form of a shared doing? Bertie wondered while becoming more horrified. She could see that, whatever the connection was between Marty and David, it was abnormal and unhealthy. She felt afraid and began wondering if her life was in danger. David next kissed Marty's naked shoulders and neck. Marty responded with a dreamy smile. Her eyes were clear and focused, as if she was a predator raptor bird looking at Bertie from very far away.

Bertie knew that Marty did not do drugs. And this look she was getting from Marty was not the look of a confused person who had lost control of her faculties. It was a cold, willful look. Marty's eyes told Bertie that she was seeing Bertie from some far-away place. It was some place that Marty desired to be; where she could now see Bertie from afar without having any feelings for her; but Marty had never before revealed this mysterious place to Bertie, not once in all their hundreds of revealing conversations. Bertie briefly hoped that this might be some prelude to yet another insightful reveal from Marty; but she quickly dismissed that hopeful thought. This was a different Marty she was seeing. This was a Marty unknown to her; a Marty that had been concealed from her; until now.

Suddenly Bertie hoped that she would never see the rest of Marty's full reveal. Her subconscious mind told her the full reveal could be terrifying. Bertie closed her eyes and said a silent prayer: *'Please no. Please make them stop.'* Marty's head fell back, now completely relaxed on David's shoulder. She smiled at Bertie. But it was not the smile of a friend to another friend or a lover to another lover, or a student to her coach. It was the evil, heartless smile of a reptilian predator; a lizard, about to ravage her vanquished prey.

"We should make her feel like she's part of our ritual, Marty," suggested David, matter of factly. *"She'd feel more involved if she had an intimate connection to her murderess. That would make your experience more meaningful and more memorable, don't you think?"*

Bertie strained against the ropes that bound her to her stake. The mention of murder had sparked her worst fears.

"Oh, yes David. We should make her feel like she's a full participant. I agree," nodded Marty. She smiled encouragement to Bertie, choosing not to comment about her coach's distress. In Marty's

already altered mental state, Bertie had already ceased to be a real living person. Marty's childhood turmoil roiled her mind. Her memories of abandonment; being shunned by the religious WEX day students; the loneliness years; the comfort love of stones; her immersion into promiscuity, swirled and tossed like a fragile raft on a raging sea. But David was quelling her rain storms. Somehow, David was calming her; assuring her that what she was about to do was normal and necessary.

When Aztec priests ripped their victims' hearts out and held them up to their Sun God, they believed they were only doing what was normal and necessary. They believed sacrifices sustained their way of life. They gave no thought to the plights of their victims.

Marty's mind now reached out across time and space, miraculously bonding with the mind of the ancient Aztec priest. Through the magic of ethereal time travel, their thoughts achieved concordance! Both minds were about to perform sacrifices. Both were about to murder their victims. Both would offer their victims' hearts to their God. The Aztec's God was the sun. Marty's God was David's penis. Both Gods would observe sacrifices to their greater honor and glory this day. And both Gods would be pleased. The Sun would attain its highest height in the sky; and beam warm approval to its loyal, murdering priest. David's penis would also attain its highest height; and signal its approval of Marty's sacrifices by pressing its hardness against her buttock.

Marty's eyes were cold and lifeless. They revealed nothing of what was about to come to Bertie. David had conditioned her mind to be numb to the plights of Bertie and George; the same like-minded numbness of the Aztec priest. Marty accepting her duty to sacrifice her friends. David's conditioning had succeeded.

Marty's mind was far away from her task at hand. This entranced mindset, not her own, only dreamed of what pleasures were to come; what glorious rewards she would receive for performing her dastardly deeds. The stimulus she felt from David's pressing penis and cuddling embrace ignited her nymphomania. Her thoughts dreamed of what was to come:

'Mmmmmm. Yes. I love how David is holding me; swaying my body with his. Mmmmm. I'm thrilled that his penis is so hard. I love how it feels pressed against me. Mmmmmm! I can't wait to complete these murders so we can have our intimacy. David will finger me soon; like he has before. I know he will. He knows I like that. I know I'll please him by murdering Bertie and George. He'll like that. That will please him. He'll love me for committing their murders. I'm sure he will. Afterwards, he'll finally see me as his equal; a complete executive. Yes! We will then have our intimacy. I can envision everything.

'Mmmmm. We'll go upstairs to his wife's bedroom. I'll be naked. I'll spread my legs widely for him. Mmmmm. He'll place his head between my legs. Yes! I'm going to cherish that moment. Mmmmmm. Then, his lips will kiss my outer lips. His tongue will vibrate rapidly between my outer lips, alternately touching them; teasing them; tempting me into frenzied desire. I love it when a partner does that. Mmmmmm. It sets my vagina on fire. Mmmmm. Then his penis will tap my outer lips, seeking permission to enter me. I'll be so thrilled to tell David: 'Yes, I want you to. Please enter me.'

'Then, I'll take his penis in my hand. I'll guide it to my inner lips. I'll rub it against my inner lips and guide its penetration. Mmmmmm. David will be so anxious to fuck me, his penis will dribble semen drops upon my inner lips. And then! Mmmmmm. Penetration! I'll feel his shaft entering me. Beautiful, lovely penetration! So lovely! Yes! I'll tell him: 'I love having you inside me.'

'So, erotic! My mind will float away. While we fuck, I'll tell him how beautiful he makes me feel; how much I love our intimacy. We will be so gloriously sinful together. Just the two of us. Finally in our own complete world. We will have each other and our Firm. We

won't need anyone else. We will have our love. We will make love for hours. And I will finally be David's equal! Mmmmm. Yes! I'm ready to begin the murders!'

"Good," continued David, *"I thought we should make our ritual as erotic as possible. It will heighten the experience for both of you. Here is a tube of estrogen cream. Go ahead and insert a liberal amount in her vagina."*

Marty applied the vaginal cream to Bertie's vagina. *"There, David. All done,"* she turned to David and smiled.

"Good, now we'll wait a little while. Here, I brought this dildo. I'd like to watch you fondle her breasts and kiss her nipples while you use the dildo to bring her to an orgasm. Do you think you can do that?"

"Oh, David, of course I can. Bertie and I have done that dozens of times."

Marty proceeded to titillate Bertie's nipples while using the dildo to bring her to orgasm.

"She's moaning, David. I can feel her wetness, too. She's having a very nice orgasm. I know her body well. She's feeling very aroused now."

"Good, but how do you feel?"

"I'm very stimulated and wet, David. I feel extremely close to her. This is the most intimacy I've ever felt with her. It's beautiful, David. It's really beautiful."

"Excellent work, Marty, are you ready to begin, "He asked?

"I think so. Honestly, I'm a little afraid, David. I don't know how I should feel about doing this. I mean, what's going to happen when I stab her? Will she be able to hurt me somehow?"

"No. She can't hurt you. She's very securely tied fast. She won't hurt you. I promise. I'm right here. I won't let anyone hurt you. Can you stab her now?"

"Yes," I think so. I think I'm ready to begin. I feel it's time," Marty replied.

"That's good, be sure you feel ready. Don't be afraid. You'll do just fine. I'm right here to help you if you need me, okay?"

"Okay, David," Marty nodded. She looked at Bertie with trancelike eyes now. Bertie's eyes widened; she was horrified.

"Be brave." David kissed Marty's neck again. He placed a long sharp knife in her hand. *"Be careful, it's very sharp. I don't want you to hurt yourself. Always keep your hand on the handle so you don't cut yourself."*

"Okay. I'll be careful." Marty lifted her head high and stretched her neck, inviting more kisses from David. He kissed her neck from her jawbone to her shoulder.

"Go ahead," he said.

Marty began. Her first stab penetrated Bertie's breast. Shock and fear registered in Bertie's eyes. Marty raised her dagger to stab again, but David caught her arm and held it. He then lowered her raised arm and placed his hands on Marty's shoulders; then he massaged her shoulders a while and kissed her neck again while his hands relaxed her tensions.

"That was beautiful, Marty. You did extremely well. I'm very proud of you. How do you feel?" He hugged her waist and kissed her neck again. *"Tell me."*

Marty took a deep breath then another, making herself light-headed. *"I feel excited. That was very stimulating and erotic. I feel kind of thrilled. I'm grateful that you've set everything up like this. Seeing her bleed like that is giving me the urge to make love with you."*

"Those are all really good feelings." His arms slipped down and wrapped around Marty's waist. He gave her a tender, loving squeeze. *"Take your time. Look at the blood flowing from the*

puncture. See how freely it's flowing? It's beautiful. You did that all by yourself. Don't you feel pride in yourself that you were able to do that?"

"Yes, I do feel proud of it. It was a very clean sort of direct stab, wasn't it? And, you are right again, as always, David. I could do it all by myself. It is beautiful; very sexy; very stimulating. Do you think it's beautiful? Am I doing it the way you wanted me to do it?"

"Yes. It's beautiful. You're doing fine. It was a wonderful first stab. You're doing very well. We're not in any hurry. You don't need to do this quickly. It's much more pleasurable when you do it nice and easy; slowly. Take your time. Can you see the terror in her eyes? Enjoy that expression. That's her way of giving away her power to you. She can't hold onto her power any longer. She knows you now have complete power over her. Appreciate the glory of your power. I want you to be completely relaxed while you're doing this. You should be feeling aroused. Can you feel your sex getting wet?"

"Yes, it's happening. My sex is highly aroused. Did you know that would happen?"

"I thought it would. I know you have deep emotions. I thought this would help you bring them out; feel them; let your body relax and enjoy them. That's the excitement of your newfound power and control. It feels good, doesn't it? Can you feel it? It's a beautiful, wonderful thing, isn't it?"

"Yes, I do feel it. I'm very aroused. It's like when I feel lust; only it's a different sort of lust. It's deeper. It's a more permanent sort of lust. I can tell it will never leave me like my lust for a man's cock fades away and leaves me. It's a new kind of lust for me. It's exciting, wonderful, and highly stimulating. I feel like I can do anything to her that I want to do. Does that make me a bad person?" Marty giggled. "Imagine me asking you if you think I'm a bad person. I'm being very bad now, aren't I, David? I'm being about as bad as a girl can be. Isn't that true? How can you know my feelings so well? You're

such a naughty boy, David. And, how did you know I was getting wet?"

"Yes, my dearest Marty. You are being very bad now; but that does not make you a bad person. You are a very good person. You're taking care of a loose end. You are simply doing what every good executive does when a problem is encountered. You're taking care of the problem and correcting a mistake. You are being very, very good. I am very proud of you."

Bertie shook her head furiously. David removed the tape from her mouth. Bertie screamed. *"Stop, please, Marty. That hurt me. Look, you two have had your fun. Now bring back our clothes and let George and me go home."*

"Your clothes are being eaten by my goats," smiled a sinister David. *"I haven't fed them for three days. They were practically starving. Your clothes are already in the process of being digested. It's okay. You won't be needing your clothes because you won't be going home."*

Fear's cold chill of realization swept over Bertie. She knew she'd been tricked. She and George were trapped in David's abyss. They couldn't escape. No one could hear their screams. The only way out of their dilemma was persuasion. She turned her loving eyes to Marty and pleaded:

"I love you, Marty. You know I love you. I've been like a mother to you. You are family to George and me. You're my precious daughter. You are the daughter I've always wanted. Please, Marty. We're the ones who truly love you. You can stop this madness. Don't listen to him. He's a sick man. Don't let him make you sick. Please, get me to a hospital. I won't prosecute you; I promise. You are not being yourself. Listen to me, Marty. Please." Bertie cried and pleaded for Marty to stop.

"I'm not your daughter, Bertie. Stop trying to confuse me." Marty smiled a knowing smile to Bertie and shook her head, telling

Bertie that her ploy wasn't going to work. Marty had agreed with David to do these murders. She was not about to change her mind.

"Then, what are you, Marty? You can't tell me that what we have together means nothing to you. Can you honestly say that? Remember, I've made you into the most famous porn star in the entire world. You wouldn't be nearly as famous without me, Marty. We need to stay together, Marty. There's no telling how much more famous and desired I could help you become!" Bertie's voice was hoarse and desperate. Fear and anxiety were taking their toll on her comportment.

"Why Bertie, you really do surprise me! After all our time together, don't you understand what I am? I'm a totally immoral whore, Bertie. I'm your finished product. Can't you tell? I can project convincing feelings of intimate love while I'm creating my porn films; even while I'm feeling absolutely nothing inside. You've taught me very well. I appreciate that. But I was never your daughter, Bertie. Amanda was your daughter. I'm simply a butterfly. And I'm finished with you now. I need to flutter on to my next flower.

"Besides, you called me, remember? You needed me to flutter into your life. We joined our lives together and we played together. The three of us had fun. You and George taught me some things. And I brought you some happiness. So, we're even, Bertie.

"But now it's time for me to flutter away, Bertie. Dom and Gwen are my sponsors now. I'm sure you've seen my Ruby Butterfly Bikini promotion for my Premium Bikini clothing line. My businesses are doing very well. My face and vagina are synonymous with many world-famous brands now. And Gwen gives me all the oral sex and creature comforts I could ever want, Bertie. You see, I've outgrown you, Bertie. I'm a butterfly that's finished with you. I've sucked dry your flower. I've taken all the nectar you could give me. And don't flatter yourself, Bertie. I have others who do my hair and make-up perfectly; and I have assistants who prep me perfectly for my explicit

scenes. I also have the best directors and camera crews. They do an exquisite job of capturing my most promiscuous smiles and my most erotic seductions. Don't worry about me, Bertie. I'll continue being the world's top porn star long after you're gone. So, Bertie, as you can see, you're of no further use to me. I'm going to flutter away from your life now. Goodbye."

David wrapped his arms around Marty's waist and gently rocked her back and forth in a playful swaying motion. He spoke softly in Marty's ear.

"That was eloquently spoken, Marty. I didn't know that you could be so cold and heartless. That's how a top executive must be sometimes; and I can see that you've got what it takes. I'm very proud of you. Now, I'd like you to focus on her murder. Remember, you are the one in complete control. You have all the power and she has none. She's helpless. It can help you if you can imagine, in your mind, that she's already dead. That way, killing her becomes less personal and more of a performance; kind of like a human sacrifice. The early Pagans performed sacrifices to mark the changing times in their lives. Now you are about to have some important changes in your own life, so this is a perfect way to commemorate your new life.

"I know you can do this. Remember, her screams won't save her. They are harmless. No one but us will hear her screams. The room is soundproof. Think of her screams as her soul protesting that it's giving up its power to you. When you think about it that way, her screams will sound beautiful to you. They are immorally religious. Enjoy yourself when you hear her screams. They should uplift you. They are her way of letting go of her frustrations over losing her control of you. She knows you're taking her power away from her and she knows that she can't make you give it back."

David kissed Marty's neck again. That sent chills of eroticism through her entire body. She reached her hand behind her and rubbed David's cock through his pants.

"I feel you're getting hard, David. That tells me you like watching me doing this, don't you? I could do this all day, every day, David. You know how much I want to have your cock inside me, don't you David? You understand everything about me, don't you? How did you know that this would excite me like this? You're such a bad boy, David."

Marty giggled as she wriggled her body tightly against David's. She sensed she was on the cusp of something profoundly euphoric. She wanted to savor every moment of it. She reached her hand to the top of David's pants. She reversed her hand to allow her fingers unfettered access to his penis; then, she began sliding her fingers lower. Her intention was to hold his bare cock, stroke it until it was fully stimulated; and then face David. Her goal was to drop his pants, interrupt Bertie's murder while she performed felatio. But David lifted her hand out of his pants.

By his reaction she understood that he'd read her mind. It confirmed everything that she understood about David. He was a linear thinker and doer. Always, he put first things first. She must commit murder now; and wait for her playtime later. She settled for massaging his cock through his pants. He allowed that. His kisses on her neck seemed to say he understood her needs and feelings; but that they needed to wait for the right time. She believed it was David's way of telling her that their love had to be special; a love that transcended all her other loves and relation-ships, even her love for Bob; that their precious love should never be blended with any other task or emotion.

"I understand peoples' feelings; that's how I knew you've gotten wet. I want you to feel wonderful about yourself, Marty. I want you to feel happiness, high self esteem, power, invincibility, all those things at once. Can you feel them?"

"Yes, David. David, I love you in a special way that's so much greater than all my other loves. I have a very difficult time feeling sexual about you and not making love with you. I really want you, David. You can understand that, can't you?"

"Yes, I understand. I know you do. And I appreciate that, Marty; honestly, I do."

David deflected Marty's suggestion for seduction:

"I'm extremely proud of you, Marty. Oh, goodness! Listen to her screams. She's entertaining us, Marty. Isn't it beautiful to hear her screaming like this? No one outside this room can hear her. She's being ridiculous. It's amusing to hear her expecting help to come, isn't it? Do you understand why she's really screaming?"

"I'm not sure. Tell me." Marty snuggled her back against David. She arched her back and lifted her shoulders, inviting David to kiss her there.

"It's actually not because you are murdering her." David kissed Marty repeatedly across the tops of her shoulders. He could tell that he pleased her by her deep breathing and the way her hand firmed while stroking his cock. *"She may think that, but that is not the real reason.*

"She's screaming because she knows you are betraying her trust and she's losing control of you. She's giving you a deep understanding of her psychology. She desperately wanted to believe in you. She wanted to believe you could be completely immoral, destroying other peoples' marriages and lives; but she believed that while you were being immoral towards others, you would always be true and faithful and loving to her and George. Now she's understanding that she is not an exception to your immorality. It's painful for her to know that you are only loyal to yourself and that you have no further use for her or for George. It's beautiful to watch her discovery of your betrayal. See it? It's playing on her face. Enjoy it. It's fascinating to watch. I'm sure you'll agree."

"I do see that now. Thank you for explaining that for me. That helps a lot. Her screams don't bother me now, except that they are kind of annoying."

"But they don't make you feel guilty, do they?"

"Oh no, David, not at all; not while I know I'm pleasing you. Why would I feel guilty?"

"Good, Marty. You shouldn't feel guilty. She was using you for her own reasons. You should enjoy this. Look at her blood dribbling down from her breast. After we decapitate her, you'll be able to make love in her blood. Doesn't that excite you?"

"Please, Marty, don't do this. I'm begging you, please." Bertie was terrified. Now, she begged for her life.

"Yes, David, it's very stimulating. I feel like there's nothing wrong with what I'm doing. I'm lifting myself up. My self-esteem is soaring." Marty answered David's question, ignoring Bertie's plea. She was as cold hearted and detached from Bertie's pleas, and as completely immoral as any ruthless serial killer could be.

"I feel something beautiful is happening within you," affirmed David. *"Your excitement should soar. That's when your adrenalin will release. Allow me to stimulate you. Then, while she screams, instead of being annoyed you'll feel even more pleasure. Her screams will reinforce and amplify your pleasures. You'll enjoy watching her descend into madness. She'll envy your pleasures while knowing she's losing her power over you. And you will feel an inner celebration of your ultimate power over her."*

Marty nodded her head in a trance-like agreement. David squeezed her tightly from behind and, again, repeatedly kissed the back of her neck. He inserted two fingers into her vagina and stimulated her. He pinched her nipples with the thumb and forefinger of his other hand. Marty's eros responded. An electric-like flash coursed through her veins, making her vagina burn erotically hot and creamy wet.

She nuzzled her head against David's shoulder. She loved the sensations she felt. It was like she was on stage, performing live explicit sex before thousands; only much, much more sensational. She was the star of this rarely staged performance. She relished the imaginary limelight. All tensions left her body, making her like putty in David's hands. His kisses had completely relaxed her.

They reassured her that he had assessed Bertie correctly; and that she was justified in murdering her former teacher.

Her hand again reached inside David's pants and found his cock. Passions controlled her now. All her reasoning about why they needed to wait became suspended. She wanted him. She wanted to try again. Perhaps now? His cock was as hard as naked bone. He wanted her, too. If only David would tell her that it was time! She stroked it while smiling a sincere smile to Bertie. Her smile was a smile of triumph. It told Bertie she was completely confident in David's opinion; fully in accord with it, and willing to proceed with her murder.

"Oh, David," Marty spoke as if they were discussing the simple matter of ordering office supplies, there was no emotion in her voice; only in her hand that stroked his cock. *"I understand what you mean now. Her screams heighten my pleasure! They really do! I love how you're always so right about everything. Oh, I'll really love stabbing her now. This is so thrilling! I know I'll love it. It's beyond wonderful and marvelous. How can I ever thank you for this?"*

"That's very good, Marty. Just take your time. Do each stab carefully and deliberately; and then remember to pause between stabs. You'll enjoy it more. Murder should be enjoyed; never hurried. Have patience while you commit murder. It should help you reflect upon your ascendancy over another person. It's one of those special passage occasions in life. It should be meaningful for you. It should give you a feeling of accomplishment. And, it should make you feel pleasure and be enjoyable. Now, look into Bertie's eyes and tell her one more time that you don't need her anymore."

Marty did as she was told: *"I don't need you anymore, Bertie."* As she spoke the words, David lowered his hand from her breasts to her abdomen, and then lowered it to her vagina. His hand rubbed her sex in a slow circular motion, complementing the fingers of his other hand which stimulated her inside her vagina.

Marty moaned. For all the hundreds of men who had touched her sex, David's touches were the touches she'd always yearned to feel. Now, finally, he was using both hands, touching and stimulating her. She felt elated, closer than ever to her goal of bedding him.

"Are you feeling good inside and all over about what we're doing to her?" David kissed Marty's cheek and her ear.

"Oh yes, David. I feel wonderful inside myself and, inside my sex, too. This is fantastically erotic. I absolutely love it. I love all of it." Marty was in her element. As she did on her porn sets, she clearly voiced what she wanted her partner to do, in order that she would experience the greatest pleasures. *"Please, reach your fingers deeply inside me. I want you to feel me. Feel me, David. Reach deeply into me and touch my clitoris. Feel how much I love what you do to me."*

"Like this, Marty? Can you feel me now?" David stimulated Marty with his fingers. He found her clitoris and massaged it.

"Yes, David, oh, yes, yes, yes. I can't wait to make love with you. I could do this forever. I want to come. Yes, I'm feeling you, David. I'm coming. Oh, this is so wonderful! Oh, I love what you are doing, so much." Marty moaned. Her blood raced with the same whore lust that her mother had felt while she fornicated with Marvin and murdered his love for Eloweiss.

Lust built upon lust, making Marty's passion for murder grow until it was insatiable. She felt David's fingers caressing her clitoris. Deliciously evil lust controlled her soul now. Ecstasy shot through her veins and reached her limbic mind. There the ecstasy raged and flared and tingled, while it worked its magical spell. Nirvana she could never have imagined existed before this sublime moment made all her nerves and muscles tremble.

She was enthralled; propelled forward into the most heinous debauchery imaginable: orgasming while in the process of murdering her closest friend. Her heart leaped with her joys of discovery. Her transformation into remorseless she-devil was happening. It would complete her. She believed it would make her acceptable and pleasing to David. She was proving to him that she had reached the ultimate attainment of immorality.

She was in the process of perfecting herself as his ideal executive; and he would love her as his equal. Yes, she was proving herself to be the ultimate immoral, blood thirsty whore. Finally, her test was ending; her soul's journey to its perdition was nearly complete. David would surely see that she was irrevocably committed to pleasure, evil and to him. Her mind was in a serene place. She was pleasing herself and David; and he was appreciating her. They were doing the ultimate evil deed, together. She was experiencing euphoria.

Bertie again pleaded for Marty to stop. She tried reasoning with Marty; tried convincing her that she was under David's power, that she was not herself; and she didn't know what she was doing. But, again, David took charge.

"Tell her you know exactly what you are doing, Marty," David's voice sharpened. *"Tell her you're going to murder her. You need her body, so we can decapitate her. Tell her you will make love in her blood. Tell her you'll send her spirit to your father's spirit. Go ahead, tell her."* David applied more pressure as his fingers rubbed Marty's clitoris. He kissed her neck and cheeks and intensified his stimulation.

The effect on Marty's body was electrifying. The rubbing from David's fingers sent trembles of ecstasy from Marty's sex, through her legs; and up into her heart, warming it; then flooding its shooting nirvana sensations through her brain, spurring her quest for even more blood lust. She was coming with a stronger flow now. She loved how David was making her feel. She would do anything he asked now, absolutely anything to make her exultant feeling last.

"I need to murder you, Bertie. I need you to accept what I'm doing. I need your blood for my ceremony. You've always told me you love me. If you meant that, please relax now, and be quiet."

"No! No!" Bertie cried. But her cries fell on deaf ears. Marty simply smiled at her with orbs that looked as dark and vacuous as a snake's eyes assessing a cornered mouse. All humanity was gone from Marty's eyes. Only death and the fiendish love of murder remained. Her vision didn't see Bertie's heaving breast or her bloodied wound. She looked past it as if it was not there. She only imagined seeing herself standing upon an elevated stage, wearing a silk lace nightgown. She was waiting for her partner. They were about to perform. He joined her onstage. He was a statuesque black man, impossibly handsome; better muscled, with a more striking adorable face than any man she'd ever seen before. And his skin tone was golden bronzed, as if he'd stepped out of ancient Arabia and traveled across continents to be with her.

And his cock! So marvelous! It was huge and hard. It glistened, anxious to be with her; to explore the inside of her. She saw the scene, imagining it was real. She blocked out Bertie's pleas, seeing herself being embraced by her bronze god; then kissing him while his hand found her vagina; then tasting his delicious hardness in her mouth; and opening for him as he gently laid her upon a pillowed, white satin day bed; then wildly reveling in the ecstasy of his cock as it enraptured her and chased away her mind's inhibitions. She had to have him. She would kill to have him.

Each stab Marty placed was accompanied by her overwhelming sensation of love; love for an imaginary man whom she had just met a few minutes before; love with no past or future. She imagined feeling the love of the immoral now and the erotic touchings of his flesh. It was a free-falling, tumbling love that absorbed all her sensibilities. It was a love of making love for the feelings of life that lovemaking brought to her. She understood it now in a new way.

It was the same love lust that had switched on in her mother's DNA when Susan had first let Marvin know that she wanted him. Nothing else mattered in her mother's life from that instant onward. It was that same love lust that Marty knew she would display for the cameras and her audience; a switch turned-on instantaneous love; a love that flowed with its hot passion madness through her blood. It was nymphomania love; love that could never be quelled or quenched; an uncontainable thirsty blood lusty passion love that she lived for kind of love; not an orderly, controlled kind of love; a madness, must have it now, love. It was even a more intensely real love than the true love she felt for Bob.

Why? If asked to explain herself, all she could honestly respond would be that her fantasy bronze god was here and now. And she had to have him. She had to fuck him. She was born to do that. She had to let him have his way with her; make him mad with desire to have his way with her. Her mind saw it all happening; unfolding, becoming more real with each stab. His cock wanted her. She knew that. His hands wanted her. She could intuit how they felt touching her. His lips wanted her. She imagined tasting how delicious they were. He was giving her a love that she could feel right now. She could swim in it with all her emotions; give all of herself to it.

She could visualize it all. She imagined the camera lights amplifying her thrusts and capturing her facial euphoria perfectly. She was fucking his cock so wonderfully! Taking all of it inside her! Amazing all the thousands of eyes that watched her spectacle; spellbound, focused on her thrusts; subsumed in her passionate whoring. Her live audience was captivated and breathless. Reviews would laud her as the most sensational femme; most provocative, mesmerizing sex goddess of all theater and film venues. She would find her perfect bronze god and personally direct her seduction vision and make this magical dream become real.

She knew 'Seducing the Bronze Statue' would become her most stunning seduction performance ever, because she would be deliciously murdering Bertie, remembering her glorious murder deed in her mind's eye; taking Bertie's life from her again and again, while she gloriously received the semen flood from her bronze god partner.

She intuited that David was right. He was always right. He understood people. He gave her this breakthrough revelation. She understood that didn't need Bertie anymore. Besides, by killing George and Bertie, Marty would inherit their properties and their securities portfolios; easily worth two hundred million. David would get rid of their bodies and also provide her an alibi. It was all so perfect! David always arranged their murders so no one could link them to their victims. That genius was what she admired most about David.

With every stab, Marty felt a tremendous weight being lifted from her. Release! Freedom! No consequences! Fabulous riches! Each stab further absolved her of the loose ends she had created. With each stab, Marty blamed Bertie for her own moral shortcomings. None of this would have happened if Bertie hadn't asked so many questions. Everything was Bertie's fault! With each stab, Marty replaced her guilt feelings and self-doubts about murdering her friends with a newfound pride in the righteousness of her immorality.

After all, a girl is entitled to make a mistake now and then. David had assured her of that. She was only human. And David was helping her correct her mistake; turning it into a learning experience:

'With each stab I'm vindicating myself and my whoring. With David's help, I'm simply correcting a mistake. Every insertion of my knife to its hilt; every touching of my closed fist's grip to Bertie's dying flesh puts more distance between these two and my mistake. George and Bertie were very good to me. They taught me many things. They promoted me until I became the world's most notorious, most sought

after porn star. But David is right. I don't need them anymore. I will always honor their memory by creating ever more glorious, spectacular porn films. I'll make each film more erotic, more sensational, and more memorable than the one I made before.

Yes! I love what the two of them have done for me; what we three accomplished. But I am the star! I am the one the world craves to see more of; not Bertie. My semen creamed, oozing, pulsing whoring vagina is the grand finale that my fans always salivate over, not Bertie's lighting and her props. I am now the undisputed queen of pornography. We successfully rebranded explicit sex. Intimate artistry is now the rage of the cognoscenti set. And I, Marty, am its unrivaled, iconic star.'

After murdering Bertie, the glory of her breathtaking explicit escapades would all be Marty's: hers alone! She believed she was doing a righteous deed. Bertie should share none of her glory and fame. Bertie should only receive death! Marty, only she, was the ravishing temptress. She was the one the film goers worshipped. It was fit and right for Bertie to understand in her death moment that she would receive none of the glory for the work they had done. Today would finalize things. Bertie, soon dead, could never develop another protégé to follow after Marty. No one would be trained in all the subtleties. Noone would be developed to upstage Marty's unrivaled debauchery. Marty would reign, unrivaled, as Queen of Porn; High Priestess of Immorality, for many years!

Marty's spirit soul felt vindicated and forgiven for every wrongdoing that she had ever done in her life. The act of stabbing Bertie purified her soul; cast away every tinge of guilt. Marty began smiling as she stabbed. The act became cathartic and transformative. It made this murder special. And she enjoyed it!

'Didn't David say I should enjoy my murders? Didn't he tell me that they helped me become a more accomplished executive? Surely,

he can now see that I enjoy my duties. Surely, he now knows I am highly qualified top executive talent!'

With each stab, Marty's knife transported sins from her body into Bertie's. Every act of adultery; every previous murder; all money sums she redirected from hapless wives to herself deposited her guilt into Bertie. Stabbing freed her conscience. Guilt and shame exhausted themselves. The fruits of her whoring and adult film performances would now all be hers; royalty free; shared with no one. The woman who had been like a mother to her now hung mortally bloodied and bound to her stabbing post. Her mutilated body was giving Marty its final gift. It was reposing her sins.

"Beautifully said; very good, Marty," David spoke softly. His voice tone was like that of a proud adult, holding a bicycle seat while giving encouragement to an uncertain child. He studied the horrified look in Bertie's terrified eyes, taking in the full measure of her fright. Then, nodding his approval and smiling, his eyes followed the air between the two women to Marty's head. He studied the young whore's cheek. He nuzzled it and kissed it while he gently cupped and massaged her breasts. He could tell by Marty's moans and the lift of her cheek jowl that she was smiling; into the moment, and enjoying herself. He correctly intuited that her blood relished the spirit of the execution.

Murder had always brought out a certain fascination in Marty, but this murder was different; special; significant because it represented her split and release from Bertie's cocoon. David was opening a new window of freedom for her. She could flutter through this new window and perform her newly discovered talents of torture, sadism, and prolonged cruelty. David sensed his disciple loved her new world. She could dominate here, in his dark murder chamber, without fear of reprisal or discovery. She could confidently inflict the most heinous horrors upon her victims, without concern for feelings of penalty or recrimination. She need only concern herself with her own pleasure. Marty's sense of macabre empowerment was thrilling her in ways she never experienced before. David noted.

David could feel Marty's thrills through his fingers. Her vagina squirmed and thrusted against them, seeking to capture the same persecution pleasures within her loins that were already gleefully dancing in her mind and her blood. She loved what she was doing to her former teacher. She loved seeing Bertie's tormented face and horrified eyes. She was cherishing her moment of mock, smiling into Bertie's eyes in response to the older woman's deeply felt sense of incomprehensible betrayal. It was more than cutting off a loose end for Marty. It was also payback for those times Bertie forbid her from performing contortion porn and for disallowing sloppy wet fucks with multiple partners in their films. Bertie hadn't allowed any slut porn scenes in any of their films. She took them out. Bertie had wanted them in. She loved performing them; loved being a profligate hard-core whore; not just an upscale, soft porn whore. Those restrictions had chafed Marty. Tonight, she was casting off her collar.

Marty was achieving her rapture state while committing this murder. She was fluttering above all that was moral and human. David gleefully perceived that Marty was losing her soul, and gaining something more. She was becoming more like him; more evil. She was sharing that same exhilarating something with him that, before today, he thought he alone possessed. It was willful aloneness, that sense that whatever happened to another being was none of his concern or responsibility, even when he was the cause of it.

Marty was achieving that same singular aloneness which David had achieved in his childhood. And he loved her for it! He empathized with her feelings; her absence of empathy for her victim. Adoration for Marty and her heinous deed swept through

David's soul. He clasped her tightly to him as if making the two of them become one, united in their beautiful evil. He felt himself loving her without reservation. She was family to him now.

"Let's prolong your pleasure," he whispered in her ear while kissing her neck. *"Imagine you are doing this to her on a stage while your audience applauds you. Imagine that her murder is your appetizer before you perform spectacular explicit fornications in an orgy. Lose yourself in those thoughts while you stab her. Watch her eyes while you express your thrill. Live these moments of your ecstasy. These are special moments. She'll understand. Trust me about this. She'll love seeing how you feel while you do this. She'll love its effect on you as much as you do. She wants to be part of your ultimate pleasure. Her mind doesn't want to be part of her body anymore. It wants to separate from her body and enjoy her own murder. I know that's true.*

"Now, before you stab her again, wipe your fingers in her blood. Taste. That's her life's blood that you are taking from her. Then, with her blood, draw large circle around where her heart is. Keep your stabs outside the circle. We want her to stay alive through the entire ritual, until the very end. You'll see. We'll kill her later. I'll show you something very special. You'll experience incredibly beautiful stimulation. It will boggle your mind. I promise. You'll always remember it. Make sure her heart keeps beating until the very end, okay?"

"Wow, David; sure, of course." Marty raised herself up, straightening her spine and leaning back, snuggly into David, inviting more kisses on her neck. *"This is so exciting. I want to thank you for this. You always think of everything, don't you? This will be a new murder game for us, won't it? You want me to have a new, fun learning experience, don't you?" You're so thoughtful and considerate of my development, David. I do so totally love you. I love what we're doing. I really do."*

"Good, Marty, I'm very pleased. You know how deeply I care for you. Now, stab her deliberately and slowly. Choose your spots. It's

good to stab her in her sides, too; also, in her legs and her buttocks. Listen to her squeal and beg you to stop. Just avoid stabbing inside the circle. Make one firm well aimed stab at a time. Plunge your knife all the way into her; then pull your knife out, slowly. Watch the fresh blood come out. Then, take your time. Look at your work and decide if you like it. See if you've stabbed her where you intended. Think about the different places you'd like to stab her and adjust your aim for your next stab. That way you won't stab her repeatedly in the same place. It's more fun if you spread out your stabs. Space them out around her chest and stomach. Think of it as a kind of puzzle game, where you're placing evenly spaced punctures all over her body.

"And don't rush yourself, Marty." David kissed the back of her neck as if to emphasize that her own pleasure was the most import-ant aspect of the murder. *"We're not in any hurry. Remember to relax. That's important. This is for your enjoyment and pleasure. Think of it as your special treat. I want you to feel comfortable and enjoy yourself. Take your time. I want you to savor every stab. Feel yourself taking control of her and her body. Watch her blood flow.*

"Imagine you are creating a beautiful work of art. Her body is there for your masterpiece. It's your canvas. Think of the delightful orgy you'll have after you complete your masterpiece. Allow me my pleasure of hugging you and kissing your neck while you're stab-bing her. Make us both proud of your work. We don't need to rush. She can't go anywhere. Enjoy the pain she registers on her face after every fresh stab. That should stimulate your sex even more than the way you're feeling now. Go ahead, pick a good spot, and stab her again." David smiled his most sinister smile at Bertie while he con-tinued stimulating Marty's vagina. His smile to Bertie messaged: *'The contest for Marty's affections is over. I have won. You have lost.'*

His smile carried a second, twisted message from David's demented mind. Bertie intuited David's psychosis. She discerned that there was a dangerous message in David's face but she could not fathom the thought it masked:

'I'm torturing you, Bitch, like I tortured helpless ants when I was a child. You are no smarter than they were and you are as powerless as they were. There is no difference between you, a human, and an insect. I'm proving that. Through my control of Marty, I can do anything to you that I want to do.'

For the next five minutes Marty casually stabbed Bertie another ten times. With each stab Marty vindicated and reaffirmed the rightness of the choices which she had made on the journey that had brought her to this point in her life. Flashing before her mind's memory paraded her many eventful decisions:

'How did I get here? Let's see: Encouraged Donny's hand play with my vagina; did lesbian love with Maria; butterfly tattooed my thighs proclaiming my promiscuity; seduced other women's beaus; invaded other women's marriages; seduced my teacher; turned professional prostitute while still in high school; lost all inhibition and defiled decency during Rita's orgies; murdered Carl's wife, very creative, that murder; defied social norms__ pushed out Fred's wife and Ed's lesser whores; did porn to broadcast my salaciousness; worked diligently with Bertie perfecting my explicit artistry and branding my promiscuity; promoted my brand internationally; developed Firm's Sex for Sales marketing; committed many murders with David. I have unique resume; indeed. And David endorses all of it!'

With each fresh stab Marty validated the rightness of all her immoral choices. The stabs affirmed her life. All second guessing's about her path forward departed her. Her doubts rode upon her knife's blade. Her stabs delivered her doubts to Bertie's flesh. There they stayed, reposed inside her mentor, after she casually withdrew the blade.

This murder was Marty's most special. It had redeeming qualities. The act freed Marty of her executive mistake. It memorialized her learning experience; taught her to not create loose ends. While performing the murder act, she understood and accepted that she was affirming who she needed to be, for David; a coldly realistic unfeeling, uncaring, ruthless top executive:

'I'm freeing myself from all feelings of guilt. I'm affirming every immoral choice I've made. I'm making myself more acceptable, and I hope, desirable to David. And didn't David often tell me that he admired Adolph Hitler for his ruthlessness, his lack of human empathy, his determination to be at the pinnacle of power? Surely, David can see that I, like him and Hitler, have the same heartless, immoral qualities.

'This murder exhilarates! I feel myself losing all concept of sin; forsaking all my childhood religious teachings; walking away from guilt and morality; no remorse; not looking back. I have entered a new, free will chapters of my life; left my fanciful childhood silliness and religious fairy tales behind. I truly do love what I am doing. I'm relishing my placement of every stab. David's insight was spot on. When I see these stabbings as a game sport, it becomes very enjoyable. I am having fun now, putting Bertie and George behind me. I need to move on. It's time. I'm the ultimate porn star now; the most adored, most notorious, immoral whore in the entire world! I don't need them anymore.'

Bertie moaned after each stab; all the while keeping her eyes focused on Marty's eyes. Hers were soft, understanding eyes; eyes that said to Marty that, while she could not comprehend why this had to be, she nevertheless continued to love Marty. Her mind struggled to understand the meaning of God and her own moral center. Yes, she had cursed God for what happened to Amanda. Yes, she had championed Marty's immoral whoring and all her destructions.

But now, contemplating her own death, Bertie's mind's eye drifted back to her Christian teachings about loving one's enemies.

Her glance shifted to David in hopes of understanding him. But there was nothing. Only this empty void in David's eyes. Black shark's eyes expressed more compassion. All she discerned was emptiness; not anger; not revenge; not happiness; only a deep, vacuous, abysmal nothing. Nevertheless, with all her remaining will, Bertie tried to speak through her failing eyes to David. Her eyes were pleading now, beseeching him to love and take care of her precious Marty child as she herself had loved and cared for her. This was the best her waning strength allowed her to do. But only David's nothingness stared back.

In her death role, Bertie proved that David had assessed her perfectly. Young Marty's immoral pleasures and stardom were Bertie's vicarious satisfaction. Through her pain, she marveled at the glorious, magnificently debauched, gore-lust of her protégé. She heard David complementing Marty's stab placements. She watched with dimming eyes as David gave Marty his approving hugs, while gently rocking her body back and forth; swaying rhythmically with her; smiling and kissing her neck while she giggled between every stab. And all the while, noticing how he was fingering her clitoris, maintaining her orgasm's seemingly inexhaustible flow. Bertie understood that David had thoroughly defeated her. She knew she was doomed. She steeled herself, accepting her murder; waiting patiently waited for death to mercifully take her.

Her dimming eyes became gray and cloudy. Shrunken in their sockets, they peered out from their pain, meeting Marty's face one final time. Perhaps, just perhaps, they would discover some measure of compassion or remorse. After all, she had loved the young whore with all her heart and soul; had given her every advantage she could. But her dying hope was not to be.

Her eyes saw only the wan smile of willful heartlessness. Marty's understanding, certain eyes stared back into Bertie's eyes. Marty's look of remorseless nothingness pained Bertie more than

Marty's stabs. Not one iota of doubt or regret was communicated. There was none. She had no influence over Marty; none. David had complete control of her. With certainty of cold, calculating purpose, the fateful deed was being carried out. Bertie thought:

'God, you are now forsaking me for a second time. Why? I did as you asked. I made her into a star. And this is what I get? This is my thanks? I hope to talk with you about this someday.'

Bertie knew Marty's life would move on; and her life would end here. The relationship of the two women had come to this. Yet Marty somehow managed an unhappy smile. Marty's smile was a willful, unrequited self-assured and self-reinforcing smile; one of confidence, rightness, and smugness in the immoral deeds Marty had already done; was now doing; and knew she would continue doing after Bertie's final demise. Marty's knowing, far seeing smile ascended above and rejected all things moral. It told Bertie everything. She glimpsed the terrible horror that festered inside Marty.

The smile declared that the murderess who wore it would not be bound by the moral ties of the Ten Commandments. She would lie without conscience whenever it suited her; freely steal others' assets; feel only disdain for her own living mother; casually murder without a scintilla of remorse; freely, willfully seek adultery; and needing no god, become her own. Nor would she be restrained by secular law. David provided Marty with perfect cover for her to conceal her crimes, even her murders. Marty feared neither criminal court verdicts nor civil judgements; not for this murder, nor for her many others; not for displaced wives or pillaged housholds. She would freely flutter wherever, whenever and with whomever she pleased. Bertie knew her protégé was now a fully-fledged, murderous blood dripping butterfly, devoid of conscience; untouchable by law. She wished her eyes were not seeing this. She wished her heart would stop beating. She wanted her torment to end.

While Bertie's body clung desperately to its last vestiges of life, Bertie heard David gave Marty her final instructions.

"Now you're going to complete your power over her, Marty. I'm going to instruct you how to perform the Japanese seppuku maneuver. I'll walk you through it. You'll need to firmly grip your knife with both hands."

"Must I take my hand off your cock, David? You're so hard now. I love touching it and stroking you. Couldn't we pause for some intimate pleasure? I'm very excited. This is so stimulating. I'd love to suck you. Wouldn't you rather stop this for now and let me suck you? She's not going anywhere. Heee, Heee. Are you, Bertie? No? See, David, Marty mocked her hapless victim, *she's not going anywhere. Maybe she'd like to watch us! I think a pause would reenergize me. Come on, David. I'm in the mood. Wouldn't you like me to suck you?"*

Marty sounded chagrinned. She naturally resisted everything that distracted her from her nympho compulsions. Her question implied that she was willing to pause during her heinous murder debauchery to slake her immediate gratification impulse; retreat from the task at hand and enter her happy world, the world of limbic bliss. She was perfectly willing to gleefully pause Bertie's execution to perform fellatio with David, uncaringly prolonging Bertie's pain and agony while forcing the older woman to watch her suck David's cock, all the way to its ejaculation.

"Marty, Marty, for this, I'm afraid we must delay our pleasures, you marvelous unrequited whore. We need to proceed with our task before we think about playtime." David quashed Marty's plea and refocused her on the business at hand. *"You'll need both hands to perform this ritual. Bertie should do this herself; but obviously she isn't up to it. You'll have to do it for her. Before we begin, you need to wipe her blood from your hands. You'll need dry hands for this. Rub your bloody hands through her hair and then wipe the remaining*

blood on her arms and the sides of her torso. Your hands shouldn't slip off your knife. They must grip the knife tightly."

Marty did as she was told. Her hands smeared Bertie's hair and body with Bertie's own blood. Bertie became transformed. She appeared to be the feminine version of the bloodied impassioned Christ, not nailed to the cross in the light of day, after being scourged and freshly stabbed by the Romans; but bound to a metal execution post in a dark, recessed murder chamber from which no light or sound could escape. Nevertheless, Bertie was a pitiful spectacle to behold. David was pleased with Marty's work thus far, and he told her so. Marty then leaned back into David, pressing her tush against his groin. *"I'm ready, David."*

"Good." David kissed her neck and massaged her clitoris lovingly with his fingers, overwhelming Marty with his approving stimulations. Bertie, still barely able to dimly see, was about to witness her own horror; more explicit than anything she had ever seen on any screen. Marty summoned up her resolve to complete her murder. She paid attention to David's instructions:

"First, you need to place a stab deeply into her belly. Make your stab a clean incision about two inches below and three inches to the right of her naval."

"Okay." Marty nodded eager to obey David. She plunged her knife into Bertie's lower abdomen, as instructed. *"Like that, David? Did I do that right?"* She turned her head to David and smiled, seeking his approval.

"Yes, you gorgeous, adorable whore. You did that perfectly." David returned Marty's smile. He kissed her cheek and hugged her. *"You're following instructions perfectly. You're a fast learner. That was the perfect spot to insert your knife. You're doing very well. Now, keep your knife inside her, right where you stabbed her. Leave it where it is. Don't take it out. That's right. That's very good."*

"This can't hurt me, can it, David?" Marty's childlike question voiced her fear of the unknown, much like a little girl seeking reassurance that there were no monsters lurking under her bed.

"No, Marty. There's nothing to worry about. She can't hurt you. Nothing will jump out of her to hurt you. I'm right here. You're perfectly safe. This isn't that hard. You'll see."

"Okay, David," Marty turned her head, kissed David's mouth, and smiled into his eyes. *"What do I do next?"*

"Concentrate on your controlling your knife. Now, use both your hands and slowly pull your knife all the way across her belly horizontally, calmly, and slowly. Don't rush your pull. We're not in any hurry. Keep your knife all the way inside her belly the entire time. Pull it across her belly steadily. Let your knife do the cutting. It's very sharp. It will perform very well. Just use a steady, gentle force to pull it and it will cut perfectly for you. Don't try to rush it. Patiently let it do its work. Her belly flesh and muscles will give way before it. Just take your time. She'll feel more pain if you take your time. I want you to enjoy the feeling of causing pain to someone else. It's good for your executive training. The knife will cut through her muscles and her flesh. Go ahead, don't be afraid. If she shifts her body around or moans, just ignore her. She can't make you stop. Remember that. You are in charge, not her."

"Okay, David. I'm ready." Marty voiced enthusiasm.

"Good girl! That's the Marty I like to hear. I'm right here with you. Nothing can hurt you. Don't worry about her. She'll feel some sensations that very few people ever get to experience. I'll hold you. I won't let you make a mistake. Everything is okay. Go ahead."

Marty slowly pulled her knife across Bertie's belly, making a horizontal slice cut across her lower abdomen. Bertie moaned; aware that her demise was certain. David kissed the back of Marty's neck while she performed the horizontal cut. David whispered his approval into Marty's ear.

"Beautiful! That was beautifully done. See, Look how easy that was. I knew you could do it." David sounded more like a parent approving of a child's first ride on a two wheeled bicycle. He hugged Marty tightly, fingering her to enhance the pleasure of the momentous experience while guiding her body in a steady, reassuring, gently swaying motion. Marty writhed in ecstasy. She intuited that the final moments of her murder were near.

"Marty, you did that perfectly! Do you see the blood spill out of her? Wasn't it fascinating? You opened the flood gates of her blood reservoir! You were outstanding! Spectacularly done! Look how bloody she is! See how pure and white you are? You're perfect, Marty. You've bested her! Remember, she tried to usurp your fame and glory. You're now delivering your divine justice to her. You're performing a holy rite!"

David kissed Marty's neck again, sending shivers of erotic stimulations through her entire body.

"How are you feeling? Does this excite you?" His fingers massaged her clitoris. He delivered his stimulations more rapidly now. He wanted to cause her to orgasm, thus memorializing this murder performance. *"Do you feel like you are most ravenous, immoral, decadent woman in the entire world, now? I hope you are feeling that way, because you are, Marty. There is no other woman in the world like you. You're so beautiful, Marty. I adore you and I love you. I feel like you are family to me now. I'm very proud of you. Are you okay to continue?"*

'Oh, how wonderful!' thought Marty. *'I'm finally seducing David! He gets his thrills from watching me commit murder. And I'm now, finally, performing the most intimate murder he's ever seen. And he loves me for doing it; for giving him the most enjoyable murder scene he's ever witnessed.'*

"Thank you, David. Yes, I'm very excited." Marty blurted out her enthusiasm for the heinous crime she was committing. She

couldn't contain herself, knowing she was pleasing David. Finally, she understood what she needed to do to seduce him. His sense of morality was horribly perverse, macabre, sick with morbidity; but now, understanding the key to David's heart, she intended to unlock it. The lives of her friends gave her no pause. Seducing David meant everything to her. Her pelvis convulsed with an unexpected, involuntary orgasmic release. She felt sublime. She intuited that, soon, she would be sharing corporate power with David, as his equal! Her orgasm affirmed to her that she was in her element; and fully in control of her seduction scene. Her body trembled. She steadied herself by leaning back harder into David's chest and gently squeezing his penis. When she was ready to continue, she whispered softly, seductively, while stroking David's penis.

"This is the first time I've ever murdered this way. It's so different. It's so intensely personal; and I feel so intimate with my victim. I totally love it. It makes me feel like I'm completely in charge of her. My heart is racing from the excitement of doing this; and I've gotten completely wet inside. This is the most immoral thing I've ever done. Am I making you more than proud of me? I feel your penis pressing hard against me. Do you like the way my fingers are squeezing it? I hope so. I love touching and feeling your penis. I hope you want me, David. I hope you'll want to come inside me. Do you want me? Will we be making love after this?"

"Of course, I'm proud of you. Yes, absolutely! Of course, I want you. I'm so up for making love with you now, after this exquisite murder. You are fantastic, Marty! Absolutely, we'll make love soon, I promise; but it must not be today. We must make love when we're alone, just the two of us, without our assistants. I want our first time to be extra special. Be patient, my love. We will have our love. I'm glad you're feeling in charge because you are. I love it when I see your confidence. You're my most outstanding employee, Marty. You are setting a wonderful example for the Firm. I'm thrilled that you

are willing to experiment with new ideas. That's the trait of a top executive. Always feel in charge. You're feeling exactly the way you should feel. I'm so happy for you. You're making fabulous progress.

"Now we've arrived at the crucial part. Keep your knife inside her and twist the blade until its sharp edge is pointed upward, okay?"

"Okay, I've done it, David," affirmed the ever-obedient Marty. She held the knife with both her hands now. *"I have the blade pointing up now."*

"I see, very good."

Marty took a deep breath and leaned back into David, soliciting more of his neck kisses. He lovingly gave them. She convulsed again, in a semi-controlled way. David's fingers and the erotic nature of this new murder experience were giving her yet another spontaneous, uncontrolled orgasm. She moaned. *"Oh, David, I love you so much. I love what the two of us can do together."*

"I know. I feel it too. Everything you're doing is excellent. You're doing extremely well. We only have a little further to go. Are you all right to continue?"

"Yes, I'm sorry. I couldn't help that. My feelings just came up on me so suddenly. I'm loving this so much, David. I've never felt like this before."

"Good, that's okay. If you need to come again, just go ahead. I'll help you. I want you to express your feelings. It's fine that you need to come like you do. I'll be patient. It's okay. Feel free to enjoy your pleasures. This is a beautiful experience."

Marty experienced even another, her third, unexpected convulsion. She turned to kiss David on his mouth. Their lips met briefly; and then David pulled his mouth away. He continued kissing her neck and stimulating her. After another minute, Marty's latest orgasm subsided. She was ready to continue.

"Okay, you're doing wonderfully. Now, I want you to take your time and pull your knife upward, steadily, and slowly. Pull it smoothly

higher in an upward, diagonally slicing motion. You're going to be cutting all the way up through the inside of her abdominal cavity until you feel your blade touching against her ribs, high up above her abdomen, right below and close to her heart. Do it nice and easy. Take your time. There's no rush whatsoever. The important thing is that you stay firmly in control of your upward cut."

David again kissed Marty's neck several times, reinforcing his enthusiasm for the murder she was committing.

"Don't become frustrated when your knife meets resistance. Just relax. That's only natural. You'll be cutting through her stomach muscles. Don't worry. They will eventually give way. Your steady upward pressure on the knife will cut through them. Her natural bodily movements will give your knife all the motion it needs to cut her muscles. She'll be naturally helping you. Just enjoy it and let your knife do its work. Remember to keep your knife all the way inside her. You'll be slicing all the way up her abdominal cavity, right through her liver. Good, that's it. You're doing it perfectly. Your knife is moving upward very nicely and steadily.

"That's excellent. You're doing very well. Beautiful, Marty; you are beautiful and your work is beautiful. You are being a very accomplished executioner. We're in no hurry. Just concentrate on cutting her all the way upward across her belly through her stomach and its muscles; and all the way up inside her, until you arrive at her heart, okay?"

"Yes, David, like this?" Marty continued her upward slicing motion with deliberate, studied intensity. As instructed, she maintained steady pressure on her knife. Bertie moaned. Gurgling sounds of blood came from her throat and abdomen. David kissed Marty's shoulders. He resembled a patient golf instructor, standing behind his female client, arms wrapped around her; guiding her motions for a perfect golf swing. Marty's strength and confidence

were bolstered by his presence, as she patiently and methodically disemboweled her mentor.

"Yes, that's perfect, Marty. You're doing extremely well. You're cutting her perfectly. Your work is steady and methodical; very focused; not hurried at all. I'm very proud of you."

Marty finished her upward slicing movement. Bertie's innards hung down from her body, spilling onto the floor. She was still alive; but barely. Her horrified screams had stopped; now, only sounds of gurgling blood and weak moans came from her dying body. Her eyes implored Marty's, begging the answer to why this horror needed to happen. Even after her evisceration, those loving eyes registered not anger, not hatred or revulsion; but compassion for Marty, as if they beheld her murderess as her own daughter.

"Oooh," squealed Marty, *"I never looked inside a human person before this!"* She turned toward David and hugged him again. *"Can you believe I did this all by myself? Thank you for teaching me how to do this, David."* Her excitement was effervescent, like a child's that perfected a new dance step.

"Wonderful. Now, Marty, I'd like you to reach high up inside her chest. Use your fingers to feel your way until you can feel her heart."

Marty set the knife down. David's hugs reassured and emboldened her. He continued stimulating her vagina with his hand and fingers.

"Can you feel it?" David whispered in Marty's ear.

She felt inside Bertie with one hand. Her other hand returned to David's cock. She stroked it through his pants. Two opposite measures of elation, life, and death, simultaneously coursed through Marty's feelings. She experienced nirvana's promise of triumphant love making, while gripped in the wonderment of her murder.

"Yes, now I feel it. I have it! I'm touching it! It's moving a little. Her heartbeat seems weak, but I can feel it. It's still beating. She's

still alive, David!" Marty's voice expressed alarm. She gripped his penis tightly.

"That's all right. She won't hurt you. You can relax, you've almost murdered her. Now, do you remember how you described to me what that Aztec priest did to his victim? You were explaining your feelings while you hypnotized Carl's wife. Remember? You said you had a similar feeling to the feelings an ancient Aztec priest felt when he ripped out the heart of his victim. Remember telling me how you looked into the eyes of Carl's wife and imagined you were seeing her eternal soul; and that you were taking her life from her? And that you were convinced she was going to go away and die?"

"Yes, David. I remember. I remember those final moments while I interacted with her. It was beautiful. In a way, it was a transference of her life's powers to me. I loved feeling that rush of power."

"Wonderful, Marty. You're making tremendous progress on your path of executive development. Now, I'm going to coach you while you take this next, very crucial step." David kissed Marty's neck while he rubbed his fingers more rapidly over her clitoris.

"Oh, David! Mmmmmm. That feels so wonderful. I'm starting to come. Can you feel how wet I am? I really, really want you, David. I want you to fuck me, right here in front of Bertie. That would show her who has the control in our relationship. That would let her see she has no power over me anymore! Mmmmm. Will you, David? Mmmmmm. Oh, please, David. Will you please, please, fuck me?"

"Marty, dearest. You know being a top executive requires self-control. You know we need to finish what we started here. There will come a time in the near future when we will finally have our intimacy. I promise. But first, you need to take the ultimate final step on your journey to being a top executive."

"And what would that be, David? Tell me."

"I need to hold you in my arms while you experience the exact same feeling the Aztec priest felt. I want you to know that ultimate power feeling, for real!"

"How, David? Tell me. How I can have his same feelings?"

"Okay. Now listen closely. Place your fingers around Bertie's still beating heart."

"Okay, David," Marty did as she was told. *"I've got my fingers around it now."*

"Very good, Marty. Excellent. You're almost there. Can you feel the excitement?" David massaged Marty's breast while he fingered her clitoris and kissed her neck. *"Are you ready for the ultimate stimulus; the most erotic feeling you've ever experienced in your entire life?"*

"Yes, David. I'm ready now. Mmmmm. You've got me soooo slippery wet. What should I do next?" Marty backed her tusche hard against David's groin. Bertie, with every bit of strength and awareness she had left in her dying body, barely, discernably, lifted her head. Her eyes met Marty's, as if they were telling her to finish it; end her misery.

"I think you can guess, Marty. And Bertie! Welcome to our little executive training session!" David's enthusiasm betrayed his manic love of evil. *"I see you're still with us. Here's your question, Bertie: Can you guess what Marty is about to do? Can you tell us what's going to happen next?"* Bertie's eyes widened slightly. She stared into Marty's eyes. She could no longer speak.

"Okay, Bertie, I see you don't want to tell us. So, Marty, you tell Bertie. Tell her what you're going to do next. And say it like you mean it. Remember, you're the one in control now. You have the power over her life. You've turned the tables on her."

Marty looked into Bertie's eyes for a long few seconds before she finally spoke:

"Bertie, I'm not taking orders from you anymore. I don't need you, anymore. I'm going to rip your heart out now. This is good bye, Bertie." Marty smiled a final smile into Bertie's eyes. Bertie blinked her eyes as if to tell Marty that she was thankful her ordeal was about to end. Then, Marty pulled her hand down, suddenly, and

forcibly hard, ripping Bertie's heart away from her body. She then held the heart in her hand and proudly showed it to David.

"David, it's still beating slightly. What do I do now?"

"Just hold it in your hand. That's just a natural, involuntary reaction. It will stop soon." David and Marty stared at the heart. It quivered slightly; then went still.

"How do you feel, now? Have you ever felt more in control of another human being in your life?" David massaged Marty's clitoris more gently now. Her orgasm was winding down. He had accomplished what he set out to do. He knew Marty's power trip would make her feel beholden to him.

"You've performed a masterpiece." David's voice was reassuring, confident, consistently praising Marty's casual, unrepentant immorality.

"You enjoyed the splendor of a human heart dying while you feel its life going out of it. You were her heart's last connection to life. Think about that. That's your power, Marty. You received the last of Bertie's power now. Her soul is in your soul now. Her powers are now yours."

Bertie's eyes had glimpsed Marty's for the last time, but they had no longer seen Marty. As she closed her eyes for the last time, Bertie saw an image of women climbing a ladder upwards into the sky. They were struggling to escape from the confining cloth bags that held them in, like they were human butterflies leaving their cocoons. One by one, they stepped out of their confinements. All were scantily clad in thongs and jeweled bikini bottoms. They were gracious and beautiful. They walked majestically down a long runway that had adoring men on both sides of it. The men reached out to touch them and hand them money and jewels and property deeds as they walked past. The women then ascended a small staircase onto a huge circular platform. There they took their places upon their throne beds where they would soon perform their prostitution rites.

Bertie imagined the sky above her vision was turning crimson as the sun was moving toward late afternoon. Torches were being lit on the platform; incense bowls were lit, adding sacred mystique and aphrodisiac fragrance to the sacred ceremony. Handsome men were going to the women, kissing them, massaging them, and openly fornicating with them. Bertie saw that a host of spirits watched over the sacred prostitutes. These spirits played harps and blessed the believing people who were paying tribute to their tribe's fertility.

Bertie smiled a soft, happy smile; her last. She knew she had made prostitution and pornography acceptable practices and beautiful art forms once again. She had pushed back the boundaries that had limited women's role in shaping human destiny. She had restored whoring to its time honored, rightful acceptance and necessity. It was no longer seen as an immoral, disgusting profession. It was now considered honorable and necessary and integral to humanity's need for connectivity, peace, and love. She felt happiness for all she and Marty had done together. Together, they had changed perceptions. Pornography was now hailed and honored as intimate artistry. She died knowing she had vindicated her life's purpose. She had obeyed the mandate of the butterfly that had visited her while she sat on the lakeside bench mourning her dead daughter.

Marty held Bertie's heart. She stared at it, spellbound by its determination to continue beating. It beat very slowly, then erratically for a few spastic final beats; then it became still. *"It's really stopped, David. It's not beating anymore."* Marty seemed relieved. A feeling of comforting warmth swept over her. All the goodness that resided in Bertie's heart had departed from the dying woman and transported its benevolence and forgiving loving spirit into Marty. Marty felt Bertie's warm, loving spirit enter her. She believed she was being accepted by the spirit world as a good soul who was not capable of any wrongdoing. And, in her distorted mind, she hadn't done anything wrong. She simple had followed the instructions of her boss and mentor. Above all, she felt that she was now loved more by David than ever before; and she was innocent of any wrongdoing. She felt accomplished as an executive now. She believed she had successfully passed an important milestone in her executive development; that she had every authority and moral right to do what she did; and that all her deeds were blessed. She felt more loved and adored in these moments than she had ever felt in her entire life. She appreciated David more than she had ever appreciated anything or anyone. She continued stroking David's cock, and with more ardor than she had ever stroked it before.

"Very good, Marty. She's dead now." David turned Marty around so he could face her. He hugged her close to him and smiled a proud smile into her eyes. They kissed each others' cheeks. *"You were sensational. You were beyond fantastic! You were wonderful! You are the most daring, incorrigible, and lovable, immoral whore in the entire world. I'm so glad to have you with me. I'm thrilled with you. I loved watching every minute of your work. I adore you. You showed no fear. You had no qualms or hints of squeamishness about murdering her. That was your best murder, ever. Don't you agree?"*

"I agree," nodded Marty. *"I felt myself getting totally into it. I really loved doing it; absolutely loved committing murder this new way. I felt as though I was performing a sacred rite. I feel so complete and pleased with myself, David. I feel like a totally grown up, confident, powerful accomplished woman. You've taught me something amazing! I never imagined murder could be so profoundly erotic and enjoyable. I became so wet inside. I never wanted to fuck so badly in my entire life. My urges were driving me out of my mind. I felt this romantic specialness about committing murder with you; the way you guided me through it; how you held me and stimulated me. I came so beautifully; so naturally; like I'd done murders this way*

for thousands of years. Even my orgasms felt different. They were so emotionally rewarding, like they were holy and divinely blessed."

"Wonderful. How do you feel now? Do you like this?" He removed his fingers from her sex and rubbed his palm over her vagina. He hugged her closely and again kissed her cheek. His fingers then returned to her wetness and again found her swollen clitoris. He tenderly massaged her again, bringing her libido to a frenzy. *"Are you loving this? Are you pleased knowing that the forces of morality have no hold over you now; and they never will?"* Marty clutched David tightly. Her orgasm flow was never far from presenting itself when her limbic senses were engaged this way. She was experiencing nirvana again. Her eyes rolled up into their whites; her orgasm flow resumed.

"Oh! Yes, David. I'm loving this. Mmmmm. Yes, I'm pleased to be free of morality. And I feel no guilt; only wonder. It was a good experience for me to murder that way. I needed to do it. You knew I needed to do it, didn't you?"

"Yes. I knew."

"I appreciate you so much, David. You helped me find an inner self I didn't know I had. I never felt such wonders before. I loved doing every part of it. I absolutely loved committing murder this way. I was a little afraid at first; but after I started, I loved every minute of it. Thank you for helping me, David. You're a wonderful man, David. You're so loving and understanding. You've taught me so many amazing things. I don't know how I can thank you enough. Oh, David, if you only knew how badly I want to make love with you right this minute. I desperately need you to come inside me, David. I need to fuck you, David. I really do."

"I know Marty. And we will, but let's wait until we're alone, please?" Tell me how you feel about Bertie now that she's dead."

"Well, I feel closer to her now than I've ever felt while she was alive. While I was pulling my knife up, I was remembering a flashback to the

time when the two of us looked at a hundred of my best porn films. We picked out over a hundred cum shots into my mouth and my vagina, and then we created a compilation of our work and spliced them into a continuous film where I was holding my partners' balls and kissing their cocks' heads and lavishing my tongue over their cocks' heads and fondling their balls, while cock after cock spurted its cum onto my tongue, into my mouth and into my vagina. Bertie and I had so much wonderful girl-fun making that film. It was surprisingly successful; and we didn't incur any production costs."

"We were just two best girlfriends laughing together, imagining how many millions of men would masturbate while watching our compilation. Bertie raved about how glorious I looked with all that cum shooting into me. It was non-stop, ejaculation after ejaculation. Later, the two of us read hundreds of letters and emails from fans praising that film. They complimented me as the most sensational erotic romance actress ever. They called me the goddess of explicit intimate film art. Some proposed marriage; others offered gifts and many new members joined my member service. The male world went wild over that film.

"That's the day Bertie told me my eroticism was living majesty. I owe her so much! I'll be forever grateful to her, David. Before I met Bertie, I always thought of myself as just another porn star. But she taught me to think of myself as someone who was above that description; and to always be very proud of what I did. That's when I started believing in myself. That's when I started believing my performances were special works of art. Now I see myself as a dignified, exquisite star of intimate explicit erotica, bringing sexual joy and lifting the spirits of millions of men worldwide. Now, I believe in myself, David. I have confidence that I bring a special talent to the world. My explicit film work sets males' limbic zones on fire and makes them feel more alive. People look up to me and respect me now. Many even worship me.

"It's ironic, David: While Bertie and I had martinis after we created that compilation, she remarked that lots of men would die to be with a woman like me. That compliment really boosted my self-esteem. That's when I reassessed my self-worth. That's when I knew I was the envy of many women and highly desired by most men. I could just hug her. I really appreciated what she did for me. It's unfortunate she had to die like this. Poor Bertie. I'll miss doing fun things like that with her.

"But now I can love her in a whole new way. She dedicated her life to helping me become a mature woman; and today she's even helped me become a more accomplished murderess. She has always been there for me, always putting my interests ahead of hers, always helping me improve. She's been a true friend. I feel like a goddess that has Bertie's love and power captured inside me now. Even by dying today, she helped me become truly proud of myself, David. I feel so proud of what I did, and how she helped my through this, I could cry. I am truly blessed, David.

"David," Marty paused with a new child-like thought, *"if Bertie could come back to life, do you think she'd be pleased with me, for learning this new way to commit murders?"*

"I'm certain she'd be pleased, Marty." David wore his most serious face. *"I'm sure her love for you transcends what happened today. Never feel guilty about what you did. It was beautiful. I'm sure Bertie's soul is pleased with you. I'm positive her soul loves you with no hard feelings. But we have more work to do. We can't forget George. We must also murder George."* David wasn't much for lingering on sentiment.

"Have you noticed George's cock, Marty?" David's eyebrows lifted as he smiled in amusement. *"I dare say, Marty, I believe watching you murdering his wife has turned George on. Look at how stiff his cock is!"*

"I've noticed it, David. He has a full hard on. It's as big as I've ever seen it! George is highly aroused!"

"Do you understand why he's so hard?"

"No, David, I'm not sure. Why do you think he's so hard? I haven't even touched him." Marty shrugged her shoulders. Her eyes searched David's for an answer.

"He's hard because he watched you murder his wife. He saw you take her power into yourself. He lost his amorous feelings for Bertie during the process. Whatever amorous feelings he ever had for Bertie have now attached to you. They have amplified the amorous feelings that he already had for you! He now associates you with power and conquest as well as erotic love. He adores your immorality. He even projects the love he had for Amanda, his dead daughter, onto you. You have become George's whole world. Believe me when I say this: George intensely loves you. I mean he's insane with the passions he's feeling for you, right now. He's never loved another woman as much as he loves you, right now, at this very moment."

"Poor George, all that love for me and now I'm going to murder him."

"Yes, but you don't need to murder him right away. We're not in any rush. Perhaps he'd appreciate one final intimate experience with you. That would help him stay engaged in the murder process. You could do that much for him. Would you like to do that?"

"Oh, yes, David. Marty squealed. I'd love to suck George's cock one last time before I murder him. Thank you, David. You know how much I love performing felatio, don't you? Would that be all right with you, George?"

George nodded. Marty removed his mask. *"Is there anything you'd like to say, George?"*

"Yes, simply this," George spoke rapidly with a high-pitched, nervous voice. *"Marty, our whole involvement with you was Bertie's idea, not mine. I was simply a prop. I'll gladly sign a paper saying that I was the one who murdered Bertie, if you'll just let me go. I don't want to die. You don't need to kill me, Marty; really, you don't.*

I'll stay silent about all this; honest I will. And I'll continue loving you, forever."

Marty looked at David to see whether he wanted to spare George. David gave a slow shake of his head, signaling that George needed to be murdered also.

"Nice try, George," Marty smiled and shook her head, *"But I guess I won't be sparing you. Besides, you wouldn't want to spoil my fun, would you? You know this is a special day for me, don't you? I'm learning a whole new way of committing murder! It's exciting. You wouldn't want to spoil my fun, would you? You wouldn't want me to go on with the rest of my life knowing that you were a witness to what I did to Bertie, would you, George? When you really, truly love someone, George, you try to shield them from anxieties. I know you know that. And, you've often told me that you love me, George. You should be ashamed to even suggest that I let you go, George.*

"You know I have special feelings for you, George. It wasn't your fault that you got caught up in Bertie's world. Tell me, how did you feel while you were watching me murdering Bertie? Did you feel sadness for her? Did you want me to stop?"

George pursed his lips before he lifted his eyes to meet Marty's. *"This is the time for honesty, isn't it?"*

"Yes, George. Be honest. I need to hear it. It would mean a lot to me." Marty nodded her head. She gave George a kiss on his lips.

George took a deep breath. His eyes searched Marty's, seeking her understanding and compassion. *"No. I did not feel sadness for her. I'm being honest. I felt a twinge of pain when you stabbed her with your first stab; but that's all I felt for her. Honestly, I knew you were going to murder her and there was nothing anyone could do about it. As soon as I understood that, I stopped seeing her as my wife, or even as a human person at all.*

"I stopped thinking of Bertie; entirely stopped thinking of her. My only thoughts were of you; seeing your face; watching your vagina

while David fingered you; relishing your orgasm convulsions while you were murdering her. This capacity came over me. It made me appreciate that I needed to take it for granted that Bertie was in the process of being murdered; and that I should appreciate the beauty of the pleasure that her murder was bringing you. And I did appreciate that. I saw the nirvana in your continence while you stabbed her. I saw the exquisite delight in your face as you orgasmed while cutting her across her belly.

"I became fully absorbed in my adoration of you. I was splendor-struck by the glory of your immorality. And I loved you for it. I was in adoration of your mind and the thoughts that it harbors; how it embraces promiscuity, shamelessness, and murder simultaneously; how it feels no remorse in the destruction of another human life. And I was riveted spellbound by your beauty. That was the moment when I accepted a profound truth about myself. And that is that I, too, am immoral. And that I, immoral man, fell in love with you, immoral woman, that first time we made love. And that I no longer cared about Bertie after that moment. I know now what I knew then. And that is that I love you; all of you; everything about you."

Is there anything you'd like me to do before I do what we both know I need to do?"

"Yes," George's voice dropped to a low, sad whisper. *"I'd like to die not thinking about Bertie's terrible fate. I watched what you did to her. I'm okay with what you did. Frankly, her obsession about you has been difficult to bear. I'm relieved that it's finally over. But, if I must die, I'd like my last thought to be of you and the fun times we had together. I regret they must end; especially this way. But if you would permit me to kiss your glorious vagina one final time and then suck me off, one last time; and then, kiss me one last time before you begin, I'd much appreciate that. I think that will help me accept my fate. Would you please do that for me?"*

"Of course, I will, George. For you, I'll gladly be your kinky, immoral, loving whore to the very end! What are good friends for, anyway? I'm very honored and pleased that it's not some memory of Bertie that you want as your last memory. You want me on your mind, don't you George? You want the tastes of my incorrigible, whoring, wanton cunt, and a kiss from my immoral semen drenched lips to be your last memories. I don't understand. I mean, all the ejaculations, the orgies, the hundreds of cream pies. Are you wanting to vicariously become a part of all that, George?"

"Yes, a thousand times yes. I want my tongue to feel the throbbing of your clitoris throughout the ages while it is showered in thousands of ejaculations and bathed in hundreds of cream pies. I want to be one with all your lovers as you helped them discover their freedom inside you. I want to commune with your divine freedom lust; your wondrous immorality, in your holy of holies and thereby fully know you. I want to be one with you while you attain your rapture and while you bask in your ecstasies. I want to experience complete acceptance of you, adoration of you and take those nirvana feelings into my soul."

"But tell me why, George."

"Because you are the essence of life, Marty; beautiful, adorable life. And because I wish to enter death clinging to my memories of life. And, I will be hopeful that, while I must leave this life, I will somehow enter another; and, hopefully my soul will find your soul in our next lives. That's my why, Marty."

"But I live such a sinful life, George."

"Doesn't matter; not really. I don't care. There's moral life and sinful life. But it's all just life. You live yours as a whore. But yours is an adorable, precious, beautiful life, just the same."

"Oh George, you're so sweet. You've always been so sweet and loving to me; even now. I'm going to miss you. I wish there was some other way. But absolutely, you shall have your last wishes, George.

I'm sorry our fun must end this way. I will always love you. I want you to know that." Marty tied her hair back in a pony tail and smiled a knowing smile to George. *"We both know how I hate having my hair falling in my face while I'm sucking a cock, George. It distracts from my concentration. There, now I'm ready. We can start."* Marty nodded cheerfully while making her comments to George. Then, without further hesitation, she pushed George down to his knees. She stepped forward and presented her vagina, resting it upon his face. George slathered his face in her lips and kissed her earnestly with his mouth and lips and tongue. She responded with a slow orgasm build and a trickle of her fluids greeted George's mouth.

After he had eagerly supped from Marty's vagina, she stood George back up. *"Did that work for you, George? Did that take you back through time? Could you taste my thousands of lovers? Could you feel my clit throbbing while basking in all those cream pies?"*

"Yes. It was everything I imagined it would be, and more; so much more. I could keep going forever. Must we stop?"

"Yes, I'm afraid we must stop, George. Sorry. That was your last supper. Now, it's time for your grand send off." She then dropped to her knees before him. She performed her exquisite felatio on George, repeatedly kissing and lavishing her tongue upon the head of his penis while expertly stroking his shaft with her fingers. George ultimately surrendered a voluminous stream of semen into Marty's mouth.

Suddenly, Miss Promiscuity realized the significance of George's ejaculation. She didn't want this experience to end; not ever. She loved sucking George off. She felt compelled to say something; something that would persuade Marty to spare George:

'Oooh, his semen flow has such creamy smoothness, delicious taste, and silky texture. And, he's so dependable; always eager to please you. And, he understands and accepts you. He adores everything about you. He's like everything you have wished you would

have in a father. And now you have it. It's like casual, accepted, understood, loving incest. And what's so terrible about that? You and he have mutual feelings of genuine love. Admit it.

'*How many times have you bounced your vagina on his face? How many times has he practice thrusted his tongue over your clit? Did he ever complain about the demands that you and Bertie placed on him? No, he didn't. He was always loyal to both of you; but especially to you. He genuinely loves you. Murdering him will be like murdering your own father. Tell David you can't go through with it. Tell David: Make some kind of airtight deal with him; bind him to silence; get him involved as a co-conspirator that you and David can trust; but don't kill him.*'

Miss Iniquity became alarmed. She knew she needed to step into Marty's mind and muzzle Miss Promiscuity. Marty's adult voice took command:

'*Stop your dream thoughts right this moment. David is right behind you. If you linger much longer, he'll sense something is wrong. You can't risk that. You told David you were good with murdering both of them. You'll never be David's equal if you waiver. Now is not the time to have remorse or regrets about your decisions. Think abstractly, like you did when you were a little girl, at WEX school. Think: George is just a stone that you used. You imagined it loved you. But then, you dropped it and moved on to a new stone. Your George stone has fulfilled its purpose and now you must drop your George stone, and forget your George stone; and move on to your next stone.*

'*The world is filled with stones; all of them just waiting to love you; all of them eager to hold you and kiss you and fuck you and ply your clitoris with their tongues. All of them have their individual circumstances that you can involve yourself with. After George, you will be free to immerse yourself in many new worlds; many new men; many new penises. And there's David. He's waiting patiently for you to murder George; waiting for you to drop this stone; anxious to hold you in his arms and kiss your neck and finger your clitoris while you murder. You know that pleases him. So, get on with the task, at hand.'*

Marty stood before George. She smiled to him with her mouth and eyes before she burbled his semen prize on her lips before swallowing it.

"Was I tasty enough for you?" grinned George, hoping to take Marty's mind off her gruesome task at hand.

"Of course, you were, George. You've always been a fabulous protein shot," Marty nodded as she smiled her coquettish smile.

"So, you enjoyed it, didn't you?" George nodded in hopeful apprehension that somehow Marty would not go through with his murder.

"Absolutely, I did, George. You know how much I love sucking cock! Cum guzzler, through and through; that's me! Whore to my core!" Marty nodded a toothy smile to George, extending her sincere friendship across the heinous deed that she was about to perform.

"Then, how, after all our intimacy, after sharing our honest love, can you be so cold-hearted? How can you go through with this?" George hoped against hope that his last cum shot into Marty's mouth would not be his final one.

"Simple, George. Stones. Remember? I've told you about the stones." Marty's face was serious, dashing George's hopes of a reprieve.

"Stones? I don't understand." George scrambled for dialogue; anything to forestall his wretched fate.

"Well, it's like this, George. I told you before. When I was a little girl, I felt the need to be loved. So, I picked up a stone. I imagined it loved me. And I imagined I loved it back. But after a while, I realized the stone and I couldn't be in love anymore. So, I dropped the

stone and began looking for another stone. My Premium Members are kind of like stones. I love them until they can't pay me anymore. Then, I drop them and go find another stone."

And there it was, just like that. Marty's stone-cold heartlessness, her matter-of-fact disposition passed over her face, chameleon-like, changing her mood like a chilling autumn cloud chases away summer's warmth. Her friendliness and playfulness were gone.

"But I was never one of your Premium Members." George protested. He sensed Marty's heart was growing cold. He desperately wanted the warmer, loving version of Marty to return. *"You and I had so much more than that. We are special together. We are so close to each other, Marty. We've done so many things together; created beautiful work; laughed; played. We're Intimate. We're in love. You know we are."*

"I know we are, George. But we can't be in our love anymore. That means you've become a stone. And I can't carry you along with me any further. I'm going on from here, George. And you can't come with me. Sorry. Now it's time for me to drop you. Try not to worry, George. You'll soon be with Bertie in your afterlives. You'll be okay. She loves you, too."

"Marty, no. Please. Don't" George's eyes begged for his life.

"I'm sorry, George. This must be. I will miss you."

"Please, don't. I'm begging you." George looked into Marty's eyes. Through his building tears, he searched desperately for her humanity and compassion; but found only nothingness. Her soul's love spark had guttered out. She looked right through him, now, as if he no longer existed.

The soft warm pools that had first seduced him were gone. Her eyes were somehow darker and colder; lifeless, like those of an emotionless shark. George sensed that Marty had just become a different person than the heartthrob he had known before; yet just as young; just as beautiful. She was even more beautiful now. Murder somehow brought the full vitality of blood lust into her skin. The rosiness in her face animated her; filled her with vibrant life; but her eyes told him that she was not going to share her joys of life with him; instead, she would take life from him. The resolve from behind her face told him that she was resolved. She was going to end their love and his life; end all of it; drop him like a stone. Her persona had become transformed into something that sent chills down his spine. This gorgeous minx, this love of his life, had become a soulless, trance-like killing machine.

Marty kissed George's mouth with a long, soulful kiss from her semen glossed lips. She held his head in her hands and looked into his eyes one last time. *"Goodbye, my sweet love. Be brave. Goodbye, George,"* she whispered.

"So now you will be taking my soul into your soul, won't you?" George swallowed hard, hoping against hope that Marty would relent and spare his life.

"Yes, George. I'm afraid so. There is no other way."

"Then promise me that you will love it; that you will remember me; that you will love me again in another life."

"Of course, I will, baby." And with that, she gave George another kiss. But this one was not soulful. It was more of the sort of kiss that a mother imparts to her child as she shoves it out the door and sends it off to school. At the end of their affair, after invading and destroying the lives of Bertie and George, Marty was proving herself true to her credo: Herself first; herself only. Her kiss and her farewell were simply her sexy, unforgettable way of delivering her indelible sensuous mock to George's unsettled mind; nothing more. Then, she smiled her final goodbye to George and turned to face David. She pressed her breasts against David and hugged him tenderly.

"David," Marty whispered, *"have I finally become a naughty enough bad girl; a thoroughly immoral enough bad girl; an incorrigibly*

enough bad girl for you? You know I'm becoming the most uninhibited, immoral whore there ever was, don't you?"

The warmth in Marty's eyes had returned. Her loving brown pools searched David's eyes. They pleaded for his approval of her unhesitating plunge into the lowest depths of her debaucheries. Sex; sex before, between and after her incidental, heartless murders; but always erotically beautiful; uninhibited, passionately intimate sex was always foremost on her mind, anxious to do her bidding.

Her hand now reached down, inside David's pants, to find David's hardened cock. It pleased her immensely to discover David's member was still fully sized, very large, and very firm. His cock gave her confidence that the truth she sought was here, in concordance with her now; adoring her cavalier wickedness; completely accepting her, likely as an equal. Clearly, David approved of her licentious debauchery. She intuited, correctly, that her wickedness thrilled him; that he was willing to plunge into her abyss of eternal immoral sin with her. She stroked his hard cock while kissing his neck and hugging him.

"You are, Marty. You are my truest love and my precious naughty darling." David kissed her cheek and neck. *"You are beyond any doubt the most magnificent immoral whore in the entire world. You are adorable and incorrigible. You are the embodiment of shameless immorality. You are perfection of all that is wonderful and evil. I idolize you. I always have and always will. You are my dream goddess. May I have the honor of holding you again, while you perform your next murder?"* David hugged her body tightly to his, reassuring her of his devotion.

"Oh, yes, David," Marty squealed. *"Let's start. Hold me close while I place my first stab into George."* The fear Marty had when she had first stabbed Bertie was gone now. She eagerly thrust her first stab slightly below George's right shoulder. George didn't

flinch. He stood stoic, speechless, with his eyes closed and his mind steeled against all senses of pain. But tears escaped his eyes and rolled down his cheeks. He knew Marty had reduced his status to that of a worthless stone. But even now, as he began his passage into his after-life, he loved Marty. He willed that his soul should be joined to hers in eternity. His tears were for him and for Marty, and for what they had once had together. As he entered the process of dying, he clung to the love they had. The love, the good times he had with Marty, were George's everything.

Marty had already let go of George's love. She had departed George's dream world. She turned to David, smiled, and hugged him. All her feelings for George instantly evaporated.

"This is deliciously erotic, David. I understand why you wanted me to learn this new method. It's stimulating! I love doing it. I could murder this way, often. I'll never be able to thank you enough."

Marty then murdered George, using the same manner of stabbings and disembowelment that she had performed on Bertie. David closely spooned his body to hers while kissing her neck and rubbing and stimulating her vagina. He guided her through the stabbing and disembowelment processes a second time. She continued stroking David's cock between stabbings. After She removed George's heart and it had stopped beating, Marty turned to David and hugged him tightly. Her eyes found his, sending him all the warmth and love she had in her soul. She kissed his lips. And while kissing David's mouth, she felt his arms tightening around her; hugging her closer; feeling his body pressing hard against hers.

"I hope you enjoyed that, David. I did it for both of us. You know that. I really, honestly love you, David. You know I love you more than any man I've ever loved. You've taught me so many wonderful things about life and people and myself. You helped me understand

how duplicitous Bertie and George really were. I'm so glad I finally saw them for what they were. I had no idea they were simply using me to advance their own pleasures. I'm proud that I've murdered them. You are a wonderful man, David. I'm so thrilled that you believe in me. I feel we have the most special bond that two people could ever have. I can't wait to thank you in a more intimate way. I'm anxious to consummate our intimacy."

"Tell me, you gorgeous whore, what were your real feelings about George? How do you feel now that you've murdered the man who was like a father to you?"

"We became lovers, David. We practiced my porn scenes; so, naturally we fell into love. But it was never going to go anywhere. It was never going to be anything more than that. So, I feel fine about murdering him. He was no longer of any use to me." Marty's eyes peered into David's in a quizzing way, betraying her coquettish carefree smile.

David noted the discrepancy. That prompted him to explore his line of questioning. *"But what I'm reaching to understand, Marty, is whether you felt connected to George in a soul-to-soul sort of way? I'm trying to understand whether you and he held your feelings for each other in your hearts? And, now that You've murdered him, do you still feel that his soul carries his love for you in his heart?"*

"Oh, I see what you're getting at. Well, I suppose George's soul may still love me in its afterlife. George was a very sentimental man. He had deep feelings for Bertie, and his daughter, Amanda; and for me. Yeah, I could see that his soul is still clinging to our love."

"My take on George is different," sneered David.

"Different in what way?" Marty's eyes, while still questioning, now betrayed a touch of defiance.

And David caught that, too. *"You see, Marty, to me, George was not a real man. He was what I would call a 'Putz.' That's someone who doesn't know why he's on Earth; someone who doesn't know his own mind and who doesn't care to develop it. I've listened to you many times talking about George. You've told me how he grieved endlessly over his lost daughter. You've told me how he allowed his wife, Bertie, to jerk him around and be her 'yes' man; and how he allowed you two women to use his dick for porn practice. George was a useless, spineless, pussy-whipped wimp; a nobody. And how a glorious, vivacious porn star and exceptional top executive like yourself, could feel remorse for such a schmuck escapes my abilities to understand human behavior. I think you still hold feelings for George. I think you feel some need to believe that George or his spirit soul is out there in eternity, caring for you. Am I wrong?"*

"Well, maybe you are right. I did feel an attachment to George. But it's nothing like the feelings I have for you, David." Marty increased the pressure of her hand on David's cock as she continued stroking it.

"Marty, I'm only going to tell you this one time. If you want to be a successful executive, you must be able to divorce yourself from sentimentality. George has no use to you. He never did. A penis is just a penis. That's all he was to you: A penis. You should have no regard for his life or his soul. You should purge him from your thoughts."

"Yes, David. I know you are right. You are always right." Marty held the head of David's penis against her vagina and rubbed it against her outer lips. Her juices had her dripping wet. She wanted David to understand how anxious she was for penetration.

But David had a different agenda in mind. *"Then, let me suggest that you completely purge George and all thoughts of him from your life. Let's see you do that before you move ahead to intimacy. Let's do first things first, step by step, like a thoughtful executive does, shall we?"*

"Well, yes, David, of course. I will purge him from my thoughts. I promise you; okay?"

"Not okay, my dear. I'm looking for deeds here, not mere words."

Marty frowned her perplexed look. *"Deeds? I don't understand. What deeds should I do?"*

David's face broke into a grin. This was his willing disciple. This was the Marty he loved most; the adorable whore who was always willing to do the most extraordinarily heinous criminal acts to prove her worthiness. This was the Marty he adored. He held her closely to him. He reached his fingers deeply into her vagina while he kissed her full on her mouth. He groaned, trying with all his willpower to not give in to her; to not penetrate her vagina with his penis. Finally, after their long, passionate kiss, he looked into her eyes and spoke slowly:

"Do you remember how you described the sacrifice conducted by the Aztec priest?"

"Yes, I remember."

"Do you remember how the priest showed total disdain for his victim?"

"Yes. He cut his victim's heart out and held it high for the crowds to see that the victim had no life. Then he severed his victim's head and threw it down the temple steps to show the people that the victim had no power. Then he rolled the victim's body down the temple steps, and ordered his body be fed to their dogs; showing the people that they should have no respect for the victim; that his only usefulness was as dog food."

"Very good, Marty. Well, then, tell me: Does George or his body and soul have any more use to you than that dead victim had for those Aztecs?"

"No, David. Of course, not."

"Then, I think you need to prove that; not to me, but to yourself."

Marty chuckled and smiled, placing her forehead against David's forehead while rubbing the head of his penis against the inner folds of her juicy vaginal lips. *"What are you suggesting, my dear mentor and master?"* She held George's heart in her hand, and stared at it. *"Well, David, here it is."* She stated, matter of factly.

"Don't you think you should do something symbolic with it? Like the Aztec priest did with his victim?"

"I suppose so," replied Marty, looking doe eyed into David's eyes. *"But what can I do? I cannot throw it down the temple steps. We are standing on a basement floor."*

"Well, symbolically, you could prove to yourself that his soul means nothing to you."

"How, exactly? What do you suggest?"

"If George's life and his soul truly meant nothing to you and mean nothing to you now, you could demonstrate that by stepping on his heart with your foot and squashing it like the useless insect that George truly was."

Marty's jaw opened. Her revelation came over her. It was suddenly clear to her that she was breaking clear of her past with George and Bertie. They were gone forever. Only she and David remained! Her world was now ordered the way David wanted it ordered. She dropped George's heart to the floor and stepped hard upon it; then forcefully squished it with a downward, rotating pressure movement of her foot, squashing, and shredding it. George was finally out of her life, forever.

"Now Marty, I want you to look at their corpses. See them standing before you, bound to their execution posts, their body cavities opened; their hearts torn out. Look at them."

"Yes, David. I'm looking. What am I supposed to see?"

"Not what you are supposed to see, you glorious murderess; but what do you feel?'

"Feel? About what, David?"

"About what you've done. When you look at them, do you feel guilty?"

"No."

"Hatred?"

"No."

"Remorse?"

"No."

"Pleasure?"

"Perhaps a little. I know I passed a milestone. Their bodies prove that. That pleases me."

"But what do you feel when you look at them? What feeling do you have for them; for what you put them through while you murdered them?"

"Oh, I see what you're asking me now, David."

"Well then, tell me, looking at their eviscerated bodies, how do you feel, now"

"Indifferent. David, I feel indifferent."

"Indifferent to their horror; their pain; their suffering; their loss of their lives?"

"Yeah, David. I feel indifferent. They were of no further use to me. So, indifferent. Yes, that's the word for my feelings. That describes my feelings best."

"You have no empathy for them; for the horrors you put them through?"

"No, David. None."

"Now, go to them. Hold open their eyes and look into their eyes. And hold open their mouths and look at their tongues."

Marty did as David commanded her. *"Now, Marty, realizing that their eyes will never see again and their tongues will never speak again, answer me: Do you feel inspired to pray for their souls?"*

"What? No, David!" Marty laughed a contemptuous laugh. *"Don't be ridiculous! Why would I pray to God? I don't believe in God. I only believe in myself. The only inspiration I feel is in my own confidence. These murders were very helpful. I believe I can do anything now. And I will. I will go forward without Bertie's help.*

And I will create the most exquisite, mouth-watering porn the world has ever seen."

David held Marty in his arms and hugged her tightly pressed against him. *"Marty, that's the perfect answer. I am so proud of you. You are not only beautiful and more desirable than any other woman in the world; you also have the debauched soul of a heartless, murderous, incorrigible whore. Now, think Marty. Are you certain that no one else knows about our murders? Are you certain no one else knows?"*

"Yes, David. But the assistants know."

"I'm not worried about them. Our friends from the drug cartel brought me exactly what I specified. Their vocal cords have been severed and their frontal lobes have had laser work done. They are simple eunuchs now. They can't tell anyone anything."

"What do they do when they aren't making love with me in the murder chamber?"

"Oh, simple house cleaning and work around the compound. They muck the barnyard and plant trees on the berms. They tend the rose bushes; pick up dead pigeons and burn them in the incinerator; odd jobs and simple things, that's all. I never challenge them. They can't process logical thoughts."

"But what do they do when they aren't working?"

"Mostly, they watch nature films. Those relax them. And, before we do a murder, I prepare them by showing them your porn films, and giving them pills that cause them to have full erections. Those erections last for hours. Have you noticed?"

"Yes, David. They are fantastic lovers! Thank you."

"I modified their frontal lobes so their minds would always be under their emotive limbic influence; always responsive to stimulus from their amygdala glands; always beholden to you and eager to make love with you. Do you find them excited to make love with you? Do they please you?"

"Oh, yes, David! They please me very much! They are so young and virile. They have incredible stamina. I love how they fuck me for hours; such pleasures! They totally drain me. They are perfect lovers. They never talk about silly things like football. Their minds are always focused on giving me exceptional, enduring pleasure. They are wonderful! The tall one is especially sweet. He always seeks to place his head upon my breasts and suckle my nipples. Does he think I'm his mother?"

"That may well be. Our drug cartel friends told me they got them when they were very young boys, after the cartel murdered their mother and father. The tall one is a year younger than his brother. I suppose he may have still been nursing? I just don't know. But after they were no longer suitable as boy prostitutes, the cartel decided to get rid of them; so, I bought them. Maybe the tall one associates you with his memory of his mother."

"Well, if he does, I don't mind. I love the way he suckles me. He's very sweet and endearing. I'm glad you bought them, David. And, thank you for modifying them for me. They excite me more than my porn partners because they share our murder experiences with us. And, they are so, totally, into the wonderful world of uninhibited sex. They are willing innocents. I can tell they adore me. When they put my Ban Wa balls inside me and take turns using my vibrators while fucking me on the murder table, they send me into nirvana land. I experience my most fabulous sex, ever! I don't know a better way of explaining this; but I think of them as my personal, living, human sex toys. And I totally love fucking them."

"And they love fucking you, Marty. They live for that. They know you as their God. That's how you should think of them, as your loyal subjects. They adore you. And, I adore you for who you are and I also love you in more ways than I can express in words." David was masterful at concealment. He did not reveal to Marty that he had frequent fellatio liaisons with the assistants. Lying by misdirection

and omissions were major tools in David's skill set. He had perfected these slights of truth since childhood.

"Oh David, I do truly love you. You've enabled me to have such a wonderful life!" Marty whispered, clinging tightly to him while accepting his compliment. Her moistened lips found his.

"Your life is about to get far more wonderful, Marty. Your share from your latest film will be 250 million; and that's just the down payment!"

"Film? What film are you talking about, David?" Marty broke from her kiss and held David at arm's length. Her frown communicated doubt; her eyes terror.

"Relax. I have everything under control."

"I was filmed committing murder?"

"Two murders; beautiful, stunning unforgettable murders."

"You filmed me while I murdered Bertie and George? How? Why?" Marty's eyes flashed distrust and anger at David's unexpected revelation.

"Relax. I told you to relax. No harm will come to you. This is about money."

"What are you saying? Whose money? What have you done, David?"

"I have a friend named Ep. He did a few things for my dad; and now he helps me, sometimes. He's paid me 500 million to film Berite's and George's murders. Your half is 250 million."

"So, you're telling me there's a film of me stabbing them; cutting through their stomachs; tearing their hearts out? Why would you let him do that?"

"Ep has a client, a Mideasterner. He's a porn aficionado. He has all your films. He adores you. He's paying Ep one billion for this film. But don't worry. Ep will have the film specially treated so it can never be reproduced; not even from a film of the film. It's a special process Ep developed. The film can only be seen by wearing a special headset."

"But why does Ep's client want a film of my most horrific murders?"

"Not just any murders, Marty. Your murders. The client has this thing for you. He regards you as the reincarnation of Ashera, the pagan goddess of life. He wants to connect with the emotive limbic feeling that Ashera stirred in her subjects when she fornicated and murdered the enemies of her people. He regards you as the most holy goddess of iniquity and immorality. He adores you. The man worships you."

"But aren't people like him supposed to be very religious; pray several times a day and all that?"

"Oh, yes, to be sure. He is very religious. And he enforces all the religious laws; makes sure his people follow those laws to the letter. But this constant religious life wears on him; makes him feel confined and stressed out. He sometimes feels this overpowering need to set his limbic mind free of religion and worship the one thing his natural tendency demands that he worship. He must heed this need or he'll go insane."

"And this need is what, David?"

"It's you, Marty. It's your exquisite pornography; your lovemaking; your ravenous, insatiable, fuck loving vagina. You see, the man worships you. He obsesses over you. He is smitten with lust for you. Your films have made him into an addict. He must have you. He'll do anything and pay any price to have you. Can you understand?"

"Yes, David. I know all about addiction. I'm a nympho, remember?"

"Yes; but in his mind you are not just some ordinary nymph; not like any other porn star. In his mind, you are the one."

"The one?"

"Yes. The one. He believes you are the one true God. In his mind, you have reemerged from millennia past to guide us mortals. You will lead our return to our natural immorality and reacquaint us with

our ancient worship practices. We will worship your fornications and your murders. We will look to you to show us how to drive out our antiquated religious practices and replace them with the new Modern Morality Standard practices that you command us to follow."

"Me? I'm supposed to do this?"

"Yes, Marty, you. You must be humankind's natural leader. You are the ultimate in humanity's creative expressionism. Your intimate artistry surpasses any works ever created by any artist or writer or film star. You are more stunning than the Mona Lisa or the ceiling of the Sistine Chapel; more profound than the written words of any biblical prophet or any author. You are humanity's living, divine artistry. Everything about you is divine; your fornications; your fellatios; especially your murders where you perform sacrifices to your greater glory. Ep's client wishes to fully immerse himself in the reenactments of those glorious, ancient tribal worship services which you, as Ashera his true God, led. He wants his spirit soul to relive those ultimate worship experiences."

"Led? Me? Led what? Relive the experience? What do you mean, David? How?"

"He will pay your service another billion dollars, Marty. Your share will be five hundred million. He needs you to do these things with him. He's wanted to do them all his life."

"He's an interesting fellow, Marty. Beneath his veneer of piety and modernity, he still believes in the old tribal ways. You will be flown to his palace in the Middle East. There, before his most hated mortal enemy, he will watch your murder film. Then he will make impassioned love with you. He told Ep that he lives to savor these precious moments with you. You are his living idol. He wishes to cherish your cherubic innocence and glorious fornication in front of his hated enemy. And while the two of you make love, he will have you witness the beheading of his enemy. The man's head will be given to you as a trophy; a symbolic gift, which expresses his

adoration for you; his way of honoring you for being the world's most beautiful, most incorrigible, and most immoral woman."

"So, he's into barbarism."

"Definitely, right out of tribal ways of twenty thousand years ago; especially prostitution worship and murder of his enemies. The man's head will be his token way of expressing his love for you; his willingness to take another man's life for you to witness for your enjoyment; to please you; heighten your libido, so to speak."

"Stimulate me to make me fuck even more enthusiastically? Just like back in the good old days, right?" Marty's chuckle conveyed her sense of amazement and incredulity. *"What are you getting me into, David?"*

"You only need to humor him; play along. Pretend you have come to him from across the millenniums to be his goddess queen. Consider the gift of the man's head as your personalized Salome moment. And be gracious. Recall the pleasures Salome must have felt when the head of John the Baptist was presented to her. Like you, Salome was the preeminent goddess of immorality of her time."

"And to express my gratitude, I'm expected to fuck him with unbridled enthusiasm, right?"

"Of course."

"Okay. David, is this sheik fellow some kind of nut?"

"No. He's not a nut; just a bit eccentric. And fabulously wealthy. He has hundreds of thoroughbred horses, race cars, and a fleet of private jets. Ep knows him, somehow. Says he loves to fantasize; imagines he relives scenes from times past to escape the tedium of religion. Ep said you should not be surprised if he wants to reenact events from the past with you."

"Like what?"

"Well, sometimes he imagines he is Pharoah Mentuhotep, who made Sara his concubine. You can expect you'll need to ride horse-back into the desert where he has a tent pitched."

"Why would I do that?"

"To humor him. He wants to fantasize that you are the modern-day reincarnation of Sara, Abram's sister, and wife. He will have you meet his two sons in the tent. According to Ep, they are very virile, handsome, strapping teenagers. You will be the object of their attentions while they reenact ancient history. You will pretend to be Sara; and you will have an orgy with him and his two sons, while they pretend to be Pharoah and his two sons. There will be some painless flogging to titillate you; and they will all perform cunnilingus with you, because they think of your vagina as the most holy place on Earth. Okay?"

"Kinky; but okay. I could get into that. Then what?"

"Expect him to shower you with gifts, like Mentuhotep did with Sara. He'll probably load you up with gold and silver; probably throw in a Lamborghini and a horse or two. He's obsessed with speed; sports cars and race horses. He'll be a great client for you."

"This seems unreal. How did he make his money? Does Ep know?"

"Ep said he inherited it. His great, great grandfather was a Bedouin Sheik who pitched his tent on top of one of the world's biggest oil fields. Some oilman showed up at his tent one day and gave him some papers to sign. The rest is history. This sheik has more oil than all the water in Lake Michigan."

"And he loves to fantasize and do kinky sex things; and he has unlimited money, right?"

"Yes. And a bit perverse. He loves observing while his security people throw homosexuals off the tops of skyscrapers. He's a bit sadistic, too."

"But he's into women and sex, right?"

"Yes, He adores women; especially porn stars. He keeps a harem of thirty wives; but he obsesses over you as the grand prize; the ultimate femme; the most splendid whore in the entire world. He

revers and adores you above all. He literally prays to a picture of your vagina."

"What? You're not serious?"

"Yes. Serious; prays that he and his mouth and penis will be acceptable to you, his redeemer from religion's rigid constraints."

"Goodness. That's too much. The man really needs me, doesn't he?"

"Yes. Badly. So, do you think you'll be able to pry yourself away from Bob, from time to time, to play fantasy games and to fuck and suck with him?"

"Oh, absolutely, David. I am a whore, you know. This is all so profound and wonderful, David. Mmmmm. I already imagine fucking him. Oh! But wait! Let me think! My head is spinning. Back up a moment! You and I know about our murders." Marty's eyes widened, revealing fright from her thought. *"You say Ep can be trusted because he took money to film the murders; so, he's part of your scheme? And this sheik, this wealthy client of Ep's can also be trusted because I will witness him commanding a beheading murder, right?"*

"Right."

"But David, how can you be sure you can trust Ep?" Now Marty's lips pinched together, revealing her distrust. She could not control the subtlety of her reveal. She could not know that David, ever attuned to everyone's slightest tell, could see her soul trembling within her eyes.

"Oh, that's simple," David immediately sought to assuage her fears, *"I already have Ep checkmated. Game over. No game at all. He can't touch us. I filmed Ep raping a twelve-year-old girl."*

"Well, that's not exactly foolproof, David. It could have been consensual on some offshore island where America has no jurisdiction."

"Yes. I saw the girl. Ep filmed her. I watched her fuck. I'm sure she wanted the sex. She was highly consensual; absolutely she wanted it. Loved to fuck like a mink. Ep raved about her; highly promiscuous

little tart; very slippery sex pot; knew she had sex appeal and used it; flaunted it; totally loved sex. She would fuck several men in one afternoon; loved doing it; different positions; multiple partners; couldn't contain herself; couldn't get enough sex; no morality whatsoever. Ep got her from a procurement guy named Celt. Took her in like a father figure. Then he took her to his island hideaway where she consented with over a dozen noteworthy celebrities, billionaires, and political types."

"*Well, she could talk.*" Marty squinted her eyes. Now they turned accusatory; probed David's eyes, seeking answers to why he would take chances that they might be discovered for their murders. A hint of anger from her sense of betrayal was carried by her voice: "*That twelve-year-old girl could turn on Ep, David. She could link us to Ep and he could link us to our murders. That girl could be a ticking time bomb. You know there's no statute of limitations on murder!*" Dismay caused Marty to shake her head.

"*No. She's never going to say anything.*" David spoke calmly. He was about to explain himself, something he resented doing for anyone. "*The girl is dead, Marty. After her last tryst, Ep took her on a helicopter ride. A thousand feet up, over the ocean, he stabbed her in the stomach; then pushed her out the door. She fell into the Caribbean, twenty miles from the nearest shore. With her blood trail, there's no doubt the sharks finished her.*"

"*Wow, David. That's amazing.*" Marty's eyes brightened. A wan, pleased smile now graced her face. Her tensions subsided, relieved knowing that the link to her murders had been dispatched.

"*Don't be amazed, Marty. What Ep did to her was only natural. Humanity is merely in the evolutionary process of returning to its natural, pagan roots. Murders and prostitution rites will become our normal cultural fare as we move forward in time. Prostitution worship and murder rites will become glorified in our new, normal society. Religion and morality will become relics of the past.*

"Our friend, Ep, did nothing new. He merely borrowed a page from Roman Emperor Caligula's playbook. Caligula had orgies with promiscuous, underaged boys and girls on his ship and at his cliffside palace. When he was finished with them, he had them wounded, then had them tossed off the ship or from the cliff's edge into the ocean below. The sharks ate them, too.

"You see, Marty, human life is meaningless; practically worthless, actually. People like you and I must think in terms of simply using people as long as it pleases us to do so. Then, when we have finished with them, we simply dispose of them in whichever way is most convenient for us. You must not concern your beautiful mind with trivial matters like that young girl. You need only worry about acquiring more wealth and pleasuring your glorious cunt in every way imaginable and with any partners you desire. Think of yourself as the queen goddess of all whoredom. Believe that everyone is here to serve you.

"Trust me. You need never fear loose ends, Marty. You know I always think of everything. The pathway has been cleared for you to perform your glorious whoring. Noone will ever interfere with your pleasures. I'll always look out for you. I promise. You know how much I applaud your lack of morals. You know I love you for being the bad girl that you are. Now, all you need to do, today, is go to your assistants; beam you sweet, innocent, loving smiles from your gorgeous angelic face while you create more exquisite intimate artistry for Ep's special film."

"Oh David!" Marty's tensions now relaxed; she pandered with delight: *"You are so incredibly wonderful. You do think of everything! You really do! I will always do as you say. I will always follow your advice. I will gladly visit the sheik and play fantasy games with him. I will entertain him with the most amazing sex he has ever known. I'll do orgies with him and his sons. I'll prepare myself with my most erotic scents. My pheromones will overwhelm them and*

drive them insane with lust for me. I'll cradle the sheik in my arms and legs and French kiss him; and joyfully fuck him; immerse him in my eternal bliss, while he's watching his enemies being beheaded. I'll applaud his immorality and assure him that his depravity gives me immense pleasures. I'll laugh alongside him and stroke his cock while we watch homosexuals plunging to their deaths. I'll assure him that he's providing me with the best, most memorable entertainment I have ever had; and I will reward him by giving our sheik the most delightful, unforgettable fellatio he's ever had. When he spurts his semen onto my tongue, I'll assure him that I love the taste of his ejaculation and I'll tell him I must visit him often to share his entertainment pleasures with him; and to suck and fuck him more often. And, I promise you, David, I'll bring billions of new assets to the Firm for management. Thank you, David, for this wonderful opportunity and for being so thoughtful! And for being so smart!

"David, David, David! It's happening. Mmmmmm. David. Please. I need you. I need you inside me. I feel it!"

"What's happening?"

"My loins are on fire! My nymphomania is raging! My spirit soul has returned to me from across the ages. I feel my spirit soul becoming embodied in my flesh as Sara, daughter of Terah, wife, and sister of Abram. I can see my past and my future. Everything is all so real! As I am now, I was then; the world's most glorious, most sought after; most glorious whore. And you, David, are my reincarnated Abram; sending me to whore with Pharoah and his sons. I will joyfully go to our Sheik and his sons, bringing them my gift of unimaginable pleasures. They will be my modern-day Pharoah and his sons; and I will pleasure them with my divine whoring; raise them to heights of ecstasy more wondrous and beautiful than anything they have ever known before. I will set their limbic minds on fire with insatiable lust for me. They will become as smitten as kittens clutching their gifts

of fresh catnip. They will become delirious with adoration of me. And they will love me. Mmmmmm, Mnnnnnnn. I can already feel myself fucking them. So sensual' so pleasing. They are glorifying me; honoring me; loving me. I can already feel their penises sliding over the lips of my mouth and tapping the outer lips of my vagina; begging to penetrate me. Yes! I want them. I already know we will enjoy wonderful lovemaking. I can already savor the tastes of their semen on my tongue; and I already feel their hot ejaculation flows coursing and spurting endless semen streams over my clitoris. I already know I will love them and treasure them as lovers. I will cherish my time of insatiable whoring with them.

"Within me, my spirit soul is also awakening as my past incarnation of Queen Isabella. Yes, David. I feel her flesh becoming my own body. I will delight in performing fellatio with the Sheik and his sons. Their souls will return to me as the souls of my courtiers, when I was Isabella. As I did then, I will do again. I will joyfully receive semen life onto my tongue and into my mouth and vagina while my ears are pleasured by the tormented cries of my kingdom's deplorables.

"I will feel the ecstatic, divine pleasures of life's semen seeds entering me, while I'm dually pleasured by the screams of the sheik's undesirables, as they plunge to their deaths; or as they writhe while they burn alive; or as they frantically gasp for air while they drown in water tanks before our eyes. Oh yes, David. I'm so excited! Mmmmm. I can't wait! I will entreat our sheik to the greatest earthly pleasures; the most memorable times he will ever know. And he will adore me for my complicity in debauchery. The sheik and I will bind our souls together with our glorious sins; and we will become inseparable lovers."

"You can foresee all these things? You can recall your past lives this way?" David was dumbfounded and perplexed. Marty's past lives had hitherto been unknown to him. He finally understood her uniqueness. He stared into her eyes while regaining his

composure; telling himself that her revelations could not, must not, disrupt his plans.

Marty smiled her most incorrigible smile to David. Her eyes now telegraphed her confidence in the committed whore she was. They told David that she was a change agent who had, in lives past; and who would, in lives not yet lived, change the course of human history. And that she was now on a mission to bend the course of history once again. Those eyes also telegraphed that she knew she was the consummate femme fatale; uniquely endowed to deliver pleasures; and supremely confident in the intimate artistry that she, alone, could create in the minds of others.

"Why yes, David. Of course I can foresee those things. I am woman. I have powers that my sex has imbued within my soul. As a man, you can only sense it as the 'feminine touch,' but you can never fully understand it. That's okay, David. Don't worry about my methods. I assure you; everything is under control. I am going to join my assistants now. I will create the most spectacular mouth-watering intimate artistic film ever made. It will please you and Ep; and especially Ep's sheik friend. I promise you.

"And after he watches this film of my murders and he sees how I love sucking and fucking my assistants; how I revel in my pleasuring, he will to go crazy to have me. I assure you; he will crave intimacy with me. He will desire having me more than all the jewels and gold in the entire world. Thank you for this fabulous opportunity, David. Thank you for pimping for me. I truly do love you, David. I must leave you now, David. My inner senses are telling me that I must do what is wholesome and natural and morally right for me. I must go to my assistants now. My disease compels me, David. I must set my nymphomania free! I must fuck now!" Marty rushed to her assistants and joined them where they waited for her on the murder table. She began her foreplay with French kisses while she stroked their penises and pressed her naked body lovingly against theirs.

'I've almost completed her!' thought David, watching her walk to the table where her assistants waited for her with hardened penises. *'My work is nearly finished! Her behavior is now as ingrained as mine, I've made permanent the attachment disorder that Susan and Dad inflicted upon her during her childhood. She showed no tinge of sadness for that murdered twelve-year-old girl; no feelings for her whatsoever; and no feelings for men like me. She's almost as narcissistic as I am. She has no empathy for other human beings, except possibly Bob. She has no feelings of guilt about creating her morality destroying pornography; or about crushing the life out of peoples' marriages; or even about murdering people in new creative ways.*

"I'm sure she'll laugh and party with the sheik while they watch homosexuals being tossed from skyscrapers, plunging to their deaths. No feelings for others; none. She's living proof that an authority figure can command people to do unthinkable things; and they will unquestioningly do them in order to gain approval. She has no remorse and feels no contrition whatsoever over butchering Bertie and George, two people who genuinely, honestly loved her; and who did their utmost to advance her career. After their tireless devotion to her; after leaving their entire estate to her, she had zero regard for their lives; no shared feelings with them over their lost daughter; no empathy whatsoever; no gratitude. And she's so proud of herself; so, pleased with her evil deeds!

'She is devoid of anyone's needs besides her own. Her narcissistic lust has fully blossomed into heinous criminal, evil acts. She feels nothing. No remorse. No conscience. She personifies immoral perfection. I've made her mind my most fabulous creation, molded in my own image. She has become, like me, a feelingless human insect. She's now much like me in almost every respect. But she does retain feelings towards me. Perhaps it's her blood? I don't know. But obviously, she needs me. She lives to please me. She will

never completely transform herself while she thinks that way. She can never be exactly like me. We are not quite the same. She can never be that. But she has become everything that I need, to perfect my own self. I, David, am alone. I alone, need no one. And I will perfect myself very soon.'

After David had again counseled Marty to be patient and to wait a while longer for their rendezvous with intimacy, he decapitated Bertie's and George's bodies with his guillotine. He watched Marty while she dutifully performed her spirit rituals with the severed heads. He then carted away the bodies and severed heads.

Marty reveled that day in her reward orgy with the assistants. Writhing and fornicating in Bertie's and George's blood sent her confidence soaring. She became ecstatic. Nymphomaniac urgings surged through her blood. She imagined herself with David, bound together in intimacy. Pleasing him had always been her most important earthly need. She knew he knew that. And today, he had told her that she pleased him. And he again had promised her that they would make love; soon.

Her loins were on fire with lust. Her nymphomania raged as she dreamed that she and David would soon affirm their intimacy. She reassured herself that whoredom was her wisest career choice. She was affirming her decision. This life was right for her. It felt right. It paid fantastic money. She purged every doubt and equivocation from her mind. She vowed to plunge herself ever deeper into whore-lust and debauchery; and to revel joyfully in her sinfulness. She silently assured herself that a marriage and family would merely be inconsequential nuisances to her whoring lifestyle; but she would tolerate them to humor Bob.

Marty snapped out of her recollections. Her thoughts abruptly returned to the present. She remembered that she was still with

Consuelo at the Adult Films awards ceremony. She placed the flashback of George and Bertie's murders in her rearview mirror. She compartmentalized her thoughts and explained, for Consuelo, how she had mastered her performance techniques without one single mention of Bertie's coaching help:

'I would, Consuelo, I really would love to; but it's hard to explain. I've studied myself for hours. I've closely examined my past work; then I thought about how I could do things better. I've looked in mirrors. I've taken selfie photos of my face. I've studied how my eyes and lips looked, how my smile looked, my facial muscles, everything. I've thought about every scene in every film, every frame; and how it would look if I did it slightly differently, that's all. I've thought about how I felt lying naked next to my orgy partners; before, during, and after our scenes, imagining how my feelings were projecting to my fans. With everything I think and do, I commit to creating more beautiful erotic intimacy.'

As Marty finished her acceptance speech, a lone Monarch butterfly fluttered to her face. It alighted upon her nose and fluttered briefly; then it spread its wings. Tiny droplets of blood dribbled from its wings. One droplet fell on Marty's upper lip. Obviously, the delicate creature had set down somewhere and gotten splashed with blood. It seemed to be recovering. It lifted itself up and briefly hovered before Marty's face.

Miss Iniquity spoke to Marty: *'Well, there's your blood omen. Bertie's blood drips form the trademark of your craft. There's your proof. David has disposed of Bertie and George. The secret you share with David is safe forever. No one will ever know the two of you commit murders together. Your secret is sealed by that butterfly's blood. David is a good partner; but, again, I remind you. Be cautious around him.'*

A voice which Marty had never heard before spoke softly. It was the butterfly's spirit voice:

'We butterflies feel pain when someone we love hurts another person that we love. Bertie and George were good to you. They loved you and wanted the best for you. Under David's influence, you murdered them. You have disappointed us. We understood your spirit need when you murdered bad people. But, the murders of Bertie and George were not for your spirit need.

'Our spirits were in their spirits and we felt the pain they felt when you betrayed their love for you. You must never murder again. We will prevent you. Do not ask me how. We understand things that you can not understand. We have our ways. Now, lick Bertie's blood from your upper lip and taste her blood. Remember her taste. Hold her taste precious in your heart. Love the memory of her and her goodness and her love. Remember, we sent her to you to help you. Remember how you have shamed yourself. Now, I must go.'

Marty smiled a puzzled smile to the butterfly. She marveled at its coincidental appearance as it fluttered from her face. She licked the droplet of blood smudge from her upper lip. She felt a change but didn't understand its significance. A tear formed in her eye. She wiped it away. She continued speaking with a slight waiver in her voice:

"To all my loving fans watching this show, I want to express my heartfelt, sincerest, very special thank you. I've just finished wrapping my latest film. It's my best, most innovative work ever! It brims with provocative seduction and orgy scenes of fabulous intimate artistry with wonderful partners. Please look for it or pre- order it now. I'll be releasing it soon!"

"Thank you, Marty," Consuelo stepped in to rehabilitate Marty. The host sensed the change in Marty's demeanor had something to do with her encounter with the butterfly. Confident that Marty would rally after a brief pause, Consuelo sounded upbeat in her praises.

"We here at WORLD INTIMACY BEAT are certain you will have another fabulous year, Marty. All of us at BEAT are highly

supportive of your beautiful intimate artistry and we anxiously await your next film. As you know, our next edition will be our annual calendar edition. Our editorial board scoured many web sites to find the very best still pictures for inclusion in our calendar. We're pleased to tell you that six of our twelve photo selections will be of you, Marty, posed in six different erotic, explicit intimate scenes, specially selected for publication by our editorial board.

"Congratulations! We want you to know that we are all grateful for the fabulous intimate art films you create and we all wish you and your sensational career continued success as you blaze new trails in the wonderful exciting world of intimate performance film art; and we look forward to catching up with you again in the future. This is Consuelo Lovely, saying good bye for now from WORLD INTIMACY BEAT at INTIMATE ARTISRY PERFORMACE APPRECIATION MAGAZINE and WORLD INTIMACY BEAT TV. And, reminding all our listeners and viewers: It's time to 'GET INTIMATE!'

"That ended the piece," said Barbara.

"Now I understand why she sometimes leaves me for a weekend or a week or two. She wasn't getting away to give herself time to think and meditate like she said, was she?" Bob was going through a sobering reassessment of Marty's truthfulness.

"No. Face it, Bob. I'm afraid not. She was getting away to do her serious business of whoring and making her intimate erotica films. It's in her blood. She can't help herself. She's the most immoral, unprincipled woman I've ever known," disparaged Barbara.

"She ceaselessly promotes her debauched lifestyle and gleefully destroys marriages to collect divorced men for her fan base. It's like a hobby or an amusement game for her. She displays their wedding rings like a mess of caught fish on a string line. Can you just imagine how Dom's wife felt when she read that interview? Who would

taunt another woman to needlessly hurt her that way? How could one woman be so cruel to another, after destroying her marriage? I doubt whether Marty even knows what love is, Bob. She's an anomaly. I've studied her. She has no feelings; no empathy for anyone else. She's like an emotionless insect. I've never encountered anyone like her, even in books. It's dangerous to get caught up in her world."

"She's really that bad? You don't think she even has a heart, do you?"

"Oh, Bob, I know you've seen another side of her. I know you and she share true feelings for each other; but Bob, Marty is badder than bad. If there were literary and film genres for intimate romance performance art, her work would skyrocket to the top of the charts.

"But, her ideas of love are perverse and wrong-headed; I shudder when I realize that so many young women are eager to follow her example, and that so many men idolize her. She's immersed herself in her world of lust. She's completely at home with it. She convinces that camera that she offers a man the most erotic love in the world. Whoring is an art form for her. She strives to master every aspect of it. The minutest detail does not escape her attention. She's been coached and practiced to perfection by someone who understands performance standards. That epiphany came to me when I closely studied her movies and compared her still frames. Her films keep getting better and better. She even uses different sets of tinted contact lenses so her eye allure matches the background in many of her films. Her productions are extremely detail oriented.

"While she bantered with her partners, she was bathed in pale soft glow lighting that made her eyes appear to be creamy, innocent blue. They looked like a soft morning light blue sky, with the sun barely above the horizon. Those eyes promised a refreshing glorious day ahead. When foreplay became earnest, as her partner began stimulating her with his fingers, heightening her desires for intimacy, the lighting changed. The producers placed a blue tint film over the lights.

"*That little touch changed the color of Marty's eyes. Her irises assumed a deeper azure blueish hue, the same coloration you see in mid-ocean, looking into the Pacific deeps on a bright sunlit day. It's a mysterious, endless sort of coloration. It's a look that says it wants you to dive your soul into it; immerse yourself inside it; completely forget everything else and lose yourself in it. It's a drawing into it magnetic pull that tells you nothing else in the world matters other than going into it; loving being within it; loving becoming hopelessly drown in the depths of it.*

"*That same enticement in her deep blue pools is what makes sailors lose their sense of reality. That same mesmerizing pull of the mysterious beckons sailors to jump overboard and drown themselves in the ocean deeps. That same blue captivates Marty's fans. It bids them to drown their souls in her immoral sea and never look back.*

"*Marty knows exactly what she does and the effects she creates in the limbic zones of men. Her performances are far above and way removed from ordinary pornography, Bob. She works tirelessly to perfect her appearances, moves and sounds. Everything she does is calculated to steal men's affections away from their women and families and hold them captive to her spectacular body and alluring eyes. Her efforts pay hugely, getting her fame and lovers. It's also self-addicting and self-reinforcing.*

"*She has feelings for you, Bob, but she also has a switch that she flips. It allows her to be heartless and uncaring about others. That's sordid. It's her way of punishing the little girls who shunned her at boarding school. She's psychologically trapped in those years. Seductions are how she gets back at those girls. Getting back at them makes Marty feel good about herself. That feel good inspires her to seduce the next man and the next.*

"*She has the emotional maturity of a ten-year-old, packaged in a face and body that every man wants to date. Men don't under-stand the nymphomania aspects of Marty's behavior. Men are her unknowing, eager enablers. All they know is Marty enthusiastically welcomes them into her panties.*

"That deep psycho stuff controls much of your Marty's behavior. That is your real Marty. You are her reprieve from her private mental torture. You are her sanctuary. That's why she comes to you. She needs you. I don't know why, exactly. It may be that you are her Daddy substitute; for whatever reason, you are a type of therapy. And, until she defeats her addiction, Bob, she will not be a mentally healthy woman. Her mind lives in a world that is far apart from yours.

"Watching the ways she positions and accents her vagina for the cameras, inviting men into her with that butterfly tattoo, I can't imagine any male not wanting to go to her, embrace her, kiss her, perform cunnilingus with her, make love with her, and become lost in delirious lust with her. She's irresistible, beautiful, and she loves fucking and sucking cocks. That part of Marty is not an act. That is who she is. It's a powerful combination which most men can't resist." Barbara's eyes looked into Bob's, hopeful he was seeing the difference between mental illness and love, between what he had with Marty and what she, Barbara, was offering him.

"How can I tell if she loves me? Sometimes I wonder whether I'll lose her to someone she falls in love with on a porn set." Bob's feelings were still in Marty's grasp. He had trouble letting go of her. *"I mean, how am I supposed to know whether I'm her therapy crutch? I mean, when she flips the switch to me, is that time with me a different her, or is she the same her, getting her shot of normalcy? Am I some kind of prescription drug?"* Bob's eyebrows went up and far away from his mind. He was lost in the incomprehensible world of things that happen inside another person's head.

"I don't know. I'm not a shrink. But I don't think you'll ever lose her to another love interest. She has discovered intimate romantic love with you, Bob. It's the real love that every woman needs. Even porn stars need love."

Barbara turned her back to him, miffed that he still seemed to hold out hope that he could somehow transform the world's most notorious whore into a docile housewife. Then, Barbara reminded herself that Bob was a guy. Understanding women was doubly hard for men. She rallied and turned back to face Bob.

"But you will never know for sure, either. Will you? That's a problem for you, isn't it? Every time you boink her you'll have to wonder whether you're getting the real thing or whether you're just getting used as her practice round; her warm up prep for her next big porno scene, won't you? Is that how you want to live your life?"

"You hate her, don't you Barbara?"

"Yes, I do. I hate her guts. She's an asshole." Barbara's pain flowed openly. Then she rallied her composure. *"No, not really, I shouldn't have said that. I don't hate her. I have no right to hate her. I know her more as some new kind of animal that I've come across; and I am trying to learn its ways. Maybe she's destructive and dangerous, like a wolverine. Maybe she feeds on the helpless, like a snake that eats mice and rabbits. Maybe she has no pride or ethics, like a rat; and maybe she's like an amalgamation of all those animals. I don't know what she is.*

"Can't you understand, Bob? I'm trying to understand someone who is uniquely immoral and unashamed of being that way; actually, being proud of it. It's hard. I resent what she's done to us, but I do not hate her. She carries some tremendous emotional hurts inside her. I can't hate her for that. I'm being honest.

"Mostly I fear for her. Her life style creates enemies, even deadly enemies. Some people hate to lose and they repay destruction with destruction. In that respect, I fear for you because you may have her taken from you by someone who has an agenda. Then, you'll feel devastated and perhaps wonder why you didn't get out now and make a different choice.

"Bob, listen to me." Barbara placed her hands on his shoulders, *"I understand her childhood void and her psyche. My people try to understand. When you understand someone, really understand them, it is very hard to hate them. So, this is not about my hate. Because I understand her, I cannot hate her. I actually admire her perseverance and determination. I love seeing that in any woman, no matter what field of work she chooses. And I respect her grit. It helped her put her childhood into her past. She doesn't wallow in her tragedy, like many others do. She found a way to make money on it. She's quite amazing.*

"Honestly Bob, I envy her. Sex is an aphrodisiac for everyone, including me. I sometimes wonder how I would feel if I were as prurient as she; having so many lovers and all that notoriety. It must be a real trip.

"But I can't bring myself to be like her. My rearing was filled with love and nurture from wonderful parents. My moral code has pointed me in the opposite direction. I love children and family; and when I see what Marty does and how she revels in her victims' misery, she disgusts me. 'Why hasn't she chosen a different path?' I ask myself. 'Why did she choose this path? Why is she taking this path to perdition?'

"My feelings for her are a jumbled, mixed-up bag, because it's you that I care about. I sometimes try to make myself think about life the same way Marty does; but I just can't. I try to hate her, but I can't do that either. I sometimes try to love her, mostly out of compassion for her, but I can't quite get there either. I just throw up my hands and give up trying to understand her choices. But, finally, on some level, I find myself feeling for her, as if she's my mixed-up sister, trying to make it in a man's world. And I sometimes pray for her. And here we are, Bob; two friends caught up in Marty's sordid, erotic world." Barbara took a deep breath and sighed, holding back tears.

"True confessions, Bob. I've done more than just watch her movies. I've studied many of them, three or four times. I can not detect

a single skip in any of her films. There are no take outs or sudden jumps. Every film is flawless. What does that tell you?"

"What, that her mind enjoys her work?" asked Bob.

"Yes, and her body enjoys it too," answered Barb. She was confronting her reality, head on. *"Those films told me she wasn't acting. The Marty on screen is the real- life Marty. The camera men, set people and directors must love working with her. Her performances hardly need editing. From the first second until the last second of the last hour of every film, she gives and receives non-stop, breathtaking erotic pleasure. She could not do that unless she had tremendous focus. Teasing, foreplay, fucking, and sucking are her entire life. She's focused. She loves her experiences; and she doesn't let anything or anyone distract her.*

"She performs the most seductive scenes of all adult film stars. In several films she displays her wide-open vagina after several men have released inside her; their creamy white flows out of her. By studying her face while she performed those scenes, I knew she'd had multiple orgasms. She didn't fake her orgasms. They were real. I could tell. Then the camera focused on her vagina while she stimulated herself with a circular hand motion. Her vagina squirted from a fresh orgasm. I witnessed lust delirium."

Barbara recalled the film she was critiquing. She relived her viewing experience:

'Well, that was a nice surprise, how wonderful,' Marty giggled after her masturbation.

"The camera spotlights her beaming face. Her mouth is wide open; her beautiful red lips are pulled back, revealing her perfect white teeth and extended tongue. The hand not used to stimulate her vagina strokes one huge black cock after another as they shoot copious streams of white creation juice onto her tongue. She receives these spurts into her welcoming mouth, swallowing that first cock's cum to slake her lust, then savoring the rest of them like the connoisseur of semen protein that she is."

'Oh, you are so tasty delicious. Yummy, let me have all of you. That's it! Yum,' she whispers to the cocks.

"Each cock head receives her mouth's adoring congratulatory kisses, coaxing it to surrender more of its precious white to her. Her lust still unsatisfied, her sin loving lips suck out all remaining cum from its hosting shaft, like she's casually drinking a milk shake from a straw. The cock's life force is spent. Her grateful lips kiss the vanquished cock as if she's putting it to bed like it's her little baby. As cocks' erections fade, they shrink back into slumber. Proudly now, smiling comely from her beaming face, her lips kiss the head of a newly arrived cock."

'Oh, here's a beautiful new friend who wants to play with me. You'd like to play with me, wouldn't you? Oh, you would? She asks while the cock bumps up against her lips. 'Well, okay, I want to play with you, too. Come here my big strong handsome lover, let me kiss you,' she whispers with her sincere come-hither persuasion.

"Her lusting mouth opens, revealing her welcoming tongue. Her viewers believe the cock on the screen is their own. They watch in enraptured wonder, their own erections all very hard.

"Her scenes impress viewers with how much she enjoys stimulating herself and her partners and how she passionately loves cock sucking. She's masterful in the ways she preens and stretches out her body for the camera while using her props. The many ways she uses her tongue to coax cum from a penis is more sensuous than any other film actresses.

"Her methods to bring a cock to ejaculation are highly practiced and finely tuned. In her hands and mouth, the penis is constantly attended, coddled, and coaxed. She relates to the cock on its own terms. She understands what it loves and provides it. The cock rewards her mouth with its semen eruption. She continues loving it long after it erupts. By her kisses, tongue licks and head sucking, she coaxes its reservoir completely empty. The cock surrenders all it has to her mouth."

'Ohhh, Ahhh, Teee-Heee,'

"She laughs and giggles, making her sounds of joyful surprise and pleasure the entire time. Her fans know sex is her joy. There can be no doubt. Competing actresses approach cock sucking as if it's a chore. Many hurry their performances and their fans lose interest. They assault the penis to force it to comply. Marty is quite the contrast. She never hurries; she treats the cock with loving patience, like it's her best friend. There is nothing fake about Marty's feelings. She adores cocks. And she loves romancing them."

The inheritors of unfulfilled renown rose from their thrones, built beyond mortal thought. Far in the unapparent. (Percy Byssie Shelly: Adonais)

Alligators can't fly and butterflies can't swim, but with plane tickets and swimming pools, they can both do both. And, even choir girls can become whores if they'll just put their minds to it. (Rosemary Ness-Bitner, author)

What makes a great artist? That's all over the place, I suppose. The ones that stick in my mind are the ones that can make their work show me things the way my own mind would wish them to be, especially when that is not possible. (Rosemary Ness-Bitner, author)

I imagined being sentenced to read only romance novels day after day, and thinking I would surely go mad; but then I watched a determined buffalo plodding through deep snow, going forward, all by himself. He was going his own way. I don't know whether he knew where he was going, but I believe he must be a lot like me. (Rosemary Ness-Bitner, author)

CHAPTER EIGHT

Behold, a virgin shall conceive and bear a son, and shall call his name Immanuel. (Book of Isaiah, Chapter seven, verse eleven)

Behold, I was shapen in wickedness: and in sin my mother conceived me. (Psalm 49, verse five)

Who's your Daddy? (Title of a song by Toby Keith)

IMMACULATE ARTISTRY

"Marty's scenes are masterful and spell binding," continued Barbara, leaving her film review thoughts and returning to Bob's awareness lesson.

"One recent film is causing a sensation and her porn star ranking has skyrocketed because of it. It opens as her orgy partners lift her into position above a male partner's face. She demonstrates her abilities as a contortionist by performing an amazing mid-air side split, revealing her widespread butterfly wings above her partner's eager mouth. Her vagina hovers slightly above her partner's face, like a butterfly flutters above a flower. His tongue reaches up to her vagina, licking and stimulating her outer lips.

"The action portrays a butterfly's proboscis probing a flower to taste its nectar, but the sensing stem is anchored to her partner's mouth, the imaginary flower, instead of to the butterfly. It's opposite from the way butterflies suck nectar from their flowers, but Marty and her partners perform this act so convincingly that you can't tell the difference. The camera angles create the imagery of a proboscis

tongue anchored inside Marty's vagina, not in her partner's mouth. The film producer and the camera crew must have worked very hard to create that illusion. It's brilliant, spellbinding intimate artistry. The viewer imagines her vagina's movements control the rapidly probing proboscis tongue. Of course, the partner's tongue is controlled by his mouth.

"While she's being stimulated by her partner's tongue, the camera frames a close-up of Marty's smiling face. She rolls her eyes back into her upper eyelashes until only the whites of her eyes show. These frames capture her feelings of ecstasy. Marty often uses her eyes this way. Her fans recognize the significance of her eyes' roll up. It's her signal that her limbic mind has taken control of her feelings and the actions of her body. It's her way of saying she's become helpless; unable to hold herself back from committing sin. In this limbic mode, she cannot possibly be a wrongdoer. Her inner nympho self has taken control of her. She's become a victim of her own lustful wantonness. Her fans go crazy when she projects this image of herself. They empathize with her. They adore her. They eat up her act and beg for more of her.

"Suddenly a dry ice mist floods the stage. The Virgin Mary, as Marty, disappears. Then, the mist slowly dissipates. Marty is no longer the Virgin Mary. She reappears in a different costume. She is now Aphrodite, bedecked in an opened vest jacket of gold, diamonds and rubies, revealing her scintillating breasts. Two turtle doves perch on her shoulders, symbolizing her fertility. She wears her diamond studded cestus seduction belt, certain to make her irresistible; certain to beckon all who seek sinful intimacy.

"Next, her lovers appear from out of the retreating mist. They come to her. As the mist evaporates, Aphrodite Marty removes her vest, bearing her succulent breasts and up lilted, cherry red nipple buds. She stands, smiling, before the cameras; a sensuous nymph wearing only her cestus seduction belt. Her partners come to her and *surround her; twelve exceptionally handsome, naked men; all with beautiful, splendid penises.*

"Their penises salute Aphrodite with their fullest, eager to please, erections. The penises move closer to her, inviting her to touch and partake. Marty, as Aphrodite, greets each penis by standing before it; then bending down, and kissing it's adoring head. It is a preview of the scenes that soon follow. The first partner stands beside Marty, while Aphrodite Marty's eleven other partners leave her to take up their positions. The eleven lie down on their backs along a garden pathway. Their penises stand at full erection, like so many skyward pointing statues.

"The film next enters its highly dramatic, attention gripping phase. Marty challenges religious orthodoxy. When the camera returns for close-in viewing, her vagina is positioned above her first partner's penis. It's fully erect; eager to consort. Marty next performs a perfect ninety-degree, Chinese side-split movement while slowly lowering her cock craving, iniquitous vagina over the anxious awaiting cock.

Unbeknownst to Bob and Barbara, while Marty was creating her flawless performance; producing the most erotically intimate film ever made, Miss Shameless was whispering these words of encouragement to Marty:

'Remember: You are gorgeous; stunning; beautiful; desirable. You are lust obsessed. But be patient and deliberate. Think only of the cock in front of you. Focus. Concentrate on it. Lavishly praise it, love it, and speak your true loving feelings to it. Feel how you completely enjoy each and every cock while you copulate with it. Release your feelings with wild abandon.

'Enjoy every moment with every one of your cocks. Millions of awed men will see your performance. For the first time they will fully appreciate a woman's sexual capacity; and for the first time many will understand the truth that it is the woman who chooses

when to conceive; and which man or men she selects for that honor. Your performance will show that it was this woman's truth that brought forth the holy child, not the concocted imaginary tales, spun by bewildered imbeciles. Perform with love in your heart. Have conviction. Savor each cock. Project your ecstasy. Orgasm freely. You will be brilliant. My love is with you.'

"Film viewers hear Marty softly voice her gratitude to her partners:

'I'm glad you answered my plea for help,'

"The camera shows them lying on their backs before her, spaced along the garden's pathway, their penises eager to pay homage to Mary as Marty. The immoral scheme, masquerading as divine virtue, is about to unfold. Penises are all standing tall; firm and fully erect; awaiting their moment in history; seeking to make their contribution to religious glory.

"Each splendid cock is willing to assist. Each cock strains mightily, knowing that it was specially selected for its magnificent size and splendid beauty. The vessels within these living phallic statues pulse with blood's hot lust. Every drop of blood and semen within their columns aches and yearns to surrender unbridled lust to the beautiful sacrilegious goddess of uninhibited immoral love and unrivaled beauty. The cocks now resemble budding crocuses, each one rising majestically out of the earth, straining upward towards the sunlight; each eagerly yearning to be kissed by life-giving morning dew.

"But these phallic columns do not aspire to drink dew's cool water droplets; rather, they seek immersion within the heated slippery passion channel of the purposeful immoral whore who hovers over them. Marty, as Virgin Mary, smiles, contemplating her cock garden. Her eager lips part in a lust thirsting smile. Each cock is mindful. This day it will take its place in history. Each cock has prayed that it would be worthy to play its part in this grand mysterious destiny. Each penis silently wills itself to do its utmost to

please the beautiful, insatiable, unchaste whore who is playing the role of virgin. Each faithfully swears to attend to every whim of her delicious guiltless immorality. Each vow never to falter or fail the glorious whore during their precious erotic moments together. The cocks hear her spoken words:

'Thank you for offering to help me in my time of need,' speaks Marty's Mary. 'You know I desperately need your help. I want you big strong men to help me become pregnant, because my future husband, Joseph, can't make it happen. We have tried but nothing has happened. I need your semen sperm to help me make a baby.'

Marty's coquettish face pleads to the camera. Her lips pout. Her eyes blink convincingly. After all, what's a woman who desires to have a baby supposed to do?

'You'll all help me, won't you? You'll all fuck me really good, won't you? Please fuck me really good. I really need to be fucked. I must be fucked. Please don't hold anything back. You wouldn't turn away from a woman who needs your help, would you?'

"Each man, to a man, shook his head and pledged not to deny her. Then each stated his enthusiastic willingness to perform the conception miracle with her. Every man was anxious to inhale her heavenly scents and immerse his crocus stem in her conception vessel. Each cock understood that it was specially selected to enter Marty's Mary's sacred covenant place of holy procreation. Every man and cock pairing were resolute to perform at the highest level of pleasure, relieving the anguish that plagues this comely, distraught woman."

'Oh, thank you, and give praises to the Lord,' gushed Marty's Mary. 'I prayed so hard that you would all answer yes to my prayers. Let's make our love now. I'm ovulating. Let's not delay a moment longer. I want every one of you to come inside my vagina. Please give me everything that you hold within you. Spare nothing. We must not leave anything to chance. I must have your semen; all of it; from every one of you. I need all of you to ejaculate all your cum inside me."'

"Thus, being direct and innocent of any pretense, Marty's hips gyrated ever so slowly, all the while maintaining her perfect split. Her pink outer vaginal lips glistened with their natural moisture and lubrications as they conjoined with the first cock. Once she felt her vaginal lips touching the cock's head, she slowly guided the head into her pink inner lips in a gentle circular movement. She resembled a butterfly settling onto a flower.

"Such a beautiful scene had never been attempted before. Within the limbic zone of every viewer, a blissful rush of awe and an affirmative: *'Yes, that's it. You've got it. Now, thrust inside me. Yes, yes, yes. Fuck me. Oh, yes! Fuck me,'* message of empathetic love poured out for her. Empathy for the Madonna's plight was transformed into pornographic adoration. Ironically, the Holy Virgin's conception scene was being spectacularly played by the world's most incorrigible godless whore. Everyone observing Marty quenching her insatiable lust fires poured out their sympathies for her. Everyone watching her insemination scene profoundly loved her. It was pornographic; but it evoked empathy and it was spellbinding. It dazzled viewers; throttled their imaginations; evoked sympathetic love. They loved the performance and they loved Marty. In their eyes, she was no longer a profligate whore, but a desperate woman doing what was necessary to conceive. They forgave her 'bad girl' reputation. They projected only love and innocence onto her. They became crazed over her. Viewers instinctively knew they were seeing an honest portrayal of the truth. Abstinence was not the father of the holy babe! Unrepentant whoring by a desperate wife did that miraculously beautiful deed; and did it so breathtakingly beautifully."

Miss Shameless whispered to Marty again:

'Feel the stirring of delicious sexual freedom rising within you. Let its song sing through your entire body. Let its appetite resonate as you Kegel and twerk upon this cock. Coax the cock to reward you.

Smile. Hear your inner voice of lust. Radiate its joy. It's the song of conception's happiness, coming from your heart. It's beautiful. And, you are beautiful.'

"*While studying Marty's face, I saw a transformation taking place,*" described Barbara. "*Deep within Marty's bosom something breathtaking and primal stirred. Making love was more than fornication for pleasure. She underwent a profound change. I glimpsed her primal instinct to achieve pregnancy. The urge to conceive swept over her entire body. It reached a ravishing intensity. It radiated from her face and her entire body. I felt her warmth.*

"*I asked myself if I was witnessing the truth. Was I seeing nature's finest wonder, a beauty-blessed human woman transporting her feelings back through time; offering her body as more than a prostitute's workplace, but as the vessel of the holy procreation? That's when my revelation came. Marty was not performing this scene to incur rancor from Christianity. She was doing the opposite. She was being helpful to the Church. She realized that many, like herself, believe the Church's version of the Immaculate Conception story is based upon early Christians' ignorance and superstitions.*

"*The early church adopted those early beliefs and branded those who challenged these gospel orthodoxies as heretics. Witches, disbelievers, and Jews were burned at the stake if they dared to disagree with Church dogma. Worlds and civilizations were conquered and destroyed in the name of Church dogma. Marty, through her performance, sought to bring truth, remorse, and a more compassionate heart to the Church's teachings; and, actually thereby, to enlarge Church membership. By showing a more scientifically plausible explanation for Christ's conception, many who previously were skeptical about the entire legacy of Christ could, through Marty's realistic truth version, now accept the Church's faith on their own terms. After all, Christ did lot of good in the world. Challenging the Roman Empire took the courage of a true messiah. Look around you today, Bob. It is a rare man who stands up to the nonsense spewed by government bureaucrats. Think of the faith and courage that Christ needed to take on all of Rome! The Savior was no sissy.*

"Marty was already widely known for her previous film works. She was already acclaimed and honored for her whoring artistry at social events and awards ceremonies, Bob. She did not need to risk her fame or reputation for excellence by performing this difficult feat. But she did. She sought to unblind the Church by making a direct appeal to its followers. She sought to pry open orthodoxy to accept more than one explanation. She is a driven woman; never content to rest when a greater erotic challenge presents itself.

"For her role she changed from being a pleasure-seeking sex partner into a primal animal, relentlessly driven to conceive. Shameless lust and her unquenchable thirsting for cocks to impregnate her, threw off every other feeling that cloaked her inner essence. She was primordial, holy, beautifully spontaneous; and so very attention riveting. She detained my emotions; captured them within her cradle of lust. I knew I wasn't watching standard porn fare, Bob. I was observing a recreation vision of the conception miracle. I was spellbound; wonderstruck by how, through her acting, Marty could create sin art so divinely erotic; so convincingly real. She took my mind into that scene with her. I was there with her, watching her, praying for her impregnation. I emoted with her; adored her effort; and I believed it was all real. Maybe it was. I could think of nothing else.

"She emerged from her inner transformation, as if reborn and thirsting for new life, drawing her strength from some force deep inside herself, like a regal Monarch shedding its cocoon. She awed her viewers with her unbridled craving for cocks. Her film craft evoked ancestral stirrings of primal mating. Every viewer yearned to join his straining cock to her conception quest; like dogs panting to inseminate a craven bitch. While her viewers can't physically join her, they can slake their desperate limbic yearnings by purchasing

her film; and by joining her premium member service, for those who can afford her rates.

"The viewer imagines it is his proboscis that is securely anchored within her sex, protruding from her perfect open split. His is the feeding organ of her fluttering butterfly tattoo. Her beautiful butterfly vagina masterfully controls her partner's cock. She slowly raises and lowers her vagina making it appear to the viewer that the cock proboscis is dipping and raising within the flower's style, drawing nectar from the flower's ovary; while instead, the cock reaches from below, probes the depths and sidewalls of Marty's vagina; then retracts, after bathing in her delicious fluids. She and her partners perform their intimate dance of sexuality; relaxed, unhurried. Partners thoroughly probe her, much like a butterfly probes a flower's style and ovary with its proboscis, tonguing and prick-touching every recess of her feminine flower; savoring and basking in her tastes.

"The genius illusion Marty and her partners create is that the males are being deflowered. Only cocks' semen eruptions give lie to that illusion. Finally, the wide-open tattoo lowers itself slowly; but this time it does not lift back up. It fully engulfs the captivated penis. It rests upon the male partner's lower torso while Marty rolls her pelvis gently back and forth over the cock. Her butterfly is now flush against the flower beneath it, Kegel sucking every drop of nectar from it. Marty gently rotates her pelvis with her encapsulated penis in her slow circular motion, as if her butterfly's proboscis is scouring the inside of the male flower, drinking in its tasty nectar. The sensational stimulations which the cock receives deep inside Marty's vagina are irresistible. The cock spurts its white surrender fluids; and tries mightily to maintain its erection:

'Ohhh, that feels so wonderful! You're shooting inside me,' Marty marvels while heaping praises upon her partner and his cooperative cock. *'That's sooo good, baby. I'm cooing like a dove. Yes, yes! Oh, that's soooo loving, sooooo lovely. You're rewarding me for being*

a naughty girl, aren't you? You're making me so happy because you know that I love being naughty. You're being so good to this naughty girl. I love you for that. You're soooo good to me.'

"The cock continues rewarding Marty, as Holy Madonna Mary, with voluminous damn bursts of pulsing hot semen. She Kegel squeezes her precious prize while slowly moving her hips in a rolling, rocking motion. Her viewers watch, breathlessly anxious to witness the cock's capitulation.

"The camera close-up captures her softly squeezing, slight liftings and insertions of her illusory proboscis organ; as her tattoo alternatively smothers itself upon the male's body, then lifts to reposition her thirsting organ for its next downward envelopment of the cock.

"The camera alternately pivots from close ups of her vagina performing its wonders to zoom close ups of her smiling face. It captures the unbridled ecstasy in her beaming eyes. Her eyes visualize the captured cock as it thrusts high up, inside her; pulsing its semen; straining mightily to impregnate her. Her face is serene, contented, joyful and confident. She knows that her historic conception secret is safe. While her butterfly is drawing its sustaining nectar from the surrendering cock, the camera records the proboscis tongue-cock and her tattoo, moving together, rhythmically, in slow motion. Then, her life creating motion intensifies. Her face radiates with its fullest divine expression. The viewer now becomes one with Marty's face and body. The male flower surrenders its fluids! Marty has her own shuddering climax! Marty is magnificent and beautiful while she portrays this holy act of conception. She is transformed from mere mortal to Holy Madonna. She creates erotic intimate film at the mysterious pinnacle of wonder-awe.

"Its purpose finished, the first proboscis-cock gently detaches from its tattoo winged hostess, revealing the pink, open underbody of the nectar-thirsting butterfly, once again. Miraculously, Marty maintains her perfect Chinese split. The viewer sees her butterfly vagina has *now been filled with white nectar taken from the first male's depleted flower. Her fingers hold her butterfly's underbody lips open widely for the camera's breathtaking close-up. The unapologetic, shamelessness of her deed! Her vagina quivers from her pulsing muscle contractions, sending ripples through her captured semen pool. The subliminal message to the viewer is that the butterfly remains unsatisfied. It thirsts for more. It must search out another flower.*

"The camera rivets the viewer's focus into a seductive close-up of Marty's cherubic open mouth receiving cum paste from her fingers. Her semen filled mouth occupies the entire screen. Smiling her winsome open mouth smile, she rolls cum upon her tongue and rolls her angelic eyes heavenward. Giggling, she swallows the nectar she lovingly extracted from her partner's flower. The coquettish child-like smile from a delightfully naughty girl's wholesome, radiant, joyous face slowly fades. Her face becomes a puzzled wonder. She asks:

'Oh, dear, I wonder if that will be enough to get me pregnant?' She teasingly asks the camera, leaving her fans pining for more of her. During this brief pause they remain bonded to her ecstasy. 'I'm not sure. How can I be sure I'll get pregnant unless I make love with every one of these men? Yes, now I understand what I must do! I must create a love child. The Spirit told me that my love child would save the world. So now I must harvest all the cocks in my garden to make sure I become pregnant. I must create a child that will save the world from sin!'

"Marty's female assistants, portrayed as mythical sex goddesses Athena, daughter of Zeus, and Hera, wife of Zeus, lift her from her first cock, now spent. Her assistants kiss her mouth and pinch her nipples as they carry her, like a fluttering butterfly, to her next encounter.

'Wheee, this is fun!' she giggles to her assistants. 'I want to do this forever. The two of you make me feel immortal! Oh! Yes, and yes! Kiss me! Did I excite you? Was I beautiful? Did you like watching

me do what I did? Were you proud of me? You ladies are so strong! When I finish having all these flowers, may I have you, too? I can't believe I'm having so much fun! Take me to another flower!'

"Another male takes his place beneath Marty's cum-thirsting butterfly. Athena and Hera shed their robes, revealing their white bodices. A male wearing a golden crown joins the scene. Marty arches her back, presenting her perfect button nipples to the mythical goddesses on both sides of her. She throws her head back; her face looks to the sky. She opens her mouth to receive incestuous kisses from her newly arrived king Zeus while her two supportive women stand firmly beside her. Their hands lovingly caress her torso and back.

"Her body quivers like an excited fluttering butterfly about to drink from another flower. Her worshiper-handlers position her perfectly above her next flower. As she again performs her breathtaking Chinese split and flutters her nectar-seeking vagina over the second cock, her two companion nymphs kiss her cherry-button nipples, stimulating her with their loving tongues. Their loving hands support and position her pelvis over the cock. They then assist her by gently supporting her pelvic rhythms as she rocks her insatiable vagina back and forth and gyrates sensually with the penis safely captured inside her.

"Marty has transformed. She has become Aphrodite, daughter of Zeus and eternal goddess of love and lust, daughter of Zeus and Hera. Her spectacular relentless whoring is blessed and championed by the kisses of her helpful immortals. The film projects Marty's insatiable cock-lust as a naturally necessary craving, inspired by heavenly forces. She is in the process of being transformed from a mere earthly woman to a divine, sexual being; part goddess, part mortal. She is becoming the mythical human bridge between mortals' life-seeding flower cocks and the erotic procreation needs of the gods.

"Mocking virginal innocence, Marty dons a head wreath and a garland neckless fashioned from white gardenias, symbolic of her

virgin goddess status. Her serene smile tells the viewers that her mind hears a song of holiness. Divinity is blessing the unquenchable lust forces building inside her. These forces are stronger than simple love. They cause a deeper craving than an orgasmic passion burst. They are the wildness of Marty's untamable love of lust itself. They flow out of every pore of her body with sin-loving radiance that men seek to possess as their own. Marty is playing Mary, captured in the throes of her transformational passion. She plays the part brilliantly. She's a natural.

"Marty's love of lust's passions also streams from her eyes. It's a hypnotizing look of overwhelming enticement, summoning males whose eyes meet hers to come to her; kiss her, love her, cavort shame-lessly with her, and forsake their very souls to become one with her; if not in body, then vicariously, in mind. And, many do fall in love with her. They cherish her and the cavalier debauchery she person-ifies. Their minds drink from her well-spring of eternal, glorious, shameless sin. They savor the explicit images she affixes to their minds, Bob. She is their dream goddess, their perfect love.

"She performs her spectacular routines to the sounds of the Ave Maria, signifying divine glory of her lust. Her ecstasy hardened nip-ples respond to kisses from her lust crazed sister, Athena, and her incestuous mother, Hera. Like their ancient namesake goddesses who hated Troy, these modern enablers confirm their disdain for moral decency. Marty smiles serenely. Her enablers' kisses have relaxed her limbic ordering. Her mind becomes obsessed with for-nication. During the brief respites between cock flowers, Marty's attending goddesses apply copious helpings of lubricating jells to her vagina, thus ensuring that, as Aphrodite, she experiences continu-ous sensual ecstasy from every cock she pleasures in her imaginary virgin's vagina. The cohorts apply their lubrications while laughingly bantering with Marty, expressing enthusiastic approval of her insa-tiable whoring. They tease about the seriousness of her impregnation

mission; stimulate her with their fingers while kissing her cheeks, lips, and nipples; dramatizing their encouragement. They perform their sex-worship with joy and honor. The divine virgin whore has entrusted them to keep confident her task.

"Handmaidens Athena and Hera champion the virgin's whore-lust, suckling her as if to stimulate her future milk flows; fondling her to reassure her sexuality while she seduces one mortal man after another. While writhing to the touches of her companion goddesses, Marty again fashions the image of a proboscis thirsting cock, drawing semen-nectar into her insatiable butterfly. She perfectly, repeatedly, performs this optical illusion. It is stunning in its artistic originality and more erotic than any film scene ever created. Viewers are left awe-struck and breathless. Their minds expand, trying to grasp that one woman copulated with twelve cocks in succession while maintaining the erotic splendor of every seduction. It's hard for viewers to fathom the never-before performed explicit eroticism they just witnessed.

"The beautiful sexuality of Marty's theatrical performance lifted my mind to another time and place, Bob. I thought I had to be dreaming. I had to be imagining more than I was seeing. Aphrodite's spirit in Mary, played as Marty, was being attended to by Hera and Athena, and I was suddenly there, whoring with the three of them. But we were no longer on a film set. We were outdoors in the open air, laughing together on a hilltop grove of riot colored cherry and dogwood blossoms, feeling the new life of springtime breezes dancing across a soft undulating meadow of fresh spring grasses.

"I was touching my fingers over Marty's creamy white skin, kissing her inviting nipple buds, and her mouth with my mouth. My fingers were inside her and hers were inside me. I kissed her neck and hugged her close to me, and our faces and eyes met where our foreheads joined. We smiled and laughed briefly. There I was, moral monogamous me, telling the world's most immoral whore that I loved her, that I loved watching her perform, and that I adored her

shameless debauchery because it made something within me come alive, like nothing else ever could. Then, I snapped out of my trance and reassembled my composure. But I continued watching her, wishing I could free myself from all my taboos, so I could go to her and love her, for real.

"Like Aphrodite, film goddess Marty's Mary encouraged her performing mortals to consort with her. Imitating Aphrodite's insatiable passion lust, Marty wanted to take from every man his seed, his life-giving essence. She whispered soft audible words of seduction to each of her cocks:

'Send your life-giving seed up my probe. I need to feel your hot gushing cum shooting into my womb. I want every single drop. Give it to me. Give it to me. Give it to me. I want all of it, all of it, all of it. Let me feel your life inside me. Love me. Yes, love me now. Love me. Love me.'

"After she drew the fertility giving semen from a vanquished cock, it softened and wilted. It was a spent force. Aided by her handlers, Marty moved to the next cock. Her vagina was once again positioned perfectly over the glistening erection tower which was anxious to join her in passion lust. Her viewing fans are spellbound, enraptured by the tireless, shameless feats of their insatiable whoring nymph-goddess. Like Aphrodite, Marty has zero self doubt and zero reflective guilt. Look closely at her face, Bob. This is the woman you love. Doesn't it affect you the least little bit to see how much she loves having sex with all these different men? Her face, Bob. That wide smile, those tongue flicks, those giggles, and laughs! Clearly, she loves fucking cock after cock after cock. There's no inhibition or guilt or self-consciousness in that face; no consideration whatsoever that what she is doing is sacrilegious and immoral. None. She's flaunting her opposition to all things moral, Bob. She's challenging the foundation of the Christian religion and the very concept of morality. She's open and confident about her whoring."

"Yes, Barb, I see it. I do, okay?" Bob was uncomfortable. Part of him, his limbic mind, adored what Marty was doing in that film. The other part, his conscious mind, resented being forced to admit that the woman he loved was a shameless whore who seemed indifferent between making love with him and making love with her porn partners.

"Oh, do you? Keep watching her, Bob. Notice her beaming face? That's success, pride, and glory you are seeing. That's a woman's face who is silently announcing that she's on top of the world, Bob. Your darling Marty has the world by the tail. She gleefully promotes her immorality. Like the goddess she portrays, Marty is supremely proud of her whoring; confident she is unrivaled, atop the highest pedestal of sin-craft; and confident-certain that her performance will draw her fans ever closer to her. This film, more than any of the ones she made before, shows her certitude about the rightness of her life choices.

"She's a fuck manic, nymphomaniac whore, through and through, Bob. She's into her profession. Having a family is the furthest thing from her mind. You come second in her life, Bob. Those men in that film, her flower cocks, they come first. Her compulsion to fuck all of them comes first.

"Because of this film, she knows her fans will love her more than ever before, much, much more. After all, how many porn stars can perform a perfect Chinese split? How many can hold that split while they fuck twelve different cocks? How many others have made film that can show their pussies gleaming and thirsting for cock after cock like Marty's film shows? Not many. Likely, not any. Those gleeful smiles from her eyes bespeak the pride with which she flaunts her deliciously beautiful fornication-crazed vagina. She captures every emotive passion in her fans' souls, leaving them erotically addicted to her.

"Think of this, Bob. Every night and day, millions of men bask in awe's adoration of this breathtaking explicit performance. Their blood becomes passion-crazed. They are hotly aroused to a state of

desires that no other erotic actress has ever caused them to expe-rience. They are anxious for the next film installment that Marty will release. They crave more and more of her limitless lust. It's an infinite, endless craving; an abyss of immorality that can never be filled. It's adoration. It's insanity. Her millions of fans cannot get enough of her.

"Maintaining her open vagina, revealing her Chinese split, Marty artfully portrays the image of a joyful carefree butterfly in a spring meadow. She visits cock flower after cock flower. Dutifully, happily, she partakes of the nectars eagerly offered up to her by every anxious cock. Her face is angelic, irresistibly beautiful, heaven blessed. She smiles a gloating smile of satiation while her genitalia savor every semen shot from every cock. As divine Mary, she is obey-ing the Genesis commandment to become fruitful and multiply. She is sowing the seeds that make life possible. She is serenely happy as she flutters from cock to cock. Like a butterfly's face enthralled by an endless supply of nectar, Marty's mouth beams a grateful smile for the bountiful supply of semen she harvests from the cocks. The camera focuses on her lips as she speaks:

'I am soooo happy,' she coos. 'I'm savoring delicious nectar sips from each fresh flower. I am making love with my dozen cock flow-ers in my lovely cock garden. I love feeling their delicious hot semen pulsing up inside me. The cocks all feel soooo wonderful! I love the love they are giving me! They all LOVE ME! They are wonderful! I LOVE FLUTTERING WITH THEM!'

"Her erotic portrayal of a rapacious, nectar thirsting butterfly is glorious. She creates masterful erotic artistry. This latest creation is a believable depiction of a historical event. It creates 'buzz,' that word of mouth follow-through that causes many viewers to watch the film more than once. Some viewers are so addicted to the inti-macy, the artistry, and the profound messaging of this film that they will see it ten times or more.

"For Marty's finale she maintains her split while dropping to her elbows before her last cock. This scene begins the most controversial segment of the film. It revisits time and reinterprets history. Marty is a contortionist with amazing strength and body control. She holds herself open, displaying her sex high in the air, flaunting her oozing, creamy white semen pool. The camera zooms to focus upon her elevated underside, as if viewing a nectar filled butterfly from underneath its wings; and then it takes the viewer to a close- up of Marty's smiling open mouth as it welcomes the ejaculation of the cock she lovingly caresses in her hands. She smiles a sweetly innocent coquettish smile to the camera as it conducts a close-up exploration her radiant face. The close-up reveals Marty's breathtaking beauty and her pride in her shameless on-camera whoring. She portrays the holy Madonna as a glorious, uninhibited sexpot who craves to fornicate even more:

'I must now find my future husband, Joseph,' she declares to the cock, as if she is speaking with a real live person. 'I must become a good and dutiful wife. I must run to him and make love with him. I must make Joseph come inside me. If I have become pregnant today, Joseph must believe my child is his; and who could ever say that it is not his?'

"The Ave Maria sanctifies Marty's fornications as Mary. By inseminations from many lovers in her orgy's cooperative effort, she portrays the promise that her vagina is the only true, real, and sacred, Holy Grail; and that the baby she will birth will save the souls of all humankind. Her film challenges the Church's Immaculate Conception story. She stands religious orthodoxy on its head.

"By her film imagery, Marty unashamedly proclaims that her vagina has more logical validity and right to explain mankind's salvation than the Church's version. Instead of one mythical spirit causing the miraculous insemination of Mary, her film suggests that multiple human participants were involved; and that her deed was *psychologically and morally appropriate. Since all the world's sinners must be saved by Mary's son, it is only fitting that many sinners must contribute to the challenge of human salvation. Her body will take the insemination product of their collective sins and transform those sinful products into a righteous child. Her performance provokes us to consider that real, plausible human need caused Mary's Holy Grail to receive its insemination from a multitude of cocks, rather than from a mysterious ethereal spirit.*

"The radiant beams from Marty's beautiful face, her mirthful eyes, smiling lips, and joyful tongue now romance the last adoring penis. Her unbridled happiness sharply contrasts with the dour pusses that don the somber faces of many priests. Her personal beliefs must have compelled her to include this final scene. She obviously possesses great conviction that her beliefs are as strong as any priest's.

"After Marty's mouth receives the ejaculation from the last cock, a naked man wearing a carpenter's belt appears. He plays the role of Joseph, her husband. His member is erect and hard. Watching Marty fornicate with twelve men has gotten him excited. He is nearly out of his mind, bursting with adoration and passion's love lust. Marty, as Mary, rises and stands naked before him.

'Joseph, dearest lover of all my lovers,' she looks sheepishly into his eyes, 'the Spirit came over me and told me I must bear a child to save all mankind. Help me obey the Spirit. Make love with me. And, Joseph, I must be known as the mother of the child that saves the world, and not as an incorrigible whore who loves to fornicate. I need you to become my husband, Joseph. My holy child must be seen to have a virtuous mother. Will you become my husband and take me as your wife? I am ovulating. This must be our time, Joseph. Will you try again? Will you father our child?'

"Marty opens Joseph's carpenter's belt and lets it fall away from her hand to the ground. She opens her arms and embraces him. He returns her embrace. The two kiss long and soulfully.

'Yes, Mary, I will honor you. You shall be my wife to hold and to keep, and our child shall save the world from sin,'

"Joseph speaks to her with prideful eyes. He beholds Marty's stunning beauty. He knows the woman he is about to marry is an unrepentant, unapologetic, shameless whore; but he does not care. Love streams from his eyes. She is a living goddess and his wife to be. He tells her what she longs to hear:

'You shall become known as the most virtuous woman among all women. I am proud of you for honoring the calling of the Spirit.'

"In Marty's version of the Immaculate Conception story, Joseph's eyes do see Mary as a whore, but that does not for one second dissuade him from marrying her. Au contraire, she will be his adored and loved wife. He decides to play along to get along; and, no doubt, to also get a lot. Mary will become the holy Madonna who bears his child. Joseph accepts and blesses her many fornications. He cherishes Mary, appreciates her efforts to conceive and loves her with the whole intensity of his being. She will become the mainstay of their household and a continuing presence in the mortal life of their son.

"Now grateful for Joseph's acquiesce, Marty, as Mary, teases Joseph's penis against her sex, wildly stimulating him into a frenzy state. Joseph's lust waxes intensely through his loins. Marty understands her sexual powers very well. She kneels before Joseph and kisses his penis. He holds her head in his hands. He throws his head back. Moans of anticipation escape his throat. He is wild with desire. Marty has engulfed his cock in her mouth and is performing exquisite fellatio. He is more than willing and anxious to perform his part in the Conception Story. He is so excited to make love with Marty, he can barely constrain himself; but he must wait and follow the script of the story.

"Marty, role playing Mary, draws Joseph down to the ground with her, assumes the missionary position and lies with him. There, amidst the dozen expended flower cocks, the two kiss passionately *and make love, sweetly, lovingly. When Marty thinks the cameras have seen enough foreplay, she gently wraps her legs around Joseph, pulls his cock deeply inside her, cradles him within her legs and gently rocks his body back and forth. They are a believable, loving couple, fornicating lovingly as if they are on their honeymoon and discovering love for the first time.*

'I feel it had to be this way,' thinks Marty as Mary, as she strokes the back of Joseph's neck, 'I'm feeling its majesty myself, here and now. A feeling of goodness and holiness is coursing through my blood. I'm having more than a passion high from sex now. I'm being lifted from my own body by some invisible hand. It's raising me higher to meet a spiritual presence. This divine presence is kissing my head; and now my mouth. It's speaking silently to me. Its thoughts are going into my own thoughts.

'It is telling me that what I have done is good and wonderful; and that my portrayal of the Immaculate Conception is true and accurate; and that I'm performing a great service to the world. It is telling me that I'm freeing many minds from their mental prisons. OOOOHHHH, the Spirit's hand is inside my vagina now, stimulating me, massaging my clitoris. How marvelous! Now, it is lifting me up! I feel my insides tumbling over and over. These are wonderful feelings which I've never felt before. I must have more of what I'm feeling. And the Spirit is telling me I will have those feelings with this man called Joseph.'

"Marty, as Mary, now changes positions with Joseph. She mounts him, sitting astride his hips, her vagina yearning for his cock. Slowly, methodically, she rocks her vagina over his cock while leaning backward and smiling her thoughts to the heavens:

'Bless me, Holy Spirit for what I am portraying here today. More than acting out, Spirit, I am feeling a closeness to you like I've never felt to anyone before. May my fornication with this man, this Joseph in my film, be pleasing in your sight.'

"One by one, Mary's disciple partners now come to her and kiss her mouth, neck, shoulders, back, and torso as if to sanctify her conjugation with Joseph. They suckle her breasts to stimulate milk flows for her future child. They hold her torso to help her lift and descend upon Joseph's penis. They seem to understand that her whoring has now become a holy act, commanded by the Spirit.

"Gradually, almost imperceptive in her subtle sensuality, Marty begins to twerk her sacred jewel upon Joseph's cock. Her slow movements quicken until her thoughts transcend into a subliminal other-worldly nirvana state:

'Oh, this feeling inside me is like no other. I've fallen back in time to a happening that took place over two thousand years ago! How can this possibly be? It feels so true and so right! Oh, my sex! I feel something I've never felt before. I feel as if my sex is on fire. My God! My God! Please forgive me. I have become a crazed woman! I must have this man. I must have his cock, forever. His name is Josh. Yes, Josh plays the role of Joseph. I must remember him. Yes! Oh, how MUCH I love making love with him! This is all so BEAUTIFUL! What a wonderful, splendid loving man. He's SO strong. He stays SO firm inside me. Oh, yes! I can feel him filling me. I know he must LOVE me. He loves me for who I am! He wants a life with me. Yes, yes, he does.'

"Oh, my darling Joseph, I love what your cock is doing inside me. Oh, yes, Joseph, have me as your wife, and love me." Marty whispers and moans. Then, she becomes lost in her thoughts again:

'This must be exactly how the Holy Madonna felt. My blood feels these raging flames. My arteries tingle like they're going to burst, and my brain is pounding and buzzing like I'm going to have a stroke from so much sex. I'm having a runner's high; but this is so much higher! It's like a runner's high, combined with a niacin overdose blood rush. I'm exhausted from all the sex I've had. My body is telling me I must stop, but I CAN NOT stop. I CAN NOT. I love this high that I'm feeling from making love with Josh, as my Joseph, so much *so, that I SIMPLY CAN NOT stop myself. I CAN NOT stop loving this partner, Josh. I CAN NOT. I WILL NOT. I LOVE him. I MUST have him. I want more of him; all of him, forever. Oh, GOD, I love his hot throbbing cock soooo much! I'm going to push myself beyond my physical limits. I don't care what happens to my body. My body will have to accept my overwhelming need to continue making love.'*

"*Bob, the film has one telling blooper. I heard the camera man whisper to the director. He asked if he should stop filming. It was obvious that the scene had spiraled off script. You can hear the director telling him no. He tells him to keep going. He knows what their filming is capturing. Marty was becoming a woman consumed with sex. She was a nympho suddenly consumed in a lust frenzy with her favorite performing partner, Josh. She could not bring herself to stop fucking. She was going to fuck until she collapsed. It was rare to capture a scene that intense, on film.*"

Marty's limbic thoughts took possession of her mind, pushing away everything other than her love making:

'I am consumed with love for this man Josh, my Joseph! Oh, my dearest Joseph, you used your mouth sooo well' Marty was tumbling freely through another world with her thoughts now. *'My love! My body heat is raging like an inferno of wonderment for this man inside my loins. I am so in love with this man. Something more is happening than sex on a film set. I feel this wonderful magical power running through every cell in my body. Can it be? Can I be experiencing the same holiness that the true Madonna felt? Oh, my GOD! YES! I am! I feel it! I'm going to come soon. Oh yes, I'm going to release everything inside of me very soon. It's here. I'm ready now. I'm going to pop. I can't hold back any longer. Soon, soon, SOON! NOW! OH YESSSSS! OH, MY GOD, YES! OH YES! OH GOD, that feels SOOO GOOD! Here I am, my sweet Joseph. I'm yours. I'm yours forever. Here I am!'*

"*Marty moans, open mouthed, her loud, almost inhuman primal moans; then she trembles. Her body convulses in her orgasm ecstasy.*

Her twerks come faster. Her stimulation is enhanced by a disciple using his hand and fingers to stimulate her crown and clitoris while Joseph's cock strains mightily to reach full length and thickness.

"More touches, more kisses and hugs of encouragement follow from her disciples. Trembling body convulsions and orgasm after orgasm continue until Marty, as Mary, experiences twelve orgasm raptures of heavenly intimacy with her betrothed. Joseph joins his semen to her sacred conception pool. He cries tears of joy. He has performed his task.

"He knows she wants him to claim that her love child is his. And he will claim it; feeling fully justified doing so. After all, when the world is taxed in the following year, Joseph will report his taxes to Caesar on a LIFO, or Last in, first out, tax basis. (According to Joseph's CPA and Caesar's latest amended and revised Internal Revenue Service tax code for child care credits, Joseph was last man to pump semen into Mary's vagina; so, the child, surely, had to be his!)

Exhausted now, our Marty's Mary lifts her insatiable honey pot from Joseph's cock and nestles it lovingly upon his mouth. His semen is already racing up her fallopian tubes. In the chaotic race of sperm, one of Joseph's edges out all the others' sperms before it. Despite the other sperms' head starts, Joseph's seed is the winner. It sprints to the finish line and impregnates Mary's egg.

Marty suddenly feels something a woman is not supposed to feel! She felt like a sudden weather front had suddenly passed. It dropped her body temperature one degree. It was a subtle feeling, but real. She knew she felt it. Tenderly she caresses Josh's head, as Joseph, while his tongue titillates and savors her magnificently insatiable clitoris. She cannot help but wonder:

'Did I actually just become pregnant; for real?'

Marty shelves her thought about pregnancy. She's too enraptured with her feelings of sexual satisfaction to dwell on the consequences at this time. She completely surrenders this new feeling of divine love to her film partner. Josh has witnessed her immoral whoring with her disciples. He understands that their exhortations, kisses, and touches during her love making with him were all intended to give their blessing wishes to her immaculate conception should the child be not his, but one of theirs.

Josh watched while Marty, as Mary, slaked her passions. He is not jealous, nor does he feel inadequate in any way. He adored the beauty and glory of her procreation effort. He now reveres her as his sexually completed wife. And he loves her! He knows that what happened on set this day was a spiritual experience for both of them. She is his consummate sex partner. She's inspired him and throttled his imagination. Could she be someone more than his inspired film-mate, playing honored wife and Madonna to be? Could they build on this love?

He wants to see her away from the film set and continue being her lover. He whispers honest desire to her ear:

'You've set me on fire, baby. I can't get enough of you. Can we talk later? I want to see you; date you. What do you say?'

Marty's eyes look lovingly into his and she nods her head in agreement. She wants to see him again; alone, just the two of them; and no cameras. She can't say no. He ignited her fires like never before. She has orgasmed but she can not come down from her high.

She slides her slippery, sweated, naked body onto her Joseph partner, still holding his shrinking penis inside her. She kisses him wildly, desperate to prolong her euphoric sensations. Unscripted, Marty holds her partner's head between her hands. Her eyes find his.

"I've fallen in love with you, Josh. I love you, Josh. I totally love you. I'm completely in love with you, yes, absolutely I want to see you." she openly declares, her words captured by the still open microphone.

Barbara, ever alert, caught the faux pas in the film: *"By calling her partner Josh instead of Joseph, Marty strayed off her scripted lines. Her fans have momentary confusion. Did she muff the name of Joseph and confuse it as Josh; or is Josh her film partner's real name? Is Josh her nick name for Joseph? There's no doubt the film contains a blooper; but it is so titillating and erotically stimulating, the producer leaves it in, uncut.*

"It's not clear whether she speaks as a woman who just found love with her performing partner, a man named Josh, or whether she speaks as a confused Mary to Joseph. Either way, Marty's fans go wild. This sex scene is beyond anything they've ever seen before. The eroticism of this film scene floods over her fans, as they comprehend what she's done. So many lovers! So many orgasms! She has her fans eating out of her hand. She can do no wrong! She is their goddess.

"Then, after she declares her love to her partner Josh, the camera zooms to a close up of her face. It's Marty's same angelic porcelain doll face, but this time there's a slight difference in her appearance. Her make up is slightly smudged and her mascara has run a little. Her smile has her same Mona Lisa-like look, but now there's something different in her eyes. They are looking far away into the distance, like they are trying to behold the wonders of life by gazing at a faraway star.

"That scene was another epiphany for me, Bob. Of course! It was suddenly obvious to me! Marty's mind and emotional make up are wired totally opposite most women's minds. A normal, mentally healthy woman sees romance as a prelude to intercourse, marriage, kids, and family life; but for Marty sex is the prelude to romance. That's it! There's no follow through. There's no marriage. No kids. No family life; just a short, fast cycle, like you get from a short cycle washing machine. It's just sex, then romance; and then sex again and romance again; and so on without end. That's what love is like,

inside the mind of a nymphomaniac! It's instant gratification, dead-end love!

Meanwhile, Marty's fans are left confused, titillated, wondering if possibly, just possibly, their beloved Marty has fallen in love for real; right there on the film set; and before their very eyes. Could it be? Her fans are left dumbfounded: did real true love finally happen for Marty?

'Did we just witness that?' they ask.

Many hope that love did happen for her because her fan base truly loves her and wants only happiness for her. But many other fans selfishly hope not. They fantasize that they will some day make love with her, themselves; and they do not relish the idea that she might someday give up her promiscuous ways; or, at the very least, they hope she will continue creating porn, producing many more erotic romance films to stroke their fantasies.

Finally, the frenzied love making scene ends. The on-screen lovers sit side by side. Marty hugs Josh and lovingly rubs his back. She feels warm, complete, and pleased that he, as Joseph, understood Mary's sexual needs. Something is going on that transcends the film art they've created. Fans who study Marty's every move know they just witnessed something profound. They intuited that she cherishes and adores her film partner Josh, who played Joseph. He is her loving, understanding, perfect husband on screen. They intuit further; likely he will also be her lover, off screen.

This film and its strong undercurrents of romance drive Marty's fans totally crazy. They obsess over it. Its reviews are through the roof; positive. The film is acknowledged as the ultimate masterpiece of erotic romance. Without having copies of it in their erotic film libraries, her fans feel they would fail Marty and be incomplete human mortals. The film becomes their sine qua non. Many fantasize, pretend imagine, that they are Josh and that they have finally attained love with their dream woman. Thousands will watch this film a dozen times or more.

"Marty did something huge with this film, Bob. Most erotic stars make films of themselves making love with the gardener or the auto mechanic or the delivery man. But Marty reached back into scripture and reinterpreted it! That's likely the direction she'll take in her future work as well. She'll have a wealth of material, reinterpreting scripture, the classics, nostalgic films, fables, all sorts of materials are there for her choosing. I see where she's going with this. She's going to make billions! Her latest film was pure genius!

"The symbolism that film conveys is clear. Whether the child who Mary conceives will be Joseph's or not, all that matters to Mary and Joseph is that her love child 'could' be his child. The married couple now lie there contented, looking skyward, hugging, smiling, and kissing. They are erotic romance film performers, but they are also now one with Adonai, the Hebrew God; complete in their love. They have fulfilled their holy obligation. Copulation in their biblical day was considered holy, good, and beautiful. Today's reenactment of life's mystery was spellbinding. The film will become known as a work of theological and intellectual art, a controversial masterpiece to be pondered through the ages.

"Their performance honored God, in Mary's interpretation, as Mary and Joseph were commanded. The original performers of the actual Immaculate Conception could not know on that holy day; but they did something more profound than shatter moral inhibitions. They created, out of their love, a splendid young man of conviction. And they set him upon a path that would rock Caesar's mighty Roman empire; and shake it loose from its foundations. Their son would grow into a man who changes the belief system of the world. The beauty of the film is that everyone already understands its profound significance. There's zero significance in erotic films that portray a housewife screwing her milkman!

"*The camera focuses again on Marty's face. She is smiling a glowing divinely inspired smile. The Mona Lisa's face pales in comparison to Marty's more beautiful tightly pored, peach complexioned face and beguiling smile. Marty's is the contented smile of a holy Madonna who knows she is blessed in a sacred way, and who also knows she has a loving, understanding husband. Her face tells all. She obviously loves her set partner dearly. Their sex fest could not have been faked. It had to be real. Marty is obviously confident and certain of set partner Josh's unconditional love for her as well. As Madonna and in real life, Marty knows she is doubly blessed. Despite Mary's storied difficulties at becoming pregnant, surely, she will now conceive, completing the biblical story; and possibly, as Marty, she has conceived for real, in the here and now.*

"*Marty's Mary knows she honored and fulfilled Adonai's overriding mitzvah: to conceive, multiply and fill the Earth. Through her film art Marty relived and obeyed the most holy of all commandments. Marty feels secure in the knowledge that, as Mary, she portrayed her mitzvah duty perfectly and found favor with God.*

"*Marty inhales a deep breath, lifting her fantastic breasts for another camera close-up. Her cherry pink nipples display her inviting sacred nub crowns atop their perfectly rounded white mounds. They glisten with wet excitement from the lavish attentions of the actresses who played Athena and Hera. Marty's fans are enthralled by her delicious buttons, wishing they, too, could suckle them. They must be satisfied with using their imaginations; for Marty's buds are for her actual lovers and performance partners and for her fictitious love child, the holy infant. Marty, Joseph's Mary Madonna, one and the same, believe in the conception story from this moment until long after her child achieves manhood, becomes crucified and buried, and is resurrected. Biblical Mary could not know it this day; but centuries after birthing her child, the Church will declare her to be the Holy Mother of God.*

"Mary will attain sainthood. Her deed this day will be declared holy. Today her chest, represented as Marty's chest, fills with wonder and pride. She can not know that her fornications with her orgy partners will be blessed by future Popes as a miracle of faith. She rejoices in her beautiful deed of conception. She is pleased with herself. She has achieved glory. She whispers:

'Thanks be to God.'

"She knows she will conceive. In her soul she also knows that the deep abiding love which she shared with Joseph and her consorts this day will change the world forever. Nine months hence the Savior of the World, the Christ, will be born.

"Marty's stunning film performance is a bold assault on established religious doctrine; but no less offensive to the laws and customs of biblical times than Jacob's assault on the birthright of his brother Esau. The film is controversial, a vile heresy to many millions; but it offers a refreshing, more credible, perspective to many other millions. Who can point to contemporary writings, not scrolls penned hundreds of years after the Holy Birth, that the Church's version of conception events is true? No one can! Is Marty's version that a religion was born as the fruit of an orgy any less credible? It's actually a more believable and realistic version.

"Think, Bob. If you were a woman and if your man couldn't father a child with you; and you, woman, wanted one, what would today's woman do? Well, there were no sperm banks two thousand years ago. Nevertheless, Mary did her best. And she got results! If Marty's version confuses today's males, that does not concern her. Men didn't understand a woman's needs thousands of years ago so they created a fantasy story to explain it. Today's males are no different. Tomorrow's males, like today's males and yesterday's males, will not be able to psychologically grasp that a male's inadequacy is not sufficient reason for a woman to give up her goal of motherhood. Males will cling to their fantasy story version. It's their refuge

from understanding a woman's compelling need to create life; to give birth. It's also the source of male power. Its illogical fantasy will live forever.

"Marty's work provokes far reaching thoughts and comments about the meaning of love and holiness. Jacob stole Esau's birthright to become a patriarch of the Hebrews, did he not? Does anyone really care that trickery was necessary to get results? Israel survives. The tribe's transitional patriarch was a clever con artist, a ruthless back stabber. That is true; but so, what? Marty knows, as her portrayal of Mary shows, results are all that really matter. The end does justify the means. Laws only exist to be broken."

"But, Barb," interjected Bob, "didn't Rebecca, mother of Jacob and Esau, show Jacob how to steal Esau's birthright?"

"Yes, Bob. And just as Rebecca showed Jacob the way to successfully get the birthright, Susan showed Marty how women can also succeed by using immoral behavior. Jacob's behavior sets the accepted human standard for morality, not Esau's. Winners write history, not dupes and losers. Just as we sing praises to patriarch Jacob today, so we will sing praises to immorality goddess Marty tomorrow. Marty understands this concept. She totally gets it. Her immoral behavior crushes the moralizers.

"Her Modern Morality Standard pulverizes decency and morality as surely as a groom shatters a crystal wedding glass when he stomps upon it with his foot. Marty's glorious sinful whoring is destroying all past morality. She knows this. She enjoys every facet of what she's doing. She's capitalizing on it hugely and becoming wealthy by doing so. Her whoring rides atop a tidal wave that is sweeping away all past standards of modesty and decency. Bob, your sweet darling Marty is the world's consummate whore magnifique! And her latest film is destined to become a spectacular marketing success, a classic!"

"So, Barb, you believe that Marty is the leading edge of major societal change, don't you? You're sure of that?" asked Bob.

"Yes, I absolutely believe that; and yes, I am sure. Realize what she's done, Bob. She's the de facto spokeswoman for this Modern Morality Standard craze whose followers essentially believe that puritan type morality is old fashioned. Immorality, like Jacob's back stabbing, and immoral sexual liaisons, like Marty's version of biblical Mary's, are now accepted, preferred social conduct. Whoring is perfectly acceptable. It's an honorable profession now. Marty's body of work says it all, Bob. She just created the most poignant consequential film art ever made. It stands head and shoulders above all other films, whether labeled erotic film or general viewing film. She brilliantly combined her beauty and sheer artistic talent with the controversial content of the film's message.

"And Bob, near the end of that film, I noticed the artful way Marty pivoted from sitting next to Josh to perfectly cupping her vulva upon his mouth. She sat bolt upright on Josh's face, looking away from his body, while he clasped her thighs in his hands. Her compliant galley slave worked his tongue strokes to propel her lust ever onward. She positioned her arms akimbo and backward angled. Then she leaned and peered forward, confidently looking far ahead, as if to declare the natural rightness of cunnilingus. I intuited that her forward lean best positioned her clitoris for Josh's stimulation.

"Her position appeared to be that of a forward-looking bow sprint, a maidenhead leading her ship. Figuratively speaking, she is leading the way for her dauntless vessel, her majestic ship, Immorality, as it transits males' seas of moral indignation. The camera closes in. It shows her eager shipmate, Josh, pleasuring her soft vaginal lips and clitoris with oral sex. Her pleasure moans and writhing torso exhort Josh to continue his erotic wonder lust. I visualized all El Mare's endless depths and expanses parting beneath Marty's lusting keel, helpless to slow her progression. Her charm and confident bravado are parting the world's customs and orders.

"Astounded moralist males can only look up, bedazzled by the erotic spectacle passing over them. They yield to her, many wishing they were Josh. Invincible Immorality sails victorious over them, not even pausing to acknowledge them. Marty's cool assuredness signals she is ever forward looking; and she will never consider the consternation she inflicts upon the ocean of social morals. That would detract from the spectacular grandeur of her immoral purpose. Righteousness and morality are perverse outmoded concepts to her, things she tramples beneath her dignity.

"It also occurred to me that Marty and Josh were well practiced partners in cunnilingus. His soft tissue mouth-flesh paired perfectly and naturally with her soft tissue genitalia. They were so matter of fact and comfortable with their roles I was certain they have often performed sex in this position. Marty obviously enjoyed it immensely.

"When Marty said:

'I love how you do me with your mouth. Oh baby, that's it. Yes, oh, yes. I love this. Your tongue is touching me perfectly now. I'm coming again! I love the way you know how to love me with your mouth, Josh. Don't stop,' *"that moment was revealing to me on many levels. It made me think."*

"Revealing what? How?" Bob's head was spinning.

"Well, after the sheer physical exertion from all her previous fornications and orgasms Marty had to be exhausted. But the way she suddenly lifted herself up onto her knees, pivoted her body over Josh's; and then so quickly slid her vulva into place over Josh's mouth and nestled it there, suggested to me it was partly done out of fear of losing Josh's interest, but also partly done out of Marty's desire for dominance. She was demanding that Josh perform oral sex and please her even more. I saw the entire transformation of human civilization in that ten second scene. I watched control of the world pass from men to women; and I saw morality transition from straight

sex orthodoxy to Marty's Modern Morality Standard. I swear, at that moment, Marty didn't know who she was; or who she loved; or whether she loved you or her film partner Josh; or whether she equally loved every man who was ever intimate with her. I believe she was so perplexed she didn't know her own mind.

"But I saw something more in that scene. Something was also happening in Marty's mind that terrified her. I saw some sort of reality check. It was in that look she had after her lower torso and pelvis convulsed from her orgasm. It was so intense and far away! I felt frightened for her. I thought she used the scene to block out something else. It's hard to explain what I saw, Bob. It's like I was watching someone who sensed a foreboding. I'm sure that part of the film was unscripted, too.

"I think she wants to create great intimate film art because she fears something. There's an emotional component to Marty that she needs to hide from the world. There's an instinct at work within her that's driving her to produce her legacy. I think she knows some deep secret that she needs to keep bottled up; and if it ever gets out, she knows something terrible will happen to her."

"You mean like me?"

"No, not you Big Horse, she knows she has you under complete control. She knows she can count on your love, no matter what she does."

"Then who would she be vulnerable to?"

"I don't know, maybe someone who has something on her or some dark secret or danger she senses."

"Like who, Barbara?"

"I told you, I don't know. But I think David has some mysterious hold over her, like a shared secret or something dreadful that he knows about her; or maybe Marty suspects David knows something about her; but she's afraid to tell anyone about it."

"So, cunnilingus is her outlet for that?"

"Yes, it might be that simple. Oral sex might be her psychological release from deep pain. Maybe she needs oral sex to get her mind into a good place. Try to think like a terrified female thinks. Cunnilingus can message submission or dominance, depending on the partners' mind sets. It's also an act that messages trust and love in a male partner. Maybe while Marty came into Josh's mouth she was in a world where she's in charge. Maybe she found comfort in that. Maybe it's her way of shouting out to her fans that cunnilingus is wonderful; that it's her preferred form of sex, like it is for so many women. I don't have all the answers, Big Horse.

"In that film she also delivered a second subliminal message. It was her subtle way of saying that her pagan lust movement now trumps religious traditions. Her Immaculate Conception film declares she does not even spare the Christian Advent season. Her alternative interpretation is now documented and widely disseminated. Her film is blowing the doors off all box office records and sweeping all awards venues. It's those brilliant subtleties and hidden messages that she brings to her films, and how well she performs them while bursting with unbridled shameless lust that make her fans worship her.

"While I watch her films, my heart nearly pounds out of my chest. I start imagining that I am she, feeling the same sensations she feels. She sends my libido into orbit, Bob. She is not a mere mortal adult film star. She's the transformational goddess of our time, a messianic presence in her own right, expressing herself and messaging us through her intimate film art. She represents creation's undeniable living force, as an enigmatic transcendental touchable being; present among her fans; adored by them; existing in her incarnate goddess-made-flesh space; existing somewhere between we mortals and the spirits. Is she really any less significant than the biblical prophets, or a Gandhi? Because she is a woman, does that make her less significant than them? Really?

"*Her unbounded wellspring of sinning destroys morals, families, dogma, and decency; and she does it so naturally, effortlessly, uncaringly. She's like a relentless, unstoppable lava flow that suffocates entire villages of unfortunate innocents. Only with Marty, it's not fire and lava that destroys. It's her insatiable vagina! The way she uses it overwhelms. Thank goodness, the destruction she inflicts isn't fatal, like lava.*

"*Her destructions are intangible. Marty destroys psyches and souls; or, perhaps I should say, she reorders them. And she destroys with cavalier joy. There's not a scintilla of guilt or caution or reflection or any pause to consider the moral consequences of what she does. She simply floods into a man's life and drowns him with sex, like it's her right to take him and make him her own. The thought that anyone could possibly stop her from what she does or that it might have unforeseen consequences never enters her mind.*

"*With her, it's all perfectly good and right and wonderful; and everyone is just expected to accept whatever she does with another woman's man. Marty's spectacular debauchery is every bit as overwhelming as a lava flow. It pulverizes the self esteem of the other woman. I believe Marty knows her sexual onslaught is crushing the other woman and her home, but Marty simply doesn't care. Like mindless, uncaring lava, she suffocates the other woman's spirit with her overwhelming immoral flood. The other woman sees immorality as unforgiveable sin. Marty's behavior is beyond her comprehension. She reacts belatedly; halfheartedly. She's quickly trapped and buried; smothered beneath her horrible fate. Marty displaces the other woman's life, like lava displaces flesh. The hapless wife stops believing she's a woman. She's reduced to an empty shell with no further purpose; a paralyzed hulk of her former self.*"

"*Is that how she's made you feel, Barb?*" Bob's empathy for Barbara was real.

"At first, yes. But I'm resilient. I'm a fighter. I don't give up. And I think my Big Horse is smarter than most men. I know you have self-respect. You don't want to be just another horse in a whore's stable of horses. And now, you have me.

"We can live the way we want to live. We can make choices. Look around you, Bob. Sickness stalks American society. States pass laws that encourage drug addiction, abortion, and infanticide. People fornicate and defecate shamelessly in public places. Immorality ascends ever higher. Evil doers are rewarded, glorified, unpunished. Police are vilified. Politicians champion anarchy. Depravity is commonplace. It's accepted. Thieves' cunning is admired. Honest, gracious, fair-minded people are scorned. Jackals among us are emboldened, venerated. Our currency is dishonest. Our word means nothing. Dishonor masters us. Americans have all become Jacobs; stealers of others' birthrights to honest money and an honest society. We live in the time of Sodom. I do not believe that that is what you want for yourself or your kids. Do you?"

"No." Bob shook his head. He saw that a future with Marty would be problematic.

Barbara had Bob's attention. She didn't let up. *"Soon, prostitution will be legalized everywhere. Worshiping with temple prostitutes will be ritualized; mainstream, like it was thousands of years ago. Whoring will become America's honored, preferred, state sponsored, subsidized religion. You see the beginnings of it. Some governments want to pay prostitute to service convicts. So, what's the incentive to not become a felon? Marty's work leads us. It champions humanity's desire for sex worship. It embodies the spirit zest for new life and passion lust. Her fans hail her as their regal Queen of Intimacy, Bob. She proudly wears her crown while flooding the world with her morality suffocating eroticism.*

"My head is spinning, Barb. It's hard to believe all this is happening. I totally fell in love with her. Are you serious about all this? And,

do you believe David controls her behavior? Does she have David on her mind more than she lets on?"

Even with these revelations, Bob still cared about Marty. Love clings to its grip on a human heart long after logic leaves love behind.

"I'm totally serious, Bob. You're not the only man who loves Marty's sex-love cycle. And, yes, Bob, I'm certain David is in her crazy mix somehow. Whatever wrongs Marty has done, I suspect David has committed ten wrongs more. He's the most devious man I've ever encountered or read about. I suspect he's at the center of Marty's behavior. He fills her needs somehow. I don't know everything yet. I'm still piecing it all together. There are things I must research and trails I must follow. I must go alone. I can't discuss these matters with you, yet."

Barbara now mocks Bob's love of Marty, showing him how he was completely duped. *"But, just look at how far Marty has come in her career, Bob!"* Barbara's voice lilted higher on her breezy wit of sarcasm. *"Look at her popularity and momentum. Wow! Why, in nine years she'll be old enough to run for President. If she runs, she'll easily win by a landslide. Her base of support, females as well as males, is totally devoted to her.*

"Think, Bob, instead of a President who consorts with and pays off prostitutes, we'll have a prostitute President who consorts with her voters! The White House will become the nation's official whore house. We won't just have money prostitution taking place there. We'll also have the real thing! People could buy ten minutes in the Lincoln bedroom with their President! Intimate donors would get a signed photo of themselves with your sweetheart, Marty, their President. They could frame it and put it in their offices. Just think, Bob: Across the country there will be thousands of men with photographs proving that they fucked your precious Marty. And all their friends will know they've fucked your Marty, the most famous and the most powerful whore in the world! The whole world will know that everyone has fucked your precious Marty!"

CHAPTER NINE

I dreamt that somehow, I had come to Topsy-Turveydom! Where vice is virtue and virtue vice, where nice is nasty and nasty nice; where right is wrong and wrong is right and white is black and black is white. (Sir William Schwenck Gilbert: The Bab Ballads)

Times are stranger than they seem. Pussies purr and lap their cream. (Rosemary Ness-Bitner, author)

It's fine to be abnormal. It's normal. Nobody can make you conform. You can't be forced to become a communist. (Rosemary Ness-Bitner, author)

NEW NORMAL LOVE

"You're being way too cynical, Barb."

"I'm not trying to be cynical, Bob. I'm frightened that our country has become so corrupt, so immoral and so stupid. Hear what I'm saying. Your sweet, precious, lovable Marty is capable of anything, maybe even more than I can imagine. She knows no boundaries and nothing can stop her.

"Words cannot describe how confidently glorious she appears while she smothers traditional godliness. There is no hint of self-doubt or uncertainty in that beautiful smiling face about the 'rightness' of her performances. She needs no one's approval. Her conscience is clear. She needs no justification other than that it pleases her to perform. She happily, wantonly personifies love and life embodied in all her immoral splendor.

"Her film art shatters inhibitions and tramples moral qualms. Her viewers believe in her and her message that there is no need for morality. There is only life for pleasure's sake. Fans pour out their heartfelt love for her. Their feelings are genuine, enduring. She's a part of their lives, if only vicariously. They pay handsomely to see her films and a lot more to consort with her, Bob.

"They escape the drudgery and political madness of their lives; they duck their responsibilities and morality by going to Marty. She embraces these social refugees, hugs them, and loves them. She reins sex goddess supreme in their hearts and minds. They dream of her; of kissing her, touching her, making love with her; many of them obsessively so.

"They eagerly await her newest films. She takes their minds cavorting with her as she journeys ever deeper into the dim, murky realms of debauchery. They worship her, follow her every utterance, believe her messages; and many emulate her acts and mores.' She is their supreme idol goddess, their exemplary standard bearer magnifique!

"Her newest viewers are mesmerized. Their opinions of good and evil and morality are shaken to the core and reexamined. An inner determination comes through her work and connects with many of them. Her life's progression, from frustrated child to full expressive self, completes its journey in her film art. Hear her, Bob:

'Look what you have made,' the inner voice from her performances cries out. 'See what a child that lived without love can become!' her acts intone. 'You want this finished product that you helped to create, don't you? Now, you want to take back this love starved child, whom all of you abandoned, don't you?' she proudly implies through her smiles.

"As I studied her salacious body of work, I found my mouth watering and my own sex becoming moist. Marty oozes sex. Her testosterone and oxytocin sex hormones are overwhelming. Her lust *seemingly pours from the screen and captivates her viewers. I discovered my heart was racing. I craved her. I, your Goody Two Shoes Barbara, started going crazy out of my mind. I, prim and proper Barbara, got wildly excited, slippery wet. I wanted sex with her.*

"I also came to appreciate that, despite her seductive words; she doesn't actually love any of her partners. And, honestly, she does not love you, Bob, or any of her private member clients, at least not in the traditional sense of the meaning of love. Marty has redefined the meaning of love. For her and her followers, love and lust are an indistinguishable blur. It a pantheistic sort of sex-love mishmash, where friendships are consummated with intimate fornications. And that casual, widely ranging, all-encompassing intimate reach is accepted by everyone in her circle. These people fuck as casually as you and I eat potato chips.

"Marty stopped feeling connectedness or care for humanity long ago. Love for another person drained out of her soul when she was abandoned as a child. The only object of her ardor now is the cock. She needed something dependable to love that would love her back. And she found it. The cock fills her love void while she makes love with it. She worships the cock. She has learned to love it. She really doesn't know how to love anything or anyone else.

"When she was young and in boarding school the young men brought her the love she so desperately needed through their cocks. In her damaged psyche the male cock became sacred. Now, she communes with the cocks when she takes inside her vagina. And when they ejaculate, they reciprocate her love. That moment is Marty's sacred communal time, her personalized Holy Mass. Fucking has become sacred to her. That explains why she uses religious background music for her films.

"As I studied her film art, I asked myself: 'What is it, specifically? What is it about this woman that draws men to her in such a way that they can not resist her?'

"*I was seeing man after man lose his soul into her bottomless abyss of lust, much like a fly loses itself to the stickiness of the flypaper or a moth loses itself to the dazzle of an open flame. And what, specifically, was it that they were they finding at the bottom of this bottomless abyss of lust, I asked myself? It wasn't just sex. What was it? And then I had my answer.*

"*It is a basic truth that they were seeking and finding in their intimacy with her. It is that singularity that knows that the entire world is phony and corrupt and one must not be fool enough to place one's trust in any one; but by consorting with Marty, they know they will obtain an absolute truth. And these men know that they can place their trust in that truth. And that truth is that we are all, at our core of being, base and lustful creatures.*

"*At once, I understood Marty and her driving force. Each, and all her lovers descend willfully into her abyss. They bring their voided souls to her; offer their souls to her; and entreat her to join their voided souls to hers; to absorb their souls, the very essence of their humanity, into her immorality. They crave to feel her tongue licking them from the bases of their necks up to their ears while her sensuous fingers tease their chests with seductive rubs. They adore the way her face and eyes dream away into another dimension while her orgasms gush with their penis strokes. Her magnificence is incomparable because it is real. The empty void from Marty's childhood welcomes and absorbs their voided souls. Their souls enlarge her void, making her immoral void all-encompassing; and emptier still.*"

"*You're not exaggerating, Barb?*"

"*Oh, Bob, no. I'm not. You have no idea how far the dimensions of this reach. Her admirers deify her. They obsess over her. Her nymphomania is contagious. It becomes their contagion. They memorize her films. They vividly recall every explicit scene; every embrace she gives her lovers; every foreplay touching; every hand and finger stimulation; every penis she guides into her vagina; every cock she kisses,*

licks, strokes and takes into her mouth; every single scene, every set-
ting and every position in her films with her multiple lovers; every
lift, decline and rotational movement of her pelvis; every display of
her vagina while receiving cunnilingus; every spurt of semen into
her mouth and vagina; every semen shot pulsated over her breasts;
every convulsive orgasm she has; and on and on.

"Her ardent fans imagine they are right there with her, joyfully
partnering with her in all those explicit ways; and, for them, it
becomes a constant, living memory. In their obsession, their other
worlds fade into nothingness. She becomes their narrowly focused
world and their reason for living. Other interests, marriages, girl-
friends, all fall away. Marty becomes ever present in their mental
dream world. Her presence in their imaginary world is their comfort
place. Their dream world occasionally erupts with bursts of pas-
sion-lust; but those bursts are for her, in the forms of masturbation
or of having sex with women whom they imagine to be her.

"But her growing fan base does not relieve Marty's condition.
The more lovers she takes to her bed, the larger and more insatiable
her void becomes. It has already become a cavernous, unquench-
able vortex of unbridled, uninhibited, shameless lust. I asked myself:
'Who else understands this phenomenon as I now finally under-
stand it?' And I thought about that, too.

"And now I understand why she and David share a mysteri-
ous bond which no one else can know or penetrate. David somehow
came to understand Marty and the forces that shaped her life. He
alone understands all her needs. I believe he understands them even
better than she, herself, does.

"I know of no other woman as immersed in whoring, as commit-
ted to immorality, or as enthusiastically enamored with debauch-
ery as Marty. She venerates sin and glorifies evil. She beholds those
twins as desirable, beautiful, and irresistible. And she's visibly joyous
when she snares a vulnerable soul and delivers it to those twins.

By satisfying those twins she becomes more acceptable to them and becomes one with them. Their acceptance enables Marty to bring her unique quality of delicious erotic splendor to her whoring; and that splendor lifts her film craft above all other porn. It transcends ordinary promiscuity and soars into an ethereal world of carnal majesty.

"She's proud of herself, too, Bob. She's fine tuned her body to be a zealous pleasure giving sex machine, performing at the pinnacle of her craft. Her body language seamlessly communicates temptation, seduction, and fornication. She knows she is viewed by millions; she beams those cherubic smiles from her innocent looking, angelic face into the camera, confident that her performances are erasing goodness and virtue from millions of susceptible minds.

"Her semen filled vaginal scenes, paired with the stunning beauty of her saintly face, captivate many such minds, inviting them to embrace her interpretations of holiness; ensnaring them in her web of unbounded lust. She knows many of these viewers will join her private membership. She relishes meeting them and getting their feedback to better understand why they joined. She enthusiastically welcomes them to her carnal world.

"After seeing her draw and swallow semen from over a hundred lovers' cocks and entertaining hundreds of cocks in her films, I can not imagine she'll ever want to nurture a child, Bob. She is driven to be hailed as the world's greatest whore and adored by millions of fans for who she is. She's not about to let pregnancy enlarge her body; nor would she even remotely consider wasting her precious celebrity time on a child. Her zeal for creating her film art won't abate until she's ranked the undisputed world's number one adult film star. She craves that notoriety and power. From that exalted platform she knows she can influence millions to reject their religious teachings. There, she can aggressively promote her culture of whoring and champion society's return to Pagan worship."

"Why would she want to do that, Barb? It makes no sense to me."

"It does if you can get out of your own mind and put your mind into hers. Her mother rejected her when she was a child. Society also rejected her. The kid got a double whammy. Marty was on her own. She needed a way to cope. She psychologically declared herself independent from society, and all its norms. That carried through into her behavior. It gave birth to her nymphomania; but also, into her messaging as an adult film star."

"I don't understand."

"I think I do. She understands human emotions. You see, her films always depict love and loving as their central theme. They are never about violence. You'll never see a gun in any of her work. You'll never see anyone hitting anyone. Women in her films are never demeaned in any way. Her partners occasionally, lightly slap her tush to sexually stimulate her. But she won't allow face slaps or choking. Those actions demean womanhood. Men do not slap or choke goddesses. Instead, her partners kiss her tush; lovingly pet it; they tickle it with feathers. They touch and they lovingly rub her there. They tease her vagina from behind, with their tongues. These ways, her work always accentuates loving; never brutality. She'll perform BDSM for her private clients, but only the softer versions of BDSM; never anything that involves actual physical pain. She only does pretend domination within strict limits.

"Her work never detracts from the dignity of a woman; not in the slightest. It always portrays her body in a reverential way. Her fans eat it up. You always see her freely giving and receiving love, through intimate sex. And it's always loving, romantic sex; never coarse sex or anything that degrades or humiliates a woman in the slightest. It's always about the woman enjoying pleasure. Even her orgy films are about the immense pleasures the woman receives from multiple partners; not about a group of men ravaging a woman; not about the pleasures men get from sex; not about the mental problems men

overcome or the camaraderie they develop by having group sex. Mar-
ty's work rejects Hollywood's concepts and its violence, bland scripts,
mediocre directing mind-numbing pyrotechnics, and animations; its
ridiculous faux love scenes; stupid car stunts and butchered grammar.
Many movies show people murdering other people. You can't watch
a movie or a TV show without seeing some idiot peeking around a
corner with a gun in his hand; or half crazed people shooting at each
other; or cars crashing; or buildings blowing up, can you?"

"No, I guess you can't."

"Well, that's because Hollywood and TV are controlled by men-
tally ill males; testosterone crazed, sex-starved nut job sickos that
are angry with themselves and the world they inhabit. Their shoot
'em up, bang, bang productions poison peoples' minds. They are the
root cause of murders, suicides, assaults, rapes, and robberies. Our
problems are symptomatic of Hollywood's dehumanizing messaging
failure, overlain on our foundation of dishonest money. That dys-
functional messaging is to blame for countless deaths, because many
dummied down American minds believe it is perfectly normal to kill
other humans. Our entire country operates on the moral premise
that it's okay to go to the other side of the world and kill millions of
people, if they happen to piss us off. Face it, Bob, we're a nation of
neurotic nut jobs.

"Look at the drug abuse. Look at the suicides. Look at the hatred
of cops. It's all totally irrational. It's all because of Hollywood. Every-
thing that's wrong is Hollywood's fault. They've dehumanized people;
brainwashed them; turned them into thoughtless imbeciles, without
grace or graciousness. Americans are easily manipulated puppets.
Why? Look at the messaging.

"Marty's work sends a different message. It says it's okay to love
freely; to make love and be loved. Marty cries out through her work,
that we should love each other; cherish and respect the other per-
son; and yes, to do so in explicit, sexual ways. In her personal life,

if another woman resists Marty's immorality, Marty crushes that woman. But, through her work, she expresses only the pleasurable side of what she represents. It's the side of her message that people want to hear. They listen to that message and crave what it says:

'It's good to make love. It's not bad. It's wonderful. It's beautiful!'

"I think she happens to be right. If culture put an X rating on every movie that had a gun in it, I believe gun violence would go the way of the Dodo bird; and if society put a G or R rating on all movies that had explicit sex in them, I believe the population would become much happier, more loving, and less neurotic; even if many women lose control of their husbands. People would be more open to discussing their feelings with each other honestly; much less likely to pick up a gun. Society and Hollywood need to rethink everything. They need to sweep everything they are doing off the board and make films that deliver Marty's message. What have we got to lose?"

"So, you think she's on a moral crusade? You think that's her motivation?"

"Yes, I do, Big Horse. That's part of it. She believes in her cause, I'm sure of it. But, there's another behavioral driver. It is a more personal one. I'm sure of it. She wants to upstage her boarding school rivals. She needs to prove she's superior to them. You can expect that, some day soon, the world will recognize her. She will reach her goal. Images of her film scenes will be burnished into the minds of every male in the world. She's making terrific progress, Horse.

"Prepare yourself. Porn trade venues will soon proclaim Marty number one; the greatest, most wonderful fuck bunny of all time. Nothing and no one can prevent it. Her face is the trade's most beautiful; her body is its most sensuous, and her will is its most determined. I'm surprised you haven't noticed her out of office career, Bob.

"She's the poster girl for yacht sales and big game safaris. If you research just a little, you'll see her semen filled vagina and smiling

face adorning the head of a dead elephant. You'll see her naked derriere beneath a skirt climbing a ladder into a private jet and on the bed of a stateroom on a yacht. Her vagina advertises the dream of an upper-class, sybarite lifestyle, Bob. Your lady's vagina is world famous! Your Marty is a secret workaholic, Bob. She has a workaholic's love of fucking and producing erotic film. She's becoming world famous, Bob. I'm sorry to be the one telling you this. Get ready to accept it.

"Ask Yourself: How will you feel when she no longer has time for you? How will you feel when she gets calls from billionaires, movie stars, world leaders and world class athletes? They will call her, Bob. They are the world's most aggressive alpha males; and they will gladly pay many millions of dollars just to spend a weekend with her. Her hourly agency rates will skyrocket. These men will all want to discover for themselves what hundreds of cocks already know; that Marty is the most wonderful, most unforgettable, most adorable fuck their cocks can ever know. Men are like that. You'll see.

"She will not say 'no' to them, Bob. When they call for her, she'll go. She will fuck and suck their brains out. Then, they'll call constantly, inviting her to exotic places and public venues where they know they'll be seen with her. It won't stop, Bob. It will be a feeding frenzy. She'll be the coveted World Cup of trophy whores; beaming her winsome smile to her latest partner; hanging on his arm; openly, shamelessly stroking his cock with her caressing hands. And, make no mistake, Bob. He will be fucking her. They'll both want the world to know that he is the lucky guy who is currently fucking her. He'll hold her angelic face in his hands; kiss her cherubic lips in public, and press his body to hers. It will be great publicity for both of them.

"Marty will do thousands of seductive photo poses. She'll flash her beautiful mouth smiles and perfect teeth; blow her kisses to the masses from the covers of the tabloids. She'll be positioned in pictures, hugging, and kissing her rich and famous lovers; flashing

*shots of her inviting derriere, opposite a picture page of her lovers'
disheartened wives. Unlike Marty's lustrous well rested angelic smiling face, the wives' drained, stress-exhausted faces will look like they
were smashed by a wrecking ball; then run over by a freight train.
Lead articles will breathlessly proclaim how Marty has suddenly,
unexpectedly, found herself enmeshed in the turmoil of a troubled
family, through absolutely no fault of her own.*

*"Her publicists will write those stories as if the marriage break-
ups were healthy, necessary things. They'll portray Marty as somehow
innocently getting caught up in a family's long festering problems;
and how she helped the besieged husband through his turmoil by
serving up her compliant vagina to him.*

*"World famous men and government heads of state will explain
how they couldn't resist her charms. These dutiful buffoons will serve
up incredulous nonsense quotes to their legions of witless morons.
They'll say idiotic things for public consumption, like they suddenly
discovered they had something in common with Marty. Those stories will prompt more alpha males to call. She'll be notorious in the
world's top social circles. She'll receive invitations to everything, all
expenses paid. Men will surround her at public gatherings. And
women will circle their wagons.*

*"She'll become known as the adult film star that top cocks run
to when their marriages are troubled. She will embrace and comfort troubled men; fuck their brains out and obliterate their tenu-
ous marriages. She will take each new lover away to some secluded
place for a week or two. When they emerge, they'll announce their
new found love to the world. The man will explain how it has
become impossible to reconcile his domestic issues. Oh, a few may
try to reconcile, but they will fail. Marty will embed her sex in the
man's mind and never allow his hapless wife back in. She'll shamelessly starve him of time for his home life by gorging him with sex.
And she'll win.*

"Whenever she appears in public, paparazzi will chase her for sound bites to go with a story or photo. She'll drop you in a heartbeat, Bob. She'll leave you in her dust. She does not 'love' you. But she does love fucking you, I admit that. But when someone wealthier or more powerful calls to take her away from you, she will leave you. She loves money, power, and fucking; and that summarizes all that she loves.

"If anyone ever writes about Marty's life story, how she rose from abandonment to fame, she will immediately become the highest ranked, number one adult film star in the world, by a factor of ten; far away and above all others. She'll be the ultimate, the world's premium, most glorious, heart stopping femme fatale. She'll be irresistible box office catnip. Chief believes there's more to her story than we know. So, maybe when her entire story is told, it will be even more remarkable.

"Her fame will garner her more invitations than the First Lady of the United States receives. People love stories about seductive fallen women that live on the dark side. They crave stories about family break-ups. She'll appear on TV talk shows. Everyone will want to see the angelic-faced beauty that caused the multibillion-dollar divorce.

"And, she'll dispense banal commentary for mass consumption in her most seductive purring voice:

'I just can't help it that his wife couldn't please him,' whispered Barbara in her most sensuous, pretend Marty, mocking voice, 'Her problems aren't MY fault; not little ole me!' She'll open her palms and shrug her shoulders and look doe-eyed into the cameras. 'She made his life a living hell. Poor man' She'll continue: 'I didn't WANT to get involved, but what could I do? The poor man reached out to ME for help. I felt so sorry for him after I heard how hard she is to live with. I can't imagine why she wanted to make him so miserable? He's such a sweet, loving man.'

"She'll lay it on so thick that women hearing her act will rub *their pussies in envy. No one will find fault in her behavior. They'll lap up every word she says:*

'What's a girl supposed to DO when an attractive man WANTS her SO BADLY?' "*She'll continue in her whining, sympathy seeking voice:*

'Everything just happened so FAST! He's irresistible; so smart and powerful. He overwhelmed me with LOVE and HOT PASSION. Oh my God, there was so much HOT PASSION! He showered me with gifts and took me to all those lovely places. I just COULDN'T say no to him. I'm SO HAPPY that we found each other. I feel like he's the first and greatest love of my whole entire LIFE! I'm all bubbly inside; like I'm the girl who never got noticed and then suddenly I got asked to be prom queen!

'And, he makes LOVE so SWEETLY! I can't get enough of him. He fills me up, Teee-Heee. We're SOOOO happy. We LOVE our time alone. We are head over heels in love. It's beautiful.'

"She'll make herself sound like she is the innocent party in that family break-up; but if truth be known, not one woman in a thousand can withstand the tsunami waves from Marty's relentless whoring. She slams her sin honed battering ram against the marriage door until it smashes down the marital partners' trust. Then, Marty opens the floodgates. Her sexual tsunami floods its pervasive destruction through their marriage sanctuary, mocking that institution; drowning it in her ruthless debauchery. Once she's broken through the marriage gates; once the public is noticed by the paparazzi that the marriage is in play, Marty's flood waters deepen. She cavorts openly with the husband; obliterates the wife's hopes of retaining him; washing away his marital memories; replacing them with thoughts of her. She immerses his sensory organs and cerebral cortex in thoughts of her; only her. This requires intensive intimate therapy. Marty provides that, freely and lovingly. Her relentless immoral flood displaces the marriage

from its connubial foundation; separates her victims from their home and sweeps them away.

"She is not unlike a prey animal or an avian raptor. But she doesn't behave this way because she needs to feed her stomach. Contrary to laws of nature and nurture, Marty uses her wantonness to spite the instincts of ordinary women; thwart their life goals and lifestyles. She artfully persuades her paramours to lend their cupidity to her drowning of their mates, and their family values. That is the true measure of her genius. She is, in this respect, an artisan of moral destruction; a fabulous, magnificent whore; nonpareil.

"Few marriages can withstand her predatory remorseless destruction. Methodically, dispassionately, her all-consuming vagina relentlessly tears apart a family's flailing attempts to restore fealty. Her relentless sex offerings cull the husband away from his family, friends, and support groups; separates his thoughts from them; plunges his love for them into her wanton sex thirsting vortex where she drowns his past.

"Marty's onslaught is like a tsunami which batters a wife's home until it's severed from its foundations. At the flood's first wave, the wife may feel she can resist the catastrophe. She may falsely believe that by being a nicer wife, a more sensuous wife, a more caring wife, Marty's immoral flood waters will recede. She may think that her home will somehow resettle, unchanged, upon its displaced foundations. But the wife could not be more wrong. She is a reactionary fool. She has a fundamental misunderstanding of the naked savagery that exists at the core of being of every man and woman.

"The wife's ordered world has turned on her. It is no more. Her first hint of Marty's involvement with her husband should be her 'wake up and smell the coffee' moment. But the wife doesn't even understand that coffee has been brewed. That wake up occurs the night when her husband does not come home. It's a sudden, bitter realization. The wife is now very suddenly aware that she is the

outsider; the other woman. Her husband's ardor has attached to another. The wife is suddenly swallowed under a fast-moving stream while her friends and neighbors simply stand aside, jaws agape. They watch her drown; helpless to save her; disinterested in her troubles. Marty and the husband emerge as the new power union, hell bent to destroy the wife. The husband obeys Marty now. With Marty's guidance, he becomes much like a reptile that eats its own children; thinking only of feeding his own needs.

"Marty's destructive legacy remains in the husband's heart and mind no matter what the wife does. The wife's life becomes like a home after a flood. Memories of weddings, anniversaries, births, parties, events, and awards won by their children have been swept away; replaced with thoughts of home wrecker Marty; like a flooded home's furnishings are swept away; replaced with debris and mud filled rooms. The wife wonders why Marty captivates her husband. She asks herself: 'How can making love with Marty be that different from making love with me?' She does not appreciate the many subtle ways determined, notorious whore Marty invades and possess a male's limbic zone.

"Perversely, the wife's children become realists. They read tabloids' accounts of the family break up. Fear of worst fears: in some cases, they find themselves in agreement with the digs Marty gives their mother. 'Yes, Mom was too controlling,' their unformed minds opine. 'Yes, Mom didn't love Dad nearly enough,' they agree. A transformative metamorphosis of opinion takes place. They perceive Marty as their freedom card from Mommy's jail. Their innocent hearts welcome the world's most incorrigible whore as their new best friend. They are happy for Dad when he disappears for hours or days or weeks. They perceive that Daddy needs something that Marty gives him; something Mommy doesn't have.

"The wife's ultimate demoralizer comes when she loses her children to Marty. Infrequent conversations with her children reveal

that they secretly root for Marty. Horrors of horrors! The wife notices her daughter's betrayal. Her child has changed. She now rejects family values and morality. She stays out late; does alcohol, and drugs; flaunts her budding sexuality. Apparently, her child's womb will not grow to womanhood as the bedrock foundation for a happy home with a good husband and praiseworthy children. The wife's hopes of grandchildren diminish. She hears her daughter ogle fine fashion clothing and jeweled bracelets, lavished upon her, compliments of Marty! 'But she's not ready for adult accessories,' protests the wife. No matter. Father and Marty have assured the daughter that she's ready for grown-up things. Wife learns daughter has secretly obtained copies of Marty's latest intimate film. She overhears her daughter tell her friends that she wants to become a whore, like Daddy's girlfriend.

"The mother fears her daughter aspires to learn whore-craft from the world's most notorious whore. Moralizing sermons fall on deaf ears; fail to reverse her daughter's trajectory. Daughter tells Mother morality is the old formula for losers who lose in life; promiscuity is the new formula for winning. Mother taught Daughter that her vagina was precious; to conceal it and save it for when she is older and for the perfect, right young man. But Daughter rejects Mother's old-fashioned teaching. She embraces Marty's new dictum. Marty proclaims that whoring is wonderful, exciting, and profitable; and sex feels good. The child has thoughts:

'Marty's ways are trumpeted and lauded in pop art and music. Mom's ways are the stuff of dusty, incomprehensible old fashioned literature. Mom's ways are tedious and boring. I have no time or patience for them; nor do I see the cultivation of my mind as a pursuit that holds any worth. Marty's ways get boys and young men to pay attention to my every whim. Marty tells me my vagina is a phenomenal asset; that the more I use it, the more valuable it becomes; and, the more popular and loved I become.'

"Grown men discover the daughter. They spend money on her and take her places. She comes home late and disheveled. The mother's efforts to discourage her daughter's behavior by grounding her or taking her wheels away are ineffective. Her daughter threatens to run away and live with Dad. Daughter checkmates Mother.

"Mother sees her entire life as a lost cause; a colossal mistake. Mother has become her daughter's reactive past. And she knows it. She approaches her daughter differently now. She may no longer criticize or suggest; only praise and compliment, lest she be completely cast into Daughter's darkness; never to see her again. Mother holds her tongue while watching Daughter primp and preen, adorn herself in skimpy clothes that suggest 'come fuck me' to eager males.

"Mother now bites her lip when daughter comes home late, or not at all. Mother knows her once precious baby, whom she suckled and loved, has become a budding fuck bunny; a promiscuous whore. She stays silent while knowing that Daughter is likely screwing her brains out in the back seat of some boy's car; or that her precious child is an orgy's center piece in some hotel room. Mother blocks these terrors from her mind and pretends all is well, lest her child-woman leaves her to live with her father and Marty. Mother aches inside. She pretends that she still has her mother role to play. But she is delusional. Marty has invaded her home; seized her husband and snatched her daughter's mind.

"Eventually the mother acknowledges her fate. Her options have narrowed. She flees to her new life. Perhaps gardening, romance novels and book clubs? Possibly drowning her misery in vodka and gin martinis? Mother's choices do not concern Daughter. There is no outreach from daughter to mother; no compassion, no feeling, no love; nothing. Daughter has other priorities: Clothes, baubles, and bling; parties to attend; and above all, boys to kiss and cocks to fuck and suck. Graciousness has lost. Marty's way, the immoral way, has won.

"But Mother knows better, because Mother knows best. She is wise in the ways of the world. She knows the gala days of American indulgence are numbered. She knows that immorality is championed by the socialist phalange to upend the moral ways of the nation's founding. She has read what happened to Eastern Bloc nations as communism swallowed socialism in post-war Europe. She knows those socialists' assertions that the new American socialism will be benign, like Sweden's socialism. She knows those are canards, because without America in opposition to communism there would be no Swedish or European buffer state between communism's and capitalism's opposing ideologies.

"Mother harbors great anxiety about her daughter's fate once the American socialists have control. She knows the time from socialism to communism in America will be short, and horribly brutal-swift. People will be disappeared, tortured, and shot if they resist the new, drab, brain-dead world that communism imposes upon a once free people.

"She fears her daughter will be a target of vile, heartless, power-crazed communist create nothing, destroy everything, thugs. Daughter will be singled out as an example of all that is wrong with America. Her precious child will possibly be sent away from her; or worse, made to whore for communist party elites; whoring and watching soullessly as her friends are murdered before her eyes. Mother's stomach churns in nightmare nights. Mother grinds her teeth. She curses Marty's name. Marty's ways now invade the mother's psyche; even her physical health. The whore has destroyed the wife and mother.

"The wife's life will never be the same, even if she gets her man back. But odds makers would bet heavily that the wife will not get him back, and they would win those bets nine times out of ten. Why? Because, day after day, night after night, the wife's husband is betraying his family. He is Marty's ardent suitor now. He willingly partakes

of Marty's bottomless pit of hot slippery lust. Her limbi-addictive fellatio from her expert mouth and tongue reinforce the allure of her marvelous, insatiable vagina. The husband's interest in his previous family life fades away; slowly at first; then, suddenly, it vanishes. No matter what romance novelists encourage their readers to pretend or deny, love dies. Reunification of wife with husband never happens. Marty has done more than win. She has devoured the wife and her marriage.

"Marty's twisted mind metes out revenge on those boarding school girls who had normal, family centric lives. And, she simultaneously offers her lifeline of love and sweet assurances to rescue the family breadwinner from his responsibilities to his wife and kids. She doesn't care that their home is inundated with the mud and debris of separation and divorce. She's no fool, either. During her destruction process, Marty keeps her eye on the family's money.

"After Marty's vagina has submersed her detested marriage in her sex flood, she willfully holds it under water until she drowns all marital hopes that struggle to resurface. She portrays the man's marriage as his unfortunate disease, an unsightly blight on his life that must be scrubbed and flushed way, setting him free. With photo op after photo op; and social engagement after social engagement, Marty relentlessly fawns over the husband and ruthlessly assaults his wife. If murder were a legally accepted means to rid herself of the nuisance wife, Marty would murder her.

"Once the husband is in Marty's clutches, the other family members could lie bloated on the beach, being eaten by dogs, their eyes pecked by birds and their remains carried off by jackals. Marty couldn't care less. She sees them as worthless losers that deserve their fate. She is heartless, and as deaf and indifferent to their pain as a tarantula is to a small mouse that squeaks in terror while succumbing to the spider's poison. Marty has what she wants. Her psyche has progressed from her frustrations as an abandoned child; to her seething anger at her impossible childhood situation; to her burning *jealousies of the other boarding school girls that did receive familial love; to her raging hatred of familial love itself. She attacks marital love with a raging inner vengeance. She is a proud, righteous warrior; driven by zeal for battle; certain her cause is just.*

"Her marriage murdering craft has evolved, Bob. She is no longer the clumsy school girl hastily removing her panties and seducing boys in back seats of cars. She is now a calculating, vixen predator at the top of her trade craft; and equally masterful is her management of public perceptions about her cruel processes. All the while she's engaged in her lust battles. she only concerns herself with her public image and her own pleasures. She enthusiastically introduces her newest swain to new sexual experiences, positions, and props. She subtly brainwashes him to adopt her new Modern Morality Standard. Incidentally, once the new lover accepts her dogma, he can hardly protest when she leaves him for another lover.

"In her boudoir she'll assure the estranged husband that he'll see his kids all he wants. "You're not losing anything,' she'll whisper to him, 'and now you'll have me.'

"While she French kisses him, licks his neck and fondles his testicles, she'll coo in his ear; reminding him that he won't have to listen to his bitching wife anymore. She'll help him recall that his wife was impossible to live with. If he shows any sign of vacillation, she'll encourage him to postpone those thoughts. She'll rehabilitate him by fucking him all week long at some secret hideaway. While refocusing her lover's new lifestyle she'll keep her focus on her grand prize, which is his divorce. Her new man will receive the greatest sexual experiences he's ever known in his life. She's determined to redeem his pledges of divorce gifts to her. The coveted family beach house will be remodeled as a love nest to suit her, and gifted to her for helping him through his troubled time. His wife's cancelled credit line will be reopened, with Marty's authorization on it. Whoring, as a business model, pays big.

"Investment sales are only a front for her, Bob. Her core competency craft is a savage, heartless, sordid business. She'll freely acknowledge to the tabloids that she had a wife opponent; and she'll seek to emblazon in the minds of her public that she has vanquished that hapless wife and destroyed her. For the wife's spirited participation in their public contest, Marty will honor the estranged wife with the same back handed respect a victorious gladiator displays while running his sword through the guts of his vanquished opponent. Crowds then, and now, cheer for the victor. Marty knows this. She milks it. She's ruthless.

"The public fixates on her triumph. She is their newest heroin. Their mind's eye visualizes a beautiful woman and her victorious vagina, graciously spread widely open, winner of the husband, magnet home for his love-thirsty cock. They hail Marty's anatomy as the lifeline for a distraught husband and lust's triumphant symbol. Many, seeing the tabloid story, will buy Marty's films. They'll become her fans and well-wishers. Their image of her will be shaped by the carefree innocence; the openly immodest, brazen joyfulness she heralds.

"She knows she is the living harbinger of the new immoral culture. She's pleased in her role. Her shameless promiscuity is on full display in her films, inviting converts to her New Morality Standard. In the minds of her fans, and those newest to her film art, Marty can do no wrong. She cannot possibly have a trace of evil within her. She's too beautiful, too innocent, too joyful in her lovemaking to be anything other than a goddess. Yes, they are convinced. She is the merciful goddess of love. Where I see the rhythmic thrusting's of her vagina and the semen spurts that cavorting cocks lavish upon her outer lips as dangers to civilized order, others worship those same thrusts. They adore her cavalier promiscuity, so much so that they seek to perform cunnilingus with her; hoping to place their faces and minds ever closer to her sinfulness. To these

masses of fans, her vagina is the champion's trophy. It's his hard-won prize. He's earned it. Its image and deeds are proudly held high; blessed, even publicly kissed by the unfortunate sex starved husband. He now stands as the lone survivor, atop his family's ruin, caused by his spiteful wife.

"This mob believes Marty has rescued this man. The poor fellow is safe in her arms now. His estranged wife and kids are publically humiliated, scorned, marginalized, abandoned in the cold deeps of publicity's unforgiving sea; while the public glorifies Marty's wondrous rescue lust-Vag. The public laps up every banal fact about Marty's latest escapade. They ogle the tabloid photos of her scantily clad body on warm beaches; desperately trying to imagine what it's like to be her, or to be her lover. They dream of what heaven might be like, kissing her adorable, whoring vagina; and fornicating with her. Marty's lewd behavior is showered with blessings from tabloid columnists, and effusive congratulatory praises from movie stars and pundits of stagecraft and film. Her latest exploits are lifted aloft and hailed as the latest triumph of humanity's immoral calling. Media gossips rave their praises. They exalt her sexuality and wanton whoring in their columns. They love her and the culture she represents. Their public can't get enough of her. There's a whole culture that loves this sinful debauchery, Bob.

"Marty's family destroying whoring also earns her latest film considerable publicity and rave reviews. Critics praise her latest release. It's hailed as a cutting-edge, state of the art orgy film where she plays compliant sex slave for an entire Roman Legion. In the film she rises to prominence as the concubine of the emperor through her unparalleled prowess in the boudoir. She tells her media followers it was inspired by her empathy for the pathetic homely wife, the latest victim to buckle under her dogged determination to win at all costs.

"Her marketing genius pays off. Her new feature length adult film will rake in a billion dollars in its first month. The film will

be hailed as the first of its kind, a true blockbuster. It will tear the public away from its archaic moral anchors. The film and Marty will be box office sensations. Helen of Troy and Cleopatra will fade as lesser lights in the mind of public lore. Marty's dazzling appeal to unbounded lust will trump them both.

"Viewers see something they have never seen before. They see more than a woman making love. They see a writhing, purposeful organism. All its emotive energies pour out seduction messages from its face and eyes. Its every nerve, muscle, sinew, and bone are harnessed and yoked for one purpose only. Their task is to provide focused emphasis and spectacular viewing realism for Marty's raging, insatiable lust-cunt. The viewer is spellbound. The thrusts and gyrations of Marty's glistening, polished and waxed vagina strike her lust fire's branding iron to the viewer's mind, capturing him into Marty's kingdom corral.

"He is hers now. She owns him: heart and soul. The images of Marty's ravenous, semen-thirsting vagina pleasuring a cock are forever burnished into his limbic mind. The explicit images become part of his daily thoughts and life. He wants Marty; no other woman. Her. He becomes obsessed. He dreams of Her; pines for Her as his sensibilities depart from him. His fascination becomes adoration. He is smitten; lovesick. He becomes her fan for his lifetime. He buys her four hundred other films and joins her Premium Member Service. He loads thousands of her porn pictures onto his computer. He views them many times a day. His mind never strays far from her. The film he first viewed will be followed by twelve more, all full-length feature films. He eagerly awaits their releases and preorders all twelve. He is not alone in his obsession. Males worldwide throng to Marty's films, like attracted iron filings race to a magnet. Every one of her new full-length films will gross over a billion dollars at the box office; and all of them will produce over thirty billion dollars in Marty's brand label sales of jewelry, clothing, luggage, lingerie, and exotic scents."

"Barb, how do you know all this, especially about her porn pictures?"

"Chief."

"Chief? I don't understand."

"I asked Chief to help me understand Marty's spirit. She is an important piece of the puzzle that is the Firm. Chief and the chiefs of the Black Feet, the Hopi, the Navaho, and the Arapahoe all helped me in this understanding. They watched Marty's movies and studied her porn pictures. By doing this they intoned her spirit and made sense of how The Great Spirit of All Living Things enters Marty and causes her to be the way she is."

"So, the chiefs studied her films and pictures? What did they conclude?"

"Chiefs of Black Feet, Navaho, and Arapahoe concluded that Marty has a sex obsession. They think she likes to screw for the pleasures of screwing, nothing more. But the Hopi chief, the chief that Father believes is most wise, had different thought. He intensively studied Marty's porn pictures. He noted something in two of her picture sequences that he believed was profound. He believes those two picture sequences are a window into Marty's soul."

"What did he see that the others missed?"

"Well, Horse, understand that the Hopi chief is also a shaman. He can look at something and see the spirit within it. He is very powerful because of this. Chief, my father, believes him possessed with special spiritual powers."

"But they all saw the same pictures. So, what did he see?"

"He saw more than screwing, Bob. He saw motive for behavior. Only shaman can see this. He said Marty's spiritual essence was revealed in two of the photo sequences. In the first sequence, she was dressed in white, as a virgin bride. Her male attendants undressed her, leaving only white stockings and a bridal veil. They took turns screwing her. They ejaculated semen all over her naked breasts.

Then, a man comes to her. He kneels before her widespread legs. He places his wedding ring upon a purple satin pillow and offers it to her. He kisses her, then places his face before her vagina as if he is peering into the window of her soul. He places his wedding ring inside Marty's sex; and then proceeds to make love with her.

'Hopi chief says this photo sequence is profound. It signifies that the man's spirit was trapped and defeated when he went to Marty. The man chooses to abandon his ties to the moral world that constrained him and offer up everything he formerly believed in to Marty's spirit. This is signified by his offering of his wedding ring. By allowing this man to kiss her, Marty signifies that she is willing to convert him to her immoral ways. By placing his face before Marty's vagina, the man signifies that he understands that he will find his reborn soul inside her; and he accepts that fornicating with her represents his immersion into his new immorality. Placing his wedding ring inside Marty's vagina is a very willful, symbolic act. It signifies that he can never return to his old, moral ways. The disappeared ring transforms his old ways. It becomes a figment of his imagination, about to travel its new path in life, the path of an immoral, pagan lifestyle.

"When he fornicates with Marty, he imagines his figment becomes one of his sperm warriors; and his sperm warrior travels deep inside Marty, seeking the truth of his life's purpose within Marty's womb, taking his discovery quest all the way inside her, into her innermost Holy of Holies. There, where his ejaculated sperm finds Marty's soul, he discovers his ultimate truth. His soul becomes eternally bonded to Marty's immoral soul. His soul is now also immoral. The two souls accept each other's love. It is a mutual love that unites them in purpose and belief in the immoral way of life. After he withdraws, a photo shows an extreme close-up of Marty's vagina. It is noticeably, highly elevated. It is propped up very high and resting upon the purple satin pillow.

"The elevated pillow signifies Marty's offering up of her spirit soul to the Great Spirit and Spirit's wishes. Semen oozes from her vagina. Her semen flow is Marty's offering to the Spirit. By flowing semen upon the purple satin pillow, Marty reaffirms her bond with the Spirit. She honored Spirit's wishes by converting this man to her immoral ways. The final photo captures Marty's glorious smile. Her face radiates her expression of divine happiness. It is the picture-perfect image of honest, cherubic innocence and deep satisfaction pride with her immorality."

"I never would have thought all those things could be understood from photos."

"Shamans have powers of insight that we do not have, Bob. Tell me something. Can you remember if Marty ever went away on a safari trip?"

"Oh, yes, I believe she did. Once she was gone for almost an entire month. When she returned, she had an expensive set of luggage made from the hide of a giraffe, and an elephant's tusk which she keeps next to her bed. Why?"

"Well, the second set of photos that interested the Hopi chief shows Marty making love with different men in front of the big game animals that they shot. There are scenes where she flaunts her vagina before an elephant, a giraffe, a lion, and an ibex. Then, toward the end of the sequence, Marty strikes all sorts of naked poses upon the skins of different feline species. She flaunts her vagina in these pictures. She spreads her legs and holds herself open while lying on the skins of lions, leopards, panthers, cougars, and tigers.

"Hopi chief says the last few photos are very telling. Marty lies upon all these skins of wild cats with her vagina elevated upon a purple, satin pillow. She has semen oozing from her vagina and semen all over her breasts. It's her way of expressing dominion over all the beasts of the earth. She's intimating that, for the pleasures of her vagina, men will murder animals for her amusement. It's depravity,

Bob. It's obvious that men have ejaculated inside her and on her breasts. That's her intimation that men who will do her bidding will be rewarded by having sex with her. It's a throwback to the times of pagan temple prostitution worshippers' sacrificial rituals. In the last photo she lies on her back and has her hands held open with her palms toward the sky; and, resting upon each hand is a set of male testicles and an erect penis. Like in the wedding photo, Marty's face is the picture-perfect image of cherubic innocence. Again, her face radiates with the shameless glory of her immorality. The Hopi chief believes this final picture of the series and the final picture of the wedding series reveal Marty's inner soul."

"Well, what does he believe the pictures are telling him?"

"Not just him, Horse; all of us. Hopi chief thinks those pictures are profound. He tells Father and the other chiefs that the way Marty elevates her vagina upon a satin purple pillow is highly significant. He says the set of photos that mock traditional marriage signifies the old, moral ways giving way to the new, immoral ways; and Marty is honoring the Spirit for making her new way possible. The second set of photos shows Marty is above the Spirit's animal creations; and Marty is presenting her whoring as a glorious offering to the Spirit. By placing her semen oozing vagina upon a purple pillow, she is communicating that her spiritual connection to the Spirit is sacred and holy; and she is honored to have that connection. So, she places her vagina in a position where the Spirit can see she is acknowledging the Spirit's wishes by raising her vagina up as an offering, the royal essence of her soul and the most sacred part of herself which is a pathway to the Spirit, to symbolize she glorifies the Spirit. Hopi chief believes the Great Spirit of All Living Things accepts Marty's offerings and he is pleased with her; and Spirit has entered Marty's soul and lives within her and commands her to make the world new again."

"Make new? What do you mean by make new?"

"Hopi chief says that the Great Spirit decided to make the world, make it new, from nothing, out of a void. Then, Spirit commanded humans to make new humans out of pagan love. Then, Spirit commanded Abraham to make new, structured faiths for worshipping the Spirit. Then, Spirit told Buddha, Moses, Jesus, and Mohammed; each one of them, in turn, to make new ways of human living and make ordered codifications of human worship and conduct.

"Now, Hopi chief believes Spirit is ordering Marty to make new again. Spirit wants women to shape the ways forward for human living. Spirit has chosen Marty to propagate Spirit's desired new way on Earth. Hopi says the Spirit likes to cause change; stir things; make people think and progress toward greater human understandings and greater human acceptance of the weaknesses in other humans; and above all else, to love the humanity that exists inside all of us. The chiefs met many times and discussed the Hopi chief's interpretations. Now, they all agree that the Hopi chef's interpretations are correct; and they have smoked on it.

"So, the Hopi chief believes that Marty is spiritually inspired to change the world's morality and its ways of believing in a higher power? Am I understanding this?"

"Yes, exactly right; which is why I must not hate her. She is on her mission. It is her divine, spiritual mission. Somewhere in her life, perhaps during her years of spiritual wilderness while her mother would not see her, the Great Spirit entered Marty's soul. Now, Marty seeks to help more woman become shamelessly immoral, confident, and enthused about their callings to become whores and porn stars. Many women already perform porn and aspire to become Marty copy-cats. Marty wants to help them facilitate their goal.

"Wherever it's legal, Marty will license-franchise her brand of exclusive religious brothels, with exclusive rights to show compilations of her best film and porn picture scenes. For her franchise fee, she'll provide these films and photos; the viewing screen; a modern, *cushioned altar, suitable for fornication rites; and assorted pagan religious accessories. During these televised world-wide pagan services, millions of eyeballs will be riveted on Marty's highly prized vagina. Fascinated by her wanton debauchery, many will watch her make love and perform fellatio for hours every day, much like the continuous televised prayers for those people who are devoutly religious. Your sweet Marty, the world's most beloved, cherished whore, will be accepted, adored, and worshipped worldwide, Bob. Her pagan brand will eventually eclipse traditional religion. Millions of converts are already flocking to her, Bob. Believe what I'm telling you. Marty's world is the world of our future.*

"Her new religion applauds immorality. She'll dutifully flutter, unconcerned with the consequences, from one wealthy lover's marriage break-up to the next. The public will drool in her drama, buy her movies like crazy, and hang on her every utterance. She'll have private label designer clothing and jewelry lines, a private jet and yacht, and every cock she wants. She's going to be a sensation, Bob. That's the world we'll live in.

"In today's world, a story about a beautiful lust crazed, brazen all conquering porn star sells magazines. Marty's story will instantly bring her world-wide notoriety. She'll be mainstream media famous and she will become filthy rich. I have no doubts about that.

"How am I doing, Bob? Had enough? Have I helped you see where your obsession with Marty is taking you? Do you really want a life with her?"

"You've got my head spinning, Barb. Is this really what you see?"

"Oh yes, and more. Having kids would destroy her business model, Bob. Her ranking would slip as her films became stale-dated and other girls erode her market share. She'd lose her shot at world fame and fortune. Your idea of a life with her and children is her anathema. It's never going to happen. Her world is the world of private jets, luxury villas and yachts, masseuses, stylists, servants, fine dining, expensive

wardrobes; and endless marketing endorsements, explicit films, and tabloid adulation. She won't even consider marriage and kids, unless her career as the world's greatest fuck bunny takes a serious tumble."

"But Barb, if all this is true, why does she want me? Why does she stay with me at night?"

"Because, silly, that lets everyone assume she has a normal life. Besides, when she gets into bed, she needs to know there's a man in it. That's part of her nymphomaniac psyche thing. It's a deeply seated need; and when there is a man in her bed, she always gets an insatiable urge to have sex him. She can't help herself, Bob. If there's a cock in her bed, she's compelled to rub her vagina over it, get it rock hard, straddle it, insert it, and rock it, twerking it back and forth until she orgasms and it discharges hot semen inside her. It's her addiction, Bob. It's her deeply seated pagan nympho DNA seed. She may as well be a temple prostitute from thousands of years ago. She needs to have a penis inside her. Fucking was her purpose in that culture and it's her purpose now. It's what she lives for. It's her ticket to prominence and glory.

"It's even more than that. If she doesn't have a penis inside her, she spirals into mental turmoil. She lapses into a kind of ugly, vengefully dark depression state. She must have sex to feel she's loved; to prove she's as worthy as those other little girls in her boarding school, who were loved. When she's not having sex, she feels she's unloved and unwanted. She becomes catatonic, like a child in the fetal position; alone and afraid of the world. It terrifies her to not fuck. She can't imagine anyone loving her for just being herself. She has no 'self' outside of sex. She has no interests in art, volunteer work, theater, music, the sciences, nothing. She's a living void.

"She can't help her condition, Bob. You cannot change her; no one can. She doesn't know what love is; even after she's found it; even when she holds it in her hand. She's hard wired now. It's her fate to never feel loved even by someone who loves her; and it's her destiny's

quest to try to fill her void, while in the deepest reaches of her mind she knows she'll never succeed. That's her disease effect, Bob. She lives a tortured hellish life. Believe me, Bob, even though she's wildly wealthy and pursued by dozens of rich and handsome lovers, her life is a living hell."

"But she's always getting calls; always going places. She's very busy!" Bob conjectured.

"Oh, she tries to make it appear glamorous, but it's not. It's broody and dark and empty. She's still that little girl desperately seeking love, but never able to find it. And when she did finally find it in you, she didn't believe she deserved it. Her mental conditioning which prevents her from feeling hurt from abandonment also makes her certain that love is something she can never have; even though she already has it."

"Are you saying I tried to interfere with her fate by being with her this past year?"

"Well, not really, not on your part. I'm saying she tried to change her own fate, and yours, and mine. Perhaps she believed if she could capture you, she could change the will of the spirits. She put her sex right out there for you, I'm sure she did. I know her. That's her way. By doing that she had to know she'd be taking you away from me. She was willfully trying to change her own fate by interfering with ours. Humans should not try to change the will of the spirits. Chief says: 'That very bad. Usually causes problems.'

"But, how did she know she was interfering with our fate?"

"Oh, come on, Big Stupid Horse. She is a woman! She had to know that you and I had eyes for each other from the first day we saw each other."

"She would know that?"

"Yes, of course she knew. She is a WOMAN! How can you stand there and be so stupid? We women know these things, even when they are not spelled out for us."

"You do?"

"YES, STUPID BIG HORSE, WE DO! Oh, you men can be so stupid, stupid, stupid! Are all you men so stupid?"

"So, she deliberately tried to keep us apart?" Bob didn't answer Barbara's question about stupid.

"YES! Listen Horse, my mother explained to me when I was a little girl that men are drawn to a woman's vagina like bees are drawn to a flower. They come for it and they go crazy over it. They have to have it. Well, didn't Marty shove her vagina at you? Didn't something come over you when you first saw her sex? I'll bet she set you buzzing like a bee, didn't she? Come on, think about it. Didn't she?"

"Yes, thinking back over that year, yes she did."

"She got you so steamed up you could hardly think of anything else, didn't she?"

"Well, I did think about you, Barb, honest I did."

"Oh, RIGHT! Give me a break, Big Horse. I'm not some hay seed that just fell off the wagon, Horse. While you were fucking Marty you were thinking of me! Really! Ha! Am I supposed to believe that? Do you think I am also stupid like some stupid Big Horse? Don't answer me. I just want you to see she was interfering with the will of the spirits, yours, mine, and her own."

"Okay, I see your point, Barb. I'm sorry I didn't see it that way, that spirit stuff, while it was happening."

"I couldn't expect you to, Horse, just like I couldn't expect a bee to stay away from a flower. You are a man. Chief explained all this stuff to me the way a man looks at it. Look, I know you have feelings for her. I do too, but can't you see the difference, Bob, between a woman who genuinely loves YOU and a sick indiscriminate whore who aspires to be known as the world's most notorious cum dumpster? When you shot your cum into her sex pit, that cum bucket was already overflowing from hundreds of her other lovers, you stupid, stupid Big Horse! You must have known something?"

"*Why are you saying indiscriminate? You mean like a street-walker?*"

"*YES, stupid Big Horse, she is indiscriminate about a man's character. All she wants is his money or his sales for the Firm. If he has serious money, it doesn't matter if he is a total pig. She'll happily fuck him for his money. What I detest about her is that she goes after men and stays after them until she drains all their money. She's not about quick affairs or one-nighters. She is a willful predator, determined to work on a man until she turns his pockets inside out. She needs mental help, Bob. But as long as she's beautiful and desirable, she will not get that help. She'll continue to fuck her way through life. Her sickness will drive her to destroy other lives. She won't stop. She doesn't think she needs help. She'll keep going until somebody stops her, perhaps by killing her.*"

"*This is depressing, Barb.*"

"*Yeah, so what? How many families do you suppose she's already destroyed? How many children live in broken homes, abandoned by their fathers because of her behavior? How many little girls lost their daddy because he spent his family's assets on cum shots into Marty's vagina? How many fathers missed their sons' sporting events while Marty sucked the semen out of their pricks and swallowed it down her cum thirsty gullet?*

"*She's as heartless and ruthless as a cold-blooded viper with its head in a nest of terrified chicks, leisurely devouring those helpless little lives, one by one; and gloating over the carnage she leaves behind. She has never cared one wit about the turmoil she caused in any little kids' life, Bob. She enjoys destroying a household nest.*

"*How many kids never saw their daddy after he became intimate with Marty on a film set? Think about it, Bob. Those studs in her gang bangs see her as the ultimate prize. In that business it's an honor to get to work with her, to be seen with the number one adult film star. She's promiscuous, beautiful, attainable. And she adores their cocks! I have no doubt that she sees many of them away from her film sets, and away from you. Do you honestly believe she'd ever say good bye to a cock that pleased her? Can you imagine her just walking away from a stud without leaving her phone number? It's all a game to her, a perverse challenge. But sex with her is never about love. She's like a cold-blooded snake that way.*

"When she soon attains her goal of world number one adult film star, just remember she crushed little kids' lives to get there. She'll have destroyed everyone that tried to distract her from her focus. She'll be famous. They'll be ruined. She has no understanding of love. It's an incomprehensible void to her. You will not find nurture in her vocabulary."

Barbara's voice rose to shouting:

"In her twisted mind, destroying some little kid's world, messing up that kid psychologically for the rest of its life is all a fun game. She'd stomp on those kids and break their bones if she could get away with it. She'll do anything and everything to get ahead. And, she believes she's somehow getting even! She's a very sick woman, Bob."

"You can't be serious. Is she really that evil?" His eyes widened and his jaw dropped at Barb's bombshell.

Barbara was still shouting. She was furious. Bob hated it when women became this emotional.

"I am serious. I don't say things that I can't prove. And, YES, she is that evil! Her sickness has made her become evil, like a mad dog turns evil. She's the consummate bad girl, the worst kind of wicked woman."

Barb pursed her lips and leveled a gaze at Bob, nodding slightly. That meant she had the goods to back up what she was saying. She didn't blink and she wasn't backing down. She looked like she might cry for all the sex Bob had with Marty. She spoke from a broken heart.

"Why is she that way, Barb? Is it just the sickness and the money?"

"No, it is not only those things." Now Barbara resumed speaking more like a normal person, explaining her insights into Marty.

"She's not a pure capitalist. Making money is only part of her motive. Money is just the currency men need to play her game. It's only the means to her real objective of taking love away from other women. Her sickness has carried her into a perverse direction. She has a hole in her heart because her parents weren't there for her. Susan was so busy screwing Marvin that she didn't have time for Marty. Marty ended up in boarding school. She never even saw her mother.

"In Marty's child-like mind, having boys fondling her, kissing her, competing for her favors, and fucking her became her substitute for the love and nurturing she never had. Her behavior progressed into nymphomania, and then she figured out how to make money by whoring. Upstaging her boarding school peers progressed to destroying the lives of her rivals. Beneath her beautiful breasts beats a sociopath's cold dark heart.

"She's also entered a sick psychological competition with her mother. She goes out of her way to prove to Susan that she can make a lot more money whoring than Susan ever did. She knows that Susan played hell with Eloweiss by taking Marvin away from her. Marty is driven to show Susan that she can win more men to her vagina than Susan ever did. It's a psycho drive to prove she's the more accomplished whore of the two of them. It's about proving that she can hurt her mother more than her mother hurt her. It's about lots more than money. It's about body count.

"It's crazy, Bob. The more Marty whores the more she feels she's getting one up on Susan. Whoring became Marty's mother substitute. But Marty's whoring has a cruel twist to it. When she fucks a man, she intends to hurt his wife or girl friend so the other woman feels that same hurt that Marty felt as a child. There's a transference

mechanism going on, the shifting of pain from Marty to the woman she's crushing.

"Romance just happened for Susan and Marvin. Marvin never loved his wife in the first place. Their marriage was strictly business. Eloweiss's family money got the Firm off the ground; for that money Marvin needed to marry Eloweiss. Marty's M. O. is different from Susan's. She intentionally targets wives and girl friends that do have love; that do have family. She rips that love away from them to give them a taste of her own pain.

"Bob, Marty's zeal is the obliteration of family, severing and destroying every precious bond that holds parents and children together. Her life is a heartless, carefree whirlwind of destruction. She has no real ties to anyone other than her tie to you and some weird closeness to David. She just binges from one conquest and lust pleasure to another of the same. She devours entire families. She immerses men's desires in her vagina and drowns their souls inside her. She takes over their lives with no second thoughts or remorse about how destructive she is."

"But, Barb, making love doesn't feel destructive. It feels the opposite of that. It feels creative, like something wonderful is happening."

"Bob, Bob, you poor stupid dumb horse male. Try to see it this way: When a shark is eating a seal do you think the shark has any feelings for the pain it is causing the seal?"

"No. I don't think sharks feel pain. The seal feels the pain."

"Okay, Big Horse, that's very good! Well, while Marty is giving herself pleasures by copulating with a man who is in another relationship, do you believe Marty feels the pain she is causing in that relationship?"

"Well, I don't suppose she cares very much about the other relationship the man is in."

"Bingo! Of course, she doesn't care. If anything, she enjoys the pain she's causing in that other relationship. She enjoys inflicting

pain as much as a shark enjoys eating. Causing relationship destructions affects Marty's conscience the same way eating a seal affects a shark's conscience."

"Sharks don't have consciences, Barb."

"Exactly. And neither does Marty. Her heart is a shark's heart. It has no feelings for the pain of others she affects, except that she enjoys causing other relationships pain just like that shark enjoys eating. You love a relationship shark, Bob. She has no intention of building enduring relationships with any of her lovers. They only exist to temporarily slake her passion fires. She's disconnected from people like us, Bob. She'll ditch you in a minute when someone who gives her greater fame, fortune or pleasures comes along.

"Listen to what I'm telling you, Big Horse. Loving her is loving a storm. It's enchanting, fascinating and all that; but it turns you inside out and upside down. It passes you and moves on. It leaves you. It's suddenly there, on top of you. And then it's gone, just as suddenly. And all it's done is excite you and taken your feelings from you. Until Marty comes to accept her childhood and finds peace with whom she is now, her revenge quest will control her behavior. Love doesn't stand a chance in her storm, Bob. Her storm wants to destroy, not build.

"Her revenge drive tortures her mother. Susan sees the Firm's sales reports every day. Susan knows what Marty does to get those sales. And it hurts her. It tears Susan's guts out; but she can't stop Marty. Her daughter is a grown woman; and Marty now has more power in the Firm than Susan does. Susan is powerless to change Marty's behavior. She used to criticize Marty in a mild sort of way, but Marty just ignored her. Susan doesn't even bother criticizing Marty any more.

"She just agonizes over what Marty does to get those sales. But she sits in her office and keeps her mouth shut. Susan is in a kind of mental hell over this. I think she regrets a lot about her own life

now. I think she'd love to have a grandchild, but she knows that, with Marty, that's highly unlikely."

"What about David and Marty? Are they bond by agreements? Do you know?"

"I don't fully understand the David and Marty relationship aspect of the Firm's dynamics. I know there are written agreements that govern Susan's control of administration; but I don't know what agreements David has with Marty. I haven't found anything written. But I'm certain that there is something extremely powerful that binds Marty and David together. It's either a written or oral agreement; or a mutual unspoken understanding. I'd love to know those terms. Whatever they are, they seem to bind the two of them very closely together.

"My sense is that David will never fire Marty. She has a powerful hold over him. And Marty will never quit the Firm because that would displease David. She seems terrified of displeasing David. It's like there's this invisible boundary that Marty is afraid to cross. I've sensed it for a long time. It's like they have some sort of secret pact of some kind. I believe he has an even deeper, more powerful hold over her than whatever their agreement is. Chief thinks so, too. We don't know what that is. But we sense that something sinister lurks in their relationship. It's the basis of it and it is very mysterious.

"I've taken notes on the weird looks they sometimes give each other; their clipped one-or two-word messages to each other: Like 'great fun!' or 'good one,' or their knowing smiles to each other. Those two have some secret code. There's an unspoken language between them. Only they know what they mean. David initiates these messages. Marty responds. I conclude from that, that David is the dominant partner of the two.

"I've wracked my imagination trying to understand what their code is, but I always come up empty. I've talked to Chief about it. He says I need to follow my intuition about it and be observant. We agree it's almost certainly not about sex because David is so gay.

Chief says I must stay focused on the two of them; look for a clue; a track of some sort.

"Chief says that whatever the connection between Marty and David is, it's the key to understanding the whole company. Whatever the Marty-David connection is, Marty knows it's so powerful that it gives her complete immunity from any discipline by Susan. I've observed proof of that. Once I heard Susan tell Marty she should be more cautious about the way she gets sales. Marty laughed contemptuously right in Susan's face. It turned my stomach to see a daughter treat her mother that way.

"I'm sure Susan knows about Marty's adult film and her private member business, too. I see how helpless and lost Susan looks when she talks about Marty. I think Susan believed she could drop Marty off at boarding school when Marty was five; then pick her up fourteen years later and Marty would still be five. I think Susan was so in love with Marvin she simply couldn't think straight.

"Susan never understood how important parental love is to a child. She took Marvin's affections from Eloweiss because she loved Marvin. But there was no love remaining for Marty. She never gave Marty's needs more than a passing thought. She was busy being like a thirsty sponge absorbing all of Marvin's love and knowledge. She craved that. Marvin's love was Susan's ticket out of poverty. While Susan soaked up love, she drained love from Marty. Mother got a full bucket of love. Daughter got a full bucket of demons.

"Now, Marty takes husbands from their wives, not because she loves those men, but because she doesn't want those husbands to love their wives. She's the love exterminator. She was not loved. Her mind became so badly twisted that now she hates real, honest love. And she's determined that no one else should have that kind of love either. She's an emotional train wreck, a human tragedy. And so is Susan.

"Susan now feels the same way Marty felt while Marty was an abandoned child. It's painful for anyone to know they are not loved.

It hurts to have someone rub that pain in your face, day after day. And Marty spitefully grinds her behavior right into Susan's face. She enjoys seeing her mother grieve the same way she grieved over Susan's relationship with Marvin. In Marty's cold dark heart, a grudge flame burns with hot vengeance. She's a young whore giving payback to an old whore, dose by dose. It's their circle of emotional pain, an ugly private hell between daughter and mother. Each one loves and hates the other.

"And, to be completely candid, Bob, my father has a whole different take on everything about Marty. The subject of Marty came up when Chief smoked with the other chiefs. The Hopi chief believes Marty is our future. He believes we are all built from trillions of viruses that inhabit the universe; in the vacuum voids of it and in the dark and invisible matter, as well as the visible matter; in all of it. He thinks nymphomania is an aggressive dominating virus with a high contagion rate and more women are catching this virus every year. He thinks we should not think of nymphomania as good or bad. He says it's just something that is. The Hopi chief thinks Marty has a viral genetic mutation. He says she's the product of the universe's natural DNA sequencing. The Hopi chief thinks this new viral nympho DNA strand found Marty's existing DNA and naturally linked to it; perhaps by finding its way into Susan first.

"He says these viruses' twine around our existing DNA and change us. These changes are completely natural. The spirits order these things to their liking. It's been happening since the universe began. The Hopi chief thinks the new viruses are from a strain that came from a parallel universe where it bumped into our known universe and left some rocks from its universe in our universe. Those rocks carried these new viruses. These new viruses propagated and mutated in many dimensions that previously known viruses could not reach.

"They can transit through our spirit and soul dimensions, so that when a soul is reincarnated into a new physical body the viruses

from the old body reappear in the new one. So, as more and more women achieve their reincarnations, the Hopi thinks more and more of them will become nymphomaniacs. He says that explains bikini swimwear and short skirts. These viruses also travel from animals to humans and humans to animals, because the Great Spirit wants all creatures linked together in spirit ways, which are the most important ways. The Spirit is very wise, says the Hopi chief. And Chief says the Hopi chief is very wise.

"Since these viruses can propagate in many different dimensions, they will rapidly take over our Earth population. The Hopi thinks all future women will be like Marty; and that all women will become highly promiscuous and sexually very active; and that will be the new normal way of the world; and since the new nymphomania DNA virus comes from the sky, this must all be good. That chief believes that women becoming promiscuous must certainly be all good. He thinks these new mutated human organisms must be highly promiscuous and highly reproductive because we are destined to return to the stars. We must return to where we came from and many of us must go because we've made a total mess of the Earth."

"That sounds crazy; really? Do you believe this, Barb?"

"I am only a simple woman of my tribe. So, yes, I must believe. I must not question the wisdom of my tribal chiefs. Big Chief, my father, thinks highly of this Hopi chief. Chief thinks him very smart; not crazy. The Hopi chief studies astrophysics and molecular science and particle physics. He is highly educated with many advanced degrees; understands the prophesies of tribal shaman and their messages of their wisdom.

"Hopi chief says we are all sky people, like Hopi people; and this is big important stuff that is happening with many women today. He thinks women now are different than women of years ago. He thinks women are more assertive, better informed, and more sexual than they were years ago. He thinks this is good. He notes that many

women today want more sex than before; that this must come from the sky, so it must be good and must be the way of the future.

"The chiefs agreed that a movie series will be made about Marty and Susan's lives; and it will be huge box office sensation. Chiefs all discussed Marty's behavior and what it means, over several days. And they smoked on it."

"So, Barb, when we see apparitions or hear voices, it could be something real from some dimension coming to us? And the spirit that carries these viruses cares about our soul and tries to tell us something? Apparitions and voices are part of the continuous soul that inhabits us? Am I getting this?" Bob tried to make sense of his visitations.

"Yes, now you are getting wisdom like the Hopi; but not all have same sets of viruses, Horse. Take David. His viruses never took hold in his earthly soul. He may be a dead-end soul with self-contained hate viruses. He is incomplete being. His soul cannot move between dimensions. Hopi chief thinks only viruses that carry hope, love and promiscuity can be propagated. The Great Spirit of All Living Things, or 'U,' wants a happy, loving universe.

"U doesn't want many mean people like David. But U does want some mean people. They interest U. They make people change their patterns. But U wants many more nymphomaniacs; more women like Marty. U would tell you, as U told me, that Marty's soul and your soul will reunite sometime as Sheila and Danny."

Bob was shocked at Barbars's revelation. *"You talked with U? Why does U want to reunite my soul with Marty's soul in another life? What are you saying? Tell me!"*

"Yes, I have talked with U. U sees that you and Marty found true love. But Marty was so conditioned by her disease that she could not allow herself to live her life in true love. She knows it's there. But she can't take it to the next level, to build a family with it. She is emotionally damaged. U feels sorrow for the two of you. U recognizes

that the two of you discovered the greatest love that ever was or will be. U loves to see people in love.

"U told me to accept Marty and understand her soul as a soul that needs love. U ordered me to hate Marty for taking you from me. I must accept and understand and be patient. I must love her like a sister. I can do that. I can compartmentalize those feelings and accept the will of U; but, although I can love Marty as a sister, I need not love her sexually. I need not accept her behavior to love her, either; and I do not accept her behavior.

"U wants love in the universe. U wants humans to propagate, so U's solution is to have your spirit and Marty's spirit discover each other again in another life in new bodies. Don't laugh, Bob, U has U's ways about these things. You must trust that U will work all these things out in U's good time. Be patient and accept things. Do not try to fight them. Never fight the wisdom of U! You've heard the sayings: 'Hope springs eternal;' 'Love me forever;' 'I'll never stop loving you; and 'I'll love you till the end of time,' haven't you? Well, those are human feelings from the soul. The virus expresses them to another soul through human-to-human corporeal connections. Feelings validate what the Hopi chief said. This means he is correct."

"What means?"

"It means you will have Marty again. You will always have Marty. And, she will always have you. The two of you will always have the most fabulous love that there ever was. You can never lose love, Bob. You will lose your human body in this life. But you do not lose love. And Marty will never lose her love. Love can not die like a corporeal body dies. Love lives forever. You can intuit that because it's true. It's the reason most people get wary when their partner talks to an old lover or meets him for coffee. People instinctively know that love never dies. Love can not die!

"U doesn't allow love to die. It's the reason that the universe continues to expand. The chiefs say it's because there can never be space

enough to fill all the love that U wants us to have. They say that all the loves that everyone has ever had will live forever and be reborn. It's the way of U. It's why there are so many stars. Loves have lives of their own. They transcend death and rebirth as new lives and new loves. You and Marty will live and relive your great love, over and over; endless times forever, until the end of time; except that time never ends. U doesn't allow time to end."

CHAPTER TEN

Awake my heart, to be loved, awake, awake! (Robert Bridges: Awake My Heart to be Loved)

Love, yes love; and love more love; and love of every kind of love. There can never be too much love. (Rosemary Ness-Bitner, author)

Mice that chase cats and cats that sleep with dogs are animals engaged in unacceptable behavior. (Rosemary Ness-Bitner, author)

Rosemary, Haddie, if you girls are not having your way with your men, you must cry, and cry again. (Advice from great grandmother's sister, Elsie May on her 106th birthday)

ACCEPTANCE

"Barb, this is stuff that's way over my head. Please tell me why Marty had an interest in me. Where is this taking me? Am I just part of some female game? If I am, I don't have good cards. It's a game I don't understand. Please tell me what you know." Bob pleaded.

Suddenly it occurred to Bob that a loving monogamous woman could feel badly if she lost her man to a promiscuous, predatory porn star: *'What was I thinking?'* Bob asked himself. *'Oh no, I wasn't thinking. She's right! I was just fucking my brains out, like a damn fool. Oh my God, what have I done to Barbara?'*

"First you must tell me how I can be sure I can trust you." Barbara brought him back into the present. Barbara saw that Bob finally had his long overdue epiphany, but she could no longer hold back her tears:

"Boo Hoo; Whaaa, Whaaa, Whaaa. How could you do what you did when you knew I loved you? Whaa, sniffle, sniff, sniff." She wept and wailed openly. Her emotions burst through opened floodgates. She was terribly hurt by what he did to the relationship they had, here in this life. It was a tragedy to her earthly dream for the two of them. Her spirits had run off the rails somehow. She felt powerless. The pain of that train wreck overwhelmed her. Now, her pain came pouring out. She shook her head. Her whole body shuddered, as if that might rid her of the truth.

Barbara feared she'd never rid her mind of its images of Bob fucking and licking Marty:

"Ahh, owee, uhhh, uhhh, sob, sob." Her weeping became convulsive sobs. What Bob did with Marty drove her nearly mad: *"Every time he approaches me for a kiss, I'll remember his tongue spent countless hours savoring Marty's clitoris. I'll know the tongue that kisses me bathed itself in her orgasms."*

She feared Marty would always be an insurmountable barrier between them. Had Marty ruined their chance for love, before they even kissed?

"Whaaa, Whaaa, sobbb." She broke down and bawled openly, like an injured child.

Bob stared at Barbara, horrified by her hurt. Her tribal stoicism had fractured. She didn't try to contain her feelings. She had no pride; no stiff upper lip. She just let her emotions flow.

Then, standing beside Barbara the apparition of Marty reappeared. It spoke to Bob:

"She speaks the truth about me, Bob. I was a wicked woman. But near the end of my life, my soul shed its wickedness and broke free, like a butterfly sheds its cocoon. My soul flutters freely now. It will soon have a new life and it will search for honest love, like ours. Our souls will meet again, Bob. I will wait for you. I know you loved me. I found love with you. We will dance and play in the sunlight. U wants that for us. We will have our love again.

"But our love must say goodbye to us in this life, Bob. You must let go of me now. Barbara stands before you. You and Barbara knew the sweetest, most innocent kind of love. You experienced love at first sight. Barbara loves you in a good, honest way. She loves you. Her love is real. She will always love you, and I know you will always love her. You always have loved her, Bob, even when you were with me. Go to her now. Comfort her and love her. Lose your life and your soul in her life and her soul. Love her more than you've ever loved me. Have children and family with her. Find happiness with her. Love your life with her."

Bob was about to ask the apparition what was going to happen to her. But before he could speak, the apparition knew his mind and answered his unformed question:

"I am leaving Earth, Bob. You will not see me again in this life. But you will be with me again and we will have our love again. My love for you is real, Bob. That part of me was honest and good. I finally found true love. You brought it out of me. I will always love you for that. You are my special love. My soul needed your love. It will never let our love die. Remember this name: SHEILA. You will discover my soul, my love, and my passions in SHEILA'S life. You will know my intimacy again. We will become lovers again. And we will make America great again! Your soul must be patient. It must wait for me. You will be in my thoughts until we are together again.

'But Barbara loves you now, in this life, with all her heart and soul. She's never stopped loving you and she wants and needs you. Go to her, hold her tightly in your arms. Love her, Bob. It is right that you love her. Never let go of her.' As suddenly as it came, the apparition disappeared.

Life and love suddenly became clear to Bob. A hot flame blazed in his chest and quickly spread through his blood. His skin prickled with needles of hot passion. He was like a wild stallion consumed by raging lust-fire; furious with desire to sire his mare. He closed on Barbara. He suddenly wanted her. He never wanted her to be away from him again. His male wildness blocked out all other sights, sounds and thoughts. Only Barbara could bridle his fury.

He swept Barbara into his arms, held her close to him and kissed her.

"Stop this Big Horse, please stop this right now. I feel hurt. I am crying, can't you see? Must you be such a big stupid horse?" she protested.

She struggled to push him away while pounding harmlessly at his massive chest with her tiny fists. But Bob didn't stop holding her.

"You are stealing my kisses, Big Horse. You must stop kissing me. I am still trying to be upset with you." Barbara pleaded.

Bob held her even more tightly to him and nuzzled her neck like a wild mustang stallion refusing to be denied. Barbara's resistance faded. She laid her head against Bob's massive chest. And then, after briefly pounding her fists upon his back, she relented and collapsed her body into his. She surrendered and returned his kisses. Her tensions left her. Her fists opened. She hugged him.

"I have kissed my big horse," she said, whispering her revelation to herself.

Then, she spoke: *"Why didn't you wait for me, Big Horse? Didn't you know how badly my heart was hurting?"*

Barbara's body became limp in his arms. She surrendered her love to him as a quiet peace and accepting understanding came over her. She felt safe in Big Horse's great strength and love. Little Sparrow was home.

"I love you, you crazy girl. Don't you know that?" Bob confessed in a choking voice. *"I loved you years ago and I've never stopped loving you. But you made me wait. I didn't know why we had to wait. I thought I'd have to wait forever. You didn't tell me why I was supposed to wait. I'm sorry I hurt you, Barb. Forgive me. I'll never*

hurt you again. I love you. I just thought you were off-limits or on a reservation; and maybe I wasn't allowed on the reservation until some buffalo said so. I didn't know your world…."

She cut him off with a soulful kiss.

"Now you blabber spew, like a really Big Stupid Horse," she said, putting a finger to his lips.

Telling her he loved her was what she'd longed to hear him say for two years. He'd finally admitted it. She *knew* he loved her now. She *knew* she had tortured him with her denials. Barbara's kisses turned deep and soulful. The two frustrated lovers were finally together. They kissed long delicious kisses while their bodies pressed closely against each other. They had waited long for this moment; now it was here. They savored the wonder of it all. They were suddenly inseparable. They would stay inseparable for the rest of their lives.

"You're finally making sense, Big Smart Horse. I will trust you now." Barbara pulled herself back from the kiss. She had made her point. It was time for all games between them to stop. They needed to go forward. There was much to be done.

"You can trust me," promised Bob. *"I swear by all the buffalo on the plains and all the elk in the forests."*

"Well, now you're talking some really powerful heap big medicine stuff, Strong Smart Handsome Big Horse." She looked into his eyes and smiled a different kind of smile. It was her 'I'm proud of you' smile.

"Is that what you and Chief call me: 'Big Horse'?" Bob loved her smile. He grinned.

"Yes, Bob," she admitted. *"You are usually called Big Strong Horse but sometimes you have also been called Big Stupid Horse. You have interchangeable names. Consider it big honor."*

Barbara danced in a circle with her arms outstretched. She dived, swooped, and twirled her body like a bird in flight, prance dancing to an imaginary ancient tribal drum beat. She tucked her chin close to her chest and held it to one side, smiling a winsome coquettish invitation at Bob as she danced. A breeze lifted her shining hair freely away from her head. Her fine silky hair caught the sun's rays. Each strand of her hair dazzled in the sunlight. She became a beautiful, sparkling jewel, a human ornament radiating pure happiness. Her eyes caught his as she whooped and laughed a good belly laugh. Bob became her bewitched; her captivated man. He couldn't take his eyes off her. He knew he would remember this moment for the rest of his life.

He didn't understand it, but it was the Lakota woman's way of dancing her soul into her man's heart. Barbara was becoming his private enchantress; his precious gem-star. And she charmed him in her expressively honest, childlike way like no other woman had ever done before.

She opened her arms and walked into Bob's arms. As she crushed her body into his, Barbara promised herself that no other woman would ever know her man. She would never let him out of her arms again.

"And Big Horse.......," Barbara's matter of fact voice trailed off.

"Yes?"

"I love children."

"You want a papoose?"

"Oh YES, my dear Big Horse, I DO. I want many papooses," she said, putting her arms around his neck, *"I want us to make many papooses. I want to spend many, many days and nights making MANY beautiful little papooses. I want our little papooses running all over the place; everywhere. I want to hear them laughing and singing and playing childhood games. I want to teach them the ways of Chief and our ancestors, and I want you to teach them your ways. Our papooses must learn both ways.*

"I want them to go to church with us and learn right and wrong. I want you to read to them and teach them business things. And I

want us to ride horse in the prairie wind with them. And I want us to camp in the mountains with them. And we will mend their boo boos and their hurt hearts. And we'll teach them to brush their teeth; and play sports; and to shoot with bow and with rifle; and to hunt and fish; and to know the ways of the animals, the prairie winds and grasses, and the secrets of the forest and the forest animals. And we will see them grow and get married. We will love the stuffing's out of them and their children. I want us to fill the earth with our grandchildren, Big Horse. And, that's not all, Big Horse."

"What? What else is there?" Bob's head was spinning in the revolving door of his Lakota princess's moods.

"Here's what, Big Horse. I studied Marty's films. I am certain I can please you more in bed than she ever did. She's good; but I'm better; and I'm better for longer. I can get even more sex crazed than she is; only for me it must be things I do only for my husband. So, don't you think I'm being a Marty knockoff in our bedroom, when I'm just being myself. This Indian girl gets fast and wild when her motor turns on. You cannot let that frighten you. Got that, Big Horse?" She kissed him again, with a kiss that promised a lifetime of family love.

"Then we shall make many papooses," said Bob, nodding his head. *"But first, please tell me, why are we standing here in front of this vacant lot?"* Bob begged to be clued in.

"Here's what I know so far," Barbara answered. *"You must not breathe a breath of this to anyone, especially not to David. It's dangerous to let him know we know anything; very, very dangerous!"* She brought her index finger to her lips and nodded, emphasizing the need for secrecy.

"My lips are sealed," Bob vowed.

"A separate set of files exists for the company. Separate records of expenses," she explained. *"Your trips with Marty were paid for by Monument Printing. We're standing in front of their corporate headquarters, this vacant lot."*

"Huh? This looks like a vacant lot," Bob looked perplexed.

"That's because it is a vacant lot, Horse. The company's printing records show you ordered a half-million Dollars' worth of printing supplies to pay for a year-long fling with your vagina flashing whore, all over the country; from Hawaii to Maine to California, to Assateague and Shenandoah and New Orleans, New York, and on and on.

"There isn't a party you two didn't go to. And what's worse, it looks like you embezzled money from the Firm through fictitious printing bills to pay for a year of nonstop whoring with Marty. Now Marty has suddenly gone missing. Guess who this all points to, Bob? We have theft from a regulated entity; the disappearance of a company officer; your name on phony printing invoices from a fictitious company with a corporate headquarters that doesn't exist. What will you say when the authorities start asking questions about all this?"

"I didn't do any of this stuff, honest." Bob shrugged his shoulders.

"But you were screwing Marty, weren't you?"

"Yes," he replied sheepishly.

"And you were loving it, too, weren't you, Horse?"

"Okay. Yes. I admit it."

"And you loved her. I mean you were really, totally in love with her, weren't you, Horse?"

"Yes, I was. Sorry, Barb."

And, there it was! That word 'Sorry.' Bob spoke it. He attached guilt to it! Barbara's amygdala sensed this was her moment. Her kill had presented itself! All the tactics she learned from Chief; everything she retained now flooded into her logically ordered frontal cortex lobes and joined the sensations she felt from her amygdala. Logic and emotions joined. Together, they would make their kill. Bob was rightfully hers. She had his love first. Today, she would kill his love for Marty. She would take her man back.

She remembered Chief's lesson from their cougar hunt: *'Use bait, Sparrow. Apply female scent near the slain deer, Wait. Keep your crossbow ready. The male cougar will appear. While he feeds, he is distracted. Take him.'*

Barbara understood animals, including human animals. When Bob confessed his love for Marty, Barbara instantly understood that Marty's oxytocin and vasopressin hormones had attracted and bonded Bob through their lovemaking. His limbic mind joined her through a chemical bridge. In this way souls bond and individuals become inseparable soul mates, much like a male cougar becomes attracted to a female cougar and mates with her.

Her cougar was distracted by her baited deer. Could not Bob also be distracted? The human mind is different from the cougar's. It has a greater capacity for abstract reasoning and logic. Barbara understood that the way to turn Bob's attention away from Marty was to help his rational, thinking, frontal cortex wrest his limbic attraction away from Marty. But how to do this? Persuasion? Shock therapy? Barbara chose the latter.

"Horse," began Barbara coyly, *"tell me something: Could you even feel her side walls when you were busy in there, being a Big Stupid Horse? It must have been like sticking your prick into a bowl of cold mushy oatmeal; huh, Horse? I bet she was so stretched out you could clap your hands inside of her and play a set of drums, couldn't you, Big Horse? A lot of trucks drove through that tunnel of hers, don't you know, Big Horse. You're lucky you didn't have a head on collision while you were in there.*

"Did she say exciting things to you while you were doing her, Horse? Did she say: 'OOOHHH, AAAHHH; and You feel so good inside me; and YYYEEESSSS, Baby; And Fuck me! Yes, Fuck me harder! Like she says in her movies? Did she tell you how much she loved licking your cum off your cock? Or, maybe how good your hot

come felt when it gushed all over her clit? Did she giggle and tell you how delicious your cum is? Huh?

"What do you think was going through her mind while she was fucking you, Horse? Huh? Was she thinking: 'Gee, my Bob has a rally nice cock. I wonder if I should make some porn films with him? How do I look while I'm fucking him? Would my fans know the difference between him and one of my porn partners? Would he fuck me like this if he knew he was on film? Can he tell whether I'm fucking him because I love him or because I just love to fuck? Does he ever think about how stupid and shallow I am? Does he ever wonder whether I can do anything else besides fucking?"

"I don't know, Barb. She never mentioned what she was think-ing. Can we stop this, please? I don't know what good can come of it."

"No, you don't, do you?" Barbara became indignant and conde-scending. *"You poor, pathetic Horse. A porn star gets you in her bed and you think you've got something special. You don't even know what wild, white hot lightning bolts from the sky sex is like, do you Big Horse? You're just going to have to wait a little longer to know that difference, aren't you, Big Horse? My poor, poor, lovable, hand-some Big Horse. He must wait just a little longer to have great, make the mountains rock and the skies shake, sex.*

"Does Big Horse even know the difference between driving a slippery hot Ferrari and a sloppy, slow, cum-dumpster truck? You want to find out, don't you? Sure, you do. Do you really think you'll be able to handle me, Big Horse? I rev my pussy motor at very high RPM's and run my pussy motor very, very slippery wet and hot; don't you know?" Sparrow baited him. The woman within her couldn't resist taking parting shots at her absent rival.

"Jesus Christ, Barbara. It was just SEX! Marty's life was built around sex. Is a man supposed to say no?" And there it was! Bob had separated sex from love. Now she needed to recapture that severed love and make it her own, again. Her confidence soared.

She knew she could easily rekindle their limbic attraction, when the time was right. They had it from the moment they first saw each other. They'd get their passions back; and quickly. Barbara knew the amygdala is chameleon-like and mercurial. It was time to let her arrows fly. She amped up her attack on Marty.

"Well, I always knew you were honest, but I never saw anything all that special about her." Barbara liked being catty. *"Except for her porn movies, she offers nothing worth wasting your time on. I've worked with her. She's a gullible dumb shit; a punched hole with no brains for business. She's just a feather-brain, nympho fuck bunny. I guess she had to fall back on sex to get you interested, the poor, stupid thing.*

"She must have spent a lot of time on her back; huh Horse? I can't imagine she knew very much about love making, the poor, pathetic thing. At least I hope you learned a few sex things, Big Horse. I don't want some Stupid Big Horse getting into my bed if he doesn't even know what he's supposed to do there." Barbara was letting Bob know she was accepting him with all his previous baggage.

"Barb, something very strange just happened to me. I don't think we should talk about Marty anymore." Bob sounded cautious and afraid.

"What? Tell me. Why do you say this, Horse?" Suddenly Barbara's voice turned serious.

"Something like a ghost just appeared to me. It came to me twice. It was telling me that Marty is dead, but that I'll see her in another life. It was weird."

"Oh, I see. Horse, you were visited by a spirit; probably Marty's spirit," Barbara sounded matter of fact, like this sort of thing happened often. *"It's a sense."*

"You mean like when a horse stops and points its ears because it knows something is out there?"

"No Horse. That is a sense horses have for the here and now. What you had was a visit from a soul's spirit. Marty's soul told you

that your soul and her soul would be together again in another life. It was real, Horse. It has happened to me, too."

"Marty's soul came to you, too?"

"No, not Marty's soul. It was my mother's soul. She came to me not so long ago, speaking as a priest. She told me to go into your life and love you. It happened when I was sitting in a church, feeling strong emotions."

"What does it all mean, Barb?"

"I not sure, Horse. I think it means two womens' souls both love your soul."

"What am I supposed to do about that?"

"Nothing, there's nothing you can do. The Great Spirit of All Living Things decides such things. Sometimes the Spirit sends butterflies to arrange these things as secret messengers between the Spirits and the mortals. You are in this life now and your soul is in your life here, and your life and soul are now with my life and soul. It is likely that sometime in another life your soul will find Marty's soul and you two will be having sex or love again; whatever you were doing with her, you'll be doing it again."

"It's confusing."

"Not confusing, Big Horse. It is life and love. Some say it is Karma. You receive what you give out, something like that. The Spirit commands us to live life and to love. You must obey the Spirit; not ask questions. We are here now. We live now and we love now. Stop thinking, Big Horse, The Spirit doesn't expect us to understand life and love; especially not male horses. The Spirit only expects us to live life."

"Barb, I need to be honest with you. Between the time you told me we had to wait and the time I took up with Marty, I sometimes watched adult films. I would watch some woman making love in a film, especially if I saw one that seemed to really enjoy it, and I imagined she was you. I don't know how to explain it, but I used to

fall asleep praying that you and I would make love like that some-day. I loved you then and I never stopped. Honest, Barb. I've never stopped loving you."

"You needed to watch erotic movies to know you loved me? Now I'm beginning to think you are very stupid, idiot Big Horse."

"No, but it helped my imagination and made me dream of you. I can't explain it any better than that, except there's just something about watching a woman enjoying making love that made me feel good about women in general, about how wonderful you women are. It was a warm wholesome sort of feeling."

"Do all you guys watch that stuff?"

"Yes, I think so. There was a study about it. Seventy percent of all men admitted watching it; but I believe all men watch it. Many just won't admit it. They're too embarrassed to be truthful because of their backgrounds; or they're afraid it will reflect badly on them if they admit it. And I think some men won't admit it because they think lowly of women. They resent women, make fun of them, and even hate them in some cases. So, they won't admit it."

"But that's not like you, Bob, is it? There's not something you're holding back is there?"

"No, that's not me at all, honest. I love women."

"Horse, as your woman I do not allow you to love all women. We need to agree about that or I will not be your woman. Understand?"

"Yes, I do understand. What I'm trying to say is I adore women as a sex. I think women are the most beautiful, wonderful creatures God, or your spirit, U, ever made. I watched it some in that lonely year because there's just something refreshing and hopeful about see-ing a woman making love. It's beautiful and wonderful to behold. It uplifted my spirits and helped me feel encouraged that some day you and I might make passionate love like that. Watching it made me feel warm and happy for all women, just knowing that you femmes can enjoy love making that much.

"But, after Marty came along, I didn't have any desire to watch it anymore. I didn't have the time even if I'd wanted to watch it. I didn't know I was dating an adult film star. It was like being inside a whirlwind machine of non-stop love making, or, I guess I should refer to it as sex, now that I understand her and how she feels about men."

"You babble sometimes, Big Horse. You wish you still had her, don't you?" Barbara's puzzled eyes explored his, searching for hope that Marty was out of his system.

"Honestly, no. Now that I know she only saw me as just another man to be in bed with; no. What I want is a sane normal life with a normal woman."

"But if she loved you and if you knew she loved you would....................?"

Bob put his finger to Barb's lips to quiet her thought. *"No, because I know what was, wasn't true. It was because of her situation. It wasn't what I was led to believe it was. So, what could not have been true, can't be made true by pretending it was true. Can you understand that? Please, Barb. You must understand that. You must believe me. It's you I love. It's you I've always loved. I now see that my year with her was just an experience. It wasn't real or enduring. There was nothing there to build upon. Does that help you?"* His eyes looked for understanding.

"Yes, it helps, but are you sure you can leave those past feelings for her out of our lives?" She needed to see if his eyes were honest.

"Yes, I am sure. You must believe me, Barb. I'm sure it's over with me and Marty. I love you, Barb. I don't ever want to stray from you or go looking for another experience." He held her tightly to him and kissed her. *"I have the woman I've wanted all along; right here in my arms, right now. And I'm never letting go of you. I want to raise papooses with you."* He smiled his biggest, most confident, grin ever.

Then Bob looked into her eyes and shook his head. *"And I had nothing to do with those phony invoices or the phony printing company setup."*

"I'm sure it's over with Marty, too, Bob. I love you very much, Big Horse. I also believe you were visited by a spirit that had to tell you something. I believe in the spirits and I'm certain we shall never hear from Marty again. We should also not talk of Marty again, and especially never bring talk of her into our bedroom. We shall only concentrate on making papooses." She knew she could trust his eyes. They spoke truth. He loved her.

"Then it's settled?" Bob wished to put Marty behind them.

"Yes, Horse, settled and done, like a trade is settled and done. It's all old business now. And I also need to tell you something. I already knew all these invoices were phony, Big Horse."

"How did you know that?" Bob's curiosity was running wild.

"You cannot know that yet, Big Horse. It's too dangerous for you to know. But rest easy. I know you had nothing to do with it, because I do know who orchestrated the whole charade."

"You do?" Again, he was amazed at Barbara's abilities.

"Of course, I do. I am Chief's Little Sparrow, remember? I also figured out who forged your signatures. Little Sparrow flits around the office, unseen and unheard. I have more work to do to fit all these pieces together and completely solve this puzzle, but just give me more time. I'll be in touch. But I do not want you to worry. If they try to frame you for this, I can disprove it. For now, you just play along as though you know nothing. Play along with David's game wherever it takes you. Do you understand me?"

"Yes, but tell me, are you in any danger yourself, Barb?"

Bob's concern for her warmed her heart. He was a good man. Still, she was not yet ready to tell Bob the other thing she found in David's locked credenza. He might become a danger to his own life if she told him she saw photographs of Marty lying in pools of blood, holding decapitated heads to her lips, and kissing them while two men alternated kissing her vagina and her nipples. She suspected David kept those photos handy in case he needed to threaten or blackmail Marty. Barbara needed to first make sure that what she was seeing wasn't just some photo shop's creation. She needed confirmations of what she suspected.

Was it possible that her suspicions about the Firm were all true? Was it really just a false front, hidden in plain sight, buried in regulatory oversight, but all an elaborate ruse to hide murders? Was the Firm the final repository to hide the crimes of a child trafficking ring and a drug cartel; a criminal operation that disposed of the cartel's many victims? Could she prove there were gruesome murders taking place on a massive scale? Marty was tied into all of it, somehow. Was she an accomplice or just one of the victims? If Bob knew her suspicions, he might slip up and say something stupid, like a stupid Big Horse. She could not risk that.

"Not much in danger, unless some people get very foolish. Chief watches over Sparrow. Chief has powerful medicine. He's very dangerous to anyone who tries to harm Sparrow."

"But he's in Montana, on a reservation."

"Trust me about this, Horse. My father has people who work for him, who take care of what he calls 'details.' One of Chief's men is never far from me. I don't worry, so don't you worry."

Bob was astounded by what Barbara knew and how fearless she was. *"You're telling me you have a protector, a bodyguard?"* he was flummoxed.

Barbara pulled out a green plastic square from her purse. There was a red button in the center of it and it had two tiny blinking lights on one side. It was obviously a tracking device of some sort. *"I am the daughter of a powerful Lakota chief. If I push this button, an armed man who understands his business will appear within one minute."*

"You're kidding. How do you know that?" Bob was incredulous.

"When both lights blink, he's within one minute," she explained. *"When only one light blinks, he's within two minutes. When no light blinks, it will take more than two minutes. If the light doesn't blink for a long time, like five minutes, Chief will be upset with my protection and he will be replaced. A light always blinks. He's never more than two minutes away."*

"This is amazing. I've never seen anything like this." Bob was astounded.

"You've never met a man like Chief. Chief very protective of Sparrow."

"Am I in trouble for kissing you just now?" Bob was still awed by Barbara's mysterious world.

"No, Silly Big Horse. But you will be in heap big trouble if you lose interest. And you will be in very big, heap big trouble if you ever behave like a witless stray dog again. I expect we will marry some day and I insist you must be monogamous Big Horse. If you ever break that trust between us, I will be finished with you, for good. I not joke about this Big Horse. I will not tolerate an ass bumping, cock sucking porn star whore sticking her twat into my marriage."

"I'm interested. I'm very interested. And I'll be true to you always, honest." Bob assured her.

"Sparrow knows, Horse, but Horse, we must still wait."

"How long?" Bob could feel his frustrations returning.

"Not much longer, Horse," she sought to assure him, *"but not real, real soon either. Chief says we must allow a little more time for time to play its magic. Waiting is hard for me too, Big Horse. I want to start making little papooses with you. Maybe we'll make some with blond hair and some with deep brown hair. I get very excited just thinking about it. I want you badly. But Chief says we still must wait. He always has his reasons. I grew up trusting Chief. He's very quiet and very smart and very wise. And he has*

his ways. Chief very wise about the ways of people. So, we obey and we wait."

"Jesus Christ. I'd never have guessed any of this was real." Bob remarked.

"It's real, Horse. And Horse?"

"Yes, Sparrow?"

"Do not swear, Horse. It belittles you when you swear and I am a very religious woman. Swearing hurts my ears."

"Okay, Sparrow. No more swearing, I promise."

More to come.

PREVIEWS FROM
BUTTERFLY MORALS

Miss Iniquity spoke to Marty's mind:

'Very good, Marty, simply bring forward your confidence and training methods from seven thousand years ago. Adapt them to the present. Do not equivocate or hold back your feelings. Speak plainly. Do not use imprecise circumlocution.

'Tell them that the world they live in now with its stable institutions, social etiquette, high values, religious gathering places and accepted dogmas are not the true and natural state of human existence or nature. Instability, uncertainties, social predations, wars, pestilences, and commonplace horrible deaths are normal experiences to the human condition . . . . *Chapter One.*

Dom next walked me to the baccarat tables. He bought three million dollars' worth of chips from the croupier and piled them on one of the tables between the shoes. He arranged for a photographer to take photos of me lying on the table on top of this huge mountain of ten-thousand-dollar chips. The shot where I've pulled away my bikini bottom to display my naked vagina on top of millions of dollars in chips is the photo that made the covers of all the sex culture magazines. I had my vagina all plumped up, freshly waxed and oiled. It looked like an irresistible creamy white morsel, anxious for sex. That photo sold tons of your magazines." . . . . *Chapter Two.*

'And what does murder do for your pain, Marty?' The taunting voice pushed Marty toward her reality.

'It takes away my pain for a while.'

'Why does it take your pain away, Marty?'

'Because, after I murder those men, I kiss their lips and their faces and I talk to them while they still have some life in them.'

'But what else, Marty? What else do you do with them?' The voice was forcing Marty to confess to her deepest secret. . . . Chapter Three.

"Oh, sometimes my lips just do that when I have an erotic inspiration, that's all, Consuelo. It's nothing. Really, it's nothing. Let's see, where were we? . . . . Chapter Four.

"In the back rooms, behind steel doors in humidified rooms were the finest works of Picasso, Rembrandt, Rubens, Manet, Gaugin, Monet, Klimt, DuChant, Modigliani, Matisse, Gerome, Courbet, Ingres, Goya, Velazquez, Durer, Botticelli, Leonardo, Michelangelo, and on and on. It was an endless, priceless collection. Before each piece there was a velvet viewing bench. . . . . Chapter Five.

"Charles knows I love Puccini's Madam Butterfly. On every one of my visits, he treats me to cunnilingus while we listen to that opera. As I listen to the words of "Un bei di Verdremo, One day we'll see," I experience a spiritual transformation . . . . Chapter Six.

"Charles helps me feel like a butterfly. My dear sweet Charles stays with me. Oh, he does!" . . . . Chapter Seven.

'Am I really any different than a flower being visited by butterflies and bees? People do not call flowers whores or think less of them for being visited by many bees; so how, I wonder, could anyone think I am less beautiful, or my life is less meaningful than a flower's life, while I'm making love?...................... Chapter Eight.

"Dom knew it was time for him to enter his personal form of human chrysalis. His old ways of thinking about sin and lust became a kind of liquefied jell within his mind. He needed to absorb them into his new freedom loving way of thinking, just as a caterpillar needs to absorb its old body into its newly liquefied form. Every time we made love, within Dom's mind a new nervous system and a new way of thinking about life was taking place; just as within the caterpillar's liquefied body its reborn nervous system feels a bursting desire to experience a newborn freedom ....Chapter Nine.

Dear listeners, is there anything about David that is what it appears to be? Is he a man of honor? What kind of firm is David running? What inner conflict does David have that he cannot reveal to Bob?

Our next book examines how Marty, during her previous lives, caused morality to change, including how her profligate sexuality was the real reason why possessive Moses needed to invent God. Does that seem incredulous? It's more Machiavellian than you might think. BUTTERFLY MORALS© the next book of the SECRET BUTTERFLY SERIES ™, questions the origins of religious beliefs. After reading BUTTERFLY MORALS©, you may find yourself wondering whether things happened the way they were explained to you in your childhood. You may even question the religious beliefs held by your adult mind. You may wonder whether your religion was really divinely inspired? And you may ask yourself: Was religion invented by man for the most fundamental reason of all? Your beliefs may be less certain than they were before your read BUTTERFLY MORALS©.

And what about Barbara? Barbara confuses David. She seems to be a background character; yet she also seems to wield considerable power. David tries, but it seems he can't figure her out. Is she really a Miss Goody Two Shoes; or is she a mysterious enigma who makes him feel uneasy, somehow. Why does she make him feel so uncertain? How does she do that? She's a detailed perfectionist, a talent his company needs. And he knows he needs her. But he also knows Marty hates her and wants to murder her. Caught up in the conflict between these two women, David's uncertainty reveals itself. What can be done about his prized corporate Wizz Kid? And how can he mollify Marty, his extremely valuable sexpot and partner in murder?

Barbara has a closely held secret. She's about to put her extremely devious plot into motion. Does Barbara understand human behavior well enough to set her ingeniously clever trap for David? Remember, this is David we're talking about. Come, flutter on with me, Minna Morinette, your audio book narrator. Let's see what Barbara plans for David's macabre, mentally distorted world in BUTTERFLY MORALS© our ninth book of THE SECRET BUTTERFLY SERIES™.

www.ingramcontent.com/pod-product-compliance
Lightning Source LLC
Chambersburg PA
CBHW070520310726
48976CB00002BA/490